21.17

W9-CZW-913

DANTE'S NUMBERS

DAVID
HEWSON
DANTE'S
NUMBERS

MACMILLAN

First published 2008 by Macmillan
an imprint of Pan Macmillan Ltd
Pan Macmillan, 20 New Wharf Road, London N1 9RR
Basingstoke and Oxford
Associated companies throughout the world
www.panmacmillan.com

ISBN 978-0-230-52935-9 HB
ISBN 978-0-230-71131-0 TPB

1 3 5 7 9 8 6 4 2

A CIP catalogue record for this book is available from
the British Library.

Typeset by Intype London Ltd
Printed and bound in Great Britain by
Mackays of Chatham plc, Chatham, Kent

Visit **www.panmacmillan.com** to read more about all our books
and to buy them. You will also find features, author interviews and
news of any author events, and you can sign up for e-newsletters
so that you're always first to hear about our new releases.

DANTE'S NUMBERS

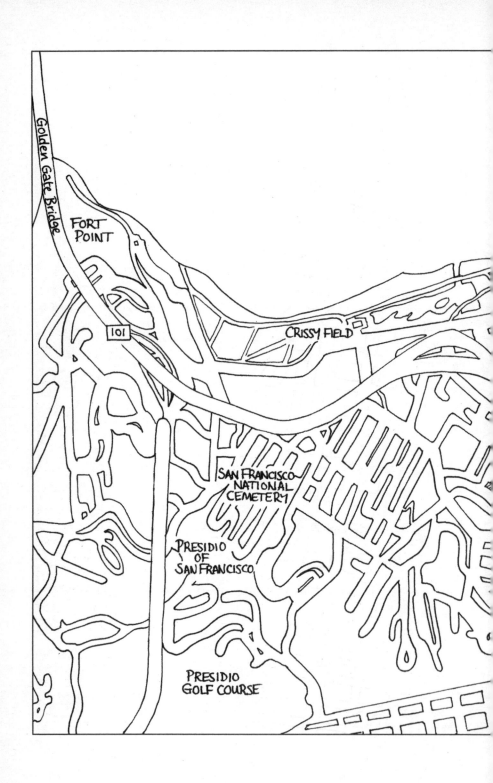

Midway upon the journey of our life
I found myself within a forest dark
For the straightforward pathway had been lost.

The Divine Comedy, Inferno, Canto I
Dante Alighieri, translated by
Henry Wadsworth Longfellow

PART ONE

- 1 -

Allan Prime peered at the woman they'd sent from the studio, pinched his cheeks between finger and thumb the way he always did before make-up, then grumbled, 'Run that past me again, will you?'

He couldn't work out whether she was Italian or not. Or how old, since most of her face was hidden behind a pair of large black plastic-rimmed sunglasses. Even – and this was something Prime normally got out of the way before anything else – whether she was pretty. He'd never seen this one at Cinecittà and a part of him said he would have noticed if only in order to ask himself the question: Should I?

She looked late twenties, a little nervous, in awe of him maybe. But she was dressed so much older, in a severe grey jacket with matching slacks and a prim white shirt, its soft crinkly collar high up to her neck. It was a look out of the movies, he thought. Old movies from back when it was still a crime to be skinny and anything less than elegant. Particularly her hair, a platinum blonde, dyed undoubtedly, fixed behind her taut, stiffly held head in a bob that, as she walked into the living room of his apartment, he'd noticed was curled into a tight apostrophe.

It was an effect he found strangely alluring until the connection came to him. Unsmiling, eyes hidden behind heavy shades that kept out the burning July morning, Miss Valdes – although the Spanish name didn't fit at all – resembled one of the cool, aloof women he'd watched in the downtown theatres when he was a kid in New York, rapt before the silver screen. Like a cross between Kim Novak and Grace Kelly, the two full-bodied celluloid blondes he'd first fallen hotly in love with as he squirmed with adolescent lust in the shiny, sticky seats of any number of Manhattan flea-pits. He hadn't encountered quiet, fixated women like this in the business in three or four decades. The breed was extinct. Real bodies had given way to rake-thin models, exquisite coiffure to makeshift mussed-up messes. Or rather the species had moved on, and he knew what kind of job it did now.

It made death masks of people. Living people, in his case.

'Signor Harvey say . . .' she repeated in her slow, deliberate Italian accent, as if unsure he quite understood. Her voice was low and throaty and appealing. More Novak than Kelly, he thought.

'Harvey's a jumped-up jerk. He never mentioned anything to me. We've got this opening ceremony tonight, in front of everyone from God down. The biggest and best movie of the decade and I get to do the honours.'

'It must be an honour to be in Signor Tonti's masterpiece.'

Allan Prime took a deep breath.

'Without me it'd be nothing. You ever watch *Gordy's Break?*'

'I loved that movie,' she replied straight away, and he found himself liking the throaty, almost masculine croon in her voice.

'It was a pile of crap. If it wasn't for me the thing wouldn't have made it outside the queer theatres.'

He truly hated that thing. It was the kind of violent fake art-house junk the Academy liked to smile on from time to time just to show it had a brain as well as a heart. He'd played a low-life hood in a homosexual relationship with a local priest who was knifed to death trying to save him. When the clamour petered out, and the golden statue was safely stored somewhere he didn't need to look at it, Allan Prime decided to make movies for people, not for critics. One a year for almost three decades. Nothing that followed gave him another nomination.

The lack of Oscars never bothered Prime too much, most of the time. From the Eighties on he'd become more and more bankable, a multi-million-dollar name who always brought in an army of female fans in love with his chiselled Mediterranean looks, trademark wavy dark hair and that slow, semi-lascivious smile he liked to throw in somewhere along the line.

Except now. He'd tried, and every time he began to crease up for the famed smirk, Roberto Tonti had gone stiff in his director's chair, thrown back his hoary aquiline head with its crown of grey hair like plumed feathers and howled long and loud with fury.

'This is what I *do*,' Prime had complained one day, when the verbal abuse went too far. He was in costume, a long, grubby medieval gown, standing in front of a blue screen, pretending to deliver some obscure speech to a digitized dragon or some other monster out of a teenage horror fantasy, though he couldn't see a thing except lights and cameras and Tonti thrashing around in his chair like some ancient, skeletal wraith.

'Not when you work for me,' Tonti screamed at him. 'When you work for me, you . . .' A stream of impenetrable Italian curses followed. '. . . you are *mine*. My puppet. My creature. Every day I put my finger up your scrawny, coked-up ass, Allan, and every day I wiggle a little harder till your stupid brain wakes up. Stop acting. Start being.'

Stop acting. Start being. Prime had lost count of the number of times he'd heard that. He still didn't get it.

Tonti was seventy-three. He looked a hundred and fifty and was mortally sick with a set of lungs that had been perforated by a lifetime's tobacco. Maybe he'd be dead before the movie got its first showing in the US. They all knew that was a possibility. It added to the buzz Simon Harvey's little army of evil PR geckos had been quietly building with their tame hacks all along.

Allan Prime had already thought through the director's real-life funeral scene. He'd release one single tear, dab it away with a finger, not a handkerchief, showing he was a man of the people, unchanged by fame. Then, when no one could hear, he'd walk up to the casket and whisper, 'Where's that freaking finger now, huh?'

Or maybe the bastard would live for ever, long enough to dance on Prime's own grave. There was something creepy, something abnormal about the man, which was, the rumours said, why he'd not sat at the helm of a movie for twenty years, frittering away his talent in the wasteland of TV until *Inferno* came along. Prime swallowed a fat finger of single malt, then refilled his glass from the bottle on the table. It was early, but the movie was done, and he didn't need to be out in public until the end of the day. The penthouse apartment atop one of the finest houses in the Via Giulia, set back from the busy Lungotevere with astonishing views over the river to St Peter's, had been Allan Prime's principal home for almost a year. It was empty save for him and Miss Valdes.

'This is for promotion, right?' he asked.

'*Si*,' the woman said, and patted her briefcase like a lawyer sure it contained proof. She had to be Italian, surely. And the more he looked at her, the more Prime became convinced she wasn't unattractive either, with her full, muscular figure – that always turned him on – and very perfect teeth behind a mouth singularly outlined in carmine lipstick. 'Mr Harvey say we must have a copy of your face, because we cannot, for reasons of taste, mass-market a version of the real thing. It must be you.'

'I cut myself shaving this morning. Does that matter?'

'I can work with that.'

'Great,' he grumbled. 'So where do you want me?'

She took off her oversized sunglasses. Miss Valdes was a looker and Allan Prime was suddenly aware something was starting to twitch down below. She had a large, strong, almost mannish face, quite heavy with make-up for this time of day, as if she didn't just make masks, she liked wearing them herself. The voice, too, now he thought about it, sounded off, artificial. *Posed*. As if she wasn't speaking in her natural tongue. Not that this worried him. He was aware of a possibility in her eyes, and that was all he needed.

'On the bed, sir,' Miss Valdes suggested. 'It would be best if you were naked. A true death mask is always taken from a naked man.'

'Not that I'm arguing, but why the hell is that?'

The corner of her scarlet mouth turned down in a gesture of meek surprise, one that seemed very Italian to him.

'We come into the world that way. And leave it too. You're an actor.'

He watched, rapt, as her fleshy, muscular tongue ran very deliberately over those scarlet lips.

'I believe you call it . . . being in character.'

He wondered how Roberto Tonti would direct a scene like this.

'Will it hurt?'

'Of course not!' She appeared visibly offended by the idea. 'Who would wish to hurt a star?'

'You'd be surprised,' Prime grumbled. This curious woman would be truly amazed, if she only knew.

She smoothed down the front of her jacket, opened the briefcase and peered into it with a professional, searching gaze before beginning to remove some items Allan Prime didn't recognize.

'First a little . . . discomfort,' she declared. 'Then . . .' That carmine smile again, one Allan Prime couldn't stop staring at although there was something that nagged him. Something familiar he couldn't place. 'Then we are free.'

Miss Valdes – *Carlotta* Valdes, he recalled the first name the doorman had used when he'd called up to her announce her arrival – took out a pair of rubber gloves and slipped them onto her strong, powerful hands, like those of a nurse or a surgeon.

- 2 -

At five minutes past four Nic Costa found himself standing outside a pale green wooden hut shaded by parched trees just a short walk from the frenzied madness that was beginning to become evident in and around the nearby Casa del Cinema. The sight of this tiny place brought back so many memories, some of them jogged by a newspaper clipping attached to the door bearing the headline, ' *"Dei Piccoli"*, *cinema da Guinness'*. This was the the world's smallest movie theatre, built for children in 1934 during the grim Mussolini years, evidence that Italy was in love with film, with the idea of fantasy, of a life that was brighter and more colourful than reality, even in those difficult times. Or perhaps, it occurred to him now, with the perspective of adulthood informing his childhood memories, because of them. This small oak cabin had just sixty-three seats, every one of them, he felt sure, deeply uncomfortable for anyone over the age of ten. Not that his parents had ever complained. Once a week, until his eleventh birthday, his mother or father had taken him here and together they had sat through a succession of films, some good, some bad, some Italian, some from other countries, America in particular, since the Disney features always seemed to play well in Rome.

It was a different time, a different world, both on the screen and in his head. Costa had never returned much to any cinema since those days. There had always seemed something more important to occupy his time: family and the slow loss of his parents, work and ambition, and, for comfort, the dark and enticing galleries and churches of his native city which seemed to speak more directly to his growing self. Now he wondered what he'd missed. The movie playing was one he'd seen as a child, a popular Disney title prompting the familiar emotions those films always brought out in him: laughter and tears, fear and hope. Sometimes he'd left this place scarcely able to speak for the rawness of the feelings that the movie had, with cunning and ruthlessness, elicited from his young and fearful mind. Was this one reason why he had stayed away from the cinema for so long? That he feared the way it sought out the awkward, hidden corners of one's life, good and bad, then magnified them in a way that could never be shirked, never avoided? Some fear that he might be haunted by what he saw?

He had been a widower for six months, before the age of thirty, and the feelings of desolation and emptiness continued to reverberate. *The world moved on.* So many had said that, and in a way they'd been right. He had allowed work to consume him, because there was nothing else. There, Leo Falcone had been subtly kind in his own way, guiding Costa away from the difficult cases, and any involving violence and murder, towards more agreeable duties, those that embraced culture and the arts, milieux in which Costa felt comfortable and, occasionally, alive. This was why, on a hot July day, he was in the pleasant park of the Villa Borghese not far from three hundred or more men and women assembled from all over the world for a historic premiere that would mark the revival of the career of one of Italy's most distinguished and reclusive directors.

Costa had never seen a movie by Roberto Tonti until that afternoon when, as a reward for their patient duties arranging property security for the exhibition associated with the production, the police and Carabinieri had been granted a private screening. He was still unclear exactly what he felt about the work of a man who was something of an enigmatic legend in his native country, though he had lived in America for many, many years. The movie was ... undoubtedly impressive, though very long and very noisy. He found it difficult to recognize much in the way of humanity in all its evident and very impressive spectacle. His memories of studying Dante's *Divina Commedia* in school told him it was a discourse on many things, among them the nature of human and divine love, an argument that seemed somewhat absent from the film he had sat through. Standing outside the little children's cinema, it seemed to Costa that the Disney title it was showing contained rather more of Dante's original message than Tonti's farrago of visual effects and overblown drama.

But he was there out of duty. The Carabinieri had been tasked with protecting the famous actors involved in the year-long production at Cinecittà. The state police had been given a more mundane responsibility, that of safeguarding the historic objects assembled for an accompanying exhibition next to the Casa del Cinema: documents and letters, paintings and an extensive exhibition of original paintings depicting the civil war between the Ghibellines and the Guelphs which prompted Dante's flight from Florence and brought about the perpetual exile in which he wrote his most famous work.

There was a photograph of the poet's grave and the verse of his friend Bernardo Canaccio that included the line:

Parvi Florentia mater amoris.

Florence, mother of little love, a sharp reminder of how Dante had been abandoned by his native city. There was a picture, too, of the tomb the Florentines had built for him in 1829, out of a tardy sense of guilt. The organizers' notes failed to disclose the truth of the matter, however: that his body remained in Ravenna. The ornate sepulchre in the Basilica di Santa Croce, with its call to honour the most exalted of poets, was empty. The poet remained an exile still, almost seven hundred years after his death.

The most famous Florentine object was, however, genuine. Hidden on a podium behind a rich blue curtain, due to be unveiled by the actor playing Dante before the premiere that evening, sat a small wooden case on a plinth. Inside, carefully posed against scarlet velvet, was the death mask of Dante Alighieri, cast in 1321 shortly after his last breath. Costa had found himself staring at these ancient features for so long that morning that Gianni Peroni had walked over and nudged him back to life with the demand for a coffee and something to eat. The image still refused to quit his head: the ascetic face of a fifty-six-year-old man, a little gaunt, with high cheekbones, a prominent nose, and a mouth shut tight with such deliberation that this mask, now grey and stained with age, seemed to emphasize: I will speak no more.

Costa was uneasy about such a treasure being associated with the Hollywood spectacle that had invaded this quiet, beautiful hillside park in Rome. There had been a concerted and occasionally vitriolic campaign against the project in the literary circles of Rome and beyond. Rumours of sabotage and mysterious accidents on set had appeared regularly in the papers. The talk, in some of the gutter press, suggested the production was 'cursed' because of its impudent and disrespectful pillaging of Dante's work, an idea that had a certain appeal to the superstitious nature of many Italians. The response of Roberto Tonti had been to rush to the TV cameras denying furiously that his return to the screen was anything but an art movie produced entirely in the spirit of the original.

The more sophisticated newspapers detected the hand of a clever PR campaign in all this, something the production's publicity director, Simon Harvey, had vigorously denied. Costa had watched the last press conference only the day before and come to the conclusion that he would never quite understand the movie industry. Harvey was the last man he expected to be in charge of a production costing around a hundred and fifty million dollars, a good third over budget. Amiable, engaging, with a bouncing head of fair, curly hair, he appeared more like a perpetual fan than someone capable of dealing with the hungry masses of the world media. But Costa had seen him in private moments too, when he seemed calm and quick-thinking, though prone to short bursts of anger.

The people he had met and worked with over the previous few weeks were, for the most part, charming, hard-working, dedicated but, above all, obsessive. Nothing much mattered for them except the job in hand, *Inferno*. A war could have started, a bomb might have exploded in the centre of Rome. They would never have noticed. The screen world was theirs. Nothing else existed.

Nic Costa rather envied them.

- 3 -

An hour after they had walked out from the private showing, blinking into the strong summer sun, Gianni Peroni's outrage had still to diminish. He stood next to Leo Falcone and Teresa Lupo elaborating a heart-felt rant about the injustice of it all. The world. Life. The job. The fact they were guarding ancient wooden boxes and old letters when they ought to be out there doing what they were paid for.

More than anything, though, it was the movie that got to him. Teresa had, with her customary guile, wangled a free ticket to the event, though she had nothing to do with the security operation the state police had in place. Early on in their relationship he'd realized the cinema was one of her few pet obsessions outside work. Normally he managed to pass over an interest he failed to share. Today it was impossible.

'Roberto Tonti is a genius, Gianni,' she declared. 'A strange genius, but a genius all the same.'

'Please. I'm still half deaf after all that racket. I've got pictures running round my head I'd really rather not have there. And you're telling me this is art?'

'All true art is difficult,' said a young, confident male voice from behind them. They turned to see a man of about thirty in the full dress uniform of a mounted Carabinieri officer, flowing cloak, shiny black boots, and a sword at his waist. 'The harder it is to peel an orange, the better it will taste.'

'I don't believe we've met,' Falcone replied, and extended a hand which was grasped with alacrity. The carabiniere had materialized unbidden and in silence, presumably fleeing the noisy and, it seemed to Peroni, increasingly ill-tempered scrum by the cinema. The officer was tall, good-looking in a theatrical, too-tanned way, with rather greasy hair that looked as if it might have seen pomade. The Carabinieri often seemed a little vain, the old cop thought, then cursed himself for such a stupid generalization.

'Bodoni,' the man announced, before turning to Teresa and Peroni to shake their hands too. 'Please. Let me fetch you another drink. There is *prosecco*. Is this a problem on duty? I think not. It is like water. Also I have a horse, not a car. He can lead me home if necessary.'

'No beer?' Peroni grumbled.

'I doubt it.' The officer shook his head sadly. 'Let me fetch something and then we may talk a little more. There is no work to be done here, surely. Besides . . .' He stood up very straight at that moment, inordinately proud of himself. '. . . my university degree was in Dante among other things. It shall be of use at last.'

He departed towards the outdoor bar leaving Peroni speechless, mouth flapping like a goldfish.

'I love the Carabinieri,' Teresa observed, just to get the men going. 'They dress so beautifully. Such delicate manners. They fetch you drinks when you want one. They know Dante. *And* he's got one of those lovely horses somewhere, too.'

Falcone stiffened. He was in his best evening suit, something grey, probably from Armani as usual. After the screening Teresa had elbowed Peroni and pointed out that the old fox had been speaking at length with a very elegant woman from the San Francisco Police Department. The entire exhibition moved on to America once the show at the Villa Borghese was over. The Californians had a team working on liaison to make sure every last precious historical item stayed safe and intact throughout. Teresa had added – her powers of intelligence-gathering never ceasing to amaze him – that Leo's on-off relationship with Raffaella Arcangelo was now going through an extended off phase, perhaps a permanent one. A replacement girl-friend seemed to be on the inspector's mind.

'I studied Dante at college for a while,' Falcone noted. 'And Petrarch.'

'I read *Batman* when I wasn't rolling around in the gutter with drunks and thieves,' Peroni retorted. 'But then I always did prefer the quiet intellectual life.'

Teresa planted a kiss on his damaged cheek, which felt good.

'Well said,' she announced before beaming at the newly returned carabiniere who held four flutes of sparkling wine in his long, well-manicured hands.

'As a rendition of *La Divina Commedia*,' Bodoni began, 'I find the film admirable. Tonti follows Dante's structure to a T. Remember . . .'

The man had a professorial, almost histrionic manner and a curious accent, one that almost sounded foreign. The Carabinieri had a habit of talking down to people on occasion. Peroni gritted his teeth, tried to ignore Teresa's infuriatingly dazzling smile, and listened.

'. . . this is an analogy for the passage of life itself, from cradle to grave and beyond, written in the first example we have of *terza rima*. A three-line stanza using the pattern a-b-a, b-c-b, c-d-c, d-e-d, et cetera, et cetera.'

Peroni downed half his glass in one go. 'I got that much from the part where the horse–snake–dragon thing chomped someone to pieces.'

Bodoni nodded.

'Good. It's in the numbers that the secret lies, and in particular the number nine, which was regarded as the "angelic" integer, since its sole root is three, representing the Trinity, which itself bears the sole root one, representing the Divine Being himself, the Alpha and the Omega of everything.'

'Do you ever get to arrest people? Or does the horse do it?' Peroni asked, aware that Teresa was kicking him in the shin at that point.

Bodoni blinked, clearly puzzled, then continued.

'Nine meant everything to Dante. It appears in the context of his beloved Beatrice throughout. Nine are the spheres of Heaven. Correspondingly – since symmetry is also fundamental . . .'

'Nine are the circles of Hell,' Peroni interrupted. 'See. I was listening. Worse than that, I was watching.' He scowled at the glass and tipped it sideways to empty the rest of the warm, flat liquid on the concrete pavement outside the Casa del Cinema. It didn't take a genius to understand that last part. The three-hour movie was divided into nine component segments, each lasting twenty minutes and prefaced with a title announcing its content, a string of salacious and suggestive headings – the wanton, the gluttonous, the violent – that served as a warning for the grisly scene to come. 'It still looked like a bad horror movie to me. Very bad.'

'As it was meant to,' Teresa suggested. 'That's Roberto Tonti's background. You remember those films from the 1970s?'

'*Anathema, Mania, Dementia*,' Bodoni concurred.

'*Dyspepsia, Nausea* . . . ?' Peroni asked. 'Has he made those yet? Or does the rubbish we just saw have an alternative title? All that . . . blood and noise.'

Bodoni mumbled something unintelligible. Peroni wondered if he'd hit home.

It was Teresa who answered.

'Blood and noise and death are central to art, Gianni,' she insisted. 'They show us it's impossible to savour the sweetness of life without being reminded of the proximity, and the certainty, of death. That's at the heart of *gialli*. It's why I love them. Some of them anyway.'

Peroni hated that word. *The yellows.* To begin with it had simply referred to the cheap crime thrillers that had come out after the war, in plain primrose jackets. Usually they were detective stories and private eye tales, often imported from America. Later the term had spread to the movies, into a series of lurid and often extraordinarily violent films that had begun to appear from the Sixties on. Gory, strange supernatural tales through which Tonti had risen to prominence. Peroni knew enough of that kind of work to understand it would never be to his own taste. It was all too extreme and, to his mind, needless.

'I hardly think anyone in our line of work needs reminding of a lesson like that,' he complained, finding his thoughts shifting to Nic, poor Nic, still lost, still wandering listless and without any inner direction two seasons after the murder of his wife.

'We all do, Gianni,' she responded, 'because we all, in the end, forget.' She took his arm, a glint in her pale, smart eyes telling him she knew exactly what he was thinking.

He and Falcone had ambled to the children's cinema earlier and seen the poster there, Peroni mentioning it to Nic in passing, noting how interested he'd seemed. Teresa's hand felt warm in his. He squeezed it and said, very seriously, 'Give me *Bambi* any time.'

'There's a death in *Bambi*,' she pointed out. 'Without it there'd be no story.'

He did remember, and it was important. His own daughter had been in tears in the darkness when they went to see that movie, unable to see that her father was in much the same state.

'This is an interesting work also,' the Carabinieri officer, Bodoni, interjected. He was, it seemed to Peroni, something of a movie bore, perhaps an understandable attribute for a man who spent his working day indolently riding the pleasant green spaces of the Villa Borghese park. The state police had officers in the vicinity too, since it was unthinkable they should not venture where the Carabinieri went. A few were mounted, though rather less ostentatiously, while others patrolled the narrow lanes in a couple of tiny Smart cars specially selected for the job. It was all show, a duty Peroni would never, in a million years, countenance. Nothing ever happened up here on the hill overlooking the city, with views all the way to the distant dome of St Peter's and beyond. This wasn't a job for a real cop, simply ceremonial window-dressing for the tourists and the city authorities.

'You can go and watch it now if you like,' Falcone said, looking as if he were tiring of the man's presence too. 'It's showing in the little children's cinema. We saw the poster when we were doing the rounds.'

'So did Maggie Flavier,' Teresa added. 'Charming woman for a star, and a perfect Beatrice too. Beautiful yet distant, unreal somehow. I spoke to her and she didn't look down her nose at me like the rest of them. She said she was going to try and sneak in there. Anything to get away from this nonsense. Apparently there's some hiccup in the proceedings. Allan Prime has gone missing. They don't know who's going to open the exhibition. The mayor's here. A couple of ministers. Half the glitterati in Rome. And they still can't decide who's going to raise the curtain.'

'That's show business,' Falcone agreed with a sage nod of his bald, aquiline head, and a quick stroke of his silver goatee.

'That's overtime,' Peroni observed. 'That's . . .'

He stopped. There was the most extraordinary expression on Bodoni's very tanned and artificially handsome face. It was one of utter shock and concern, as if he had just heard the most terrible news.

'What did you say?' the officer asked.

'There's some argument going on about the ceremony,' Teresa explained. 'Allan Prime, the actor who's supposed to give the opening speech, hasn't turned up. They don't know who'll take his place. The last I heard it was going to be Tonti himself.'

'No, no . . .' he responded anxiously. 'About Signora Flavier. She has left the event?'

'Only to go to the little children's cinema,' Falcone replied a little testily. 'It's still within the restricted area. As far as I'm aware. Personal security is the responsibility of the Carabinieri, isn't it?'

'We just get to guard *things*,' Peroni grumbled.

But it was useless. The man had departed, in a distinct hurry, glittering sword slapping at his thigh.

- 4 -

Costa's eyes stayed locked on the poster for *Bambi*, outside the Cinema dei Piccoli. An insane idea was growing in his head: perhaps there was an opportunity to spend a little time in the place itself, wedged in one of those uncomfortable tiny seats, away from everything. Before he could find the energy to thrust it aside, a soft female voice asked, in English, 'Is this a queue for the movie?'

He turned and found himself looking at a woman of about his own age and height. She was gazing back at him with curious, very bright green eyes, and seemed both interested and a little nervous. Something about her was familiar. Her chestnut hair was fashioned in a Peter Pan cut designed, with some forethought, to appear quite carefree. She wore a long dark blue evening dress that was revealing and low at the front, with a pearl necklace around her slender throat. Her pale face was somewhat tomboyish, though striking. He found himself unable to stop looking at her, then, realizing the rudeness of his prolonged stare, apologized immediately.

'No problem,' she replied, laughing. Everything about her seemed too perfect: the hair, the dress, her white, white teeth, the delicate make-up and lipstick applied so precisely. 'I'm used to it by now.'

The woman had 'movie business' written all over her, though it took him a moment to realize.

She returned his stare, still laughing.

'You really have no idea who I am, do you?'

He closed his eyes and felt very stupid. In his mind's eye he could see her twenty feet tall on the screen in the Casa del Cinema wearing a flowing medieval robe, her hair long and fair and lustrous, an ethereal figure, the muse, the dead lover Dante sought in his journey through the Inferno.

'You're Beatrice.'

The charming smile died.

'Not quite,' she said with a slow deliberation. 'That's the part I played. My name is Maggie Flavier.' She waited. Nic Costa smiled blankly. 'You still haven't heard of me, have you?'

'No,' he confessed. 'Not beyond Beatrice. Sorry.'

'Amazing.' He had no idea whether she was delighted or offended. 'And whom do I have the pleasure of addressing?'

Costa showed her the ID card. She glanced at it.

'Police,' she noted, puzzled, and nodded at a couple of distant carabinieri on matching burnt umber mares, black capes flowing, gleaming swords by their sides.

'One of them . . .'

'They're Carabinieri,' he corrected her. 'Military. We're just civilians. Ordinary. Like everyone else.'

'Really?' She didn't seem convinced by something. 'The movie . . .'

Costa pointed to the Casa del Cinema.

'The premiere is over there. This is just a little place. For children.'

She extended her arm out towards the wall and he caught a faint passing trace of some expensive scent.

'*Posso leggere*,' she said in easy Italian, pointing to the article about the cinema on the door, and then the poster for the cartoon, reading out a little of each to prove her boast.

'I meant this movie,' she added, now in English again. 'A few minutes of peace and quiet, and a fairy story too.'

'I thought you were in the fairy story business already.'

'Lots of people think that.' She touched his arm gently, briefly. 'You could join me. Two fugitives . . .' she nodded back towards the crowd near the Casa del Cinema. '. . . from that circus.'

She seemed . . . desperate wasn't quite the right word. But it wasn't too far wrong. He did recognize Maggie Flavier, he realized. Or at least he could now match the image of her in life with that on the screen, in the public imagination. Her photo had been in the papers for years. She was a star, one who'd attracted a lot of publicity, not all of it good. The details eluded him. He was happy to leave it that way. The artificiality of the movie business made him uncomfortable. Being close to so many Americans, finding himself engulfed in such a tide of pretence and illusion, had affected Costa. He would have preferred something routine, something straightforward, such as simply walking the streets of Rome, looking for criminals. The seething ocean of intense emotion that was a gigantic movie production left him feeling a little stranded, a little too reflective. It was a relief to look Maggie Flavier in the eyes and see a young, attractive woman who simply wished to step outside this world for a moment, just as he did.

Costa spoke to the man in the ticket booth. His ID card did not impress. It was the presence of a famous Hollywood star that got the small wooden doors opened and the two of them ushered into the tiny dark hall where the movie was now showing to a small audience; their tiny heads reflected in the projector beam.

'Only for a little while,' he whispered into her ear, as they sat down.

'*Certo*,' she murmured, in a passable impersonation of a gruff Roman accent, and briefly gripped his arm as she lowered herself into the small, hard seat.

He started to say, a little too loudly, 'But you must be back for the . . .'

She glowered at him, eyes flaring with a touch of amused anger, until he fell silent and looked at the screen. Bambi was with his mother fleeing the unseen hunters' guns, racing through snow fields, terrified, shocked by this deadly intrusion. Finally the little fawn came to a halt, spindly legs deep in snow, suddenly aware that he was alone, and the larger, beloved figure of his mother was nowhere to be seen.

It never ceased to touch him, to break his heart to see the

defenceless, fragile creature wandering the woods lost and forlorn in a series of lonely dissolves, searching, coming to realize, with each solemn step, that the quest was helpless. This wasn't just a movie for children. It was an allegory for life itself, the endless cycle from innocence to knowledge, birth to death, the constant search for renewal.

Perhaps this clandestine visit wasn't such a good idea. Something about this tiny place made him feel sad and a little wretched. He glanced at the woman by his side and felt his heart rise towards his throat.

Maggie Flavier, who had seemed so quiet and self-assured when he met her outside the little wooden cinema, sat frozen in the tiny cinema chair, hand over her mouth, eyes glassy with tears and locked to the screen.

'I think . . .' he said, and took her hand, '. . . we should get out of here.'

– 5 –

Peroni watched the carabiniere disappear into the crowd milling around the entrance to the Casa del Cinema. The mood there didn't seem to be improving.

'Maybe they've realized people won't like it,' Peroni wondered. 'Maybe there's – how much? A hundred and fifty million dollars and some very big reputations? – all about to go down the pan.'

Teresa gave him a caustic look.

'Stop being so bitchy. This is the biggest movie to be made at Cinecittà since *Cleopatra*. It won't fail.'

'*Cleopatra* did.'

'Those were different times. Roberto Tonti has a hit on his hands. You can feel it in the air.' She glanced at the crowds of evening suits and cocktail dresses gathered for the premiere. 'Can't you?'

Falcone handed his untouched glass to a passing waiter.

'Possibly. The critics say it could be an unmitigated disaster, financially and artistically. Or a runaway success. Who cares?'

Peroni scanned the shifting crowd. Some of them cared, he thought. A lot. Then his eyes turned away from the milling crush of bodies and found the green open space of the park.

He was astonished to see a lone figure on a chestnut stallion, galloping across the expanse of verdant lawn leading away from the cinema complex. Bodoni of the Carabinieri didn't look the fey, aesthetic intellectual he'd appeared earlier. He'd been transformed, the way an actor was when he marched on stage.

This Bodoni looked like a soldier from another time. He charged across the dry, parched summer grass of the park of the Villa Borghese, down towards the Cinema dei Piccoli.

High in the officer's hand was the familiar silhouette of a gun.

- 6 -

They sat on the wall outside the Cinema dei Piccoli.

Maggie looked a little shame-faced. 'I'm sorry I went all boo-hoo. Bag of nerves really. You're lucky I didn't throw up. I'm always like this at premieres. I took three months off after *Inferno* and it feels as if it never happened. Now I have to do it all over again. Be someone else, somewhere else. Oh, and you dropped this in your rush to bundle me out of there . . .'

His battered leather wallet was in her hands, open to show the photo there. Emily, two months before she died, bright-eyed in the sun, her golden hair gleaming on the day they took a picnic in the gardens on the Palatine.

'No need to explain,' Costa said, glancing at the picture, then taking it from her. 'I don't know why films do that. It's not as if they're real.'

Her green eyes flashed at him.

'Define "real". *Bambi*'s a bitch. Disney knew how to twist your emotions. It's a scary talent, real enough for me.' She stared at the grass at their feet. 'They all have it.'

'Who?'

'Movies and the people who make them. We exist to screw around with your heads. To do things you'd like to do yourself but lack the courage. Or the common sense. It's a small gift but a rare one, thank God. Beats waiting on tables, though.' She hesitated. 'Your wife's lovely.'

'Yes,' he replied automatically. 'She was.'

He was distracted watching what was coming their way from the

24

gathering by the cinema complex, trying to make sense of this strange, unexpected sight. He knew what the park Carabinieri were like. They were indolent toy soldiers. Usually.

The woman with the Peter Pan haircut sat next to him looking like a child who'd been placed inside her shimmering blue evening dress on someone's orders, someone who'd created her for a ceremony, or another hidden purpose. She held a damp tissue in her pale slender fingers. Her make-up had run a little from the tears.

'Did something happen back there?' he said, and nodded in the direction of the gathering. 'At the premiere?'

He could hear the distant clatter of hoofs as the horse galloped towards them with a strange, stiff figure on its back. She squinted at the sunlight and said, 'I don't think so. Allan Prime hadn't turned up to make his speech. That's unusual. He's normally dead reliable.' She registered the movement ahead of them, and began squinting even harder.

Costa stood up and said, 'Go inside, please. Now.'

'Why?'

He didn't like guns. He didn't like the sight of a carabiniere in full dress uniform storming madly across this normally peaceful park in their direction.

The rider was getting closer. She rose to stand next to him. Her arm went immediately through his, out of fear or some need for closeness, he was unsure which. Briefly, Costa wanted to laugh. There was something so theatrical about this woman, as if the entire world was a drama and she one more member of the cast.

'Let me deal with it,' Costa insisted, and took one step forward so that he was in front of her, confronting the racing horse that now made a sound like an insistent drum roll, or the rattle of some strange weapon, as it flew closer.

The officer pointed his weapon in the air and loosed off a shot. From somewhere nearby a dog began to bark maniacally. The man's insane dash across the green grass of the Villa Borghese had only one point of focus, and it was them.

'Who the hell is that?' Maggie asked.

As Costa watched, the uniformed man leaned forward in the saddle, as if preparing for one final assault.

It felt as if he'd walked unbidden onto some movie set, one with a script he couldn't begin to fathom. The carabiniere was in a crouch, racing furiously to close the distance that separated them. The sight reminded Costa of some old movie, *The Charge of the Light Brigade* maybe. Something that began as a show of bravado and ended in a shocking, unforeseen tide of bloodshed.

'Here's an idea. Let's not find out.'

He turned and grabbed her slender arm, both tugging and pushing her towards the closed wooden door of the tiny cinema. Soon there was a thunderstorm of desperate hoofs behind them and the rhythmic beat of the animal's angry snorts. He got her inside, protesting still.

'Don't cops here carry guns?' she demanded, dragging herself out of his arms as he pushed and kicked a way in, opening up the black interior in which the movie still played over a handful of small heads.

'To go to the cinema?' Costa asked, bewildered. 'Please . . .'

'Maggie! Maggie!'

The carabiniere was screaming for her as he fought to control the horse. Costa had seen enough cowboy films to know what came next. He'd dismount. He'd come for them.

'Who *is* this guy?' she pleaded, struggling against him.

'Your biggest fan?' Costa wondered, before he bawled at the attendant to call for the police.

Of course he didn't carry a gun, Costa thought. Or even a radio. They were there for what was supposed to be a pleasant social event, and to watch lazily as someone unveiled a seven-hundred-year-old death mask. Not to encounter some crazed carabiniere who rode like John Wayne, and seemed able to handle a weapon just as well.

It was a struggle to force her further inside. There was a fire exit sign on the far side. He found the light switches and turned the black interior of the cinema into a sea of yellow illumination. No more than seven kids sat in the tiny seats in front of him, each turning to blink at him resentfully.

'Go out the other side,' Costa yelled at them.

No one moved.

'*Bambi*'s not finished,' a small boy with a head of black choirboy hair objected. He could have been no more than five or six and didn't look as if anything would move him.

Maggie Flavier was strong. She fought as Costa dragged her over to the projection room, a place he'd visited once, when he was a child, in the company of his father. Then he kicked open the little wooden door, saw there was no one inside and thrust her into the cubicle, ordering her to keep quiet, then shutting the door to keep her from view.

When he turned round, he found daylight streaming through the entrance again. The carabiniere walked in, the black gun in his right hand, held at an angle, ready for use.

Costa walked up to block his way.

'There are children here, officer,' he said calmly. 'What do you want?'

'I'm not an officer, you idiot,' the man in the uniform said without emotion. 'Where is she?'

'Put down the gun. Then we talk.'

'I don't wanna talk.'

His accent was strange. Roman yet foreign too, as if he came from somewhere else.

'Put down . . .'

The man moved quickly, with an athlete's speed and determination. In an instant the carabiniere had snatched the small, complaining child from the nearest seat, wrapped his arm round the boy's chest, picked him up and thrust the weapon's blunt nose tight against his temple. The young eyes beneath the choirboy cut filled with tears and a wide-open, fearful astonishment.

'Where is she?'

Costa thought he heard voices outside. The cinema attendant

must have got someone's attention. What that meant when this lunatic had a child in his grip . . .

'Let go of the child . . .' he began.

'I'm here,' Maggie Flavier said, opening the door of the projection room at the back of the theatre. 'What do you want?'

She stood silhouetted in the entrance to the cubicle, something trailing from her left hand, something he couldn't quite make out.

The figure in the uniform turned to look in her direction. He didn't relax his hold on the child for a moment.

'I want you,' he said, as if the question was idiotic. 'Doesn't everyone? I want . . .'

Perhaps it was an actor's talent, but somehow Costa knew she was about to do something.

'To hell with everyone,' Maggie Flavier said, and tugged on whatever she held in her fingers.

It was film. Costa could hear noises coming from the projection room, frames of movie rattling, jamming, held inside the machine that gave them life. Unconsciously he'd realized what had happened to the showing of *Bambi* as the attacker entered the room. It had somehow frozen on a single frame. She must have done that. She had to be in control.

Maggie Flavier yanked hard on the snaking trail of celluloid and something snapped, came free.

The carabiniere stared in her direction, curious, angry, uncertain what to do.

Nic Costa gazed at his feet, guessing what came next. The film fell free in the projector gate. Bright, piercing white light, as brilliant as a painter's vision of Heaven, spilled into the room.

The boy in the uniformed man's arms squirmed and screamed. The carabiniere swore, a foul English curse, and tried to shield his eyes. Costa, not looking for a moment towards the projector's beam, laid a heavy, hard blow to the visible area of the man's stomach, unable, he knew, to reach the weapon, intent, still, on releasing the child. He punched again. There was a cry of pain and fury. His left hand closed on the boy's back, his right struggled to pull him free.

Costa was kicking and flailing with his feet and his legs, intent on coming between man and hostage.

Then something else intervened. A large silver circular shape crossed his vision and dashed against the carabiniere's head. Maggie Flavier had a film can and she was using it, along with some pretty choice language too.

The weapon turned to face Costa's chest. The barrel barked, the black shape jumped in the man's hand.

The woman struck again, hard, with such force the firearm fell back, still in their attacker's grip. The boy wriggled free and fled the moment his small feet touched the floor. Costa closed in, took the man's forearm, forced it back, sending the weapon upwards into one of the hot overhead lights in the low wooden ceiling.

There was a scream. Pain. Heat on skin. The handgun tumbled to the floor. The carabiniere turned and stumbled out of Costa's hold, was free again, was scrabbling, half-crouching, towards the gun, too close to it for anyone to intervene.

'Run,' Costa ordered, unable to understand why he was still standing, why he could feel no pain.

She didn't move.

'No. Are you hurt?'

'Run!'

'I don't need to. Can't you see?'

He could, and he didn't understand how he knew she was correct, but she was. The individual in the Carabinieri uniform, now stained with dirt and dust from the floor of the Cinema dei Piccoli, wouldn't come back to them. It was written in his defeated, puzzled, angry face. As if his part was over.

'Leave the weapon,' Costa barked. '*Leave the weapon alone.*'

It was useless. The man retrieved the gun, then laughed and half-fell, half-ran out of the door, out into a warm golden Roman evening.

She started to take one step to follow. Costa put out a hand to prevent her.

'That was a mistake,' he said.

He knew what happened when wild men flailed around with

weapons in public, particularly in a protected, special place, full of officers determined to guard those in their care.

From beyond the door of the tiny wooden cinema came voices, loud and furious, shouts and cries, bellowed orders, all the words he dreaded to hear since he knew what they might mean, because he'd been through this kind of tense, stand-off situation in training, and knew how easily it could go wrong.

'What's happening?' she asked and started to brush past him.

'No!' Costa commanded, with more certainty than he'd used in many a long month.

He stepped in front of her and stared into the woman's foreign yet familiar face.

'You never walk towards the line of fire,' Costa said, his finger in front of her face, like a teacher determined to deliver a lesson that had to be learned. '*Never . . .*'

He was shocked to see that, for the first time, there seemed to be a hint of real fear in her face, and he was the cause, not the madman who had attacked them for no apparent reason.

Outside the shouting ended and the staccato sound of gunfire began.

- 7 -

They heard it from the Casa del Cinema. The volley of pistol shots sounded so loud and insistent it sent every grey, excitable pigeon in the park fleeing into the radiant evening sky.

'Nic's there somewhere . . .' Peroni said instantly, alarmed.

Falcone and Teresa's eyes were on the podium. Peroni couldn't believe their attention was anywhere but the source of that awful, familiar sound.

'It's the Carabinieri's job,' Falcone answered, not looking at him for a moment. 'Nic can take care of himself.'

'To hell with the Carabinieri! I'm . . .'

Peroni fell silent. The dark blue uniforms of their rivals seemed to be everywhere. Officers were shouting, yelling into radios, looking panicked.

On the podium Roberto Tonti, with a gaggle of puzzled, half-frightened politicians and minor actors around him, was droning on about the movie and its importance, about Dante and a poet's vision of Hell, all as if he'd never noticed a thing. The tall, stooped director looked every inch of his seventy years. His head of grey, swept-back hair seemed the creation of a make-up department. His skin was bloodless and pale, his cheeks hollow, his entire demeanour gaunt. Peroni knew the rumours; that the man was desperately sick. Perhaps this explained his obsessive need to continue with the seemingly interminable speech as the commotion swirled around them.

'. . . for nine is the angelic number,' Tonti droned on, echoing the words of the strange carabiniere they'd met earlier. 'This you shall see in the work, in its structure, in its division of the episodes of life. I give you . . .'

The movie director tugged on the braided rope by the side of the curtain. The velvet opened.

'. . . the creator. The source. The fountainhead.'

The casket came into full view. Peroni blinked rapidly to make sure he wasn't dreaming. Someone in the crowd released a short, pained cry. He watched the woman next to him, some half-familiar Roman model from the magazines, elegant in a silk gown and jewels, place her gloved fingers to her lips, her mouth open, her eyes wide with shock.

The Carabinieri became frantic. They didn't know where to look, towards the children's cinema and the sound of shooting, or at the platform, where Tonti was now walking stiffly away from the thing he had revealed, an expression of utter distaste on his cold, sallow face, as if he resented the obvious fact that it had somehow stolen his thunder.

Falcone was pushing his way through the crowd, elbowing past black-suited men with pale faces and shrieking female guests.

Teresa, predictably, was a short step behind.

'Oh well,' Peroni grumbled, and fell in too, forcing his big, bulky body through the sea of silk and fine dark jackets ahead of him, apologizing as he went.

By the time he reached the small stage outside the entrance to the Casa del Cinema the area around the exhibit case was empty save for Falcone and the pathologist who stood either side of the cabinet staring at what lay within, bloody and shocking behind the smeared glass. Peroni felt quite proud of himself. There'd been a time when all this would have made him feel a little sick.

He studied the object. It appeared to be a severed head covered in some kind of thin blue plastic which had been slashed to allow the eyes and mouth to be visible. The material enclosing most of what stood in place of Dante's death mask was pulled painfully tight. So much so that it was easy to see the features of the face that lay beneath. It was an image that had been everywhere in Rome for weeks, that of Allan Prime. This was the face of the new Dante, visible on all the posters, all the promotional material that had appeared on walls and billboards, subway trains and buses. Now it had replaced the death mask of the poet himself. Sealed inside the case by yards of ugly black duct tape, it was some kind of cruel, ironic statement, Peroni guessed. Close up, it also looked not quite real – if the word could be applied to such a situation.

Two senior Carabinieri officers materialized at Falcone's side. He ignored them.

'This is ours,' the older one declared. 'We're responsible for the safety of the cast.'

Falcone's grey eyebrows rose in surprise. He didn't say a thing.

'Don't get fresh with me,' the officer went on, instantly irate. 'You were supposed to be looking after the mask.'

Peroni shrugged and observed, 'One lost piece of clay. One dead famous actor. Do you want to swap?'

'It's *ours*!'

'What?' Teresa asked. 'A practical joke?'

Slyly, without any of the men noticing, she had stolen the short, black truncheon from the junior carabiniere's belt. The pathologist now held it in her right hand and was quietly aiming a blow at the blood-smeared glass.

'Touch the evidence and I will have your job,' the senior carabiniere said, more than a little fearful.

'Same here,' Falcone added.

'This is evidence, gentlemen,' Teresa replied. 'But not of the kind you think.' She looked at each of them and smiled. 'We're in the movie business now, remember? Do the words "special effects" mean anything at all?'

The short baton connected with the top of the glass cabinet. Teresa raked it round and round. When she had enough room to manoeuvre she reached in and, to the curses of both Falcone and his Carabinieri counterparts, carefully lifted out the head and held it in her hands, turning the thing round, making approving noises.

Teresa ran one large pale finger along the ragged line of blood and tissue at the base then, to Peroni's horror, put the gory tip to her mouth and licked it.

'Food colouring,' she said. 'Fake blood. It's the wrong shade. Didn't you notice? Movie blood always is. Flesh and skin . . . it's all a joke.' The tissue at the ragged torn neckline came away in her fingers: cotton wool stained a livid red, stuck weakly to the base of the head with glue.

Her fingers picked at the blue latex cladding around the base of the neck and revealed perfect skin beneath, the colour and complexion of that of a store-window dummy. Peroni laughed. He'd known something was wrong.

'But why?' she asked, puzzled, talking entirely to herself.

She turned the head again in her hands, looked into the bulbous eyes staring out of the slits made in the blue plastic. They were clearly artificial, not human at all. It was all legerdemain, and obvious once you learned how to look.

Then Teresa Lupo gazed more closely into the face and her dark, full eyebrows creased in bafflement. She pulled back the blue plastic around the lips to reveal a mouth set in an expression of pain and bewilderment. More plastic came away as she tore at the tight, enclosing film to show the face. There was a mask there. It had been crudely fastened to a store dummy's head to give it form. She removed sufficient of the film to allow her to lift the object beneath from the base. Then she held it up and rotated the thing in her fingers.

'Hair,' she said, nodding at the underside. 'Whiskers.' Her fingers indicated a small stain on the interior, near the chin. 'And that's real blood.'

She glanced at Falcone, anxious, bemused.

'This is from a man, Leo,' Teresa Lupo insisted. 'Allan Prime.'

The inspector stood there, a finger to his lips, thinking. The Carabinieri couple said nothing and looked at one another. More of their officers were pushing back the crowd now. Peroni could hear the whine of an ambulance siren working its way to the park.

She placed the mask on the podium table and rotated the pale dummy's head in her hands, ripping back the remaining covering.

'There's something else,' she murmured.

The words emerged as she tore off the blue film. They were written in a flowing, artistic script across the top of the skull. It reminded Peroni of the huckster's props they found when they raided fake clairvoyants taking the gullible to the cleaners. They had objects like this, with each portion of the head marked out for its metaphysical leanings. In this case the message covered everything, from ear to ear, as if there were only a single lesson to be absorbed.

'*Lasciate ogne speranza, voi ch'intrate,*' Teresa said, as if reciting from memory. 'Abandon all hope, you who enter here.' She shook her head. 'Damnation in the mind of a poet. That's what was written on the Gate of Hell when Dante entered.'

A noise made Peroni glance back at the crowd. Costa was walking through looking pale but determined, a gun hanging loose in his hand. By his side was the actress from the movie, her eyes downcast and glassy.

Costa joined them, nodded at the dummy's head in Teresa Lupo's hands, and asked, 'What happened?'

The pathologist told him before Falcone could object.

'And you?' Falcone demanded.

Maggie Flavier was staring at the mask, shocked, silent, her cheeks marked by lines of smudged mascara.

Costa glanced at her and said, 'It seemed as if someone was trying to attack Miss Flavier. Then . . .'

The senior Carabinieri man found his voice.

'This is *our* case. *Our* evidence. I have made a phone call to *Maresciallo* Quattrocchi, Falcone. He was called away briefly. Now he returns. You learn. This cannot . . .'

He fell abruptly silent as Costa lifted the handgun, pointed it at the fake head and loosed off a shot. The sound silenced them all. Maggie stifled a choking sob. There was nothing new there when the smoke and the racket had cleared. No damage. Not another fresh shard of shattered glass.

'Blanks,' Costa told the man. 'This was his gun. I took it from his corpse while your men danced around it like schoolgirls. They've just shot dead a defenceless man taking part in some kind of a sick prank. Why not go investigate that?'

'Th-this . . .' the officer stuttered.

'Enough,' Falcone interjected and glanced at Costa. 'Assemble a team, *sovrintendente*. *Subito*.'

Teresa was already on the phone, and standing guard over the objects on the podium table.

'Where does Allan Prime live?' Falcone asked.

The officer said nothing.

'I know,' Maggie Flavier said. 'Do you think . . . ?'

She didn't finish the sentence.

'You can tell us on the way,' Falcone said, then called for a car.

PART TWO

- 1 -

They sat in the back of the Lancia, with a plain-clothes female driver at the wheel.

'Sir,' Costa said, as they slowly negotiated the bickering snarl of vehicles arguing for space in the Piazza Venezia. 'Miss Flavier . . . I don't understand why she should be here.'

The woman by his side gave him a puzzled look but remained silent.

Falcone sighed then turned round from the passenger seat and extended his long tanned hand. Maggie Flavier took it. She was more composed now and had wiped away the stray make-up from her face. She looked younger, more ordinary. Prettier, said a stray thought.

'My name is Leo Falcone. I'm an inspector. His inspector.'

'Nice to meet you. Why am I here?'

He gave her his most gracious and charming of smiles.

'For reasons that are both practical and political. You were the victim of some strange kind of attack. Perhaps a joke. But a poor one it seems to me. Allan Prime . . . Maybe it was a joke in his case too. I don't know and I would like to. One man is dead. Prime is missing. The Carabinieri, meanwhile, are wandering around preening themselves while trying to work out which day it is. We have no need of complications.'

Falcone stared at her openly.

'Would you rather they have regard for your safety? Or us? The choice is yours, naturally.'

'My safety?'

'Just in case.'

'What's going on here?' she demanded. 'I was supposed to be at a movie premiere tonight. People shooting blanks. Fake death masks.' Her bright, animated face fell. 'Someone getting killed.' She looked at Costa. 'Why did they shoot him anyway?'

'Because they thought he was dangerous. They didn't know any better. Whoever he was . . .'

'Not Carabinieri, that's for sure,' Falcone intervened.

'Whoever he was,' Costa continued, 'this is now a real case and it's not ours.' He caught the dismay in the inspector's eye. 'I'm sorry. That's a fact, sir. The Carabinieri were given the job of security. Also, there's the question of jurisdiction. Allan Prime is an American citizen. If he's missing, someone has to inform the Embassy and allow them a role in the investigation. We all know the rules when a foreign citizen's involved. We can't just drive away with a key witness and hope it's all ours. I should never have left the scene in the first place, or taken that weapon.'

The car came to a halt in the traffic in Vittorio Emanuele. He didn't understand why they were taking this route. There were quicker ways through the tangle of alleys behind the Campo dei Fiori. A good police driver should have known about them.

The woman at the wheel turned and smiled at them.

'The US authorities are involved already,' she said. 'So don't worry on that front. Captain Catherine Bianchi. San Francisco Police Department. Is there a better way than this? I don't drive much in Rome usually. I lack the fortitude.'

She was about forty, slim, with a pleasant, bright face, Italian-looking he would have said until he looked at her hair. It was straight and immaculate, coal-coloured with a henna sheen, tied back behind her head in a severe way that would have been rare on a Roman woman. She spoke good Italian, though with an American inflection. This was the woman he'd heard about; the one who'd caught Falcone's eye.

The inspector outlined a faster route to the Via Giulia, with a degree of patience he would never have used on one of his officers.

'Can I hit the siren?' she asked.

'No,' Falcone replied. 'That will just give them notice.'

'Give who notice?' Maggie Flavier asked.

'The Carabinieri, of course,' he answered.

Costa looked out of the window, at the people and the cars, the familiar crush of humanity in his native city.

He understood why Maggie Flavier was in the car. A man had died in the gardens of the Villa Borghese. Some strange, gruesome caricature of a human head had been substituted for the precious death mask of Dante which they were supposed to be guarding. A world-famous actor was missing, and his co-star had been the victim of an attack that seemed to be some kind of pointless prank.

There were crimes here, perhaps serious, perhaps less so. Leo Falcone clearly had no desire to try to go near the shooting. It would have been pointless. The man who attacked them had been killed by the Carabinieri. Only they could investigate themselves. What Falcone was quietly attempting to do was position himself to steal any broader case concerning the death mask and, more importantly, the fate of Allan Prime. The two principal national law enforcement agencies in Italy usually managed to avoid turf wars over who handled what. In theory they were equals, one civilian, one military, both capable of handling serious crimes. Often the decision about which organization handled a case came down to the simplest of questions: Who got there first?

'We will have to offer them a statement,' Costa insisted. 'Miss Flavier and I. We were witnesses.'

'There's no hurry,' the inspector observed. 'Neither of you knows this man, do you? Nor did you see how he died. It's better that Miss Flavier remains in our company. For her own sake.'

'Absolutely,' the American policewoman insisted from the front seat. 'No question about it.'

Maggie Flavier leaned back in the deep leather of Falcone's Lancia, flung her arms behind her head and sighed, 'I love Italy.'

She gazed at Costa, smiling wanly, resigned. He found himself briefly mesmerized by her actor's skill, the ability she possessed to turn her gaze upon someone, seize his attention, to look at him with her bright green eyes and hold his interest, make him wonder what came next. This was the way she stared into the camera lens. For reasons he couldn't quite pinpoint he found that thought vaguely disturbing.

'Why's that?' he asked.

'Here I am being kidnapped by two charming Roman cops. And why? So you can steal some case you don't understand right from under the noses of the opposition.'

At the wheel of the Lancia as they negotiated the narrow, choked lanes of the *centro storico*, Catherine Bianchi chuckled and said, 'You got it.'

Costa didn't laugh though. Nor did Leo Falcone, who was on his mobile phone, engaged in a long, low discussion he clearly didn't want anyone else to hear.

They rounded one more corner, past a house, Costa recalled, that was once supposed to have belonged to the mistress of a Borgia pope, Alexander VI. An image flashed through his head: Bartolomeo Veneziano's subtly erotic portrait of Alexander's bewitching daughter Lucrezia, ginger hair crimped, a single breast bared, catching the artist's eye with an unsmiling sideways glance, the selfsame way Maggie Flavier regarded Roberto Tonti's camera, and through it the prurient world at large. It was a strange memory, yet apposite. Lucrezia, like Beatrice, the character Maggie played, was an enigma, never quite fully understood.

The Lancia turned into the Via Giulia, one of the smartest streets in Rome, a place of palatial apartments and expensive antique stores. A sea of blue state police cars stood motionless ahead of them. There were dark blue vans of the Carabinieri in among them. Traffic was backed up on the Lungotevere by the river. A battle was looming.

Maggie nodded at a house in the centre of the tangle of the vehicles.

'It's that one there.'

'You know it well?' Costa asked.

'Allan threw parties,' she said with a shrug. 'A lot.' She looked at him, her smile gone, her face very like the Lucrezia he recalled from the painting he'd seen when he stole off from some routine immigration duty that had sent him to Frankfurt. 'Everyone likes a party from time to time, don't they?'

She paused and looked, for a moment, very vulnerable.

'You don't want me to come in, do you?' she said, and the question was asked of Falcone.

The inspector seemed puzzled.

'Would you rather stay here?'

'If that's OK.' She put a hand to her close-cropped hair, tousled it nervously, the way a child did. 'You'll think I'm crazy but I get a feeling for things sometimes. I've got one now. It's not good. Don't make me go in there. Not unless you know it's all right. I need the bathroom. I need a drink.'

'*Sovrintendente*,' Falcone ordered.

'Sir.'

'Find two women officers who can take Miss Flavier to the wine bar round the corner. Then you come with me.'

- 2 -

Gianni Peroni had enjoyed stand-offs with the Carabinieri before. Just never over a dummy's head with an apparently genuine death mask attached to it. He had four plain-clothes state police officers with him to form a physical barrier between the evidence and the grumbling crowd of smart uniforms and surly faces getting angrier by the moment. The small police forensic crew had, meanwhile, gathered what passed for some of the strangest evidence Peroni had ever seen.

What really took his breath away were the movie people. Roberto Tonti, grey hair flying as his stooped, lanky frame hobbled around the stage storming at anyone within earshot. The dark, heavily built producer Dino Bonetti, who'd pass for a mob boss any day, stabbing his finger at anyone who'd listen, demanding that the evening go ahead. And, more subtly, some quiet American publicity man backing them up during the rare moments either paused for breath. Even the Carabinieri baulked at the idea everything could go off as planned. While the arguments ensued, Teresa and her small newly gathered team worked quietly and swiftly, placing items very quickly into evidence bags and containers, trying to stay out of the mêlée. He hadn't told her they didn't have long. He hadn't needed to.

'There's been a death,' Peroni pointed out when Tonti began threatening to call some politicians he knew. 'And . . .' he gestured at the bloodied fake head. '. . . this. The entertainment is over, sir. Surely you appreciate what I'm talking about?'

The publicist took him by the arm and requested a private word. Glad to have an excuse to escape the director's furious bellows,

Peroni ordered the plain-clothes men not to move an inch and went with the man to the back of the stage.

He had seen Simon Harvey on their visits to Cinecittà to discuss arrangements for the exhibition. He seemed a professional, obsessed with the job as much as the rest of them, but, perhaps, with some rare degree of perspective. Peroni recalled that, on one occasion, the man had given them a brief and apparently academic lecture on Dante and the origins of *Inferno*, as if somehow needing to justify the intellectual rationale behind the movie, to declare, 'This will be art, promise.' This had struck him as odd and unnecessary at the time. But then the movie industry was rarely predictable, for ordinary human beings anyway. That day in the film studios he'd watched hideously disfigured ghouls sipping Coke, smoking cigarettes and filling in crosswords during their time off camera. He'd been glad to get out into the dull suburb surrounding the studio and breathe the fume-filled air after that.

'Listen,' Harvey went on. 'Forget about Roberto and Bonetti bawling you out. That's how they work, Roberto more than most. The point is this. There's big money at stake here. *Italian* money.'

Peroni stared at the man, wondering what to make of this strange comment. With his unruly head of wayward fair hair, a face that wasn't as young as it was trying to appear and an attitude that varied from servile to importunate, he didn't seem to fit at all.

'Italian money?' Peroni asked. 'What does that mean?'

Harvey cast a backwards glance to make sure no one was listening.

'Do I need to spell it out?'

'For me you do.'

The publicist placed a conspiratorial hand on Peroni's arm.

'You're a cop,' he said with a sigh. 'Please don't act the innocent. God knows it's been in the papers anyway. Bonetti has all kinds of friends. Government friends.' He winced. 'Other sorts. There's more than a hundred and fifty million dollars running on this horse. Money like that creates debts that need paying. This is your country . . . not mine. We both know there are people neither of us want to piss off, not for a three-hour private screening in front of a handful of self-important jerks in evening dress anyway. All I ask is you give us a break. Then we're done. It won't get in the way. I'll make sure. That's a promise.'

Peroni couldn't believe what he was hearing.

'Someone's been shot. They heard it. We all did. There's also the question of a death mask which, in case you've forgotten, seems to resemble your missing movie star.'

He pointed at the head, which was now on a plastic mat on the podium table, being prodded and poked by Teresa and her deputy, Silvio Di Capua. She caught Peroni's eye and he got the message straight away. It was time to get the evidence out of there as soon as possible, before the Carabinieri made a determined charge to grab it. The dark blue uniforms seemed to be breeding around them, and some of them had fancy stripes and medals on their jackets that denoted the arrival of more senior ranks.

'Ever heard the saying "The show must go on"?' Harvey replied.

'Don't tell me. It's what this absent star of yours would have wanted.'

'Precisely. Imagine. All these people can go tell their friends tomorrow they still got to the premiere, even after everything. This is the world I live in, friend. It's about status and money and one-upmanship. *Inferno* is the big release of this summer, worldwide. They get to say they saw it first. We get to keep our backers happy. You escape the phone calls from on high. Please.'

'This is a police investigation . . .'

'No it's not,' Harvey interrupted. 'Let's speak frankly. I oversaw those security arrangements. By rights this belongs to the Carabinieri. Not you. All you guys had to look after was the stuff.'

'The stuff,' Peroni repeated.

'No fun doing the menial work while others get to stand in the spotlight, is it?' The American smiled. 'This is within my gift, Officer . . . er, I forget the name.'

'Gianni Peroni,' he answered. 'Like the beer.'

He stuck out his hand. Peroni took it.

'Simon Harvey. Like the sherry. Here's the deal. You let this little show go on tonight. I'll do what I can to ensure this investigation goes your way. The Carabinieri won't argue. Not till they've phoned home, and by then you and your friends will be clear away with the goods.'

Peroni thought about this. Harvey had no idea how these matters worked. The probability was that the Carabinieri would get the investigation in any case, however hard Falcone tried to steal the job. The men from the military had been given cast and crew security from the outset. It was their call.

'Why would you want to give me a deal like that?'

The head of curly hair nodded in the direction of the dark blue uniforms.

'Because I've had a bellyful of those stuck-up bastards for the past few months and they won't cut me a deal on anything. Is that good enough?'

Peroni discreetly eyed the opposition. Some boss figure had emerged and was now bravely taking on the police forensic team, not even blinking at Teresa's increasingly desperate attempts to shout him down. There was strength in numbers, particularly when it came backed up by medals and rank. It was definitely time to go.

'You must have seen that film a million times,' Peroni observed.

'A million times is not enough,' Harvey replied straight up, and it was impossible to tell whether there was any side to his words whatsoever. 'Roberto Tonti's a genius. I'd watch it a million times more if I could. *Inferno* is the finest piece of cinema I've ever worked on. I doubt I'll ever have the privilege to get my name attached to anything better. What's your point?'

'My point, Signor Harvey, is I'm willing to let you have your little show. Provided you can help us get out of here the moment my colleagues are ready.'

'It's done,' he said immediately. 'You have my word.'

'And I want someone to come along with us. Someone from the studio. Bonetti, Tonti . . .'

The man waved his hand in front of Peroni's face.

'Don't even think about it. They don't do menial.'

'In that case you. Seen inside many police stations?'

Harvey's pleasant demeanour failed him at that moment.

'Can't say I have. Is this relevant?'

'Not at all.'

'Then what am I supposed to talk about? Dante? I've got a degree in classics.' Harvey caught Peroni's eye and nodded at the fake severed head. 'That . . . *thing*. It's about Dante, you know. The line they wrote on the skull . . . Abandon all hope, you who enter here.'

'So I gather.'

Teresa had what she wanted. He could see the boxes and bags ready to go. The pathologist took a break from bawling out an entire line of Carabinieri officers to issue a sly nod in his direction.

Harvey wriggled, a little nervous.

'You know something? We've been getting strange anonymous e-mails. For months. It happens a lot when you're making a movie. I never thought too much about it.'

'Strange?'

'They quoted that line, always. And they said . . .' Harvey tugged at his long hair. '. . . they said we were living in limbo. I never took it literally.'

'What do you mean?'

The American grimaced.

'I mean *literally*. The way it appears in Dante.' He sighed. 'Limbo is the first circle of Hell. The place the story begins.'

Just the mention of the film revived some memories Gianni Peroni hoped had been lost. Things seemed to be happening from the very opening moment in Tonti's version of the tale. Not good things either.

'And then?' Peroni asked. 'After limbo?'

'Then you're on the road to Hell.'

– 3 –

The door to Allan Prime's apartment opened almost the moment Falcone pushed the bell. Nic Costa felt as if he'd stumbled back through time. The woman who stood there might have been an actress herself. Adele Neri still looked several years short of forty and was as slender and cat-like as he recalled. She wore well-pressed designer jeans and a skimpy white T-shirt. Her arresting face bore the cold, disengaged scowl of the Roman rich. She had a tan that spoke of a second home in Sicily or beyond and a heavy gold necklace around a slender neck that carried a few wrinkles he didn't recall from the case a few years before when she had first come to the notice of the Questura. That had taken them to the Via Giulia too, to a house not more than a dozen doors away, one that had been booby-trapped with a bomb by her mob boss husband Emilio as he tried to flee Rome. She was an interesting woman who had led an interesting life.

'I thought I was past getting visits from the likes of you people,' she said, still holding the door half open. 'Do you have papers? Or some reason why I should let you into my home?'

'We were looking for Allan Prime,' Costa said. 'We thought he lived here.'

'He does. When he's around. But this is my house. All of it. Several more in the Via Giulia too. Do you mean you didn't know?'

She gazed at Falcone, thin arms crossed, smiling. Costa recalled seeing the intelligence reports after Emilio's death. They said that Adele had taken over leadership of his local clan for a while before selling on her interests to a larger, more serious mob and, if rumour was correct, removing herself from the murky world of Roman crime to enjoy her vast, illicitly inherited wealth.

'Inspector Falcone. The clever one.'

'Signora Neri,' Falcone said pleasantly, nodding. 'What an unexpected delight.'

'Quite. So tell me. Why didn't you try to put me in jail? After Emilio got shot?'

'Because I didn't think it would stick,' Falcone replied, looking puzzled. 'Isn't that obvious? I'm a practical man. I don't fight lost causes over trivia.' He got one foot over the threshold and tried to look around. 'This is nothing to do with you. We merely wish to locate a lost Hollywood actor.'

'Join the club,' she moaned, then stepped back and said, 'I'll let five of you in here and they'd best have no dirt on their shoes. This place rents for eight thousand dollars a week and for that people don't expect muddy cop prints on the carpet.'

Costa issued some orders to the officers left outside then got in first, looking around, wondering where to start. It was obvious really, with her. They let three officers begin to prowl the vast, airy apartment. There was a spectacular view of the river and the busy Lungotevere to the front through long windows, with a vista of the dome of St Peter's in the distance, and by the external terrace a circular iron staircase to what he took to be a roof garden. To their left stood a large open kitchen with the kind of fittings only the rich could think about.

He sat down on a vast tan leather sofa. Falcone joined him and they waited. She wanted to make an entrance, a point. Adele Neri dodged briefly into the kitchen and came out with a glass of blood orange juice, a *spremuta* freshly pressed, probably from one of the stalls in the Campo dei Fiori around the corner, he guessed. The memories were coming back as he looked at this attractive if somewhat hard-faced woman. Emilio Neri had been one of the most important mob bosses in Rome until his past caught up with him. Adele, more than thirty years his junior, with a history in vice herself, had been complicit in his downfall, though how much of that was greed and how much hatred for her husband they had never been able to decide. Falcone was right. Some cases simply petered out well short of a court hearing, and that of the Neris had been one of them. The gang lord was dead, his empire shattered, soon to be disposed of by his guilty widow. One crime clan left the scene, another took its place. Life went on, as it always would. He'd felt happy about Neri's fate at the time. A man had died at Costa's hand in pursuit of the answers Adele Neri had held in her smart, beautiful head all along. He had never quite shaken off a misplaced sense of guilt over that particular outcome.

'Where's Allan Prime?' Falcone asked.

'You tell me. I was supposed to have lunch with him today, at noon. I came over, rang the bell. No one answered, so I let myself in. Then some people phoned from the studio. They said he hadn't turned up for the premiere either.' She took an elegant, studied sip of the scarlet drink. 'This is my place. I can do what I damned well like.'

'You and Mr Prime . . .' Costa asked.

'Landlady and tenant. Nothing more. He tried, naturally. He's the kind who does that anyway, just to see who'll rise to the bait. It's a form of insecurity, and insecure men have never interested me.'

'You have no idea where he might be?'

Adele Neri had always seemed a very confident woman. Even for her, though, these seemed ready, easy answers.

She made a gesture of ignorance with her skinny, tanned arms.

'Why should I? He pays the rent. I indulge him with lunch from time to time. It's a kindness. He's like most actors. A lot less interesting than he thinks. A lot less intelligent too. But . . .' She gazed at them, thinking to herself. 'This isn't like him. He's a professional. He told me he was going to that premiere tonight. He moaned about it, naturally. Having to perform, for free.' The woman laughed. 'Allan's an artist, of course. Or so he'd like to pretend. All that razzmatazz is supposed to be beneath him.'

'Girlfriends . . .' Falcone began.

'Don't know, don't care,' she interrupted. 'He had women here.

What do you expect? He had a few parties early on, and I had to get someone to speak to him about that. There are some nice old people living in the other apartments. They don't like movie types wandering around with white powder dripping from their noses. It's not that kind of neighbourhood. Also . . .'

She stopped. There was something on her mind, and she was unsure whether to share it with the police, Costa thought.

'Also what?' he asked.

'Why should I tell you people anything? What do I get in return?'

The inspector frowned.

'Some help in finding your tenant, perhaps. Does he owe you money?'

'Three months outstanding. Show business people never pay on time. They think we should be grateful they're here at all. That we should put up a plaque on the wall when they're gone.'

'Twenty-four thousand dollars,' Falcone observed. 'A lot of money.'

'Don't insult me. I spend more than that in one day when I go to Milan. I'll tell you one thing though. For free. Prime and his cronies had interesting friends. I came to one of his parties. Him and that evil bastard Bonetti. The company they kept.' She smiled. 'It was like the old days. When my husband was alive. The same dark suits. The same accents bred in cowshit. A bunch of surly sons of bitches from the south who think they own you. That kind never changes. They just put their money in different places. Legitimate ones. And movies too, not that they're the same thing.'

Costa watched her, thinking, then said, 'You seem to know about the movie business.'

'I've made my contribution. Shits like Bonetti know how to screw you. "It's only a million. Think of the tax write-off. If the worst comes to the worst, you get your money back anyway." Then . . .' She clapped her skeletal hands and the loud noise they made rang round the room like a gunshot. 'It's gone, and Bonetti or one of his creatures is phoning from LA, full of apologies, promising that maybe a little of it will come back one day. After everyone else has taken their cut.'

Adele Neri leaned forward and her sharp eyes held them.

'Allan moves in dangerous circles and he doesn't even know it. I told him but he wasn't the kind of man who'd listen to anyone else. A woman least of all. That's the truth. You don't honestly think I'd be sitting here waiting for the doorbell to ring if I'd done something, do you? Why?'

'I cannot imagine,' Falcone answered honestly. 'Do you read Dante, Signora Neri?'

The unexpected question amused her. Adele Neri looked human, warm and attractive and perhaps even a pleasure to know at that moment. It lasted for a second or two, no more.

'Dante?' she asked, amazed. 'I'm going to go to the movie some time. Preferably when Allan gets me some free tickets. But reading?' She threw back what remained of the *spremuta*. 'I'm the merry widow now, Falcone. I shop, I spend, I travel and when I feel like it, when I see something that interests me, I take a little pleasure. Life's too enjoyable for books. Why leave this world for someone else's? Reading . . .' She leaned back and closed her eyes. '. . . is for people without lives. No. I know no more of Dante than you.'

'Actually, I know quite a lot,' Falcone replied almost apologetically. 'Not that it matters.'

'It doesn't?' she asked. 'Why?'

'Because I find it hard to believe that anyone would commit much of a crime over poetry. However much they might wish us to think it otherwise.'

She went quiet and asked, 'You really think something's happened to Allan?'

'He's missing. We have some very strange evidence. One man is dead for sure. Perhaps there's no connection. Perhaps . . .'

She cut the air with her hand and said, 'This does not involve me. If you want to talk any more we need to do this with a lawyer around.'

Taccone, the old *sovrintendente* Falcone liked to use, had returned from looking around the apartment and was waiting for the inspector to fall silent.

'You need to see this,' he said.

The two men got up and followed him into what appeared to be the master bedroom. Adele Neri came in behind them. Somewhere along the way she'd picked up a packet of cigarettes and was quickly lighting one.

'What is it?' Falcone asked.

Costa walked forward to stand a short distance from the bed. He looked at Adele Neri and asked, 'Didn't you come in here?'

'Why would I want to sneak around his bedroom?'

'Call in forensic,' Falcone ordered. 'Let's not touch anything. Did you find any signs of violence?'

Taccone shook his head.

'We didn't find anything. Except this.'

The bed was covered with a green plastic ground sheet of the kind used by campers. The shape of a man's body was still visible on it, set deep enough to imprint itself on the mattress below. Around the outline of the upper torso there was a faint sprinkling of pale grey powder which grew heavier around the head.

Taccone reached down and, using a handkerchief, picked up the handle of a brown bucket that had been hidden on the far side of the bed.

'It looks like clay or something,' he said. 'Made up on the spot.'

Costa's phone was ringing. He'd placed two requests with the officers left outside on Adele Neri's orders. They had news. The doorman who had been on duty that morning had gone home at lunchtime. It had taken a while to trace him. Costa listened to what the officer who'd finally found the man, in a Campo dei Fiori cafe, had to say. Then he asked to be passed to the *agente* who had handled the second inquiry.

'Seal off this room,' Falcone ordered. 'Assume we have a murder scene.'

'We don't,' Costa said simply. 'There's no CCTV in this building, but we've found one of the staff who was on duty. There are details in the visitors' book.'

He looked at Adele Neri and asked, 'Is the name Carlotta Valdes familiar?'

She drew on the cigarette and shook her head.

'No. Is it Spanish?'

Costa nodded.

'It sounds that way. A woman calling herself that arrived to see Allan Prime at eight thirty this morning. They left together around ten. Mr Prime looked very happy, apparently. Expectant even.'

Falcone shook his head in bafflement, lost for words for a moment, as if the investigation were slipping away from them before it had even begun.

'A man *is* dead . . .' Costa reminded him.

'He belongs to the Carabinieri, as you have made very clear.'

'Also . . .'

'Also the death mask we were supposed to protect is missing,' Falcone went on. 'I am aware of that. It may be all we have. A case of art theft.'

Costa struggled to see some sense in the situation. It was impossible to guess precisely what kind of case they had on their hands. The loss of a precious historic object? Or something altogether darker and more personal?

'The man who was killed in the park,' he continued, regardless of Falcone's growing exasperation. 'He's been identified. We were told by the Carabinieri as a matter of course, at the same time they put in a formal request for an interview. I need to report to them with Signora Flavier.'

'Well?' Falcone asked.

'His name was Peter Jamieson. He was an actor, originally from Los Angeles. The man moved to Rome a decade ago, principally playing bit parts, Americans for cheap TV productions at Cinecittà.'

Falcone looked ready to explode.

'Tell me. Did he have a part in *Inferno*?'

'Non-speaking. Barely visible.' Then he added, not knowing quite why, 'There's no reason why anyone from the cast should have recognized him at all.'

The inspector pointed a bony finger in Costa's face, as if he'd found the guilty party already.

'If this is some kind of publicity stunt gone wrong I will put every last one of those painted puppets in jail.'

'If . . .' Costa repeated, and found himself staring again at the powder on the bed, and the silhouette of Allan Prime's head outlined there.

- 4 -

Maresciallo Gianluca Quattrocchi was furious on several fronts. The screening had begun without his permission. Key pieces of evidence had been removed from the scene by the morgue monkeys of the state police, under the supervision of Teresa Lupo, a woman Quattrocchi had encountered, and been bested by, in the past, on more than one occasion. And now Leo Falcone had placed a team in Allan Prime's home without any reference to the Carabinieri, though the state police inspector knew full well that security for the film cast was not his responsibility and never would be.

As a result Quattrocchi's bull-like face appeared even more vexed than normal and he found himself sweating profusely inside the fine wool uniform he had chosen for an occasion that was meant to be social and ceremonial, not business at all. He stood at the back of the projection room, temporarily speechless with fury, not least because his principal contact within the crew, the publicist Simon Harvey, appeared to have been spirited away by Falcone's people too. All he got in his place was the smug, beaming Dino Bonetti, a loathsome creature of dubious morality, and two young, pony-tailed Americans with, it seemed to him, a hazy grasp of the seriousness of the situation.

While everyone else wore evening dress, the two young men had removed their jackets to reveal T-shirts bearing the name 'Lukatmi', with a logo underneath showing some kind of oriental goddess, a buxom figure with skimpy clothing, a beguiling smile, and multiple arms, each holding a variety of different cameras – movie, still, phones, little webcams of the kind the Carabinieri used for CCTV –

57

all linked into one end of a snaking cable pumping out a profusion of images into a starry sky.

Quattrocchi peered more closely. There were faces within the stars, a galaxy of Hollywood notables – Monroe, Gable, Hepburn, James Stewart, their heads floating in the ether.

'Note,' the skinny one identified by his shirt as 'Josh Jonah, Founder, Ideologist, Visioneer', ordered, 'the absence of noise.'

'I can hear *you*,' Quattrocchi snapped, to no avail.

'If we were in an ordinary projectionist's room,' Jonah continued, 'we wouldn't be able to have this conversation. There would be film rattling through the projector. Physical artefacts. Needless expense. Time and money thrown away without reason.'

'I am an officer of the Carabinieri. Not an accountant.'

'We're all accountants in the end.' It was the other American, a big muscular man with a boyish face, a pony-tail and long, wavy dark hair. Quattrocchi peered at his T-shirt. It read 'Tom Black, Founder, Architect, Corporate Conscience'. He seemed younger than his peer. A little less sure of himself too. 'In the sense that we pay for things. You'd like to get movies quicker, cheaper, easier, wouldn't you?'

'Right now,' Quattrocchi blurted out so loudly that he felt sure his voice had carried into the cinema beyond, with its audience of VIPs, 'I would like to know where Allan Prime is, why we have a dead actor in the park out there, and what the hell is going on around here.'

He glowered at their shirts again.

'Who is Lukatmi anyway? Some Indian god? And who the hell are you?'

The two looked at each other and the one called Tom Black smiled.

'That was kind of the positioning we were looking for. Three million dollars got blown there. Worth every penny.'

'We're backers,' the skinny one boasted. 'We've got money in this thing. Without us it would never have got made.'

'What . . . ?' Quattrocchi began to say.

'Lukatmi's nothing to do with India either,' the quieter American interrupted. 'It's a play on the English. "Look at me." It's a philosophical statement about not hiding away, about being a part of the digital lifestream, a star in your own right, out there for everyone to see.'

'Like YouTube,' Bonetti added, and Josh Jonah howled, 'No, no, no, no, *no!* How many freaking times do I have to say this? YouTube is yesterday . . .'

'When Google bought them . . .' Tom Black shook his head, his broad, young face so sorrowful it looked as if someone had died. 'It was all over. They don't understand the whole mash-up thing. The behemoth days are past.'

'Lukatmi is just the medium, not the message,' Jonah added, taking over, clearly the boss. 'Except for the paid-for content, we don't own a damned thing. It's not for us to dictate to human beings what they create or what they see. If you have a problem with that, don't watch.'

Quattrocchi realized he'd read about these people in the newspapers. They'd found some loophole that allowed them to be absolved of any legal responsibility for what was, on the surface, carried by their network. They were, if he understood this correctly, like a dating agency. Their computers put someone wanting something in touch with someone offering it. The relationship was consummated in a way that had, so far, allowed them to escape the attentions of the law, on the simple grounds that they never published anything directly themselves. If the material people found on Lukatmi turned out to be copyright, blasphemous, or, with very few restrictions, pornographic, they weren't to blame. It was anarchy with a listing on the NASDAQ. Millions and millions of people had flocked to their site since it went live less than a year before. The two founders had become paper billionaires on the back of a flotation that had seen staid investment houses and international banks pour vast sums of money into a company that seemed to be little more than two geeks with a big and possibly dubious idea.

One thing still puzzled him.

'What on earth has all this got to do with the movie business?'

'Everything,' said Bonetti, intervening. 'This is a revolution. Like when silent movies got sound, when black and white turned to colour. It means we can finally reach people direct, any way we want, without getting screwed by the distributors or anyone else.' He cast a sour glance at the Americans. They saw it, as the Italian producer intended. 'Except them.'

Quattrocchi massaged his temples. There was a persistent, low ache there and had been ever since the shooting. An internal investigation team was now overseeing that, following the procedures after the deaths of civilians at the hands of a Carabinieri team. He wasn't looking forward to having to face them himself. He'd been absent from the Casa del Cinema when that took place on highly spurious grounds, a call of a personal nature. That was one more secret to keep under wraps.

'Who'd want to watch a movie on a phone?' he asked, unable to take his eyes off the screen beyond the room. It seemed to be on fire. The flames of Hell licked everywhere, and through them burst the faces of grinning, leering demons, their green and purple mouths babbling profanities and obscenities at the stricken, cowering figure of Dante, who shrank back, the beautiful Beatrice at his side, seemingly unmoved by this horrific sight.

'Millions of suckers everywhere,' Bonetti crowed. 'A dollar a clip. A monthly subscription for twenty. And then they go to see it in the cinema anyway. And buy the DVD. Then the director's edition. Then the collector's . . .' His fleshy face beamed. 'It's a dream. You sell the same old junk over and over again.'

'With absolute efficiency,' the skinny one, Josh Jonah, emphasized. 'Not a wasted piece of celluloid. Not a single cassette or DVD in inventory. And this . . .'

He patted the silver box streaming light into the theatre beyond.

'. . . is ours. Every last piece gets streamed straight here for less money than it costs to produce a single cinema print. The crap the masses turn out gets fed from PC to PC for free. The people that junk brings in become the movie audience of the future, and we serve them direct, same price they'd pay in a theatre, but at a fraction of the delivery cost.'

He clicked his fingers.

'Voilà. Big money.'

'Big money,' Bonetti repeated.

Quattrocchi shook his head and grumbled, 'So much for art. Also . . .'

This had bothered him all along. The picture on the screen didn't look right. It wasn't as sharp, as detailed, as engaging as he'd expect of a movie like this. It felt wrong, however smart the toys these kids used to fool Bonetti and anyone else throwing their hats into this particular ring.

He stopped, unable to believe what he was seeing.

'What on earth is that?'

The scene was dissolving in front of their eyes. The flames faded. The faces of the demons, Dante shrinking in terror before them, now gave way to something else. Quattrocchi had seen Roberto Tonti's movie that afternoon, at the private screening arranged for them and the state police. He knew for sure that what was now emerging on the screen in front of a selected audience of some two hundred international VIPs, politicians and hangers-on had never been there before.

It was Dante again, still terrified, his face frozen in dread. Or rather Allan Prime. In close-up, grainy, as if from some CCTV camera.

An open-faced black metal mask, ancient, medieval-looking, enclosed his head, one band fetching up hard against his mouth. The man's horrified features seemed exaggerated behind its bars. His eyes were locked and rigid with terror.

There was utter silence in the project room and in the theatre beyond. Then, nervously, someone in the crowd laughed, and another coughed. A voice rose. Quattrocchi recognized it: the furious, coarse bark of Roberto Tonti complaining about something yet again.

Josh Jonah wiped his skeletal forearm over his eyes.

'Was this an out-take or something?' he asked no one in particular. 'I don't recall seeing it. Tom. *Tom?*'

The other American was staring at his silver machine, punching keys, watching numbers fly up on the monitor.

'This isn't coming from us.' Sweat was starting to make dark, damp stains across his burly chest. He almost looked as frightened as Allan Prime. Or Dante. Whichever, Quattrocchi thought. 'I don't know where it's coming from.'

'Cut it,' Jonah ordered. 'Stop the frigging thing rolling. If someone else has got hold of the stream . . .'

'Sure . . .'

'No,' Quattrocchi ordered and found he had to drag the American away from his strange projector.

They both stared at him. Bonetti too, though there was no expression Quattrocchi could read on the producer's dark, lined face.

'This isn't part of the show,' Josh Jonah stated firmly. 'It's not supposed to be up there.'

'Yes it is. Your star's missing. Someone has taken hold of your toy. What if they're trying to tell us where he is? Or why? Or . . .'

He was about to say . . . Or both.

But the words never reached his lips. Two things had happened on the screen. In the right-hand corner a digital stopwatch appeared, counting down from the hour. *59:59, 59:58, 59:57 . . .*

As it ticked away an object entered from centre left, first in a sudden movement that darted in so quickly he was unable to see what had happened, only the result, that it had inflicted yet more pain and fright on the trapped man struggling on the screen in front of them, and that blood was now welling from some fresh wound that had appeared on his left temple.

The image disappeared. After a long break the picture resumed and Quattrocchi found he was unable to breathe or speak or think for a moment. Some narrow, deadly spear, the shaft as shiny as a mirror save for the bloodied tip which had just stabbed the trapped man's head, had slowly emerged, sharp and threatening, aimed once more at his temple.

The stopwatch flicked over from 58:00 to 57:59. The spear moved on a notch towards Allan Prime's head, as if attached to some machine that would edge it forward, minute by minute, until it drove into the actor's skull.

Quattrocchi stared at this gigantic, real-life depiction of a captive man waiting to die. There were hints to be found in this sight, surely. Clues, keys to unlock the conundrum. Otherwise why broadcast it at all? Simply to be cruel, nothing more? Behind the head he could just make out some shapes in the darkness, paintings perhaps, images, ones that might have been familiar had he possessed some way to illuminate the scene.

Beyond the projection room, out in the cinema, Tonti ceased roaring. Someone moaned. Another voice cried out in outrage. A woman screamed.

Bonetti threw open the door and bellowed at an attendant, 'Clear the room, man. Everyone.'

Then he returned and stared at Quattrocchi, shocked, finally babbling, 'Find him for God's sake. *Find him!*'

'But where?' he asked, to himself mostly, as he held down the shortcut key for headquarters on his phone, praying that there was someone there who was good at riddles.

He got through. The wrong man answered. Morello. A good officer. Not a bright man. Not the one Quattrocchi hoped for, and there wasn't time to locate others. He had to work with what he had.

The *maresciallo* changed tack.

'Are we listening to our friends?' he asked.

There was silence on the line. They weren't supposed to eavesdrop on the police. And vice versa. But it happened, in both directions.

'We can be very quickly. For anything in particular?'

'I would like to be informed of any mention of the actor Allan Prime, from any source whatsoever.'

'Of course.'

'Good,' Quattrocchi said, then got himself put through to forensic.

While waiting he caught the attention of Tom Black, who stood away from his silver machine, glancing at the flashing monitor with concern.

'I need my scientific officers to see what's happening.'

The young American winced, as if afflicted by a momentary pain.

'Tell them to find a computer and tune in to Lukatmi,' he answered glumly. 'These bastards are putting it out to the public too. Through us. We can stop them, but the only quick way would mean we lose the stream here too . . .'

'Touch nothing!' Quattrocchi roared. He pointed through into the cinema where Prime was screaming on the screen again. The small, deadly spear had moved closer to its destination. 'If we lose that, we lose him.'

Josh Jonah walked up to the machine and peered calmly at the monitor.

'I can read off the URL,' he said. 'Are you ready?'

- 5 -

One kilometre away, in the forensic lab of the *centro storico* Questura, the same word was puzzling another law enforcement officer, though one from a very different agency.

'URL? What's a URL?' Peroni asked.

He thought they were in Teresa Lupo's morgue to stare at the head of a store-window dummy and the curious death mask that had been attached to it. Also, more than anything from Peroni's point of view, to talk to Simon Harvey. At the age of fifty-one, with an understanding of the cinema industry which extended to no more than a few security duties at the Cinecittà studios over the years, Peroni felt it was time to become better acquainted with the working methods and mores of the movie business, such as they were. He had an inexplicable and vague feeling they might come in useful, and that Harvey was a man who could impart much worthwhile information on the subject if he felt so minded.

No one answered his question. Harvey and Silvio Di Capua had exchanged a brief conversation and the whole game plan seemed to disappear in smoke. While Teresa and her two young white-coated trainee assistants played half-heartedly with the head and mask – finding no new information – Di Capua and Harvey had gone over to the nearest computer and started hammering the keys, staring at the gigantic monitor as it flipped through image after image.

'Will someone please tell me what a URL is?' Peroni asked again.

'Universal resource locator,' Di Capua grumbled. 'What I'm typing. Any the wiser?'

'No. Enlighten me. How is this helping exactly?'

Teresa came over and gave him a cautionary glance.

'Gianni,' she said, 'if I'd been allowed to set up some kind of a crime scene on that stage. If we were in control in any shape or form . . .' She opened her hands in a gesture of despair. 'We have nothing to work with. Nowhere to begin. If staring at a computer helps, I'm all for it. What else is there?'

'This is my fault,' Harvey apologized. 'I didn't mean to start an argument. It was only a suggestion.'

The suggestion being, Teresa explained patiently, that they use the strange, unexplained internet service owned by two American geeks who'd helped finance *Inferno* to try to find out what people at large were saying about Allan Prime.

'Think of it this way,' Harvey went on. 'Would you like to be able to tune into every TV newscast around the world that was covering Allan right now? Every little net TV channel, every vidcast too?'

Peroni shook his big, grizzled head.

'Every what?'

'If it gave us a clue . . .' Di Capua said. 'I'd take anything. This thing . . .' He blinked, incredulous at the flashing series of moving pictures on the monitor. '. . . is unbelievable. I never realized . . .'

'They bring stuff online before announcing it,' Harvey said. 'It's all part of the hype. You never know what they'll turn up with next. You just have to tune in to check.'

Teresa had her head bent towards the screen. Peroni felt like an intruder from a different century.

'How the hell do they do it?' Di Capua asked, still in a state of awe.

Harvey sighed.

'I don't really understand it myself. From what they said it's a mixture of reading keywords, transcribing speech, recognizing faces . . . All the TV stations are now online and streaming. Add to that new video material. Blogs. Small web stations. I guess they have some way of consuming it all as it appears, reading it, then serving everything up. Google for video and audio, only ten times bigger, ten times faster and deadly accurate. That's why they're worth a billion or so each.'

Peroni cleared his throat and said, 'This is *so* interesting. Is anyone going to find something for me to look at?'

Teresa stepped back, gestured at the screen and said, 'Take your pick.'

What enthusiasm he had left swiftly dissipated. The monitor was crammed with moving pictures the size of postage stamps, each with odd graphs by the side and a geographical location.

'Allan Prime's a star,' Di Capua observed. 'When someone like him disappears it's a big story.'

Peroni leaned forward and found himself wishing he could rewind the clock to enter a simpler, more straightforward universe. Each postage stamp video represented a TV channel, usually news, seemingly issuing some kind of bulletin about the Prime story. The BBC in London. CBS in New York. A channel in Russia. Somewhere in Japan, Australia, the Philippines . . .

'This can't all be live . . .'

Harvey nodded.

'Pretty much. With Lukatmi if it's going out real time it's being relayed by them that way. With maybe a few seconds' delay, that's all.'

Peroni felt he could soon start to lose his temper.

'This is of no use to me whatsoever. How many channels are there for pity's sake?'

Di Capua hammered some keys and said, 'More than four hundred sources have run a story on Prime in the last hour.'

Peroni watched as the monitor cleared again, then very slowly came back to life, painting a set of new tiny videos on the screen at a snail's pace.

When the images returned they were all the ones Peroni expected. Local and national news channels, familiar presenters reading out their scripts, all with images of the missing actor and shots from the park and the production of *Inferno* blown up in the background. A counter by the side of the screen was some kind of popularity meter. The audience seemed to be running at seven figures and rising, most of them for a single video channel, one that was blacked out at that moment.

'Why can't we watch the one that's top of the list?'

'It won't load for some reason,' Di Capua said, trying something with the keyboard. 'Too many people watching it, I imagine. Or their fancy computer system can't cope.'

'I want to see it . . .' Peroni began, and then fell quiet. Teresa's deputy had made the black window occupy the full screen of the path lab monitor. As he watched, the empty space filled, line by line, with a real moving image.

They all crowded round to see. It was a man in fear for his life, trapped inside some cruel and ancient cast-iron head restraint. The digital stopwatch imprinted by his neckline turned from 28:31 to 28:30 and the seconds kept on ticking. Allan Prime's eyes were as large as any man's Peroni had ever seen. He looked ready to die of fright even before the bright, shining spear with the blood-soaked tip reached his head, which surely would happen soon. Within less than thirty minutes, or so this strangely hypnotic little movie, surely the most personal Prime had ever made, seemed to be saying.

Teresa leaned over Di Capua and said, 'Get me some detail.'

Harvey had his face in his hands. His eyes were glazed, filling with tears. Peroni looked at him and said, 'You don't have to watch this. Why not go and sit somewhere else? I'll come for you when there's news.'

'Of course I've got to watch it,' the movie man croaked, then dragged up a chair.

There was no caption. Only the image of the terrified actor, the time ticking away and, by the side of the video, the digital thermometer that was the popularity counter. It was now flashing red. Peroni bent down and stared at it. Allan Prime's dying moments seemed to be the most sought-after thing in the world at that instant. A real-life drama being watched by a global audience that was popping into the tens of millions and growing by the second.

He pressed a finger against the screen and indicated the area behind Prime's quaking head.

'There's something there, Silvio. Can you bring it up?'

The pathologist's hands raced across the keyboard. Prime's features began to bleach out. From the dark background it was now possible to make out some kind of shape. Di Capua tweaked the machine some more. It was a painting, strange and old and, Peroni thought, possibly familiar.

'Get that to the art people straight away,' he ordered.

Teresa was staring at him. He knew what she was thinking.

'Has Nic got one of those new video phones?' he asked.

'You all have them,' she said, and folded her arms. 'Even you if you bothered to look.'

'I deal in people, not gadgets,' Peroni replied, then called Costa on the fancy new handset the department had, as Teresa indicated, issued to everyone only a couple of months earlier.

'Silvio,' he said, listening to the ring tone.

'Yeah?' the young pathologist answered absent-mindedly, still punching away at the keyboard trying to improve any recognizable detail in the swimming sea of pixelated murk that now filled the screen.

'Best give me the URL please.'

– 6 –

They went back to the Lancia in the Via Giulia. Falcone was calling people. No one seemed in a rush to go anywhere quickly. They would wait for the forensic team to arrive and watch them go through the clay dust and any other evidence they might find in the apartment Adele Neri had rented to Allan Prime. It felt better outside. Something about the information they had gleaned from Neri's widow depressed Costa. The movie world was not all glitter. Allan Prime, along with the producer Dino Bonetti, kept the company of mobsters and thieves. Costa wondered why he was surprised. There had been plenty of scandals in Italian show business over the years. It shouldn't have come as a shock to discover they spilled over into something as important and lucrative as the comeback blockbuster for one of the country's most reclusive directors.

Maggie Flavier came and stood next to him by the wall beneath the Lungotevere. The traffic made a dull, physical sound through the stone that separated them from the busy road and the river beyond. She was smoking and had the sweet smell of Campari on her breath, a lightness that might have been the onset of drink in her eyes.

She smiled at him and said, 'We all lead different lives. What's yours?'

'Being a police officer. It's enough.'

She drew hard on the cigarette then threw it to the ground and stamped out the embers with her shiny, expensive-looking evening shoes.

'In my line of work you become more conscious of words,' she said quietly. 'You used the past tense when you talked about your wife . . .'

He nodded. He liked her directness. Perhaps it was an actor's trick. Perhaps not.

'She died seven months ago.' He thought of the mausoleum of Augustus, less than ten minutes away on foot, and the terrible events of the previous December.

'I'm sorry. Was it unexpected?'

'You could say that.'

She breathed in deeply, quickly.

'I don't know what to say. I felt something, that's all.'

'Sorry's just fine.' There isn't a lot else, he thought. People die all the time. Those who survive get on with their lives.

She turned to look at the building housing Prime's apartment, now surrounded by blue police cars, with still only a handful of Carabinieri vehicles in the street.

'Do you know where Allan is yet? Is he OK?'

'He was fine when he left here this morning.' His eyes fell on Falcone, serious and intent by the door, busy on the phone. 'Perhaps he's just gone walkabout.'

She shook her head.

'When he's due to open the premiere for the biggest movie of the summer? I don't think so . . .'

The thought wouldn't leave Costa's head.

'Could this all be some publicity stunt?'

She stared at him in disbelief. He caught the bittersweet aroma of Campari again.

'Someone died. The premiere's been cancelled. A publicity stunt?'

'The man who attacked you was an actor. His name was Peter Jamieson. He was an extra on the set of *Inferno*. Did you know him?'

Maggie Flavier didn't blink.

'A movie set's like a football crowd. The only people I see are the ones I'm playing a scene with. I don't even notice Tonti. Just hear him. You couldn't miss that.' She gazed directly into his eyes, to make the point. 'I didn't recognize that poor man. I've never heard of someone called Jamieson. If I had, I would tell you. I may be an actor but I'm a very bad liar.'

His phone rang. It was Peroni, excited, trying to explain something he clearly didn't understand himself. He heard Teresa snatch the thing from him at the other end.

'Nic,' she said anxiously. 'Don't ask, just listen. Allan Prime is captive somewhere and it's being broadcast on the web. He's in danger. It looks bad. We need you to see the pictures and tell us if you recognize anything.'

'Pictures?'

'*Live* pictures,' she emphasized, then told him how to find the Lukatmi page she wanted him to see.

Costa had to cut the call to try to get the web on his phone. When he did, and keyed in the address she gave him, all he got was a blank page and a message saying service unavailable. He called her back. There was a brief exchange between her and someone who sounded like Silvio Di Capua.

'Forget that idea,' she ordered. 'Silvio says the network must be breaking up under the strain. Everyone's watching this poor bastard trying to stay alive. Listen. It's possible there's a hint about where he might be. The background to the picture is indistinct but it seems to contain some kind of painting. We think we've captured some of it. We're trying to circulate it to the art people here to get their opinion, but they're all out taking tea with their maiden aunts or something. Look at it for us. Please.'

A beep told him there was an incoming e-mail. Costa opened it, looked, thought for a moment and told her, 'It's just smudge and ink. I'm seeing it on a phone. Tell Silvio to get more detail and blow the thing up until it's breaking.'

There were curses and shouts on the end of the line. Two more images arrived, each little better than the first. Falcone came over. Costa told him what was happening while Maggie stood by his shoulder, trying to peek at what was on the phone. He showed her. Showed Falcone too. It was impossible to recognize anything on the tiny, pixelated screen.

'Bigger, brighter, louder,' he ordered.

They waited. One more e-mail arrived.

He looked at it and thought of a bright Sunday the previous autumn when he and Emily had bought ice cream from the little cafe near the Piazza Trilussa then set off on a long stroll to the Gianicolo, past the house that was supposed to belong to Raphael's mistress, La Fornarina, through the still-quiet part of Trastevere the American tourists rarely found.

The image was cruelly disfigured by both Silvio Di Capua's digital surgery and the distorting electronic medium through which it had been relayed. But he recognized those lovely features all the same, and could picture the figure beneath the face, half naked, racing her scallop-shell chariot over the surf, surrounded by lascivious nymphs and satyrs.

'This is from a painting called *Galatea*,' he said with absolute certainty. 'It's in the Villa Farnesina in the Via della Lungara in Trastevere. It's just a small museum and art gallery, not well known. Quite deserted at night, and in secluded grounds.' He thought of the way there across the river. It was perhaps four minutes if they crossed the Mazzini bridge.

'Four cars,' Falcone ordered, walking back to his Lancia. 'Leave Miss Flavier under guard here.' He opened the driver's door and beckoned for Catherine Bianchi to move. 'In the passenger seat, please,' Falcone ordered. She shuffled across immediately. Costa fell in the back.

From somewhere came the din of a siren. Falcone looked surprised, and more than a little cross. More so when it became apparent from the timbre that it was the sound of the Carabinieri, whose own vehicles were now trying to abandon the Via Giulia entirely.

- 7 -

Across town, in the control van *Maresciallo* Gianluca Quattrocchi had positioned outside the Casa del Cinema, there was excitement and amusement.

Quattrocchi put down the mike and, with the same coded instruction to Morello that he had used earlier, ordered an end to the eavesdropping. Then he closed his eyes and pictured the layout of his native city, the place where he'd grown up, where he felt he knew every brick and alley, every corner and battered statue. Falcone and his team were in the one-way street of the Via Giulia, trapped in the sixteenth-century warren that had once been created as a wealthy suburb for the Vatican across the river, a little way along from Trastevere itself.

Quattrocchi liked bridges, and had ordered officers and cars to all of the key crossings in the centre of the city, a trick he had developed and perfected in the past. The Tiber would once more be his ally.

'Close the Mazzini,' he ordered. 'And the Vittorio Emanuele. There will be only one easy way left to the Via della Lungara then. We go south to the Garibaldi. Falcone will never reach there. Not till some time tomorrow.'

This was a Carabinieri case and it would stay that way.

– 8 –

It was the smallest camera Allan Prime had ever worked with. The device hung in front of his face, dangling from a flickering light in the ceiling, a wire trailing off somewhere to the computer he'd seen on the way in. Prime never did get technology. It was tedious, even now. Nothing had ever really mattered except the monocular glass eye that watched him, never blinking, never ceasing to pay attention. In his head it had always been there. Even in the dim, dark noisome movie theatres of Manhattan when he was a sweaty teenager dreaming of stardom, determined to achieve it, whatever the cost.

Whatever the cost.

The idea provided some amusement in his present, odd predicament. He wanted to laugh alongside the sobs that came rippling up from his body, physical reactions, tricks of the trade, not conscious, personal responses. He was able to divide the self from acting. That was always the first deceit. And this *was* acting. He kept reminding himself of that. This whole exercise, once complete, would be an end to things. A wiping out of all debts, financial and otherwise, with a considerable prize in private too.

It hadn't been the decent lunch and a little afternoon delight he'd been hoping for following Miss Valdes's work on the clay mask. She had turned somewhat coy, to his surprise. Long-term, though, maybe it was for the better, a cheap deal too. Hide away for the day. Miss the premiere to stoke up some publicity. Then let her put him in some weird, sadomasochistic rig set up in a tiny museum that had been closed for renovation. The camera came out. A fake kidnapping, an act of terror played out in front of millions. A world-famous star in a one-man show that would make headlines everywhere. Hell, she sold it so well Allan Prime thought for a moment he would have paid to be in the thing. This one stupid prank would set up queues outside movie theatres everywhere, sell millions of pieces of merchandise, bring a flood tide of money into the coffers of *Inferno*, a cut of which, net after producer fees, would come his way. And the rest . . .

The performance was what really mattered, though. It always would be.

So he had allowed himself to be strapped into the black metal frame, worked with her to perfect the focus on the tiny, bug-eyed camera, and sat patiently while she faked the spear thrust into his skull – plastic point, stage blood – that was used for the opening sequence to set up the scene.

He'd done this kind of thing a million times and, given the swift, smooth professional way she went about her business, he assumed Carlotta Valdes – or whoever she really was – had too.

After that, she actually called 'Action' and he was on, moaning and writhing for the tiny white light that sat blinking on top of the camera, unwilling, and unable, to focus on anything but the tiny lens for the next sixty minutes, an hour which, Carlotta promised, would make him the biggest, most talked-about star in the world.

And then the cops would come. Rescue him. One more piece of deceit, of acting, was required to explain his abduction. It was, Prime thought, a piece of cake. He was used to faking it for millions. Fooling a few dumb Italian cops would be child's play by comparison.

The movie business was weird sometimes. It ran in uncertain directions, was diverted by fate and circumstance and, on occasion, pure luck, both good and bad. The debts were worth losing. So was the rape complaint that was still hanging over him from the weekend in Rimini three months before. What the dark suits behind Dino Bonetti surely promised – he assumed Carlotta came from them, though she never said, and he would never have expected it – was a clean sheet, a fresh start, a vast private payoff, and a mountain of free publicity and global sympathy that would make him bigger even than

Inferno itself. Plus the fringe benefits only a few – Carlotta among them – understood.

The unseen clock tick-tocked once more. The device to his left moved another notch towards his face. It would stop, she said, when the rubber tip reached his cheek, before the supposedly razor-sharp blade bent beneath the pressure, revealing the legerdemain, exposing the lie. That couldn't be long now. He felt he'd been trapped in the rig for hours. It was starting to become painful. He couldn't wait for this scene to be over, for the cameras to die, and for her next trick: his astonishing, headline-grabbing rescue.

Prime was wondering how he could vary the act too. Sixty minutes of writhing and yelling would be boring. He'd be marked, rated, reviewed on this performance, just as on every other.

So he stopped crying, made an effort to appear to be a man struggling to recover some inner resolve and strength. Then, trying to find some way round the awkward iron bar over his mouth, he began to bellow, as loudly as his lungs allowed.

'Carlotta,' he cried, not minding he was yelling out her name to millions, since it could only be a sham, like everything else. *'CARLOTTA!'*

There was no reply. None at all. Not a footstep, not a breath, not the slightest of responses. In some chilling, inexplicable way, Allan Prime came to understand at that moment that he was alone in the small, dark museum to which she had taken him in the early evening after eating ice cream together in a secluded corner of the Gianicolo.

Something else. He remembered where he'd heard her name before, and the recollection made his blood run cold.

Carlotta Valdes was a ghost from the past – vengeful, vicious.

The unseen clock must have ticked again somewhere. The invisible device to his left lurched on a ratchet, ever closer. As it did so it made a heavy, certain clunk, quite unlike that of a stage prop, which would have been cheap, throwaway stuff, its own soft, revealing sounds covered by the insertion of a Foley track dubbing menace and the hard clash of metal to lend a little verisimilitude to flimsy reality.

This is for real, Allan Prime thought.

Real as pain. Or blood. Life. Or death.

A warm, free flow of stinging liquid was spreading around his crotch. He stared at the bug-eyed camera and began to plead and scream for help, for release, with more conviction than he'd ever possessed in his life.

Somewhere at the back of his head he heard Roberto Tonti's disembodied voice.

Stop acting. Start being.

It sounded as if the vicious old bastard was laughing.

– 9 –

Falcone screamed out of the open Lancia window, not at anyone in particular, but the world in general. They hadn't moved more than fifty metres in the Via Giulia, and traffic was backing up in every side road around. Sirens blaring, lights flashing, it didn't make a blind bit of difference. These were medieval cobbled streets, made for pedestrians and horses and carriages. There was nowhere left for the civilian cars stranded in them to move to allow another past. They were trapped in a sea of overheating metal.

Costa called the control room and asked what was happening. He looked at Falcone.

'The Carabinieri have thrown up roadblocks on the bridges. They won't even let pedestrians across.'

'I will crucify those stuck-up bastards for this . . .'

'They think it's their case,' Costa pointed out. Then, before his superior exploded, he added, 'We can get there across the footbridge. The Ponte Sisto. Go over, turn right and find the Via della Lungara. It's the long way round . . .'

'How long will it take?' Catherine Bianchi asked.

Costa was getting out of the car already and signalling to two of the younger men in the vehicle behind to come with him.

'That depends how fast you can run.'

He began to backtrack along the Via Giulia, towards the shallow uphill slope that led to the Lungotevere and the old footbridge crossing, setting up a steady pace, aware he'd be well ahead of any of the men behind him. Since Emily had died Costa had got back into running, spending long hours pounding the stones of the Appian Way near his home. It helped, a lot sometimes.

He was at full pace by the time he got to the bridge, pushing past the importunate beggars and their dogs, the hawkers with their bags and counterfeit DVDs. On the Trastevere side he had to leap across the bonnets of the cars which were so tightly and angrily backed up along the river they didn't leave space for a pedestrian to get through. Costa ignored the howls of outraged drivers. It took five vehicles to traverse the broad riverside road, then he was down, pacing through the Piazza Trilussa, turning in towards the Via della Lungara.

There were carabinieri everywhere, but no barriers within the road itself yet. They were still getting into position, leaving some movement in the area to allow senior officers to decide their tactics.

Costa took out his police ID, held it high and kept on running. The sight of him took them by surprise so much he managed to get through the gates of the Farnesina and into the beautiful, secluded garden before anyone stopped him.

Finally a large gruff minion stuck out his arm and immediately launched into the customary litany of excuses that were trotted out, on both sides, when some conflict occurred in public.

'I don't have time for this and nor do you,' Costa interrupted him. 'Look at the card, see my rank and tell your superior officer this. I know the Farnesina. It's got a history he needs to understand. If you don't take me to him now I will make damned sure afterwards he gets to understand you kept me away.' Costa pointed at the small, elegant villa that had been built five centuries before on the orders of some wealthy Roman noble as a salon for artists and chancers and beautiful, occasionally dubious women. 'There are things he needs to appreciate.'

'Get lost,' the idiot said, waving him away. 'This is nothing to do with you.'

A large, ruddy-faced man in an immaculate uniform swept past. Costa was never good at Carabinieri ranks but something in the officer's face spoke of seniority.

'Sir, sir . . .'

He ran into the individual's path waving his police ID. The man looked at him as if this were an act of the utmost impertinence. Costa could see the younger colleagues who had followed him from the Via Giulia being apprehended at the villa gates, along with a furious Catherine Bianchi.

'My name is *Maresciallo* Gianluca Quattrocchi. This crime scene is in our possession. Go away.'

'I know this building,' Costa insisted. 'Do you?'

'When I wish the opinion of civilians I will ask for it. Now stand aside . . .'

Two sets of strong arms began to pull Costa away. Quattrocchi marched forward, flanked on either side by half a dozen uniformed officers. An elderly civilian was unlocking the doors, seemingly shaken by the fuss.

'It's all about illusion,' Costa yelled. '*Trompe-l'oeil*. A trick of the eye. What you see is not what's real.'

Just like the movies, he thought, as he watched the group of men stomp towards the villa's elegant entrance. Under the harsh white floods it looked like a sketch from Piranesi scribbled into life with the crayons of a giant.

Quattrocchi turned and, to Costa's astonishment, grinned sarcastically then made a coarse and sexual street gesture not normally associated with senior military officers.

Very little in the Farnesina was as it appeared, Costa recalled, as the dark uniforms of the carabinieri vanished through the doors. There were paintings masquerading as tapestries, a cryptic horoscope depicted as a celestial relief, artificial views of a lost Rome that might never have been quite as real as they suggested. It was a temple to both illusion and the sensuality of the arts.

He turned on his heels and headed for the gate. It was quieter now. Falcone was there, and for once he wasn't shouting. The game, for them, was surely lost.

- 10 -

'Make notes,' the *maresciallo* ordered as they entered. 'Take photographs. Video. I wish a record of everything. We will release it to the media when we're done.'

He glanced at his large gold watch, then at Morello, who already had pad and pen in his hands.

'How much time do we have left?' he asked, walking on.

'Seven minutes and . . .' The carabiniere held up his phone to try to see the picture there. 'No. It's gone again. Seven minutes at least. Ample time.'

'You?' Quattrocchi said to the elderly caretaker they had jerked away from the TV soccer in his tiny apartment adjoining the villa. 'Take us to *Galatea*.'

'This is the Loggia of the Psyche,' the little man said with pride, immediately falling into a fawning tourist-guide voice. 'You will note, sirs, the work of Baldassare Peruzzi and Raphael. These fruits, these flowers . . . once this would have opened onto the garden, hence the horticultural theme. And the so-called tapestries, which are painted too. The Council of the Gods, Cupid and Psyche's wedding banquet . . .'

'This isn't a damned social visit,' Quattrocchi snapped. 'Where's *Galatea*?'

'We don't get many visitors at night,' the caretaker replied, hurt. 'Not from officers of the law.'

'Where . . . ?'

Quattrocchi stopped himself, realizing the man had been leading them there all along. Now they had wandered into the loggia, which connected with that of Psyche.

He stared ahead. The painting was there, and many others too. There was nothing else. The place was empty.

The *maresciallo* muttered a curse under his breath, and found himself briefly wishing he hadn't shooed away the young police officer quite so quickly. What had he said? This was a place of illusions. The images on the web had guided them – or, more accurately, the state police – to this building, and this room. But one more trick, one more sleight of hand, still stood between them and Allan Prime edging towards death.

'Someone told me,' Quattrocchi said, 'that this villa was a place of tricks. What does that mean?'

The caretaker rubbed his hands with pleasure.

'There are many, sir. Allusions. Illusions. Codes and cryptograms. References to the stars and alchemy, fate and the fleeting, intangible pleasures of the flesh.'

'Spare me the tourist chat. Where do I look to find them?'

'Everywhere . . .' the old man opened his hands.

'Where more than any?'

'Ah,' he replied, and nodded his head as if something had been suddenly revealed. 'The *Salone delle Prospettive*. But it's closed for restoration, and has been for many months. I'm sorry. What visitors we have . . . they always ask. The matter is out of my hands . . .'

The Salon of Perspectives. Quattrocchi knew it was the place the moment he heard the name. This was part of the cruel game. Playing with viewpoint. Changing a familiar aspect of the world through a trick of the light, a twist of the lens through which one saw the scene.

'Show me . . .'

'It's closed. No one enters except the restoration people.'

'*Show me!*'

Morello had found a sign to the place and was pointing to it. Quattrocchi brushed the caretaker aside and led the way up a flight of marble stairs, breath shortening.

The younger officer was staring at his phone again. He had a picture back. Quattrocchi could just make it out.

'Time?'

'Less than five minutes.'

The door was locked. They bellowed at the caretaker until he came up with the key. Then, with Quattrocchi in the lead, they went in.

It was dark and church-like. The only illumination came from a low light in the ceiling which was focused on a mass of tangled wires, mechanical contraptions and constricting devices near the end of the room. A man – Allan Prime – was at the heart of this ganglion of metal and cable, strapped tightly into an upright frame, the open iron device around his head. A tourist print of the painting of Galatea fluttered behind him, animated by the breeze from an open window. On the floor, connected to the whole by a slender cable, sat a single notebook computer, its screen flashing a slow-moving image of something so unlikely it took Quattrocchi a moment to recognize what it was . . . the Golden Gate Bridge in San Francisco.

From behind, the caretaker, unaware of what lay before them, chanted, 'You will note, sir, the perspectives of another Rome . . . Trastevere and the Borgo . . . the *centro storico* . . . painted as if real views from real windows. Also . . .'

Coming in last, he finally saw, and stopped.

Allan Prime whimpered. Pain and relief mingled with the tears on his sweat-stained face.

Quattrocchi walked forward, as close as he dared, and took a good look around the mechanical apparatus into which the actor had been strapped, checking carefully for traps or some kind of light-signal device that might have been set to warn of an intruder's approach, and perhaps trigger the mechanism early.

He saw none, but the gleaming sharp point had now edged its way to within a centimetre of the actor's left temple.

The mechanism that held the deadly device was hidden in the deep, dark shadow outside the garish, too-bright overhead light. Carefully, barely breathing, Quattrocchi took out a pen torch and shone it on the space there. A low, communal gasp of shock ran through the small gathering of officers behind him. A full-size crossbow, of such power and weight it could only be designed for hunting, stood loaded, locked inside some ratchet mechanism that shifted it towards its victim with each passing minute. It was not just the spear – which he now saw to be an arrow – that was moving in the direction of Allan Prime. It was an entire weapon, ready to unleash its sharp, spiking bolt straight into the man's skull.

'Four minutes,' Morello said, and sounded puzzled.

'We will release you immediately,' Quattrocchi said calmly. 'You have nothing to fear. Four minutes is more than enough . . .'

'Sir . . .' the young carabiniere interrupted.

Quattrocchi turned, annoyed by this intrusion.

'Something is happening,' the officer pointed out.

He walked carefully towards the *maresciallo* and showed him the phone.

The picture was changing. Quattrocchi grappled for the correct term. Finally it came. *Zooming*. The camera was zooming out of the scene. He looked at the single grey eye of the device that had been set up in front of Allan Prime. Its glassy iris was changing shape, as if trying to focus on something new.

When he returned to Morello's phone he saw himself there, looking surprised, angry, red-faced and, to Quattrocchi's dismay, rather old and lost as he stood next to the terrified actor strapped into the deadly frame.

From a place Quattrocchi couldn't initially pinpoint came the deep, loud, disembodied rattle of a man's laughter, cruel, uncaring, determined too. Someone gasped in shock and, perhaps, fright.

A lilting voice, male, probably American, issued up from the computer, and spoke in English.

'*Say cheese. Say . . .*'

There was a sound like water rushing through air, then a scream that was strangled before it could grow into a full-throated cry.

Quattrocchi turned his back on the apparatus, not wishing to witness what was happening to Allan Prime locked in the rig behind him. On the floor of the *Salone delle Prospettive*, in a sixteenth-century nobleman's version of an illusory paradise, he saw instead an elderly caretaker who was on his knees, crossing himself, turning his eyes to heaven and starting to pray.

Something had been written on the dusty tiles in multi-coloured aerosol paint, letters a good metre high, the way teenagers sprayed graffiti on the subway. *Maresciallo* Gianluca Quattrocchi gazed at the message and remembered his lessons on Dante from college some thirty years before. The letters were ragged and rushed, but the words were unmistakable.

The Second Circle. The Wanton.

'What next?' Morello asked, unseen by his side.

'The third, of course,' Quattrocchi answered automatically.

- 11 -

Costa awoke with a start. He'd slept in Leo Falcone's Lancia, which, after much argument, had been allowed to enter the secure area created by the Carabinieri in the Via della Lungara and the streets beyond and park close to the Farnesina. The Lungotevere was closed to traffic, which explained the strange silence. There would be media everywhere, cameras and reporters, crews from around the world, switched from the year's grandest movie premiere to a terrible death, and grateful for a story that would surely occupy the headlines for weeks to come. But none of the morning hurly-burly of commuters fighting to get to work.

Beyond the window he could see Falcone, Peroni and Teresa Lupo talking to Catherine Bianchi near the entrance to the villa. Maggie Flavier was joining them, a seemingly uncomfortable Carabinieri officer by her side. He couldn't help but notice she glanced in the direction of the car after she spoke to them. He looked at his watch. It was coming up to seven in the morning. Costa turned on the car radio and listened to the news. There was only one story, and one law enforcement agency to tell it. Not the Polizia di Stato.

No one had been apprehended. The idea that *Inferno* would receive its world premiere in Rome had been abandoned. Instead the entire cast and security operation would bring forward their planned move to California. The exhibition created for the Casa del Cinema would be rebuilt, as planned throughout, at the Palace of Fine Arts in San Francisco. Once that was complete, *Inferno* would be launched there, leaving Roman filmgoers to wait weeks for a domestic public release, a decision that was already creating fury among local fans.

The name of the place rang a bell. Costa closed his eyes and recalled Emily, then unknown to him, in a room in the American Embassy displaying a picture of a beautiful, half-ruined classical building by a lake as part of the investigation that had brought them together.

Then he was brought to earth by the gruff Roman voice of Gianluca Quattrocchi giving the news his somewhat over-dramatized version of events. Prime, he claimed, was beyond rescue from the outset. The videos of him on the web – and his savage demise, which was now on many millions of computers and phones around the world – were all part of a sadistic murder plot played out with heartless deliberation over the internet. Why? Quattrocchi had the answer. The clues were there throughout. In the message scribbled on the dummy's head – *Lasciate ogne speranza, voi ch'intrate*. In the words written on the floor in front of the trapped actor, which had been instantly shared with the world as the webcam panned the scene. In the constant stream of hate-mail and dark threats sent to the production for months and now released to the Carabinieri by the publicist, Simon Harvey, who had – unwisely, Quattrocchi suggested – kept them quiet out of a mistaken belief they came from a crank.

'Cranks they may be,' the *maresciallo* went on, playing for the cameras, 'but they are also killers.' He lowered the tone of his voice to make sure there could be no mistaking the seriousness of his message. 'Killers obsessed with the works of Dante. They wish to punish those who made this movie for what they see as some kind of blasphemy. The star is dead already. We are redoubling security for everyone else involved, cast, crew, all of them. We will cooperate with the American authorities in this, and, since Italian citizens are under threat, participate in the operation in California as well.'

'Nice work if you can get it . . .' Costa muttered. Quattrocchi had never mentioned that the unfortunate Peter Jamieson was carrying a gun loaded with blanks. He wondered how that awkward fact could possibly fit in with such strangely histrionic theories.

Feeling stiff and hungry he got out of the car. Two more state police vehicles were set close to the far side of Falcone's Lancia like a wagon train surrounded by a sea of dark blue Indians. He ambled over to the discussion Falcone was conducting. Maggie Flavier looked pale and pink-eyed as if she'd been crying and lacked sleep. When she saw him she turned to the carabiniere and ordered him to fetch coffee and *cornetti*. The man slunk off with a mutinous grunt.

'Be kind. He's only doing his job,' Costa suggested.

'If I want protection I choose who does it,' she retorted. 'And I choose . . .' Her slender finger ranged over the four of them there, before adding Catherine Bianchi too. '. . . you.'

'Oh no,' the American policewoman responded, half amused. 'I'm just the captain of a little San Francisco neighbourhood police station, and one that won't be there much longer either. If the Palace of Fine Arts didn't happen to be around the corner I wouldn't be here at all. All the heavy work gets shipped to the important people downtown in Bryant Street. Frankly they're welcome to it. Guarding celebrities is out of my league.'

'There are protocols here, Miss Flavier,' Falcone added. 'You must do as the *maresciallo* says. He seems very sure of himself.'

'People don't murder for poetry,' Costa reminded him. 'You said it yourself.'

'Allan Prime's death is none of my business. Our business. That . . .' Falcone's bright eyes shone with some inner knowledge. '. . . has been made very clear to me indeed by people with whom I am not minded to argue. Besides, Quattrocchi has created for himself a very certain picture of what is happening, one that seems to fit well with his own theatrical ambitions. Far be it from us to disturb his reveries.'

'Leo . . .' Teresa interrupted. 'We have some interesting material from that place in the Via Giulia. Give us a little time and perhaps we could get something useful.'

The inspector shook his head.

'You must hand it over. It's theirs now. All of it. Everything pertaining to Allan Prime and the American actor they shot dead in the park. Besides, whoever is responsible is surely gone from Rome already. That circus trick they performed with Prime . . . I've checked with your deputy. It could have been run from anywhere. America even. If Quattrocchi is correct and this is connected with the film – and I do believe this to be true – their attentions will surely follow that too, across the Atlantic, far from Rome.'

Costa waited. He recognized that glint in Falcone's eye.

'All we have,' the inspector went on, 'is a missing death mask. A priceless, historical object. And several other similar exhibits that will shortly be crated up and air-freighted to America.' He scratched his chin. 'Is it possible they might also be at risk? If so, would it be fair to add to the Carabinieri's burden by asking they take responsibility for that role too . . . ?'

Peroni laughed, shook his head and let loose a long, amused sigh.

'I'm not sure it's a possibility I can ignore,' Falcone went on, then pointed a commanding finger at Costa.

'Your English is good, I know that already.' He peered at Peroni. 'What about yours?'

'Mine? Mine?' the big man replied, aghast. 'I spent six months on secondment with the Metropolitan Police in London, eating nothing but pies and fried potato. In some place called . . .' He thought about this. 'The Elephant and Castle.'

'A bar?' Teresa asked.

'No,' he replied, outraged. 'A place.'

'How long ago?' Falcone demanded.

Peroni shrugged.

'Fifteen, twenty years . . . They were first-class police officers. And also good . . .' He searched for the word. '. . . "blokes".'

'Your English, Gianni,' Teresa wanted to know. 'How is it?'

He drew himself up and looked officious.

'*Ecco!*' Peroni declared, pointing straight into Costa's face at close quarters. With his scarred and beaten-up face, he suddenly seemed remarkably threatening.

'Consider yourself well and truly nicked, sonny,' he roared in a thuggish London accent that Costa thought comprehensible – just.

The volume of this outburst caused the Carabinieri man newly returned with the coffees to tremble with shock and spill the hot liquid, cursing quietly under his breath.

'Works for me,' Costa murmured with an admiring nod.

'We fly out in two days,' Falcone announced. 'I have reservations already. You must be in economy, I'm afraid. Budget restraints. Now go home and pack.'

Teresa danced a little dance, sang a short burst of 'America' from *West Side Story*, and twirled around on her large feet with an unexpected ease of movement and grace.

Then she checked herself and prodded the inspector's chest.

'When you said "we" . . .'

'Happily, the financial affairs of the forensic department are none of my business,' Falcone declared, and began walking off, turning only to add, 'Since there is no death on our files I doubt even you can persuade upstairs to foot the bill for that. Of course, if you have vacation owing and the money for a ticket . . .'

'I have to pay my own way?' she shrieked.

'Perhaps we can fit you in at the accommodation Catherine is arranging,' Falcone added, barely pausing. 'The choice – and the expense – are both yours.'

Costa watched the two of them walk into the street bickering, both understanding neither would change his or her position, and that Teresa would be on that flight, even if she had to buy the ticket herself.

Maggie Flavier took a coffee from the silent carabiniere's hands and passed it over to him.

'Will they find who did this?'

'They'll try.' He didn't want to pry. He knew he had to. 'Was Allan Prime a friend of yours? A good friend?'

'No,' she answered with a shrug. 'He was a man I worked with. He tried his . . . charms, if you can call them that. Welcome to acting.' She stared at him and he knew: she had been crying, and was now allowing him to see, to understand. 'It's a solitary business. Being other people. The really odd part is you get to be alone in the presence of millions.'

'I can imagine,' he said.

She looked at him with a sharp, engaged interest that made him feel deeply uneasy.

'Can you?' she asked.

PART THREE

- 1 -

Nine days later they found themselves surrounded by a sea of storage boxes fighting for space inside a gigantic tent by the lake in front of the Palace of Fine Arts, San Francisco. Home had become a small, two-storey rented house a short walk away. It was in the oddly named district of Cow Hollow, on a quiet corner in Greenwich Street, just a few blocks along from the police station of which Catherine Bianchi was captain, head of a dwindling team, slowly running down for the unit's eventual closure at the end of the month.

Hundreds of chests and cases had been shipped by air from Italy over the preceding week. Item after item was being patiently lined up on serried rows of tables under the scrutiny of US police, private security guards, and Leo Falcone, who was clearly torn between a duty he found tedious and a desire to impress the amiable but apparently unyielding Captain Bianchi.

There was, in Peroni's words, an awful lot of stuff to unpack. Paintings, sketches, cartoons, letters, manuscripts, reviews, personal artefacts, mostly genuine, many of value. Costa was, by now, used to the painstaking cycle of work that went into assembling any moving exhibition. He had worked several in his career. Each was different. This, set in a different country, to be housed in tents during the day, guarded at night in secure warehouses nearby, was more unusual than most.

'I'll say one thing for you lot,' Teresa declared, watching Peroni hover over a set of Florentine ceramics being unpacked by a pretty young woman from the museum in Milan. 'You certainly know how to treat a woman. I blew almost two thousand euros getting myself here. And what happens when I arrive? You lot spend days unpacking all this junk at the speed of a maiden aunt. And as for him . . .'

She nodded at Peroni, who was still, in spite of the weather, dressed in thin summer slacks and a polo shirt, though the temperature was distinctly nippy, even in the tent.

'There ought to be a law against some people being allowed out of the country.'

'Your liberal tendencies are slipping.'

'I'm bored, Nic. And this is a very long way to come for that.'

She had a point. Gianluca Quattrocchi had swiftly seized control of all the key aspects of the investigation into Allan Prime's murder, sharing what information he had only with the senior San Francisco Police Department homicide team that had been brought into the case. The local force had a direct interest: Prime had owned a home in the city, a palatial house in Pacific Heights, part of a small community of Hollywood professionals who preferred the bohemian atmosphere of northern California to the frenetic commercialism of Los Angeles. Maggie Flavier was a long-term resident too, with an apartment in Nob Hill. Roberto Tonti lived in a grand, white-painted mansion in the Marina opposite the Palace of Fine Arts, where his film would now receive its world premiere. *Inferno*, it seemed, was a local, almost family, affair.

The state police had become outsiders in a crime which, in some ways, they had witnessed, briefly interviewed by Quattrocchi's surly plain-clothes Carabinieri officers, then left to take responsibility for the tasks they had originally been handed in Rome. This was strictly confined to ensuring the security of the remaining historic items for the Dante exhibition.

Costa was determined not to allow this to get under his skin. This was his first visit to America. San Francisco was a city of delights. The mundane work they had been left by Quattrocchi's team was both straightforward and easily managed. Not that any of them felt entirely relaxed about the coming round of public events.

'You bore too easily,' he told Teresa. 'There are at least ten items in this exhibition equivalent in value to that missing death mask. If we lose one more, Leo could be looking for another job.'

The inspector was with Catherine Bianchi again, finger on chin, listening to her as if she were the only person in the world.

'Try telling him that. Leo's mind is elsewhere, not that it's doing him any good. The man needs a case. A real one, not looking after antiques. There's a murder investigation here. It should be ours. Not that idiot Quattrocchi's.'

Costa was inclined to agree. With the assistance of officers in the *centro storico* Questura he had pieced together more information about Peter Jamieson, the bit-part actor who had seemingly attacked Maggie Flavier. While the Carabinieri busily briefed the media and gathered together Dante experts and criminal profilers, Costa's men had patiently tracked Jamieson's movements the day he died. They could place him at a rehearsal for a play at the Teatro Agorà in Trastevere only forty-five minutes before he appeared outside the Casa del Cinema. Jamieson was a skilled horseman, and had performed stunts when acting work was hard to find. The uniform he wore when he rode at them outside the Cinema dei Piccoli was stolen from the Teatro Agorà, as was the stage gun loaded with blanks that had brought about his end. CCTV clearly showed him travelling by bus and tram directly from Trastevere to the Villa Borghese park shortly before the strange interlude that led to his death, in uniform and with no obvious possessions. It was inconceivable that he could have found the time to replace the real mask with the fake one. Even if he had, someone else must have taken the genuine object away. The entire park area had been searched and no trace of the original found.

There the information ran out. Jamieson lived alone in a down-at-heel apartment not far from Cinecittà, had few possessions and even fewer friends. There was nothing on his computer or mobile phone to indicate an e-mail correspondence with anyone inside *Inferno*, apart from his minor role as an extra. His agent described him as a strange, melodramatic individual prone to fantasies and deeply in debt. In other circumstances, the police would have assumed that he had been acting alone. Only one unusual fact stood out: the day before he died twenty thousand dollars had been deposited into his bank account through an internet money-wire service which hid the identity of the sender. Peter Jamieson, it seemed, had been hired for a single, expensive performance, one he doubtless knew would cause trouble with the police. The money – perhaps a down payment on some promised balance – seemingly made it worthwhile. Had he behaved less rashly and dropped the gun in the children's cinema, he would simply have been apprehended as a troublesome gatecrasher and probably released with a caution or a minor fine for public nuisance.

It seemed clear to Costa that only someone inside the exhibition or movie production teams could have exchanged the masks. Someone directly involved in the dreadful fate meted out to Allan Prime, given the verse scribbled on the dummy's head and its link with the message on the floor of Farnesina. These facts appeared to be of little interest to Gianluca Quattrocchi when Costa raised them after the much-delayed interviews he and Maggie gave to the Carabinieri shortly before flying to California. They were merely awkward, minor details in a larger conspiracy.

Costa's second anxiety was more personal. Maggie Flavier had abruptly shaken off the attempts of the Carabinieri to dog her footsteps, and seemed very good at doing the same with the exasperated officer from Catherine Bianchi's station who had been assigned to take care of her security instead. She had also developed a habit of finding Costa, sometimes when he least expected it, rapidly discovering the address of the house in Greenwich Street and knocking on the door to invite him for a coffee or lunch, keen to talk of anything and everything except the movie business and the continuing furore around *Inferno*.

He was flattered. He was amused.

The large form of Gianni Peroni, Falcone and Catherine Bianchi at his side, brought him back down to earth.

'Are you two going to do anything?' Peroni wondered.

'I'm on holiday,' Teresa protested. 'Also, you apart, I try to stay away from old, dusty things.'

'Thanks. *Sovrintendente?*'

'I was thinking.'

'About what?' Falcone asked.

'About the fact there's not a lot more we can do here.'

Costa had spent two days going over the CCTV surveillance systems and the various alarm arrangements for both the exhibition and the storage areas. They were among the most thorough and technologically advanced he'd ever seen. There was so much in the way of surveillance hardware in the vicinity he half-wondered whether human beings were really needed.

Teresa looked Peroni up and down. He wasn't shivering, quite.

'Why on earth are you wearing those flimsy clothes?'

'It's California, isn't it?' he complained. 'In July.'

'The coldest winter I ever spent . . .' Catherine Bianchi began.

'. . . was a summer in San Francisco,' Peroni interrupted. 'Mark Twain. If someone paid me every time I've heard that since we arrived . . .'

'Sorry,' she apologized.

'No problem. It's a myth anyway.'

The American woman laughed. Falcone couldn't take his eyes off her. She was in plain clothes, a dark blue jacket beneath an overcoat most Romans would have chosen for autumn. Her long, hennaed hair was down around her shoulders. With her bright eyes and dark, constantly engaged features, she appeared more relaxed, more certain of herself than she had seemed in Italy. A fitting match for the elegant, upright Roman inspector, with his tanned, gaunt face and silver beard, and love for similarly expensive clothes. In Falcone's mind at least.

'It's not a myth, Gianni. I grew up in San Francisco. This is what summer's like. You should come back in September.' She glanced at his polo shirt. 'Then you'd be dressed for the weather.'

'I wasn't talking about the weather. I was talking about Mark Twain.'

They all looked at him. Everyone seemed to throw this quote at visitors the moment the subject of the climate came up.

'It's a myth,' Peroni insisted. 'He never really said that. I looked it up. I Googled it. Isn't that what you're supposed to do out here?'

'You're kidding me . . .' Catherine Bianchi looked astonished.

'A myth people take for granted,' Peroni added. 'Like killing people over poetry, perhaps.' He stared at Falcone. 'So are you going to tell us, Leo? Or do we just pretend to be museum guards for the duration in the hope that some miraculous revelation will put us back in charge? Or even find that stupid death mask.'

Falcone bristled.

'The mask of a legend like Dante Alighieri is anything but stupid.'

'Don't be so pompous,' Teresa scolded him. 'It's a piece of clay depicting a man who died seven centuries ago. You're chasing moonbeams if you think you're going to get it back and you know it. There's a market for art that can't be sold in public. It's a black hole. They disappear down it and unless we recover them very quickly the odds are they will never reappear again, not in our lifetime.' She stared hard at him. 'We're not really here for that, are we, Leo?'

'I suspect we won't see the mask again,' he agreed.

'Here's something else,' she added. 'The Carabinieri's fantasies. Is it possible some bunch of lunatics will travel the world going to great lengths to murder a well-known actor simply out of revenge for a movie they despise?'

Catherine Bianchi looked at each of them and said, 'This is California. I've known people kill someone over a can of Bud and a hot dog.'

'That makes more sense, doesn't it?' she responded. 'It's instant fury, not premeditated murder. Human emotions like that are real. Poetry. History. Art. Much as I love them . . . they're not. Not in the same way. Quattrocchi has his reasons for showboating like this. He likes the movie business. It's glamorous. These people flatter him. Also these fairy tales deflect attention from the pathetic way he handled the case in Rome. But as an answer . . .'

She shrugged.

'So where do you look?'

Costa had got this from the start, back in Italy when they were in the apartment Adele Neri had rented Allan Prime, one where the actor had entertained people with a murky past.

'This is a project with more than a hundred and fifty million dollars floating around inside it,' he said. 'At least some of which seems to have come from criminal sources.'

'That is a distinct possibility,' Falcone concurred. 'But I would be grateful if we didn't trouble Quattrocchi and his men with this thought. They're busy enough already. When we meet . . .' He glanced at his watch. '. . . and we must be going soon, we're there to listen and nothing else. Catherine? Agreed?'

'I'm an officer of the San Francisco Police Department,' she answered, astonished. 'Not one of you.'

'Of course you're one of us!' Falcone insisted with heat. 'Think of it. You're snubbed by those men from downtown, since they regard a homicide as beneath you. Your station will close at the end of the month out of . . . what?'

'Centralization,' she hissed. 'Rationalization. Putting good offi-cers behind desks downtown, in front of computers, instead of out on the street where they're supposed to be.'

Peroni chuckled and muttered, 'We *are* in the same business.'

Falcone pointed at Costa and told him to stay with the exhibition. From the look on his face, it was clear there was no point in objecting.

'I don't want anything else disappearing,' the inspector insisted. 'There are thirteen incunabula, a good number of rare books, and what's supposedly the finest copy of the original manuscript of the work in existence, from Mumbai of all places. The Indians will have our hide if that goes. Make sure it doesn't happen.'

'And me?' Teresa wondered.

'How you spend your holiday is your business. If you happen to be passing a store, could you kindly buy some decent coffee? That stuff in the house is disgusting.'

She took a deep breath and glared at him.

'So what am I supposed to do with my brain? I was on holiday when we were in Venice if you remember . . .'

'Venice was a different place.'

'Damned right. I saved your life there.'

'*Grazie mille,*' Falcone said nonchalantly. 'We must get this out of the way because I don't wish to keep repeating it. You are here of your own volition, on your own time. You're a pathologist. We're not investigating a murder. Nor will we ever be allowed the opportunity. It's hard enough for me to argue a way in to eavesdrop. I cannot do that for you and I won't waste my breath trying.'

A chill wind engulfed them at that moment, and it wasn't simply the lively sea breeze gusting in from the nearby shoreline.

The Palace of Fine Arts was a beautiful, quiet spot. Not what Costa had expected of the city of San Francisco, any more than was Cow Hollow, the small district neighbouring the Marina and the houses of the rich and famous, Roberto Tonti among them. They had landed in a quiet, genteel oasis of affluence tacked to the side of the larger, grey urban metropolis from which the Carabinieri team and the local officers Catherine Bianchi simply referred to as 'downtown' were running the investigation. And keeping their cards very close to their besuited chests.

- 2 -

To Gianni Peroni's mildly jaundiced eye it seemed as if *Maresciallo* Gianluca Quattrocchi and Captain Gerald Kelly, his counterpart in the SFPD Homicide Detail, might have been made from the same mould, one customarily used to turn out military action figures for reclusive adolescent boys. They were of similar age – late forties – similar heavy build, and possessed the same kind of sullen, heavy, clean-shaven face, that of a boxer or field sergeant perhaps, or some burly priest with a taste for communion wine. Now they sat with their respective teams, three officers each, all male, behind facing tables in the largest room the modest Greenwich Police Station could offer, which wasn't very large at all. But at least the American cast Quattrocchi the odd doubtful look from time to time when the Carabinieri man's language got a little too over the top. There might be hope there, Peroni thought. If only they had the chance to speak frankly . . .

Falcone, Peroni and Catherine Bianchi were perched on the end like bystanders. It still felt chilly outside but this overcrowded chamber at the rear of the little station was stifling and beginning to fill with the musky odour of men in business clothes. Peroni wondered, briefly, how much of his life had been passed in meetings, and atmospheres, such as this, then reminded himself that for once there was a variation from the norm.

Quattrocchi had found himself an expert. Or rather *the* expert if the Carabinieri were to be believed. Professor Bryan Whitcombe had flown from Toronto, where he divided his time between teaching Dante and writing about the man and his work, to join the team

Quattrocchi and Kelly had assembled inside the Hall of Justice in Bryant Street, a location Falcone and his men were clearly unwelcome in, since this was where the serious work took place. The purpose, Quattrocchi had let it be known in a fulsome round of newspaper and television interviews, was to gain precious insight into the mentality and intent of the Dante-fixated murderers of Allan Prime, who might now be stalking remaining members of the *Inferno* cast and crew in San Francisco. The media, naturally, loved this story, and had come to adore the handsomely uniformed, English-speaking Carabinieri *maresciallo*, a man who seemed like an actor himself and was only too happy to play up for the cameras on any occasion.

Peroni and the others had watched Quattrocchi introduce Bryan Whitcombe on the TV the previous night and found themselves wondering what the media might make of him. The man was thirty-five according to his personal web-site, though his manner spoke of someone much older. He was extremely short and slender, bird-like in appearance, with darting, expressive hands and a pinched, pale academic's face half-hidden by enormous horn-rimmed spectacles. His curly dark brown hair seemed to shoot straight out of his scalp in any direction it fancied, in the manner of a 1970s rock musician. Whitcombe clearly enjoyed the attention and the cameras as much as his patron, frequently stuttering off into academic dissertations, often peppered with obscure quotes in medieval Florentine, and never tiring of dealing with the most basic and idiotic of questions.

'He wants his own show,' Teresa had observed perceptively. The professor also seemed extremely well informed about the case, given that he'd only been in San Francisco a day. The TV reported that he had been following the story since the dreadful night of Prime's death in Rome, and had been taken onto the team after the Carabinieri had identified him as one of the world's leading authorities on the interpretation of *The Divine Comedy*.

Falcone had cleared his throat at that point and revealed something the TV station hadn't. Thanks to Catherine Bianchi, the inspector knew that Whitcombe had approached Quattrocchi personally to offer his assistance after seeing the Carabinieri officer on CNN the morning following Prime's murder.

'Toronto is six hours behind Rome,' Falcone added. 'He must watch television in the early hours.'

Seeing Whitcombe in the flesh now, Peroni didn't doubt it. The man had the nervous energy of a squirrel, even out of public view behind the guarded doors of the small, doomed San Francisco neighbourhood police station to which they had been summoned.

Gianluca Quattrocchi made the nature of the meeting clear from the outset.

'You're here to listen,' he told them as they arrived. 'Not talk. I have a duty to share with you any information I feel may enable you to carry out your guard duties professionally. Nothing more. This is an ongoing murder investigation. The less chatter, the better. Professor?'

Whitcombe nodded, as if in approval, and added, in an oddly nasal accent that was not quite English and not quite American, 'I have examined the notes and they support the thesis that these people are intelligent, informed and knowledgeable in their subject. They know Dante . . .'

'These people?' Peroni interrupted. 'I know you think the man you shot dead in the park was one of them. What makes you think there were ever more than two, one of them dead?'

'Because I am assuming we're dealing with normal human beings,' Quattrocchi said with a sigh. 'Not Superman. Now will you kindly sit and listen without interrupting?'

Peroni shrugged and caught Falcone's eye. Catherine Bianchi scratched her ear and smiled at the table.

'These *people*,' Whitcombe emphasized, 'clearly know and appreciate the subject matter. They understand this is a cycle, with form, direction and purpose. I must assure you my opinion is this: they will regard their work as only begun, not even half finished. There are nine circles of Hell, and their notes indicate only two have passed . . .'

Falcone raised a finger.

'I'm sorry. This is my first and last question. Why would anyone kill another human being over a movie, even some so-called block-buster that half the world seems to be panting to see? What does it matter?'

Quattrocchi began swearing again. The academic bristled then adjusted his glasses, a nervous habit which he repeated constantly.

'No, no, please,' Whitcombe continued. 'Let me handle this.' He fixed Falcone with a glare, one Peroni found more daunting than he might have expected. 'If I were the killing kind, *ispettore*, I would murder over this. With as much brutality as I could muster. It's blasphemy.'

'Not according to any dictionary I know,' Peroni objected. 'If Roberto Tonti is insulting anything – and he's adamant he's not – it's some ancient piece of poetry. Not the Church.'

'For anyone who admires Dante,' Whitcombe emphasized, 'this *is* blasphemy. I sat through that drivel a week ago. They flew a group of experts to London hoping we would gild their vile nonsense with praise.' His small fist thumped the table. 'Not a man or woman among us would say anything but the truth. It's rubbish. Like defacing the Sistine Chapel.' He turned and glanced at Kelly and his men. 'Or painting the Golden Gate Bridge black.'

'Neither of which is worth killing for, either,' Peroni observed.

Catherine Bianchi's light fingers caught his arm, and he found himself looking into her bright, attractive face.

'Remember what I said, Gianni. This is America. A Bud and a hot dog. Sometimes that's all it takes.'

'Let's come to the point,' Kelly cut in brusquely. 'This is all we have. If it's not some lunatics offended by what's up there on the screen, what else could it be?'

Falcone frowned at Peroni, who was about to open his mouth.

'In the absence of any better suggestions,' Kelly continued, 'we've got to run with what we have, and for the life of me this *does* sound convincing. I watched that movie. There's something distasteful about it. The thing's nasty and creepy and obsessive. Just the kind of crap that can push the buttons of any number of screwballs out there.'

'Someone hijacked that computer system,' Falcone suggested. 'Someone made Allan Prime's death an international event. That's evidence, isn't it? Not about poetry either.'

One of Kelly's men leaned forward and said, 'It's evidence that confirms there's probably a link in this geographical area, sir. Nothing more. They didn't hijack Lukatmi by the way. Not in the sense you mean. They simply hacked into the DNS servers so that particular stream got pointed to some place they were hosting it in Russia, not that we'll ever discover much from them.'

Peroni felt his head start to thrum.

'How many people could pull off that kind of trick?' he asked. 'Surely it's got to be someone from the company? Or someone who got fired?'

The men from Bryant Street looked at one another as if it were the most idiotic question they'd ever heard.

'This is San Francisco,' Gerald Kelly said with a shrug of his big shoulders. He looked a little apologetic. 'Between here and San Jose reside ninety per cent of the world's geek population. These people don't breed or have girlfriends. Their principal romantic relationship is with their iPhone. They barely eat or talk. They just spend their time frigging around with their little laptops earning a living one moment and destroying someone else's the next. Any big-name start-up like Lukatmi gets hackers going for its throat the moment someone picks up the *Wall Street Journal* and reads they've got seed capital. It's part of the game.' He stared hard at Peroni to make his point. 'We can give you more detail later if you want it.'

'No clarification needed.' Gianluca Quattrocchi was intent on reclaiming the conversation. 'This is none of their concern. We are naturally investigating employees and ex-employees in Lukatmi and Tonti's own production company. That's all you need to know. That's *more* than you need to know.'

'Maybe,' Kelly agreed. 'But understand this. Any one of a million sad nerds out there could have hacked into that system. Whoever it was could have done it on their laptop sitting in a Starbucks downtown sipping their latte while that poor bastard was eking out his last minutes in Rome. This stuff is global.'

One of the younger American officers jumped in and added, 'We have experts in the FBI trawling the web spoor.'

'The what?' Peroni asked.

'Any traces they've left in their wake on the net,' one of them explained. 'We've ten officers alone in Bryant Street working this. There are other agencies involved too, in the US and in Rome . . .'

'Enough,' Quattrocchi barked.

Falcone stifled a laugh and glanced briefly at the ceiling.

'How many officers do you have knocking on doors, staring in people's faces and seeing if they look guilty?' Peroni asked.

The carabinieri glanced at their watches. Gerald Kelly wriggled in his seat.

'Listen,' the SFPD captain responded. 'We all came up that way. Those of us over the age of thirty-five. We all know what you're thinking. Go head to head, yell at people, watch what happens. Let me tell you guys. Firstly, even if we did have a face to yell at, those days are over. In this town there'd be a lawyer in the way before you got to the second sentence. Or the civil rights people if their name's unpronounceable. Those days are past. Intelligence, analysts, profiling . . .' He patted Whitcombe on his small arm. 'Expert insight based upon years of knowledge . . . welcome to the future.'

Peroni nodded and leaned forward.

'And when you find them, will you have anyone left who still knows how to bring them in?'

'You just watch,' Kelly replied with no small amount of menace, waving down the furious Quattrocchi. 'We called this meeting to tell you the direction this investigation is heading. If those of you working the exhibition team see any suspicious individuals or come across any possible evidence, however small, we expect to hear of it, immediately. Your job is to keep those museum exhibits all together in one place. I suggest this time you get it right. It shouldn't be too hard, should it?'

He leaned forward and pointed at Falcone.

'And stop that young cop of yours hanging around with Maggie Flavier. She's under our protection. Not yours.'

'Miss Flavier goes where she wishes,' Falcone answered. 'You know that as well as we do. Speak to her. Put her in protective custody if you like. The media will love that.'

'Falcone . . .' the Carabinieri officer warned.

'What?'

'Do not get in our way. One more question. Then we go.'

'I doubt our paths will cross much, *maresciallo*. I will be happy to comply with your wishes.'

'And the question?' the man in the smart uniform added.

Falcone screwed up his face.

'You haven't found anywhere that sells decent coffee, have you? The stuff we have in our house is simply disgusting.'

'Good day,' Quattrocchi snorted and stood up.

The rest followed. The tiny room emptied in a flash. Catherine Bianchi opened every window, letting in some welcome fresh air. Peroni was pleased to notice that he could detect the scent of the ocean. Did the Pacific smell different to the Mediterranean? He thought so.

Catherine Bianchi looked at Falcone and said, 'Gerald Kelly is a good man. He's only swallowing that bullshit because he's got nothing else to work with.'

'I believe you,' Falcone insisted.

'So do you intend to tell him anything? You guys go home when this is over. I've got to keep a career, and it just might wind up in Bryant Street once they bring down the shutters on this place.'

'I can't think without coffee,' Falcone complained. 'Real coffee. Not with chocolate in it. Or cinnamon. Or anything else. Just coffee.'

She looked at Peroni, and he wished she hadn't.

'There's a store round the corner,' she said. 'They take orders. Not me.'

Then she walked out of the room.

Falcone watched her go, quite speechless. Peroni found himself a little misty-eyed with mirth and tried very hard not to show it.

'They do things differently here, Leo,' he said quietly. 'Best remember.'

- 3 -

Teresa Lupo knew she would end up gravitating to Chestnut Street. The house in Greenwich was comfortable and pretty and . . . boring. One neighbourhood store on the corner. A couple of bars and restaurants a block along. That was it. She hankered for noise and people and the bustle she associated with Rome. More than anything, she craved intellectual activity. Chestnut provided the first three, and perhaps the fourth, if she was lucky, though she felt sure that, by the time this self-assigned trip was over, she'd know every last book store, delicatessen, restaurant and cafe there as well as any back home.

It got a little quieter at the end near the Palace of Fine Arts. At three o'clock on this chill San Francisco afternoon she found herself in a small and spotless cafe trying to summon the energy to walk along to the stores. Distances in this city were deceptive. From the nearby waterfront the Golden Gate Bridge itself seemed not much more than a stroll. She'd checked on the map she'd bought. The truth: it was a long, long haul, past West Bluff, Crissy Field, then Fort Point and on to the bridge's great, arching span, thrusting out like some metal giant's arm, reaching over the water. San Francisco was deceptive, a metropolis posing as a set of villages, or a set of villages posing as a metropolis, she wasn't quite sure which. Perhaps if she went downtown . . . But the Marina and Cow Hollow were comfortable, and given that she seemed to be expected to fall into some kind of mental torpor while the men got on with being jumped-up museum guards there was, perhaps, no better place to be.

The cafe owner was Armenian. His list of Italian 'specialities' contained several items which Teresa not only failed to identify, but

111

also found quite difficult to categorize. The coffee was fine, though: a strong *macchiato*, from a proper Italian machine, good enough for her to ask him to grind some to keep Falcone happy. Though why she did that . . .

A long, low and somewhat scatological Roman curse escaped her lips.

One of two men seated at the next table shook his head and said, 'Tut, tut. We are shocked.'

She hadn't really noticed them before, and now she realized that was odd. The pair appeared to be at the latter end of middle age, average height, dressed in the same fawn slacks and matching brown shirts with military-style pockets. Each had a good head of greying brown hair receding at the front, leaving them with prominent widow's peaks. Their broad, friendly faces were tanned and adorned with walrus moustaches that nestled beneath florid, bulbous noses that spoke of beer and a bachelor lifestyle. They had the same eyes too: deep-set, dark, yet twinkling with intelligence and, perhaps, mischief.

'I'm sorry,' she apologized. 'I didn't realize anyone would speak Italian.'

'We don't,' the second one said. 'A curse is a curse in any language. It's the intonation.'

'The force and the manner of speech,' the other added.

'Observation is everything,' his counterpart continued, then dashed a vicious look across the street. Her own powers in this field were clearly on the wane. Both men were staring, with some degree of malevolence, at the fire station opposite. The doors were open revealing the largest fire engine Teresa had ever seen, a gigantic monster of gleaming red paint and mirror-like chrome that looked eager to burst upon the world seeking some blaze to extinguish merely by the force of its looming, glittering presence.

A young fireman, handsome in heavy, industrial trousers, braces over a white shirt rolled up at the sleeves, was sweating over the front of the machine with a bucket, a sponge and a leather, making it sparkle even more.

'That spot's on the fender still, I'll wager,' the first one declared. 'Dirt on the front left mudguard. Tyre walls grimy as hell.'

'Not that *he'll* notice,' the other chipped in. 'Sloppy, slutty, careless, or perhaps uncaring. Who knows?'

Both sets of beady eyes turned on her.

'Do you agree?' they seemed to say in unison.

'It seems a very shiny fire engine to me.'

'Surface shine, nothing more,' the first announced. His voice had a firmness, both of opinion and tone, that she was coming to associate with San Francisco. She liked it. 'That's all anyone requires for the twenty-first century. People don't notice detail any more. What you don't see is what you don't get. The powers of observation wane everywhere. And as for deduction . . .'

'Who said deduction was dead?' she objected.

Their eyebrows rose and the other said, simply, 'We did.'

It was a challenge and she never ducked one of those. Teresa Lupo looked at the two of them and was relieved that someone was, albeit in ignorance, asking her to exercise a little professional judgement.

'You're identical twins,' she said.

They peered at her wearing the same dubious expression, then picked up their coffee mugs, each with a different hand, and took a long swig.

'Fruits of the same zygote?' the nearer commented. 'That's quite a far-reaching conjecture from such brief witness. A similarity of features suggests relationship, I'll agree. Little more.'

'No,' she said firmly. 'It's more than that. You share the same facial features. The same build, hair colour, and a shortness of breath that would indicate some inherited tendency towards asthma. Also hardly anyone but a scientist or an identical twin would know the word zygote. Most people think babies come straight from the embryo.'

'So,' the further one said pleasantly, 'you surmise we share the same DNA and fingerprints?'

'Oh no. You can cut out the trick questions. The DNA is identical at birth. Fine details such as fingerprints . . . individual.'

'A doctor then?' the same man asked.

'Once. A criminal pathologist now.'

The other one raised his coffee mug in salute, and was followed by the second. She noticed the hands again.

'Any more?' the first wondered.

'You're mirror twins.' She pointed to the one who had just spoken. 'You're right-handed. You part your hair on that side and it curls clockwise at the crown. He . . .' She indicated the second who was listening intently, fist beneath chin, a posture his brother adopted the moment he saw it. '. . . is the opposite in every respect.'

They applauded. The Armenian *barista*, who had been eavesdropping avidly, came over with free cake by way of a prize.

'One other thing,' she went on. 'Don't take the DNA thing for granted either. If one of you is thinking you can get away with something by blaming it on the other, I've got news. DNA changes. It's called epigenetic modification. You start off the same but DNA's plastic. Different environments change it over the decades. I'd know.'

The neared leaned forward on one elbow and said, 'We've never had different environments. We were born round the corner in Beach Street sixty-one years ago. We've lived there all our lives. Before we retired . . .' He nodded across the road and added, though this was no surprise, '. . . we worked there, keeping every engine that came through that place spicker and spanner than any of those indolent young bloods know how today.'

Two large, identical hairy hands, one right, one left, extended her way, and their joint, booming voices announced in unison, 'Hankenfrank.'

She blinked and asked, 'Do you run to first names?'

They sighed. Then the one with left-turning curls said, 'I'm Hank Boynton.' And the other added, 'In case you hadn't worked this out, I'm Frank.'

'Oh . . . Teresa Lupo.'

Their grips were warm and soft and, though mirrored, very much the same.

'When did you retire?' she asked. 'From over there?'

'It's been thirty-three weeks, two days and . . .' Frank looked at his watch. 'A few hundred minutes. That poor damned engine hasn't been properly clean since.'

'And so we pass the time,' Hank declared with a flourish of his arm. 'We read. We think. We talk with intriguing and exotic strangers in cafes. Of DNA and . . . epigenetic modification.'

'Do you read the same books?' she asked out of curiosity.

They erupted in spontaneous, deafening laughter. When it had subsided and they'd wiped away the tears, still saying nothing, she persisted.

'Well?'

Hank flourished his hand and declared, 'My specialist subjects are the history of this rich and wonderful city during and immediately after the gold rush in 1849 . . .'

'He stole it all from Herbert Asbury,' Frank cut in. 'Blood and guts nonsense . . .'

'. . . as well as the works of Gilbert and Sullivan, nineteenth-century Japanese woodcuts, notably Hokusai, and, in literature, anything by or related to Sherlock Holmes.'

'Note the recurrent theme,' Frank suggested. 'Lowbrow posing as high. My . . . *things* are bebop, Edgar Allan Poe, the Impressionists and American cinéma noir from the 1940s on. These are lists in summary, you understand. The full catalogue is much more horrendous, on both our parts. We won't even breathe a word about philately.'

'As I'd expect,' she declared, pleased with herself. 'You choose opposites.'

Hank gave her a humbling look and said, 'Not really. It just gives us something different to talk about at night. There isn't a smart explanation for everything, you know. Some things just are.'

'Good point. I forget that sometimes.'

'So what do you want to know?' Hank asked. 'A little blood-curdling local history? Where to go to hear music not muzak? Two crumpled old men's advice on the last yuppie-free place to get a cold beer in the Marina?'

The question made her feel pathetic. She had no good answer. The ticket to San Francisco had cost a fortune. It was bought on a whim without a thought as to why she had to come. The four of them worked together as a team now, or at least they had since Nic had arrived. She hated feeling excluded.

'What I'd really like to know,' she murmured, half to herself, 'is where I can find Carlotta Valdes.'

Hank and Frank looked at one another briefly. Then Frank tapped his strong forefinger on his watch and declared, 'If you've got ten minutes . . .'

'. . . we can show you,' Hank added.

- 4 -

The location for the *Inferno* exhibition had proved to be a visual delight so unexpected that, when he first saw it, Costa felt he ought to rub his eyes to make sure it was real. The Palace of Fine Arts was a purpose-built semi-ruin set by an artificial lake with fountains and swans. It was a short distance inland from the beach front that led to Fort Mason, home to Lukatmi, on one side, and on the other, after a long and pleasant walk by the ocean, to the Golden Gate Bridge. The exhibition was slowly being assembled during the day in a series of peaked Arabian tents which had been erected around the central construction, a high, dome-roofed rotunda open to the elements. They stretched in a curving line through the trees along the lake-front to a group of Romanesque colonnades on the northern side, close to a children's museum housed in a set of unremarkable low square blocks.

For days the area had been overrun with workmen, security guards, uniformed police officers, and members of the *Inferno* cast and crew inspecting the temporary theatre, in the largest tent of all, that would be used for the premiere. For Costa the event had the feel of a travelling circus. The collection of rare objects – documents, letters, the manuscript from India, and, arranged in haste, an authentic replica of the original death mask – was arriving in San Francisco crate by crate. The brief for Falcone's team was clear and limited: monitor the security arrangements before the opening to ensure they were satisfactory. Then, when the exhibition became public after the premiere, hand over all responsibility entirely to the Americans and return to Rome. No one mentioned the missing death mask of

Dante. The assumption was that this had now entered the global black market for stolen art, and was probably long gone.

Costa had soon grown tired of checking the security system set up by the American organizers. So he took the time to wander through the tents and the teams of individuals milling around delivery vans and crates, building the stage for the premiere, trying out lights and projection systems, playing with shiny and seemingly very expensive toys he could not begin to comprehend. He also, at Peroni's bidding, spent some time with the publicist, Simon Harvey. The man's remit appeared to run far beyond dealing with the media. He had taken a keen interest in every aspect of the security arrangements on the ground, insisting that if another item went missing, or there was a second violent incident affecting the crew, it would be his job to deal with the fallout. It was Harvey's opinion that the replacement death mask would prove one of the most popular items in the show, for its macabre connotations. The man had even suggested that what the public really wanted to see was the actual death mask of Allan Prime now sitting in the Carabinieri's labs in Rome.

He'd listened to the American and said nothing. It seemed a cruel thing to think, let alone say. Yet he had to acknowledge that the idea contained some truth. Actors of the stature of Prime – and the beauty of Maggie Flavier – were no longer fully in control of their own lives, or deaths. In return for fame and wealth, they surrendered their identities to the masses who would dissect, reshape and play with them as they saw fit. Celebrity came at a terrible price, he felt, one that was made acceptable to those it affected only through their own ability to pretend they were unable to see its costs.

Costa was, however, sanguine about the security arrangements. The only way the original death mask could have been switched for the fake severed head of Prime was by someone on the inside, probably within the two hundred or more individuals who worked for the exhibition companies, the caterers, the crew and the various arms of the production company: publicity, accounts, still and movie photographers, make-up artistes, and a variety of hangers-on who appeared to fulfil no particular function at all. These people seemed even more numerous in San Francisco. But the items on show were to be heavily guarded and under constant CCTV surveillance.

It was difficult to see what more could be done. If some improvements were advisable, Costa felt sure that he would be the last person who could bring them about. An expensive private security company had been brought in to deal with the handling of the exhibits from the moment they arrived by truck, and to provide personal security for key members of cast and crew. Catherine Bianchi's dwindling band of officers from the Greenwich Police Station was being sidelined too. Only one, a sullen young man with bright blond hair and a curt, sharp tongue, remained at the Palace, and he seemed to take little interest in proceedings. Like the Italians of the state police, the local cops were spectators, ghosts walking in the shadows of the men of the Carabinieri and Bryant Street.

This he found deeply vexing. After checking the arrangements once more, he spent a pleasant few minutes peering at a rare Venetian incunabulum of the *Comedy*. Miller, the American officer from Greenwich Street, had followed him and made some caustic comments as Costa tried to read the explanatory material.

'Incunabulum,' the cop grunted. 'Sounds like witchcraft.'

'You're thinking of incubus,' Costa replied. 'Incunabula are just very early printed books. Before 1501.'

'So why don't they call them "very early printed books"?'

'For the same reason people call this the Palace of Fine Arts, even though it's a pointless folly made out of plaster and chicken wire. It makes life more interesting.'

He mumbled something and gave Costa a suspicious look.

'You clearly don't have to deal with the kind of shit we do if you've got nothing better to do than learn stuff like that.'

'I didn't know until now,' Costa replied, indicating the exhibit case. 'I just read the label. The same goes for the chicken wire. It's all there if you take the time to look.'

Looking was important. Falcone emphasized that often, though

Costa knew it instinctively and always had. Neither man enjoyed the modern tendency to rush in, to pull out the regulations and procedures, to try to wrap an unknown in hasty, tangible certainties.

'Yeah, well . . .'

'No worry,' Costa said pleasantly. 'Sometimes it takes a stranger to show you something that's sitting right beneath your nose. It happens to us all. If you ever visit Italy, come and see me. You can return the favour.'

It had happened in Rome, with Emily, experiencing the city through different eyes. Perspective was good, as a cop, and as a human being.

He walked outside to see Simon Harvey, Dino Bonetti and Roberto Tonti engaged in a huddled conversation beneath the dome of the rotunda. Costa went over, watched as they became silent, noting his approach.

'Something you need, officer?' Harvey asked.

'Introductions. I've seen these two gentlemen in Rome and now here. We've never met.' He extended his hand. Tonti simply stared at it. '*Sovrintendente* Costa,' he added. 'If there is ever anything . . .'

'Such as?' Tonti asked.

'I don't know. You tell me.'

The director looked even more grey and sick close up. He sighed and said, 'What matters lies with Quattrocchi and Kelly. These security guards who are eating into what's left of our promotion budget take care of the day-to-day work. Everything else is irrelevant. Including the state police of Rome.'

'Yet you have the SFPD outside your own house, sir,' Costa said, nodding at the three-storey white mansion, with gold crests and handsome bow windows, across the street from the palace. 'Not a private company.'

'I am an exception,' Tonti replied, his expression hidden behind the plastic-framed sunglasses. 'They regard me as a local celebrity, to be protected. Besides, who would want to end the life of an old man when nature is doing that for them?'

'I'm sorry to hear of your illness,' he said automatically.

'Why? You don't know me.'

'To have spent so long without directing anything. It must be . . .'

The glasses came off and Costa fell silent. Two grey, watery eyes, physically weak yet full of some unspent intellectual power, stared at him.

'Must be what?'

'Frustrating.'

'You know nothing about this industry, young man. It's the invisible people like me who make it work. Over the past twenty years I've written, produced, developed TV series . . .'

'Is that why you came here? TV?'

'I came here for freedom,' the director snapped, his grey head of hair flying around him. 'For money. For life. Rome is a village next to this. Cinecittà is a peasant's pig sty next to Hollywood. I would have made *Inferno* there if it weren't for . . .'

He stopped. His gaunt cheeks were bloodless. His breath seemed short and laboured.

'For what?' Costa asked.

Bonetti laughed and nudged the director with his elbow.

'If it weren't for the money, Roberto. Hollywood didn't want to give it you. Italy did. And your generous friends at Lukatmi. Tell the policeman the truth. More importantly, tell it to yourself.'

'Dante was Italian. It could be made nowhere else.' Tonti rubbed his eyes then returned the sunglasses to his face. 'I could have made it here if I'd wanted.'

'Of course you could!' Bonetti declared. '*Inferno* is the kind of project Hollywood adores. The pinnacle of commercial art . . .'

'Popular. *Popular art*,' Tonti screeched. 'How many times do I have to say this?'

'Popular,' the producer corrected himself. 'Like me.'

'Still, a hundred and fifty million dollars,' Costa wondered. 'So much money to reclaim before any of your backers makes a penny profit. Even with all this . . . unwanted publicity. That's a mountain to climb. Isn't it?'

Tonti waved him away with a feeble, bloodless hand.

'The movie is made. Those who matter have been paid. The rest is meaningless.'

Bonetti's face fell into a furious scowl.

'Money is best left to those of us who understand it,' the producer muttered. 'Why are you wasting our time, *sovrintendente*? Do you have nothing better to do? No idea where to find this mask of yours?'

'I . . .'

'Perhaps one of your own stole it. Have you thought of that? Who had better opportunity? You're as rotten as the rest of us. Don't pretend otherwise. At least with us they get entertainment. And from you?'

'Very little, sir. But at least we never promise any.'

He looked Bonetti straight in the eye.

'Adele Neri told me you invited some of her late husband's friends to dine in Allan Prime's apartment.'

'What friends?' Bonetti snarled. 'What are you talking about?'

'Emilio Neri was a *capo* in Rome until he was murdered. I'm talking about criminal friends. Perhaps from the Mafia or the Camorra. Or the Russians or the Serbs. We live in international times. If you knew Neri's friends, then some might assume . . .'

Harvey was coughing into his fist. Roberto Tonti, in his dark suit, behind his black sunglasses, was stiff and silent, like an arthritic crow waiting for something to happen.

'I am a congenial man in a congenial business,' Bonetti said simply. 'When you wish to raise money for a creative enterprise you meet all kinds. Our little business is merely the world writ large. You should get out more. It might make you less of a pain in the ass.'

Costa leaned forward and touched the director's thin, weak arm, and said, 'Should you need any help . . . I know that breed of people better than you.'

The man shrank back, murmuring a succession of bitter Roman curses, then finished – Costa was only just sure he heard this – with the low, mumbled words, in Italian, 'I doubt that.'

It was enough. Costa walked to the mobile van set up by the caterers, thinking that even a poor cup of coffee that had been stewing in an urn for hours might help take away the taste of that encounter. Bonetti dealt with crooks. At least some of the money – perhaps a large part – that paid for the production of *Inferno* surely came from criminal sources. Roberto Tonti appeared not to care less whether they got their investment back, with good interest, although he seemed to be aware that this nonchalance carried with it some risk. All useful intelligence . . . if they had been working on a murder case.

He got a coffee, closed his eyes, gritted his teeth and took a swig. It was as disgusting as he expected.

When he turned, she was there, smiling, bright-eyed in a white sweater and blue jeans, looking younger than ever.

'Well?' she asked. 'What do you think?'

His mouth felt dry. His head was spinning. Maggie Flavier had become a different woman. Her hair was fuller, deeper and had lost its chestnut hue. It was no longer an expensive straggly impersonation of some English page boy's. Through some process he could not begin to comprehend it had become a pure, golden shade of yellow, and had straightened into a serious, slightly old-fashioned cut falling down to her shoulders. She was changed. No, he corrected himself, transformed, almost into someone else altogether.

What took his breath away were the memories, the connections. Maggie's hair so vividly resembled Emily's, in the photograph in his wallet she had briefly seen in the Cinema dei Piccoli, that the similarity both shocked and fascinated him. She didn't look like his late wife. Her eyes were a different colour, her neck more slender, her skin a subtle shade darker, and her face possessed a more classical, timeless beauty. All the same . . .

'I hate it,' Maggie said, picking up his train of thought. 'Needs must. I'm testing for some new part. Some 1950s mystery. I'm a waitress in a diner. What do I know? A girl's got to eat.'

'You look beautiful,' he said, without thinking.

She blushed, and seemed even younger.

'I should be serving in a soda fountain from some ancient TV comedy. Please . . .'

'No,' he said, laughing, shaking his head. 'I'm sorry. It was just such a . . . surprise. How do you do this? Where does it come from?'

'Bangs,' she replied, and put one hand up to her long, soft locks, then tugged out a length with her fingers. 'Everything's fake that's not flesh and blood, and there may come a time when I can't even say that.'

The familiarity between them was strange, and had been from the start. It was as if there had never been a point of introduction, a border that was crossed between their being strangers and their being . . . friends.

'Now look what you've made me do,' she complained, holding up the hank of golden hair. 'I can't put it back myself. Nic?'

She turned. He found himself staring at the back of her neck, which bore the lightest of olive tans, so dissimilar to the pale northern skin of Emily. They weren't alike. Apart from the single physical resemblance, and the same directness and utter lack of self-consciousness.

He took the bunch of hair and found some way to pin it back in place. His hands shook all the time.

She noticed but didn't mention it.

'I can show you,' Maggie said, turning to face him.

'Show me what?'

'Where it comes from. If you like.' She moved closer and whispered, 'If we can shake off the goons. I want to get away from this place. I need to. I feel like a dummy in a shop window. Please . . .'

She turned to the man working behind the counter of the catering van and asked, 'Do you have any fruit?'

It took a moment but from somewhere a shiny red apple appeared. She took it, rubbing the skin against her sweater, and made as if to eat, then stopped.

'Food is one of life's great pleasures,' Maggie said, her green eyes holding him. She held up the apple. 'I'll deal with this along the way. So? Do you want to see a secret or not?'

– 5 –

Hankenfrank – somehow she thought of them as a single entity, and needed to work on this – led her across Chestnut, past the fire station – where a few gruff words were exchanged with the poor young officer who was unlucky enough to be cleaning the engine – then down the street towards the stores a few blocks away. As they walked she saw a building rise in her vision ahead and knew, unconsciously somehow, that this had to be their destination.

An old and probably defunct neon sign on the side read, Marina Odeon. It was attached to a grimy bell-tower that rose three storeys above the low line of houses and shops on the street. Like the building itself, the tower was clad in rough white adobe plaster.

It was a cinema. More than that, it was somehow familiar, in a way that was nagging her, exactly as the name of Carlotta Valdes had.

The two men in identical brown clothing got to the entrance. Hank hammered on the shuttered ticket booth. Frank stood stock still and yelled, 'Anyone home?'

She caught up with them.

'What do you mean is there anyone at home?' she demanded. 'The place is derelict.'

'Derelict?' Hank objected vociferously. '*Derelict?* This is San Francisco. Dereliction is a trait of character, not a notice of death. This old Odeon's just a little careworn. That's all.'

'It's a dump,' Frank added. 'The young guy who's got it inherited the thing from his uncle or something. He opens it up when he feels like it, so he can show ancient movies to ancient people like us. Good old movies, in widescreen Technicolor, with just a couple of speakers for sound, not some goddamned rock band's racket machine like you get in the new theatres.'

'Is the popcorn good?' she asked.

'We are not children,' Hank pronounced, folding his strong arms. 'But yes. It is. Do you want to see Carlotta Valdes or not?'

'I do! I do! And I want to know about this place. I've seen it before.'

Frank shook his head. His walrus moustache bristled with the pride of superior knowledge.

'No you haven't. You just think you have. In spite of appearances, this is not San Juan Bautista. That's ninety miles south, and you won't find the bell-tower there either. That was a lie as well. We're dealing with the movies, Teresa. Remember? Everything worthwhile usually turns out to be an invention. You don't sit in those hard, bald seats for the truth.'

She stared at the stumpy white tower. It was all coming back. An old, old film, one she'd loved when she was a teenager, juggling dreams of getting a job in Cinecittà, following in the footsteps of the greats: Fellini, Bertolucci, Pasolini. Even Roberto Tonti for one brief teenage summer spent spellbound by a horror flick mired in gore.

The title of the movie eluded her but she could picture it now *and it was here*. In San Francisco, an earlier incarnation of the city but one still recognizable. Some sights – the Palace of Fine Arts, the city streets, the view towards Fort Point and the Golden Gate Bridge – were scarcely changed. The colours were the same: the bright, sharp sun, piercing, relentless.

The name danced in the shadows at the back of her head.

'There's no one around,' Frank announced. 'They won't mind if we walk round the back. Hell, if they didn't want visitors they wouldn't have something like that in the garden, now would they?'

There was a particular colour that mattered, she recalled, in a way she never quite understood. It was a dark yet vivid green, the colour of a vehicle, and of a woman's flowing, elegant evening dress, all somehow iconic of a lost and deadly desire.

'Garden?'

They were already pushing their way through a battered wooden gate by the tower side of the cinema. She looked up and got a momentary fearful ache in her stomach. That was a memory too. Of a man staring down from just such a campanile as this, his face creased in misery, as if all the cares and tragedies in the history of the world had fallen on his shoulders at that moment.

'Here it is,' one of the two brothers – she couldn't see which – was shouting. 'There's a donation box. We could put something in it.'

Even for her, a Roman pathologist well used to stepping off the straight and narrow, this seemed strange. To be following two complete strangers, eccentric old firemen, well read, self-educated probably, into the unkempt back yard – it was no garden, not in her judgement – of an odd little rotting cinema in a lazy, sunny suburb of San Francisco called the Marina.

'Just like I remembered,' Frank said. She recognized his voice this time. It was a little higher, exactly half a tone. Mirror twins. Identical in most ways. Differently similar in others.

Teresa Lupo walked through what looked like a small junk yard, with an old white sink stained with rust, an abandoned refrigerator and a tangle of ancient piping, and found herself in a patch of open ground a few metres out of the shadow of the bell-tower above them. Pansies and miniature dahlias ran around the border of a bed of pale marble chips and gravel. A grey stone urn stood in the centre filled with fresh scarlet roses. A green silk sash – the colour sent a shiver through her, it was so accurate, so familiar – was wrapped around the vase neck, new and shiny.

She stared at the headstone that stood over what could only have been a fake grave and felt her head might explode.

The inscription, worn by the years and only just visible, read, 'Carlotta Valdes, born December 3, 1831, died March 5, 1857'.

'You're supposed to pay a couple of dollars to see that,' said a young man's voice from behind.

She must have jumped. She wasn't sure. This all seemed so curious: real, yet dreamlike too.

'Sorry,' she stuttered.

There was concern all over his young face. He was pleasant-looking, in his early thirties, wearing workman's overalls, and sturdily built.

'You look like you've seen a ghost.' He smiled at them apologetically. 'Sorry. I didn't mean to scare you.'

'It's our fault,' Hank said, taking out a ten-dollar bill. 'Blame us. The lady came all the way from Rome to see this. There was no one in, but the gate was open.'

'You mean Rome, Italy?' the man asked, amazed.

'There are others?' she wondered.

'Oh yeah,' he answered, nodding. He had a vigorous, simple demeanour, like that of a farmer. 'Georgia for one. Not that I've been there either. You came all this way to see *that?*'

'Not really.' Not at all, now she thought about it. 'I just wanted to put a name to a memory.'

She looked at the tower again.

'It was in *Vertigo*, wasn't it? Hitchcock. Nineteen fifty . . .'

'Shot in fifty-seven,' Frank said, tapping his right temple. 'Remember my small obsessions. Released the following year.'

'Sounds right,' the man in the overalls agreed. 'I'm not a movie fan to be honest with you. I just inherited all this stuff. If it keeps people happy and doesn't cost a fortune, it can stay for all I care. I work construction for a living and it doesn't get in the way. Besides, the last thing Chestnut needs is another yuppie bar. My uncle was a good old guy. He said he was a carpenter on the set, hand-picked by Hitchcock. That's why we got to pick up a couple of props. Then he got the movie theatre when it went bust, built that stupid bell-tower on it . . . Unique selling point, he always said. He was right about the unique part. I keep a few flowers on that fake grave there for any fans who turn up. Caught three this week, not including you.'

He leaned forward and, in a stage whisper, added, 'Tell you the truth, my uncle was a terrible liar. I reckon the thing's just a fake. But what the hell. It's the movies. Does it matter?'

'Are you showing it again soon?' Teresa asked hopefully.

'*Vertigo?* I only open the place up when someone comes up with the money. It won't pay its way every day. We've got a little festival of Fifties noir coming soon. Some bank is backing it, with a little help from the arts people. Let me try to recall . . .' He thought about it. 'John Huston. Nicholas Ray. Billy Wilder, Fuller, Fritz Lang. I think that's right. Those arts guys produce the programme. They love this place for some reason. I just smile and hand over the keys.'

'I shall be here every night,' Frank insisted, then elbowed his brother. 'He can go slurp beer and fart alongside his bar buddies.'

'That'll be nice.' The young man hesitated. He shooed away a couple of wasps buzzing around the place. 'Damned yellowjackets. I came around 'cos one of the arts guys thought we had a nest somewhere. Guess he's right. Is there anything else?'

'I really need to see *Vertigo* right now,' she said hopefully. 'Tonight if possible. Maybe a DVD. Or . . .'

Lukatmi, she thought suddenly.

'. . . I could download it off the web or something?'

Frank put the forefingers of his two hands together to form a cross, then pointed it in her direction, hissing all the time, like someone chasing down a vampire.

'Jimmy Stewart would be turning in his grave.'

'I rather doubt that, sir,' the young man said very seriously, and removed the ten-dollar bill from Hank's fingers. 'I don't know much about the movie business but I'm guessing he'd rather be watched than ignored. No idea about all that internet stuff. But there's a Blockbuster down the street if that's any use.'

- 6 -

The private security men were easily lost. Maggie led Costa round the rear of the Palace, past the children's museum, to a parking lot where she climbed into a dark green vintage Jaguar, then fired up the throaty engine with visible enthusiasm. He got into the passenger seat and felt himself sinking into soft, ancient leather.

'What kind of car's this?' he asked.

'It's a Betsy. That's my name for her anyway. She's a loan from some company trying to sell something or other. I dunno. Corporate bonds. Donuts. Who cares? She turned up yesterday morning. My agent said I can keep her for a week so long as I do a photo shoot at the end. It's all by way of thanks for some romantic slush that came out a couple of months ago called *On a Butterfly's Wing*. The boss guy liked me apparently. Did you see it?'

'No.'

'Ever hear of it?'

'Vaguely . . .'

She slapped the leather steering wheel and giggled in disbelief.

'You are the world's worst liar. I don't believe this. Here I am chauffeuring some foreigner around my home town and he doesn't even watch my movies. Will someone please explain to me why? Where's the adulation? What's my ego supposed to survive on?'

'It's nothing personal. I just don't go to the cinema much.'

She crossed the busy highway leading to the Golden Gate Bridge then pulled off to enter the pleasant open space of the Presidio. Soon they began to climb uphill, winding through a network of narrow, empty roads, past a cemetery and both modest and palatial homes, mostly set against a backdrop of lush forest.

The windows were down. The ancient engine growled and roared as the vehicle tackled the steep inclines. Costa felt as if he'd stepped back fifty years into the frame of some old movie.

'Some stranger *lent* you this car? It must be worth a fortune.'

'That's what I said. And yes, I guess it must be worth a fortune.'

'Isn't that odd?'

'This life is odd. Haven't you worked that out yet? I get given stuff all the time. I could have had three new kitchens last year if I wanted. And a condo in Orlando. Yuk. It's commerce not kindness. They hope the stardust, such as it is, will rub off and leave a little money behind. Occasionally it's some kind of trick from some sleazeball who thinks it's the price of a date with a movie star. If that's what I am . . .'

'I will watch every movie you've ever made,' he promised. 'When I have the time.'

That amused her, though in his heart he meant it.

'No need. Most of them are junk. No one's called about Betsy yet, mind, so perhaps I'll be spared that particular ordeal. What would you do? Send her back?'

He patted the upholstery and ran a finger along the gleaming polished burr walnut of the dashboard.

'I'd still wonder why he really did it.'

She burst out laughing.

'God, Nic. Don't you ever relax? I checked. This is a Jaguar Mark Eight. She was made in 1957. Only in production for two years. Allow me one indulgence, please. It came with these too. I should have put them in water but I forgot. I'm not house-trained. Not really.'

She reached over into the back seat and retrieved an odd-looking bouquet.

Pink roses set among blue violets, tied inside a star-shaped arrangement of white lace.

'That's the strangest bouquet I've ever seen,' he said. 'They look so . . . old-fashioned.'

Maggie shot him a pitying glance then threw them on the rear seat.

'Flowers are flowers. Beautiful whatever . . . Why don't men understand such a simple idea?'

He leaned back, put his hands behind his head and closed his eyes, enjoying the cool breeze, with the tang of the nearby ocean, and the peace of the Presidio.

'It's genetic,' Costa murmured over the burbling lowing of the engine. 'Where are we going?'

'I told you. To see a secret. Where this all comes from. Where *I* come from?'

He recalled the file he'd examined, guiltily, in the Questura before catching the plane.

'I thought you came from Paris?'

'When I was a child. But when I got older, became . . .' A coldness entered her voice. '. . . *saleable*, my mother moved me here. Not LA. That was too . . . louche for her. We spent a year living off fast food and flying down to studios for auditions. The week I finally got a part was the week they told her she had some spot on her lungs that would turn round and kill her in a couple of years. All that smoking while she sat outside auditions. Was it worth it?'

'What was the part?'

'I doubt it reached Italy. Quite big here for a while though. It was a corny TV comedy show, *L'Amour LA*. Sort of *The Partridge Family* but with foreigners. I was Françoise . . .' She glanced upwards, as if trying to recall something that was once important. '. . . the rebellious early teens daughter of a handsome French widower pursuing an on-off relationship with an ordinary Californian divorced mom. Ran for three seasons. Made me. Killed everyone else. My catchphrase – and I had to deliver this in a really stupid French accent – was, "But 'oo can blame Françoise?" Usually uttered after I'd done something really bad. Ring a bell?'

'I think you're right. It didn't reach Italy.'

She smiled at the view. It was hard for him to believe they could have moved from the city so quickly. Everything was so lush and quiet and beautiful.

'Why did I come the scenic route not the easy one?' she sighed, slapping her forehead. 'Oh right.' She pointed at him. 'Because of *you.*'

'San Francisco . . .' he said, returning to the subject.

'This is where I come from,' she said, serious all of a sudden. 'The real me. Not the child. I grew up juggling movie parts, smiling for the camera, even learning to act sometimes. Watching my mother shrink away to nothing. I was born here. I guess I'll die here too. Not that I like that idea. I don't want to die.'

She pumped the pedal so that the spirited engine dropped a gear and the car lurched forward into the darkness of a eucalyptus glade.

'Not ever.'

He didn't catch the last part to begin with. Costa had found himself trying to crook his neck so that he could see in the mirror, glancing back through the Jaguar's rear window from time to time.

Their route through the Presidio and beyond ran up and down, steadily climbing along empty narrow roads that belonged in deep, isolated countryside, not on the edge of a great city.

They were not alone. In the distance, briefly glimpsed as the ancient Jaguar wound its way through the forest of the Presidio, then on into Lincoln Park, past solitary golfers swinging clubs in the golden sun of late afternoon, Costa could see the same car following them, a yellow sports saloon, maintaining a constant distance, dogging their tracks.

- 7 -

While Teresa Lupo tried to watch her new Hitchcock DVD, Falcone and Peroni bickered in the kitchen over whose turn it was to provide dinner.

'I cooked yesterday, Leo,' Peroni complained. 'And the day before.'

Falcone remained adamant.

'I told you. If you want me to get food, I will. But in the way I choose.'

'I am not eating that fried chicken crap again! How fat do you want me to get?'

'I like the fried chicken. It's different. You can't get it like that in Rome. Or we could have pizza. Or Thai. Or Chinese. Or . . .'

'Just cook some pasta, put the damned sauce on it, then grate some cheese,' the big man yelled. 'Have you never, ever cooked for yourself before?'

'No . . .' The inspector sounded dejected. 'What's the point if there's only one of you?'

'There are three of us now . . . And I happen to be as hungry as a horse.'

This was impossible. Teresa turned up the volume on the huge flat-screen TV next to the duck's nest iron fireplace and bellowed, 'Shut up the pair of you and come and look at this.'

There must have been something in her voice because for once it worked. Or perhaps they were just taking a break between rounds. The two men came and sat either side of her on the deep, soft sofa. Teresa worked the buttons, keying to the scenes so conveniently tagged on the DVD.

'Here's Carlotta Valdes,' she said, and showed them the scene in the graveyard of Mission Dolores. 'Or rather the headstone.'

'Where is this?' Falcone asked. 'Mexico?'

'The original location is about a fifteen-minute cab drive over there,' she said, pointing back towards the city. 'Mission Dolores was one of the Spanish missionary outposts set up in the eighteenth century when California was being colonized. It's still around.'

The two men glanced at each other, their faces full of puzzlement and surprise.

'Rome doesn't hold the copyright on history,' she reminded them. 'Other people have their own bits too.'

'So Carlotta Valdes is buried in some old missionary cemetery in the middle of San Francisco?' Peroni asked.

'No. It's not the middle exactly. And she was never buried there. It was a fake grave and headstone they made for the movie.'

'What was she like?' he added. 'The character I mean?'

'Impossible to say. All you see is a painting of her, and a brief glimpse of someone in a dream. Hitchcock had the canvas made. Like he did the headstone. Which now, by the way . . .' she waved out of the window. '. . . is sitting in the garden behind some crazy little cinema three blocks or so over there.'

Falcone looked uninterested.

'People choose false names in all sorts of ways. Newspapers. Phone books. Perhaps the woman was a movie fan. It hardly proves anything.'

'Movie obsessive,' Teresa insisted.

'Movie obsessive. So what?'

'So it's interesting! Quattrocchi thinks this is all to do with Dante. You think it's about the mob getting restless over their investment. What if you're both wrong? What if . . . ?'

She stopped. She knew it sounded ridiculous.

'What if it's to do with an old movie somehow?'

They both tried not to laugh and only just succeeded.

'Teresa,' Falcone replied, placing a sympathetic hand on her shoulder. 'It's no more likely someone would kill over a piece of cinema than they would over a piece of poetry. Adele Neri told us all we needed to know. There's black money, from the Sicilians or someone, in this thing, and they're determined they'll get it back, with interest, one way or another. Or leave a reminder that they don't like being squeezed.'

She stared at him and said, in a deliberately censorious tone, 'You are becoming shockingly literal in your dotage, Leo. Keep quiet, watch and listen. Please.'

They did, and they stayed silent too as she showed them, by flicking through Hitchcock's eerie masterpiece, places they now knew – the Palace of Fine Arts, the waterfront at Crissy Field leading to Fort Point, beneath the great bridge, and so many of the narrow downtown alleys through which they'd wandered in delight, jet-lagged, when they arrived and had a little time for rubber-necking.

'In short,' Falcone summed up, 'this movie covers many of the locations we've seen, and a few that appear to have connections to Roberto Tonti, or his cast, his crew and his movie.'

'That and the rest,' Teresa went on. 'Tonti worked on *Vertigo*.'

She watched their faces. They didn't seem surprised, or interested.

'He was a second camera man! In America illegally, trying to pick up experience. It's in his biography. The man didn't know a thing about directing until he came and saw Hitchcock at work here, in San Francisco, in the autumn of 1957. If you look at the movies that got him some fame in the Seventies the influence is obvious. *Vertigo* made Roberto Tonti. This city left its mark on him.'

The pair of them folded their arms, an identical indication of boredom that would have made Hankenfrank proud.

'Also,' she added desperately, 'he came back and got married when his career in Italy began to hit a brick wall.'

Falcone's tan face creased in a scowl.

'It didn't work, did it? What's the man done for two decades? How's he managed to live?'

That question had also occurred to her.

'It's all listed on the internet. Directing commercials. Developing

TV programmes. Jobbing work. Lecturing. Writing. Consulting. There are always crumbs to be picked up if you once had a name.'

'And then,' Peroni ventured, 'he bounces back from the dead and picks up one of the biggest jobs around. One hundred and fifty million dollars and rising. How does that happen? Why didn't they give it to Spielberg or someone?'

'Because,' Falcone suggested, 'of the risk. It's a movie based on an obscure literary masterpiece everyone's heard of and no one's read. That's why the mobsters who put up the money are getting worried.'

She wriggled on the comfy sofa. It had to come out, however much she hated the idea. This revelation obscured her principal point.

'You're very quiet all of a sudden,' Falcone noted.

'Don't get fooled by the obvious.'

She pulled out the sheets she'd printed on the little inkjet that came with the apartment. Her assistant Silvio Di Capua had risked no small degree of internal conflict by calling in some favours from the anti-Mafia people in the DIA and asking them to run a few names through their system. Somehow what he found came as no surprise to her. It still didn't mean it was relevant.

'I got the office to do some discreet checking. No footprints back to us. That I promise.'

Falcone cleared his throat and gave her a filthy look.

'Tonti got married thirty-two years ago, here. His wife was one Eleanor Sardi. Born and bred in San Francisco. Daughter of the Mafia *capo* for northern California at the time. There have been a few . . . corporate takeovers since then. But Roberto Tonti knows the mob. Probably better than he knows Dante. The dark suits run in the family.'

'Family. So that's how Bonetti raked in the emergency finance when he needed it,' Falcone declared, suddenly animated.

Peroni looked puzzled.

'Why wouldn't Tonti get the money himself?'

'Because he's a director,' Teresa pointed out. 'Money's beneath him. Supposedly. Producers find money. Directors direct.'

'Where's this wife now?' Falcone demanded.

She wished he didn't look so enthusiastic. This was not the direction Teresa had hoped to lead them. All the same, it had to be said.

'It hasn't made the newspapers for some reason but they separated nine months ago, not long after *Inferno* got a lot of bad publicity saying it was in trouble over finance. She's living in Sardinia. In a very well-guarded villa on the Costa Smeralda. Doesn't go out much. Her father died years ago. His clan's now part of some Sicilian conglomerate.'

She saw that familiar glint in his sharp eyes.

'The wife's hostage for the mob money that went in to rescue the movie,' Falcone surmised. 'Either Tonti comes up with the goods, or she pays the price. That gives him a good motive for making sure *Inferno* grabs all the publicity – good or bad – he can find.'

'You could say that about Dino Bonetti,' Peroni pointed out. 'If he tapped Tonti's mob relatives for money. Also, remember Emilio Neri's lovely widow said *he* was the one mixing with the crooks at Prime's place. Not Tonti.'

'You could say that about Simon Harvey too,' Teresa added.

'He's just the publicist!' Falcone cried.

She picked out another piece of paper that Silvio had found.

'He's a substantial investor in *Inferno* in his own right. He took a profit share instead of a full fee. It's all in *Variety*. And he's a scholar, of both literature and the cinema. Someone who's familiar with Dante and Hitchcock. Don't forget those two odd little geeks, Josh Jonah and Tom Black, either. They've put in a stash of money too which, contrary to popular opinion, they can't afford. There are lawyers hovering around Lukatmi trying to screw them for breach of copyright, inciting racial hatred, suicide . . . you name it. And where exactly do they come from?' She nodded at the front window. 'Just over the road. A two-minute walk from Roberto Tonti's mansion. If you want to go down that path . . .'

'I still don't like the way the video of Prime got onto that site,'

Peroni complained. 'It's all very well for Gerald Kelly to claim there's a geek on every corner here. It can't be that easy. Also, think of the publicity. The publicity they're all getting. Every last one of them, even Maggie Flavier. They could all be in it together.'

Falcone looked cross.

'Oh for pity's sake. You're starting to sound like Gianluca Quattrocchi, both of you. There may well be an attempt to make everything that's happening appear complex. That doesn't mean it is. One man is dead, a fortune hangs in the balance, and everything depends on Roberto Tonti's movie being a success, which it might not be on its own merits. The more we lose sight of those basic facts, the further we are from some resolution.'

'It's not our case, though, is it?' she reminded him. 'You didn't even know this stuff about Tonti and his marital background, Leo. Don't play games. You're desperate. Best admit it.'

To her astonishment he allowed himself a brief, childlike grin.

'Touché,' the inspector murmured. 'But . . . I hear things.'

'Catherine?' she asked outright.

'Possibly.'

'Is telling you stuff her way of diverting the conversation from all these pathetic invitations to dinner?'

'I have no idea what you mean,' Falcone complained.

'Dammit, Leo. I'm not giving dating lessons here too. I told you before. This is California. Not some middle-aged playboy's cocktail shack on the Via Veneto.'

'I know for a fact that we are no more and no less in the dark than Quattrocchi and Gerald Kelly,' Falcone insisted, trying to steer the conversation somewhere else. 'It's a level playing field.'

'Not exactly,' Peroni snapped. 'They've got weapons.'

That had been a source of discontent from the outset. The rules of their security assignment precluded their carrying guns. Costa liked that idea. Peroni wasn't so sure. Falcone was of much the same opinion but his arguments fell on deaf ears.

'Does anyone want to hear about this movie I found?' she cried, before the gun debate could start again.

'A summary in no more than three sentences,' Falcone ordered.

She shook her fist in mock fury.

'You have to watch it. I don't want to spoil things for you.'

The two men made a show of looking at their watches.

'It's a work of art. This is ridiculous . . .' She'd only managed to flick through the DVD before they came home bickering about dinner. Most of what she did know was dimly remembered from two decades before.

She closed her eyes and in that moment could picture where she first saw it, on the screen of the dusty little cinema in the corner of the Campo dei Fiori, on the arm of a hirsute Milanese economics student with exquisite manners and dreadful taste in clothes.

'John Ferguson, a police office known to everyone as Scottie, afflicted by vertigo, off duty after a terrible fall that nearly killed him, agrees to tail Madeleine Elster, the wife of a former acquaintance who believes she is acting oddly, possibly suicidal and possessed by the spirit of Carlotta Valdes, an ancestor. The cop falls in love with the woman, who appears to kill herself. He has a breakdown, and afterwards meets another woman whom he rebuilds in her image, only to discover that she was the original Madeleine Elster he met, taking part in a complex murder plot to kill the villain's true wife. In the end he loses her too.'

She clapped her hands.

'There!'

'That was four sentences. And what's this got to do with Dante?' Peroni asked.

'Nothing! Everything!' she screeched. 'I don't know. You work it out. I'm on holiday, aren't I? The woman whose spirit was supposed to possess the victim was called Carlotta Valdes. The story played itself out here, in San Francisco, and Roberto Tonti worked on it. I do not believe in coincidences.'

'I'm not in the mood for a movie,' Peroni grumbled. 'I'm hungry.'

Falcone took out a coin and said, 'Heads it's chicken, tails it's pizza.'

Peroni's large, scarred head fell into his hands and he made as if to weep.

'Chicken it is,' Falcone declared, after briefly flipping the coin and letting no one see the outcome. 'I'll go.'

Teresa swore bitterly beneath her breath, then passed them a piece of paper with her scribbled handwriting visible on it.

'This is a list of real-life locations from the film. My prediction is that if something happens, it will happen close to one of these. We are being led down a merry little path, gentlemen. But not the one you think.'

She skipped through the chapter points she'd set on the DVD. A bouquet of pink roses, set with blue violets in a star-shaped lace bouquet, came on the screen. Then the camera panned up to the painting of a serious, intense Hispanic woman in Victorian dress, dark eyes staring directly out of the canvas. In her hands sat an identical bunch of flowers.

'Meet Carlotta Valdes. This scene was shot in an art gallery called the Legion of Honor in Lincoln Park, which you will find on my list. Also . . .'

She switched to a new scene, one of several hypnotic, dreamlike sequences in which Jimmy Stewart's Scottie followed the troubled Madeleine as she drove apparently aimlessly across the city, along narrow urban streets, quieter neighbourhoods, and then through endless, dark, unidentified woodland.

The two men became quiet. Falcone reached for the remote control and paused the playback. He pointed to the dark, metallic green saloon frozen as it wound its way downhill, somewhere, it seemed, near the Golden Gate Bridge.

'I saw one just like that this morning. Maggie Flavier was getting into it.'

He scratched his narrow, jutting chin.

'Where's Nic gone?' he asked.

– 8 –

They pulled up outside a building that seemed like a mirage emerging from the faint bay mist. Flat grey lines of weathered stone, perfectly placed columns, an American version of a distorted Palladian dream transplanted from some country estate in the Veneto to a green Californian hilltop running down towards the bay and the great red bridge below. The two of them got out of the Jaguar. Costa stopped and stared and smiled.

'I know this place . . .'

'You've been to Paris. I was a child there. I knew it too. The home of the French Legion of Honour opposite the Quai d'Orsay. This is a copy. San Francisco always did look to Europe, you know. Why do you think Tonti is so at home here? The pace of life. Buildings like the Palace of Fine Arts . . .'

'Piranesi should have drawn that.'

Her sharp, incisive eyes peered at him.

'Why are you a police officer? Not an artist or something?'

Costa shrugged.

'I can't paint.'

'Does that bother you?'

It seemed an odd question.

'No.'

'It would annoy the hell out of me. I'd *try*.'

'I did. That's why I know I can't do it. What else should I be? Why are you an actress?'

'Because it lets me be other people, silly.'

142

She took his arm and dragged him past a large, familiar statue, towards the entrance.

'And I get paid a lot for it. That really is Rodin's *Thinker* by the way. One of the early casts. No garbage here. Not much anyway.'

It was almost empty inside. The gallery had such space, such light, such apparent modernity. It was nothing like Rome. All his favourite places there – the Doria Pamphilj, the Borghese – had more the feeling of palatial homes decorated with pictures. The Legion of Honor was cold and clean, organized and . . . dead. A memorial, she told him, to the fallen American soldiers of the First World War.

Faces lined the walls, portraits of men and women, some in the flush of youth, others in failing old age. She seemed to know every last work in the place, every feature, every personality.

'The cruelty of man,' Maggie declared, as she guided him to a fifteenth-century tapestry that depicted peasants trapping and killing rabbits with ferrets and dogs.

'Presumably they were hungry.'

'You're a vegetarian! You're supposed to disapprove.'

'When someone's hungry . . .'

She harrumphed and took him to another canvas. It showed a young girl in poor country dress, seated by a grubby stone well. He looked at the notice next to it: Bouguereau, *The Broken Pitcher*. Late nineteenth century.

'Had you seen my movie debut, the Disney epic *The Fairy Circle*,' Maggie announced with mock pomposity, 'you might have recognized this.'

'I didn't.'

'I know that. Well, this was me.'

It was impossible for him to imagine her as this lost, sullen creature.

'How?'

Her strong hands beat the front of her sweater.

'Because I stole her!' Then, more thoughtfully. 'Or she stole me. The hair. The surly, sad look. The determination. Which won the day in the end, naturally, since this was Disney.'

He looked at this sophisticated blonde woman by his side and laughed.

'Ridiculous am I?' she demanded. 'Watch.'

She snatched the extensions out of her hair and thrust them into her bag. The urchin cut was still there somewhere, dyed but waiting. Then she did something with her hands, put her head down, shook it, as if getting rid of something bad.

When she looked up at him he felt briefly giddy, just as he had the day they first met.

Costa switched his attention between her and the painting. There was the same life, the same identity in the fierce, hard stare, the set features, the reproach to the viewer as if to say: *Can you see now?*

'Point taken. You're a good actress.'

A mild curse escaped her lips. She was back. Herself again in an instant.

'No. I'm a good vampire of paintings. Or an easy vessel for some ghost. This is what I do. It's what I learned, when my mother was down in LA, doing whatever it took to get me auditions.'

Her face turned stony for a moment.

'So I came here. I looked at these women on the walls. I imagined them into me. It's not hard, not when you try. Whenever I needed them they showed up. Look . . .'

She led him to another pastoral canvas, this one more lyrical: a young shepherdess next to a brook, gazing wistfully out of the frame as her flock wandered in the background. French again, of the same period.

'This was two years later. *The Bride of Lammermoor.* Walter Scott. Classic stuff. Here . . .'

Another portrait. French again, but clearly earlier, from the romantic style and of a rather vapid-seeming aristocrat. He examined the notice: Hyacinthe Gabrielle Roland, later Marchioness Wellesley. It wasn't easy to imagine the woman's round, naive face, with its flush of curls and gullible stare, succumbing to Maggie's talents.

'I had to put on weight for that. You need puppy fat for Jane Austen. That took me, oh . . .' She placed a finger against her cheek.

'. . . three weeks to hit the mark. You can't hurry gorging. First time I got to take my clothes off.' She cleared her throat. 'But at least it was art. Ha, ha.'

The discomfort inside her was distant but discernible.

'Why do you do this?'

'Because I like it. Do you need another reason? Being someone else. It's . . . distracting.'

She was taking him to another canvas, one he knew he would dislike the moment he saw the familiar, neurotic swirls beginning to take shape as they approached.

'This is me when I'm older,' she went on. 'Maybe not a movie at all. Maybe *me*. Whoever that happens to be.'

It was a woman in her late thirties, posed like a siren on a dreamy sea, her face tilted at an awkward angle towards a Mediterranean sky, her full body half clothed in a revealing, swirling dress that flowed over her flesh with the liquid sinuousness of the waves beneath. In the background nymphs and mythical creatures revelled in some impenetrable diversion. It was reminiscent, vaguely, of Raphael's *Galatea* in the Farnesina.

'I never much liked Dali,' Costa admitted. 'He doesn't seem to like the people he paints.'

'Agreed. She looks like a bad actress being forced to smile for the audience. If I'm still getting paid for that when I turn forty I'll be happy.'

'So this is where you come for inspiration?'

'No. I told you. I come here to possess, or to be possessed. By a dead girl in a French painting. Or a forgotten English aristocrat. Anyone so long as it works.'

She leaned towards him, as if he were a child.

'You don't honestly think they go to the movies to see *me*, do you?'

'Where's Beatrice?' he asked, avoiding the question.

Without a word she took him to another canvas. He stood in front of the work and felt, finally, at home.

'Dante came before Raphael, remember,' she whispered. 'So what do you expect?'

It took him back to Italy in an instant. The simple beauty, the placid tempera colours, the classical, relaxed posture of the figures: a winged Cupid with his bow, a young woman, in long medieval robes, reclining opposite him, staring at his tender face, in anticipation, perhaps in fear. They were in the kind of garden that might have been found in many a canvas adorning the walls of the museums of Florence: thick with trees, dark in places, shot through with light in others. In the distance three muses turned around each other, dancing.

The centuries passed, some ideas stayed the same. He leaned down and looked to see its origins. She was right: Pre-Raphaelite, Roddam Spencer Stanhope, from 1877 but fired directly by the Renaissance, and Botticelli in particular.

He turned to Maggie Flavier, now blonde, looking much, as she had first said, like an attractive young waitress from a 1950s TV show. When she wore the guise of Beatrice on the screen, under the directorial control of Roberto Tonti, she was someone different entirely: this woman from another time, a different now pretending to be a different then.

'I knew you'd ask,' she said as she retrieved some ribbons out of her bag. Costa watched as she wound the coloured strands through her hair, loosely styling them, after a fashion, in the manner of the braids on the figure in the painting. He could see her Beatrice still, beneath the dyed blonde tresses, beneath the tan she'd acquired somewhere along the way.

'You were perfect,' he whispered.

'I *am* perfect,' she corrected him. 'When I want to be.'

He looked at the nameplate: *Love and the Maiden, 1877.*

'I've nothing else to show you here,' she said. 'But there's a view. If we wait long enough we could see the best sunset in the world. Well, in San Francisco anyway. I used to love it when I caught the bus, waiting for my mother to get back from the studios, wondering what she'd say.'

'Where?'

'Through the woods,' she murmured, her green eyes never leaving his face for a moment. 'Where else?'

- 9 -

It was a short drive. They stopped in a deserted car park next to a stand of eucalyptus. Nearby there was a group of picnic tables and a site for tents alongside a campfire pit. He'd almost forgotten about the yellow car he'd seen on the way to the Legion of Honor. No one seemed to have followed them, though it was impossible to be certain in the narrow, winding pathways they drove along, the old green Jaguar swaying on its ancient suspension as if it were some ageing vessel navigating a rolling hilltop sea.

They got out and the smell of the trees – strong and medicinal – was everywhere. The grey trunks, shedding bark like bad skin, ranged around them in equal lines, disappearing into the hazy blue distance. He'd read the signs on the Presidio when he'd walked in the lower reaches. The forest was the creation of man, not nature, planted by the military who had once occupied this narrow stretch of territory to the north of the city. He liked this idea, the notion of a land that was made, not simply inherited. To him it seemed novel.

'Down there,' she pointed, to their left, 'lies Baker Beach and the Pacific Ocean. Call this a city? Four miles behind us there's Union Square and Market and all that crap. Here.' She made a circle around herself, eyes closed, smiling, face pointed to the sky. 'Here is peace and paradise. I used to pitch a little one-girl bivouac in these trees sometimes. Spend the night here when my mother never came back from LA. It's a *world*.'

'Isn't that dangerous?'

'Do you know something worthwhile that isn't?'

'Quite a lot of things, to be honest.'

'Did your wife feel the same way?' she asked nervously. 'She was an FBI agent once. She must have . . .'

He stayed silent, wondering.

'It was in the papers. Sorry. I looked. I had to. None of us has secrets any more, you know.'

'You could have asked.'

She shook her head. The blonde locks, exactly Emily's colour, fluttered in the wind.

'No. You don't want to talk about it. I don't want to make you. All the same I had to let you understand I know. Otherwise it would hang over us both. Me wondering whether to ask. You wondering whether to tell.'

He gazed past the trees, trying to guess how far it was to the beach and what they might find there.

'She wasn't afraid of danger,' Maggie said simply. 'That killed her. Didn't it?'

'No. A man killed her. A deranged man I should have stopped. But I didn't. I was too slow. Too . . . indecisive. I thought . . .'

This knowledge would never go away.

'I thought I could negotiate some solution in which no one got hurt.'

That failure almost nagged him more than anything. It was a curiously indeterminate kind of guilt.

'So you want everything to be safe from now on. You want everyone close to you to wear some kind of armour that stops them being touched by what's bad.'

'If I could find it . . .'

She stood closer to him and peered into his eyes.

'If you found that, Nic, they'd be someone else. Not who they really are.' She sighed. 'Unless of course you're in my business, in which case you have to be other people. God, I wish I could still use the word "actress". Katherine Hepburn. Kim Novak. Bette Davis. It was good enough for them. I can't stand in their shadow. But maybe one day.'

'I promise to see one of your movies. Soon.'

'I didn't mean that.'

The wind caught. It ran through her hair. For a moment she looked like the urchin, a very elegant and well-kempt one, he'd first seen in Rome. She took a deep breath of the clean, sweet air.

'I love this place. The ocean. These trees. When I was a girl I used to imagine I was a bird, a gull or something. That I could fly off this headland, over that beach, head west, on and on, free for ever. Where do you think I'd wind up?'

'Hawaii?'

'Shame on you. Are all Italians bad at geography?'

'This one is. I've never been out of Europe before. What do you expect?'

'Better. Head that way, my boy . . .' Her long, strong, purposeful arm stretched out into the wind. '. . . and you will, after a very long journey, end up in Japan.'

She bowed, like a geisha and said, '*Konbanwa*', then paused to enjoy his bafflement. 'It means "good evening". I can do small talk in a million languages. Helps when you're on tour.' The forest of slender, upright eucalyptus made a whispering sound, leaves rustling in the breeze. The scent seemed stronger. Night was on the way.

'What did you do?' he asked. 'When you camped here. As a teenager.'

A different expression on her face now, amused, mock angry.

'On a warm San Francisco night . . .' she sang. He dimly recognized the song. 'What do you think? I smoked pot. Fell into the sleeping bag of any passing stranger. The usual.'

'I didn't mean that.' It was true and had to be said. 'I didn't think it. For a moment.'

'Why? You might be right.'

'It's none of my business.'

'Oh.' She raised her finger in front of his face, in a way that Teresa Lupo might have done. 'So you do believe in intuition. When it suits you. But you're not far wrong.' The shadow he was coming to recognize flickered across her face. 'That all came later. Do you want to know what I did?'

'If you want to tell me.'

'I ran.'

This was California, he reminded himself.

'You jogged?'

Her green eyes lit up with indignation.

'*Jogged?* I ran. Like the wind. Not your kind of running. Peroni told me about *that*. Long-distance stuff. Marathons. Old man running. I sprinted. Pushed myself until I could feel my heart ready to burst. And then . . .' She raised her shoulders in a gesture of self-deprecation. '. . . I curled up alone in my sleeping bag with a bunch of Twinkie bars, feeling alive, watching the moon until I fell asleep. All alone. I liked it that way. I still do.'

A part of him wanted to touch her. A part of him wanted to resist.

'I'll count to five. Give you a start.' She nodded across the campsite. 'There's an information point with a map a hundred yards over there. I'll still beat you to it.'

'Too old . . . too tired . . .'

'Get running, damn you!'

He turned, not quite thinking right, and happy with that idea, the release of sanity, the embrace of something less rational. He could see the sign she spoke of in the shade where the trees became denser, extending into other varieties that gave thicker leaf cover.

Costa didn't move as quickly as he could. He felt a little giddy. He wanted her to win, wanted her to overtake him, laughing, childlike, racing in front of him. And then . . .

He didn't know. He wasn't sure he cared. San Francisco was a different place, a million miles from home. None of the old rules – the old cares, the old burdens – existed here. He was free of them, for a while anyway.

When he got to the sign he wasn't even out of breath. He'd run so deliberately slowly that perhaps she'd seen, perhaps he'd disappointed her already.

'Maggie . . .' he said as he turned.

There was no one there. Just a forest of grey trees standing like petrified soldiers, erect, stiff, unmoving except for the dark fluttering diamonds of leaves, rippling their aroma into the land breeze that was running through the forest, down to the ocean.

He stood and thought, realizing, with the old head he used in Rome, that he'd acted like a fool. Then in the distance, where the light was failing, he saw a figure flit through the grey trunks.

It was a man, heavily built, carrying something low in his right hand. Something black and made of metal.

'Maggie!' Costa yelled again.

There was the faint echo of her laughter from somewhere. A shape in a white sweater slipped through the glade ahead to the right, not far from the man he'd seen. Not far at all.

Costa raced towards her, at full speed this time, half tripping over the rotting branches and the carpet of crisp dry leaves at his feet, bellowing into the thin night air, summoning up all the threat and the force he could muster.

A voice wasn't much against a weapon but it was something. In the distance, a little down the hill, just off the road, stood the yellow car he'd seen earlier. Trying to stifle the fury he felt with himself, he ploughed on, half stumbling into a crater full of ferns and moss and trash, fighting to keep his balance, yelling all the time.

He didn't catch sight of the man anywhere. But the third time he called he heard her laugh again, a calm, musical sound, followed by a mild French curse directed at his masculinity.

'This is not a game,' he roared.

A flock of birds rose unseen in a noisy, squawking gaggle. The suddenness and the sheer physical noise of their presence made him jump.

'Not a game . . .' he whispered to himself, trying to still his thoughts.

Something white emerged briefly from behind a silvery trunk ten steps or so to his right.

He didn't say anything. He walked straight there. When he was close she stuck out a foot to make sure he saw.

Costa rounded the tree and found her. She was smiling, looking like a guilty schoolgirl. The apple she'd bought in the car park at the Palace of Fine Arts was in her hand. She looked ready to eat it.

'We're going,' he said, and took her arm, more roughly than he intended.

'Why?' She stood firm. 'What's the rush? Oh come on, Nic. Loosen up. Help me. Just a little. This is new to me too, you know. I'm starting to feel like I'm fourteen again. Only happy this time round.'

'There's someone here,' he warned, glancing around, seeing nothing.

'What? A peeping tom? Who cares? I don't. I've had those since for ever.'

'Well I haven't.' He reached for her arm. She stepped back, away from him. 'I'm taking you home. You're still supposed to have security.'

'Not from you, mister! You know, I could lose patience with all this. I don't usually have to beg.'

He was still scanning the grey trees for the lone individual who was surely stalking them.

'I'm sorry. Let's go back to the city. We can find a restaurant. Have dinner.'

'I don't need dinner, thank you very much.' She waved the apple in his face. 'I have this. Paid for it myself.' She took a huge, greedy bite of the fruit and screwed up her face as if it wasn't so good. 'I don't need anything from anyone. Ever.'

'Fine. So can we go? Please?'

She didn't say another word. But she moved, striding in front of him, long steps, trying to make a point. In other circumstances he might have laughed. There was a theatrical quality to her petulance. It was a performance, one that was deliberately comic.

They were just a couple of steps from the car when she fell. Costa rushed to her side. The ground was treacherous: leaves covered potholes, snarled roots of the stiff military trees lurked hidden, waiting to trip the unwary.

'Let me help you up,' he said, and offered her a hand.

Maggie Flavier rolled over on the earth in front of him. Her face seemed strange. Taut, a little swollen. Her mouth flapped open as if out of control. Her lips were a vivid shade of red, and her green eyes stared up at him in terror.

'Ow, *ow*, OW . . .' she screamed and gripped her stomach in agony.

The apple tumbled from her hand, half-eaten. Costa bent down. Stupidly, automatically, he picked up the piece of fruit and sniffed it. A strange, unexpected aroma rose from the flesh. Almonds, he thought, and the word caused alarm, for reasons he couldn't place.

A physical tremor gripped her body. She stiffened like a plank. Her head jerked back, golden hair thrusting into the dank leaves and earth, then rolled sideways. A cry of pain and astonishment and anger emerged from her lips. Then a thin stream of bile began to trickle from her mouth onto the ground, her breathing became short and laboured, her body started to arch in harsh involuntary spasms.

Someone was approaching, fast and deliberate.

His hands held hers until the last moment. Then Costa rose, turning, saw the powerful, muscular shape of a man in a red check lumberjack shirt, with something black and threatening in his hand, closing on them.

There wasn't time to think anything through. He took one step forward and lashed out with his right fist, caught the intruder on the chin, punched hard again, was satisfied to see the corpulent frame start to fall backwards, the object in his hand tumbling into the dead leaves.

It was a camera, a big black SLR.

Costa blinked, felt hopeless, uncertain where his attention ought to lie.

The man on the ground started swearing at him. Costa didn't listen. He turned and looked at the stricken woman, crouched next to her again. Her eyes were starting to roll back under the lids. She seemed barely conscious. Her breathing appeared dreadfully fast and shallow. The convulsions had fallen into a terrifying regime, one that was slowing with each diminishing lungful of air.

They trained a police officer for this kind of event. But that was on a different continent, in a different language.

Whoever the man was he wasn't a threat. Not an obvious one at that moment.

All the same, as the hulking figure in the red shirt retrieved his camera and began to edge out of the way, firing off shots all the time, Costa took one quick step towards him, kicked hard at his arm as it held the camera, heard the snap of fracturing bone.

There was a scream. The figure was on the ground again, still trying to scramble crab-like through the desiccated leaves covering the forest floor. Costa turned, stepped forward and stood quite deliberately on his shattered limb for a moment, then waited for the cries of agony to subside a little.

'*Dove . . .*' he began, then shook his head to clear it. 'Where are we? I need to know the location. Now. Before this woman dies.'

'You saw the sign,' the man in the red shirt spat at him, clutching his arm and the camera as if each were of equal value.

'Where?' Costa bellowed, and lifted his foot again, eyeing the tortured, crooked arm.

The photographer shrank back in fear.

'Rob Hill campground. Now leave me alone.'

He was only dimly aware that the man was crawling off somewhere. And that the sound of the camera was there again, diminishing as the paparazzo retreated, like the chirp of some electronic bird fading into the lowering dark.

Costa got down on the ground next to her, held her damp, sweating, twitching hand, leaned into her head, ignoring the foul smell rising from her agonies. He put his lips to her ears then, not knowing whether she could hear, whether she had any idea of the tears fast rising to sting his eyes.

He began to murmur, over and over again, 'Stay with me, stay with me, stay . . .'

Her breathing seemed to stop for a moment. Her eyes opened. Maggie Flavier's face was puffy and soaked in sweat and tears. But her right hand was jerking towards something. He looked into her eyes. They were calm, determined. As if she'd been here before.

She was pointing at the bag. He picked it up and turned it upside down, emptying the contents onto the forest floor.

The kit was there, with a red cross on the outside, instructions and a primed syringe that looked like a pen. The drill he'd learned from the medical trainers started to come back. He tore open the pack, withdrew the needle, removed the cap, bent down and in one sure, forceful move thrust the injector into her right thigh, through the fabric of her jeans.

She half screamed, half sighed, and her head went hard back again, straight into the ground.

Still he held the pen there firmly, and kept his left hand in her hair. After ten seconds, as gently as he could, he eased the needle out of her flesh before checking the drug had been dispensed. Then he threw the thing into the spent dry leaves by the empty bag.

She was sobbing. He cradled her in his arms, trying to make some comforting, wordless sounds, grappling for the phone, fighting to find the right language to use in this strange, foreign country.

From somewhere, finally, they came.

He dialled 911, waited an agonizingly long time and then said, knowing the name would make a difference, not caring about whether that was right or wrong or just plain stupid, 'I need an ambulance at the Rob Hill campground near the Legion of Honor now. I have an actress here, Maggie Flavier. She's in anaphylactic shock and we need a paramedic team immediately. I've given her . . .'

The words danced elusively in his head until he snatched up the discarded syringe package and examined the label.

'. . . epinephrine. It's serious. She needs oxygen and immediate transfer to hospital.'

The line went quiet.

Then a distant male voice asked, 'You mean *the* Maggie Flavier?'

'I do,' Costa answered calmly, and tried to remember something, anything about CPR.

PART FOUR

- 1 -

Catherine Bianchi sat at the wheel of her Dodge people-carrier looking as if she was worried about her career. Falcone was by her side, Peroni and Teresa Lupo in the back. Ahead, like ancient aircraft hangars at a decayed military installation ranged along the bay shoreline, stood Fort Mason. Three buildings were bright with recent paint. Above the central one, a good ten metres high, stood the waving, multi-armed logo of Lukatmi, neon still flashing in the bright morning sun.

The American police captain took a deep breath and muttered, 'You guys are going to get me into real trouble, aren't you?'

They had an appointment with Josh Jonah and Tom Black inside the Lukatmi HQ in fifteen minutes. If Bryant Street got to hear of it, there'd be plenty of awkward questions. It was difficult to see how interviewing the bosses of a digital media firm, albeit one heavily involved in financing *Inferno*, could possibly be justified given their tight and supposedly unbreakable brief: watch over the assembly of the exhibition, nothing more.

'You don't have to join us if you don't want,' Falcone said. 'I do think we have the right to be here.'

That got him a fierce look in return.

'The Palace of Fine Arts, with all your precious stuff, is that way. There's not a single thing in those buildings of Lukatmi that concerns you, Leo. It's just geeks and computers. We should be back where we're supposed to be.' She seemed as exasperated as the rest of them. 'Twiddling our thumbs and waiting to be told what to do next.'

Falcone leaned back in his seat and sighed, 'What we do next is look for the money.'

Teresa Lupo realized she didn't have the energy to engage in that particular argument again. The same circular bout of bitching had rumbled on all morning, in between the inquiries to the hospital, the calls from a furious Quattrocchi and an equally livid Gerald Kelly of the SFPD. It was now two days since the attack on Maggie Flavier. The temperature hadn't cooled.

In the midst of it all Falcone was sticking to his guns; somehow, somewhere, this case hung around nothing more than cash. Not a piece of poetry. Not an old movie. Money was at the root of everything. Maybe it was Josh Jonah and Tom Black protecting their investment. Maybe it was Roberto Tonti or Dino Bonetti trying to make sure the heavy mob who bankrolled *Inferno* got payback before they turned ugly, or the mob themselves doing just that. Those, as far as the inspector was concerned, were the only avenues worth exploring, not that they were supposed to.

Once the arguments began again, made yet more shrill by the howls of outrage from the Carabinieri and the suits in Bryant Street over Nic's close involvement with the actress they were supposed to be protecting, no one even bothered to ask much about Maggie Flavier's condition, which did nothing to calm Teresa Lupo's temper. A severe anaphylactic shock was a truly terrible experience. If Nic hadn't been there, it might have taken her life. Not that he was going to get much credit on that front. The media had other things to amuse them.

She picked up that morning's copy of the *San Francisco Chronicle* from the floor of the vehicle. They ran only one photo, of Nic bent over the stricken woman, stabbing the epinephrine pen into her thigh. It wasn't the worst. Some of the less fussy rags felt no such restraint. In spite of his broken arm – now the subject of a police investigation on the grounds of assault – the paparazzo had hung around long enough to capture a series of images of the actress being taken into the ambulance by paramedics with Nic, worried to death, holding her hand.

While Teresa fumed over the paper, Peroni retrieved a couple of the grosser tabloids from the floor. All over the front pages, alongside the shots of a woman in the throes of a dreadful allergic reaction, they carried a series of photos of Maggie Flavier close up to Nic, propping herself against the silver form of a grey, ghostly tree half stripped of bark, smiling, a look on her face no one could mistake. It was one step away from a kiss and everyone who saw it would surely have wondered what came after.

'If she'd died,' Peroni pointed out, 'they'd never have carried those. Not for a day or two anyway. They'd call it "respect".'

That was probably true, she thought. Allan Prime had been treated like a lost genius for a short while after his murder. Then the papers had started to find other stories. Of his financial wranglings, his debts, his association with known criminals. And the women. Young, sometimes too young. Often vulnerable. Sometimes paid off for their 'troubles'. It took less than a week for the dead actor to tumble out of Hollywood heaven and into the gutter. Teresa had read enough about Maggie Flavier's past, a very typical tale of broken love affairs, tussles with the law and the occasional drug and booze bust, to understand that she would doubtless have followed the same path had she wound up on a morgue table.

'OK,' Catherine Bianchi said. 'I shouldn't be telling you this but I will. Nic isn't going to face any charges over that guy's broken arm. He might get yelled at. No, he will get yelled at. But that's it. We're not stupid. The SFPD doesn't like that kind any more than you.'

'What do you know about him?' Falcone asked. 'The photographer?'

'I can't possibly tell you that, Leo. You shouldn't even be asking.'

'What if he's not just a photographer?' Peroni wondered. 'What if he's involved?'

The woman's smart, dark face creased with fury.

'We're not idiots. Don't presume you have some kind of monopoly over sound policing procedures. They will investigate the man.' She swore under her breath. 'Hell, they have investigated him. He's a lowlife with three cautions for suspected harassment of young

161

actresses over the last two years. He's a jerk and a creep and probably ought to get taken into some dark corner somewhere and taught a lesson he won't forget. But he is not a murderer.'

The big man folded his arms and asked, 'Where does he live?'

'Now you have to be joking.'

'His name is Martin Vogel,' Falcone announced, taking a scrap of paper out of his pocket. 'He has an apartment somewhere called SoMa. It's central. I have the address. An art district or something, I'm told. Good restaurants apparently.'

'What . . .' Catherine snarled. 'Restaurants? What?'

'I thought we might go out for dinner somewhere.'

'*Dinner?* Screw dinner, Leo! Are you seriously thinking of approaching a witness who claims – with some justification – that he's been seriously assaulted by one of your own men? How the . . .'

'His name was in the paper. You have these things called phone books.'

'Visit that man and you are on your own,' she said, cutting the space between them with her hand. 'God knows you're pushing my limits already. Martin Vogel has lodged a complaint of brutality against Nic. Bryant Street are still trying to work out how to get out of that one without some lawyer coming at us for millions. Things are complicated enough already. I will not allow you to make them worse.'

Falcone tapped his fingers on the dashboard, thinking, then said, 'Martin Vogel was in the right location though, wasn't he? Not an obvious place either.'

'He's freelance camera scum,' she pointed out. 'They'll follow someone like Maggie Flavier for days, weeks, to get what they want. Do you have any idea how much those shots will earn him? Six figures maybe. Not bad for an evening's work, and if he manages to screw compensation out of someone too, even better.'

'The Legion of Honor was on my list,' Teresa pointed out. 'The *Vertigo* list.'

Falcone scowled.

'Nothing happened at the Legion of Honor. It was a mile away in the woods. Stop clutching at straws, please.'

'But you said . . .' she protested. 'About the car.'

'It was just an old car. Perhaps the company that sent it had a movie buff on the staff. Where's the real link?'

'Carlotta Valdes!'

He had that foxy look in his eyes. One she loved and hated because it was both a rejection and a challenge.

'The idea is as ridiculous as the fairy story the Carabinieri are chasing. Unless you can prove otherwise.'

'Thanks, Leo . . .'

He gazed out of the window in the direction of the Lukatmi studios and said, 'The most likely solution lies in the money. If we can understand that, who benefits, who feels cheated, and, ultimately, who loses . . . there lie the answers.'

'You're a philistine,' Teresa announced. 'And if you hope to understand the financing of modern movies you'll be here for years.' She waved a hand at the Lukatmi building. 'I'll bet you even they don't understand it, and a stack of their money has disappeared into Dino Bonetti's pockets. Think of what you have and what you know. I'm a pathologist. I look for traces. So should you.'

Falcone was unmoved.

'You've no laboratory, no staff, no jurisdiction. Most of all you've no job. You invited yourself here. I'm glad you came but I can't change your status. You're nothing more than a tourist. Don't forget it.'

'As if I could! You remind me every hour on the hour. So tell me. How did someone know that Maggie was vulnerable like that? Would Lukatmi's computers have told them she was allergic to almonds?'

'Any computer would have told them that,' Catherine Bianchi said. 'She had some kind of attack at the film festival in Cannes three years ago. All the papers covered it. That one wasn't so severe, thankfully. It gave her the presence of mind to carry that syringe all the time.'

She eyed Teresa nervously.

'You won't tell anyone I gave you that report from the lab, will you? They'd fire me. They'd have every right.'

'Of course I won't!'

'Well? What did it tell you?'

'You have a forensic department. What did it tell them?'

'Nothing more than you read in that report. Just . . . facts.'

'And I'm supposed to give you more than that? Me? The tourist?'

All three of them stared at her in silence. And waited.

- 2 -

Captain Gerald Kelly hated press conferences. Particularly, he had come to realize, those that involved a police chief from another country, one who loved the limelight and seemed incapable of going anywhere in public without the presence of a similarly media-obsessed Canadian academic who never knew when to shut up.

Kelly had looked at Leo Falcone's odd pair of sidekicks while bawling them out the day before, one huge and old and ugly, the other slight and dark and handsome, and wished, with all his heart, that they had been on this case with him. That awkward-looking trio possessed a subtle careworn eagerness that matched his own, half jaded, half mutinous, attitude to the job. Gerald Kelly had long ago learned to live with the nagging sense of doubt and uncertainty that went with everyday police work, so much that, at times, he came to regard these feelings almost as friends, ghosts on the shoulder reminding him to ask the impertinent, awkward important questions he might otherwise have forgotten. On occasion the science people came up with a lucky certificate of proof, a conviction in a blood or semen stain, a jail sentence in a fingerprint or a string of genetic code. But when forensic failed them the answers almost always lay in lacunae, what was missing or unknown, not waiting to be discovered out in the plain light of day. He was at home with that idea, as were Falcone's men, he felt sure. Not so the artificially erudite Gianluca Quattrocchi, a man who seemed to harbour very few doubts about anything, least of all himself, shunning the interesting if difficult Falcone for the diminutive Bryan Whitcombe, who was constantly at his side, chipping in literary references at any opportunity.

165

Had this strange, prolix and seemingly impenetrable case gone on much longer, Kelly was quietly intent on telling Quattrocchi he was bringing Falcone and his men into its inner workings, whatever the Carabinieri thought back in Rome. He could live with the squeals. This was San Francisco, not Italy. It was his call. The SFPD needed all the bright intelligence he could find, and he saw that in the eyes of Leo Falcone and his men the instant they met.

Kelly grunted an inaudible curse as the TV men started heaving at their cameras. That happy outcome was not to be. Nic Costa, who was more than Falcone's right-hand man, Kelly could sense that in the bond between them, was at that very moment the quarry of a thousand prying lenses and curious voice recorders. California's dread legions of showbiz hacks and cameramen were seeking photos and interviews with Maggie Flavier. Second best, but only by a short head, would be the man who had saved her life, not long after he had seemingly entered it in a way half the male population of America envied as they pored over the photos in that morning's papers. Maggie Flavier in her prime, Maggie Flavier in her agony. And gazing adoringly at some unknown lowly Italian cop. This ravenous pack usually saved its activities for LA; now Kelly had them on his doorstep. That did nothing to improve his mood.

Kelly had seen enough of show-business cases to understand that, when stars and the movie trade came into play, every key aspect of an investigation soon had to be approved by the tin gods above him. Slowly, ineluctably, a homicide investigation was starting to follow the familiar path from tight, well-ordered police case to sprawling, unmanageable public circus, one played out daily in the papers and on the TV. He had seen this happen often enough to know there was no way of turning back the clock. Press conferences were part of the show, ordeals to be endured, grist for the media mill. He couldn't wait to get back to his office in the hope that someone, in science, in intelligence, in Catherine Bianchi's doomed little police station in Greenwich Street, even, could throw some faint mote of light on the dark, shapeless morass of possibilities that lay before them.

The conference room was packed. Standing room only. The event was, naturally, going out live, through the networks, and, he saw to his amazement, over the web too, since the crew at the very front wore bomber jackets bearing the logo of Lukatmi.

'Wait a minute,' Kelly whispered to the police public affairs officer who was watching her minions trying to keep some kind of order in a rabble of more than a hundred assorted newspaper, TV, radio and now web hacks. 'Josh Jonah's got himself a TV station now?'

'Since last month,' the woman whispered back. 'Don't you follow the news?'

'Only the stuff that matters. Who the hell let his pony-tails in here? And why are they sitting up front like they own the place?'

This was the new SFPD. When even some infobabe from public affairs got to stare out a police captain.

'I did. You want me to deny them accreditation? How am I supposed to keep them out? They're media. They've got an audience bigger than ten local news stations. Also Lukatmi are backing the movie. They're using this footage for some programme on the "making of . . ." or something.'

He stared at the woman in disbelief and pointed out, 'This is a homicide investigation. Not a reality TV show.'

'You have your job. I have mine. We both report to the commissioner's office. You want to sort this out there?'

'Listen . . .'

'No you listen. Josh Jonah and Tom Black have been on all the networks, primetime nationwide TV, telling the world what good friends they were with Allan Prime. They've delivered flowers by the truckload to Maggie Flavier. How good do you think it's going to look if we throw their TV crew onto the street after that?'

'I don't care about looking good . . .' Kelly was aware his voice was rising. The lights came up just then and he found himself getting stared at by a multitude of faces in a sea of shining artificial suns. 'And frankly,' he muttered, entirely to himself, 'I am starting to care even less with every passing minute.'

'That's your problem,' the public affairs woman said, then slipped an envelope in front of him. 'They asked me to give you that.'

'Who?'

She looked a little guilty.

'The commissioner's office. After Bonetti and the Lukatmi people got in there. Via the mayor's office, I ought to add. The governor's been on the line too.'

Kelly blinked. The public affairs woman added something he didn't quite catch and walked into the audience trying to instil some order into it. Gerald Kelly wished he were anywhere else on the planet but in this room, with these people, knowing that, in between the crap and the prurience, there'd be a few good, decent, old-fashioned reporters who knew how to ask good, decent, old-fashioned questions too. Ones he couldn't begin to answer.

He didn't even have the energy to look at the sheet of paper the infobabe had handed him. Besides, the first question out was pre-arranged: some guy from the *Examiner*, primed to ask the obvious. Was there any proven connection with Allan Prime's death? Kelly liked to place the openers. It gave him half a chance to keep a handle on things. Normally.

'Any connection is supposition at this moment . . .' he began to say after the plant rose to his mark. He was astonished to see Gianluca Quattrocchi reaching over to take the mike from him, talking in his florid English, saying the exact opposite. Kelly sat, dumbstruck, listening to the stuck-up Italian blathering on about poetry and motivation and the damned movie that seemed to overshadow even one bloody murder and now a near-fatality too.

As he reached some obscure point about the relationship between the crimes and the cycle inside the book, the pompous Carabinieri man fell silent, waving on the Canadian academic to finish the answer.

'The links are implicit, obvious and ominous,' Whitcombe announced, in his weedy, professorial voice. 'In Dante's Hell the punishment fits the crime. Allan Prime died in the second circle, that of the wanton. He was led to his death by a woman, and the publicity we have since seen seems to show that his private life merited this description. The third circle is that of the gluttonous. Ergo . . .'

Kelly muttered to Quattrocchi, 'Ergo what? Maggie Flavier was eating an apple. This is not what we agreed.'

'Listen, please,' the Italian replied, shushing him, almost politely. 'The man is a genius.'

'He's a frigging . . .' Kelly began, and then shut up.

The PR woman was actually pointing at him from the audience, her long finger erect in the bright lights of the camera, then running across her upper lip, as if to say, 'Zip it.'

McGuire, the crime man for the *Chronicle*, had started to snigger in the front row.

Kelly picked up the envelope the infobabe had given him, ripped it opened, and read the contents with growing disbelief.

- 3 -

Teresa Lupo wished the American policewoman hadn't asked about Maggie Flavier's poisoning because she hated imprecision more than anything.

So she simply said, 'The poor woman met her wicked stepmother. Or stepfather. Who knows? Unless your people find the man who gave her the poisoned apple.'

'Mobile caterers . . .' Catherine Bianchi sighed. 'They're minimum-wage businesses. Casual labour. What do you expect?'

'Not much. The thing is . . .' She felt as if she were trying to analyse a scene from a movie, one that had been ripped out of context. Without knowledge of what preceded the event, she couldn't begin to pull some logic out of what might follow. '. . . it's a very strange way to try to murder someone. If that's what it was. Particularly given the way they killed Allan Prime. A crossbow bolt through the skull. A poisoned apple given to someone with a food allergy. They don't even sound like the same person to me. What they did to Maggie was horrifying. But . . .'

The more she thought about it, the more convinced she became.

'If I was a betting person I'd lay money against her being badly affected by a cruel stunt like that, much less killed. She spends most of her time near lots of people. She knows she has that allergy and she's prepared to deal with it. Yes, she was at risk in the woods, alone with Nic. But no one could have predicted she'd be there. The chances of her dying should have been quite slim.'

Falcone finally took his attention away from the Lukatmi building.

'You mean they weren't trying to kill her?'

'I don't know what I mean. I just think it was a very odd way to go about it if that's what they wanted. Perhaps they just planned to hurt her. They certainly managed that.'

She tried to put the problem succinctly.

'What bothers me most of all is the style. Allan Prime had no chance of survival whatsoever. He died from violence of the most extreme sort, the kind of brute force we get to see ten, twenty times a year because that's the way the human race tends to go about eliminating one another. It's quick. It's easy. You don't have to do much in the way of preparation. But poisoning . . .' She'd racked her memory already, trying to find some insight that might be useful. '. . . it's rare. And tricky. I've only dealt with one case of wilful poisoning in my entire career and that only worked because the victim was dying from heart disease already. Why now? Why here of all places?'

One more thing bothered her.

'Do they grow almonds in California?'

'Of course,' Catherine answered. 'Millions of them. Merced County. About an hour south. I go at the end of February when the blossom's out. You can do a tour. It's beautiful.'

'Farmed almonds? For sale?'

'Sure. But you don't need to go out and buy almonds to get almond essence. It's on sale in any grocery store.'

'Not this kind,' Teresa answered, wishing she had her lab, and Silvio Di Capua ready to ask off-centre questions that might lead somewhere. 'Whatever was injected into that apple was home-made. There were traces of fibre. You don't get that in essence. Also there was a small but noticeable amount of prussic acid.'

That silenced them.

'Cyanide,' she explained.

'Cyanide smells of almonds,' Peroni pointed out.

'Or almonds smell of cyanide, whichever way you want to look at it. I did a little research after Catherine slipped me that report. The native, wild almond contains a substance that transforms into

171

hydrogen cyanide when the flesh is crushed or bruised. Domesticated varieties have had that mostly bred out of them, though they retain the smell. That's not what Maggie Flavier got. She was poisoned with the crushed fruit of a wild, bitter almond. You must have some here. They're used in medicine. You can still buy bitter almond essence in Rome. We use it, very carefully, in cooking. But it's banned in the US, which is why I guess he had to make it himself.'

'So she had cyanide poisoning too?' Catherine asked. 'And you still think they weren't trying to kill her?'

'Not with cyanide. It was a minute amount. They could have had exactly the same effect using standard almond essence from a grocery store. It was the allergic reaction that put her in hospital. There wasn't enough cyanide there to do much of anything. I don't get it. Maybe he didn't even know. But then why bother?'

Falcone yawned. Details that went nowhere always bored him.

The clock on the dashboard ticked over to one fifteen. They were due inside Lukatmi.

'That supermarket over there,' he said, reaching into his wallet and pulling out a fifty-dollar bill. 'We need some shopping.'

Teresa took a deep breath in an attempt to calm herself and asked, 'Are you going to do this to me every time there's someone interesting to talk to?'

It was Peroni who came back with a reply, so quickly she felt sure the two of them had discussed this in advance.

'We scarcely have reason to be in that place,' he said apologetically. 'You certainly don't.'

'So I'm supposed to shop?'

'A suggestion only,' Falcone cut in. 'I would never presume to give you orders. It would be impertinent. And also . . .' He mulled over the words. '. . . somewhat counter-productive in my experience. You fare best left on your own. Think about old films and bitter almonds, please. Just out of my earshot.'

Muttering something obscene in which the phrase 'stinking cops' was one of the milder rebukes, she got out of the car, slamming the door as hard as she could behind her.

It was a bright, cold San Franciscan summer day. The chill of the strong sea breeze soon began to make her teeth ache. She thought of walking out to Fort Point, a mile or so towards the bridge, and trying to find the exact location for the solitary, haunting scene in which Jimmy Stewart rescued Kim Novak from the ocean. Much, it seemed to her, as Nic had apparently saved the stricken Maggie Flavier. Life imitating art. Quattrocchi thought that was happening. So did she, but in a different way. While Leo Falcone . . .

Teresa Lupo wasn't sure she was right. But she was certain they were wrong, at least in part.

She walked back towards the Marina, thinking. Naturally, she'd keyed their number into her phone, under the single name Hankenfrank.

'Pronto!' said a voice on the other end.

'What the hell are you doing talking Italian, Frank?'

'What the hell are you doing being ignorant of caller ID?' the voice on the other end demanded. 'And how did you know it was me, not zygote two?'

'Because you sound different, even if you don't know it. Can I buy you coffee?'

'Only if you are in possession of interesting questions with which to entertain us.'

'That,' she said, pocketing Falcone's fifty-dollar bill, 'I can guarantee.'

- 4 -

Gerald Kelly listened to Bryan Whitcombe's droning nasal drawl and felt himself drifting worryingly close to the edge. The professor was rambling on about poetry again, things a homicide cop could never, Kelly felt, be expected to understand or take seriously. About how the fourth circle was to do with the avaricious and the prodigal, and they should expect, given the rigid adherence to the subject matter of the structure of *Inferno*, that any intended victim should somehow have fallen guilty to these sins.

'That narrows it down in the movie business,' Kelly muttered, and didn't mind that a couple of people in the front row got to hear, the furious-looking public affairs woman among them.

Someone put up their hand and asked the kind of obvious question hacks always wanted to bring up: *And then?*

Whitcombe launched into the list. The fifth circle, the irascible. The sixth, heresiarchs, which he defined as the leader of some dissenting movement. Then, the seventh, the violent. The fraudulent and the malicious, the eighth. Finally the last, the traitors.

'And after that?' the reporter asked.

Kelly snatched the microphone and barked, 'After that there's not a living soul left in the whole of California. Gentlemen. Ladies. I leave you with our Italian friends and their pet professor. Some of us have work to do.'

He walked out and went straight to his office three floors above. Not many officers in there seemed keen to look him in the eye. The conference was still going on. They were all glued to it on the internal video system. Quattrocchi and Whitcombe were fielding

174

the questions. The harpy from public affairs had press-ganged poor meek Cy Fielding, one of his oldest and softest detectives, onto the podium in his place, not that anyone seemed remotely interested in what the man might say.

Kelly looked at the letter again and swore. The phone on his desk rang.

'Yes!' he yelled into it.

It was Sheldon from the commissioner's office, all sweetness and sympathy.

'Calm down. We would have told you beforehand but you weren't around.'

'That's because I was out doing my job. Like it or not, murderers rarely walk into the office of their own accord or turn up as attachments in an e-mail. Anyone else round here noticed yet?'

Kelly hit the keyboard on his computer and brought up the video. It was live on the screen in front of him in an instant, naturally. Geeks ran the SFPD. Like they ran the world. At that moment just about every police officer inside a station in San Francisco was doubtless watching this piece of vaudeville instead of walking the street looking for bad guys.

'When a big movie company wants to lay a million dollars on the table as a reward for finding the bastards who butchered one of their stars and tried to kill another, we listen,' Sheldon said calmly. 'We have no choice. These people have clout. Quattrocchi especially. Ask him for his dinner party list, then go figure. You have to work with them.'

'A million-dollar reward,' he spat back at the phone. He put on an accent he thought came close to Quattrocchi's dainty English. 'For information leading to the arrest and conviction of anyone threatening the life or security of any cast members or associate of . . .' He paused to emphasize the next part. '. . . *Roberto Tonti's Inferno*. Jesus. They're writing the script for us now. Don't you see that? They're turning this into a freak show with every passing day. We don't need any stupid reward. Whoever did this . . . we're dealing with head cases. They're not mixed up with any street morons who'll hand them over to us, even for a million dollars. All we're going to get is a bunch of lunatics trying to lay their hands on that loot instead, and a photo shoot with Maggie Flavier . . .'

'Shut up . . .'

'No. I won't shut up. You've just taken away half my manpower. Maybe more. 'Cos now we have to field the phones listening to kooks who think their neighbour's a star-killer.'

'*Shut up!*'

That was loud, and Sheldon didn't normally do loud. So Kelly kept quiet.

'I say this once and once only, Gerry. You're too damned good to throw away your career over this. It could happen. Believe me.'

'Someone murdered Allan Prime. Maybe they tried to murder Maggie Flavier too. We are not dealing with an episode of *Columbo* here.'

'Maybe?'

'You heard me.'

'That's your problem. These guys are mine. They've got money. They've got clout. They've got the ear of the governor, the mayor, and God almighty for all I know. Do you think we're stupid? Work with the politics or they'll eat you.'

Captain Gerald Kelly slammed down the phone then rolled round his executive chair and stared out of the window.

The worst thing was, Sheldon had a point.

- 5 -

'Pony-tails,' Catherine Bianchi grumbled as they walked through the wide open central hall of Lukatmi Building Number One. It was much like an aircraft hangar on the inside too. An open space, with three galleries ranged around the sides, each housing cubicles lit by the glow from ranks and ranks of computer screens. In the centre of the hall lay vast soft sofas in bright primary colours, pinball and table football machines, places to eat and drink coffee. The staff, all around twenty-five, rarely more, wore jeans and T-shirts and either lolled in the play area or dashed about looking deeply serious, often tapping away at tiny handheld computers. To Peroni it seemed like a kindergarten for people who would never grow up. Except for the flashing, sports-style scoreboard at the end of the vast interior, set against an open window overlooking San Francisco Bay, with a rough grey chunk of Alcatraz, a lump of uninviting rock and slab-like buildings, intruding into the corner.

High above the office the electronic scoreboard displayed the Lukatmi stock price in a running ticker alongside a host of other tech industry giants: Microsoft, Apple, Google, Yahoo.

A skinny individual with greasy shoulder-length hair had been deputed to meet them when they arrived. He said very few words and continued eating a sandwich that looked as if it was stuffed with pond weed. When he saw what had caught Peroni's attention, he tapped him on the shoulder and nodded at the scoreboard.

'Watch the totals. Dinosaurs down five per cent average over the year. Lukatmi . . .'

The numbers kept on flickering. There was a big up arrow next to the symbol that had the multi-armed logo by its side.

'Sixty per cent and rising.'

Catherine Bianchi eyed him and said, 'The dinosaurs have still got more money than you. They could buy out Lukatmi tomorrow if they wanted. Or invent something that kills you stone-dead overnight. Beware old people. They don't harbour grudges, they nurture them.'

The geek pulled a sour and very ugly face.

'You know, lady, when you're living inside the *e*-conomy you soon get to realize there are some things people *outside*, old people in particular, never ever come to comprehend.'

'Does that mean you're up for sale or not?' Falcone asked.

'I code,' he said, after a bite of pond weed. 'Nothing else. My old man told me anything's for sale if the price is right. But then I earn more in one year than he ever got in a lifetime. So who'd you think I should listen to?'

'Perry Como,' Peroni suggested. 'Hot Diggity, Dog Ziggity Boom.'

Their guide looked foxed for a moment then pointed to an open suite enclosed by tinted, transparent glass and said, 'Josh and Tom's offices are over there. I will leave you three now before whatever time machine you own drags me back to the ice age too.'

The big cop watched him leave.

'Pierino Como was a fine Italian-American. What's his beef?'

'He belongs to a superior race,' Catherine guessed, then held out her hand to Josh Jonah and Tom Black, who were approaching, Black just a foot or two behind his partner.

Neither of them looked welcoming.

'What's this about?' Jonah wanted to know.

'Security,' she said straight away. 'Yours. Ours. The movie. The people.' She smiled at the pair of them. 'And the stuff. You do understand the stuff is important too, don't you, Josh? My Italian friends have lost a very important museum exhibit already. They don't want to lose any more.'

Peroni considered this strange couple. Skinny, moody, arrogant, with his long, carefully coiffured fair hair, Jonah seemed to be a fit for the type of man who'd be running a company like Lukatmi, student on the outside, shark on the in. Black . . . he wasn't so sure. They'd run through some profiles before arriving. The two of them had met at college, Stanford, not far away in Palo Alto. Black was the coding genius, Jonah the business visionary. A complementary mix, left side of brain meets right side, or so the glowing profiles claimed. Untold wealth ensued. But did that mean they liked one another? Peroni saw no sign of it. These two men had just turned twenty-three and were, at that moment, worth more than a billion dollars each, with much, much more in prospect if they managed to 'grow the company', as the papers put it, or sell the business on a high. Not that it seemed to be making them happy just then.

'How's Maggie?' Tom Black asked.

'We know no more about Miss Flavier than you've seen on TV,' Falcone told him.

'Don't give me that,' Jonah moaned. 'That was your guy with her.'

'When they . . .' Black added, before stopping awkwardly.

'If you don't know about Maggie,' Jonah went on, 'you've got no job being here.'

He stopped and barked at a passing female employee to fetch him a coffee. Lukatmi didn't look much like a new age, politically correct, do-no-evil-to-anyone corporation at that moment. Peroni had seen bosses in Italy treat women staff that way and get their heads chewed off in return.

'I'm sorry,' Tom Black said. 'This is a bad time for us. Allan's murder . . . The movie. How it got out onto the web . . . We've been working to make sure it can't hit us again.'

'How did it happen in the first place?' Peroni asked.

Jonah stepped in to field the question.

'In ways you people never could understand. Ask the SFPD tech team. It was no failing on our part. Not even on our network. Some dumb third-party supplier. Bryant Street and the Carabinieri have their names. We'll wind up suing the shit out of them. Or taking their business by way of compensation.' His hand made a dismissive sweep through the cold office air. 'That crap could have happened to anyone. Microsoft. Google. You name it. We were not to blame, and if anyone says so they'll be talking to our lawyers.'

He took the coffee off the woman who brought it and didn't even acknowledge her presence.

'Lukatmi is a busy corporation,' Jonah insisted. 'All that old stuff at the exhibition . . . it's nothing to do with us and never will be. We're investors in *Inferno*. We have a fiduciary interest in its success. That does not extend to any crap you brought with you from Italy.' He glanced at his watch, theatrically. 'Now if you don't mind . . . I'll have someone show you out.'

'What do the investors think?' Catherine Bianchi asked.

Josh Jonah's face became fixed.

'The investors are looking at a return on their money of between sixty and a thousand per cent depending on when they came in,' he replied eventually. 'How would you feel in that situation?'

'Nervous. That's paper money. The only way you can get your hands on it is to sell now. If you do that, you lose on any upside that comes after. You guys are getting big. Maybe you're the next Google . . .'

'Google . . .' Black sighed and put a hand to his head. 'That comparison is getting so tired.'

'Why?' Catherine Bianchi demanded. 'Because they're not in the red?'

The two of them stayed silent.

'You are,' she went on. 'You're buying yourselves Ferraris on dream dust. I talked to an analyst buddy. He said you're four, six quarters away from reporting anything close to a real profit, and even that's just speculation.'

'Analysts . . .' Jonah mumbled and scratched his head.

Black cleared his throat, like someone starting a lecture.

'You can't apply your old-world economics to what we do. You can't gauge our value on a spreadsheet or some stuck-up suit's assessment of our worth. Those days are past. Those people are past.'

She wasn't budging.

'Even in the new world you have shareholders, Tom. They'll still look to realizing their value at some stage, and after the last crash they know they can't do that out of thin air.'

Peroni realized he was starting to like Catherine Bianchi a lot. She hadn't mentioned a word of this before they went in. She wanted to spring it on them too.

'That's your real fiduciary duty,' she continued. 'To the people who own your stock. That's a *legal* duty, if you recall. Unless you think the law's just so . . .' She waved her hands, did a woozy hippie look. '. . . like twentieth-century, man.'

'Your analyst buddy tell you anything else?' Jonah asked.

She walked up and stood very close to him.

'He said there's a bunch of shareholders looking at a class action right now. They didn't know about you investing their money in a movie. They say it was unapproved and illegal to cut a deal like that from the funds you were raising to develop Lukatmi. When that lands on your desk your stock could go forty, sixty . . . maybe two hundred per cent south. If that happens anyone could stroll through the door and pick you up for a song. You're walking a tightrope and I think you're hoping *Inferno* will keep you upright. Maybe it will. Maybe not.'

Josh Jonah pointed to the exit.

'You can walk there or I can get someone to walk you.'

With that he turned on his heels, and Tom Black, stuttering a couple of apologies, did the same. They watched the two men return into their gigantic executive fish tank overlooking the bay.

The geek who'd been eating the pond-weed sandwich showed them to the door without saying a single word. The day was a little warmer when they got outside.

'So that's why you made captain,' Peroni said, and shook her hand.

Falcone was beaming like a teenager in love.

'It's nearly two. Time for a late lunch,' he announced. 'Somewhere good. Fish, I think. Perhaps even a glass of wine. Then I have to call Nic.'

'That would be nice, Leo. But I have a police station to run.'

'Dinner then.'

She looked at him and said, 'You can be very importunate sometimes.'

Peroni watched in awe as the merest shadow of a blush rose on Falcone's cheeks.

'It was just an idea. I'm on my own. You . . .'

'I have a million friends, some who think they're more than that.' She wrinkled her nose. 'OK. But you behave. No wandering around SoMa. No getting near to Martin Vogel. That's the deal. Gerald Kelly is a good guy. He might do you a favour one day. If you don't jerk his chain again. Agreed?'

'That's the deal,' he replied with a little too much enthusiasm, then glanced back at the Lukatmi building, with the vast multi-armed logo over the central hall. 'They're desperate, aren't they?'

'They're a couple of naive kids drowning in so much money they can't count it. They don't know what's around the corner. Of course they're desperate. It doesn't mean . . .'

She reached into her handbag and took out a band. Then she fastened back her hair. Catherine Bianchi looked more serious, more businesslike that way. It was her office look, a sign she was preparing to go back into the Greenwich Street Police Station and get on with the job.

'Someone had to handle the practical side of things, surely. My dad worked in a repair shop. He taught me mechanics matter. A lot sometimes. Arranging for Allan Prime to be abducted. Getting all that equipment into that little gallery where he died. Sure, these two could point a camera in his face and put it on the web. But the physical part . . . finding that penniless actor and getting him to threaten Maggie Flavier in the park. Coming at her again here with a poisoned apple. I don't know.'

'Jonah could do that,' Peroni suggested.

'He'd like to think so. But then he'd like to think he could run the world. I'd hate to be around if he got the chance to try. Now you go guard your old books. And stay out of trouble.'

'This analyst?' Falcone asked tentatively. 'He's a . . . friend? Nothing more?'

She rolled her head back and laughed.

'He's an imaginary friend. I made it all up just to see what happened. Companies like Lukatmi come and go, usually in the same predictable way. If they don't have someone preparing a class action somewhere, they're probably out of business anyway.'

'Oh,' Falcone said softly, then put a finger to his cheek and fell silent.

'Can I drop you somewhere?' Catherine asked. 'Such as the Palace of Fine Arts and that exhibition you're supposed to be guarding?'

'We can walk,' Falcone answered. 'We need the fresh air. But thank you.'

- 6 -

The Park Hill Sanatorium was located in an old mansion in Buena Vista Avenue opposite a quiet, green area of open space overlooking the city. Costa drove lazily through Haight-Ashbury to get there then parked two blocks away on a steep hillside street. The staff entrance was around the corner. From the ground-floor hall he could see that the front of the building was besieged by reporters and cameramen, the road littered with live TV broadcast vans. Baffled residents of this wealthy, calm suburb walked past shaking their heads, many with immaculately trimmed pedigree dogs attached to long leads. This wasn't the kind of scene owners or animals were used to witnessing. They probably preferred it on TV, beamed from somewhere else, distant, visible but out of reach. He felt grateful that Catherine Bianchi had called ahead to make arrangements for him to enter by a different door. Otherwise, he knew, he'd have been forced to run the gamut of the media mob outside.

Maggie had been transferred to the sanatorium after several hours in the emergency room of a specialist private unit in the centre of the city. He found it reassuring that Park Hill seemed more about recovery than treatment. The corridors resembled those of a fine hotel, not any medical institution he'd entered. Vases of fresh flowers stood in every corner and alcove, piped music sang discreetly in the corridors. Smiling white-clad staff wandered around nonchalantly. The place seemed timeless. He found it impossible to imagine anything more distant from the chaos and crush of a Roman public hospital. The rich and famous lived differently. Somehow the thought had not occurred to him during the brief time he had known her.

Beauty and fame apart, Maggie seemed . . . ordinary was the word that first occurred to him as he walked to her room behind a friendly, unassuming nurse, carrying in his right hand a twenty-dollar bouquet of roses.

Yet it was the wrong one. He couldn't get out of his head the image of her standing in front of the paintings in the Legion of Honor deciding which woman from the past, from someone else's imagination, she would choose for the next part, seemingly with little in the way of a pause between roles. Maggie Flavier enjoyed being possessed in this way because for a few months or, in the case of *Inferno*, a year or more, this removed from her the difficult task of defining her own identity. In the skin of others she was free to escape the drudgery of everyday existence, the old, unanswerable questions: Who am I and why am I here?

The questions Costa asked himself every day. The ones that made him feel alive. He couldn't begin to understand why she avoided them with such relentless deliberation. All he felt sure of was that she was aware of this act of self-deception, acutely, for every minute of the performance.

After a short walk he was led into a large, sunlit room. She was beneath the sheets of a large double bed, propped up on pillows next to a wall filled with flowers. The window behind her gave onto a gorgeous vista of the skyline of downtown San Francisco and the ocean beyond. Simon Harvey sat on a chair by her side, gingerly holding her hand, staring into her tired green eyes with an expression that managed to combine both sympathy and some sense of owner-ship. Her hair was still blonde, though it now seemed dull and shapeless.

'Nic,' Maggie said, smiling warmly at his appearance.

The nurse left. Harvey didn't acknowledge his presence. The publicist seemed different in America – more at home, more powerful. In Rome he'd appeared a tangential, almost servile figure, running round the set at Cinecittà doing the bidding of anyone who called, Tonti or Bonetti or even Allan Prime. Here, in Maggie's room, he didn't look like the kind of man to take orders.

'I didn't mean to interrupt.'

'You didn't,' Maggie said quietly. 'Simon's an old friend. We did a movie together in the Caribbean. What was it . . .'

'Five years ago,' Harvey answered, releasing her hand, still not looking in Costa's direction. 'Piece of derivative pirate crap posing as art-house. It bombed. At least we got paid. Not everyone did.'

Harvey stood up and looked Costa in the eye. He seemed bigger somehow in the bright, hard California light streaming through the long windows.

'I don't know whether I should shake you by the hand or punch you in the mouth. If it wasn't for you Maggie might not be alive. And she might not have got into this situation to begin with. What do you think?'

'I wouldn't advise the second. It would be impolite, and I can't imagine anyone in the publicity business would want that.'

'You're a smartass. Maybe you can get away with that in Rome. You don't have the history to make it work here. Remember that when you need me.'

'Simon,' Maggie protested. 'Will you stop being so rude? I told you, a million times. It was my idea to play hooky from all that tedium at the exhibition. If you want to blame someone, blame me.'

'I do. And him. The pair of you.'

He extended his hand out to Costa.

'But she's alive and I'm grateful for that. And now the two of you are all over the papers. So I have a professional interest too.'

His grip was firm and powerful.

'Not in me you don't,' Costa said.

'Please,' Maggie implored him. 'Sit down. Hear Simon out.' She looked at him and Costa couldn't interpret what was in her eyes. Dependence? Fear? 'He's my publicist too. Not just the movie's. My adviser. A kind of second agent if you like. I need you to listen.'

Costa sat down on the end of the bed and said, 'I need you to tell me how you are first. That's why I came here.'

She leaned back on the pillows. Her head fell into the shadow cast by the long drapes.

'I'm exhausted, my head hurts, I'm full of dope and glucose. I've had worse hangovers.' A scowl creased her half-hidden face. 'Much worse. It was an allergy, that's all. If I get that shot in me – and thanks to you that happened – I'm fine after a while.' She seemed pale but very much herself, and rather better than he'd expected. 'They say I can leave here soon. The premiere's next Thursday. I'll be fine for that.'

'Why the rush?'

'What kind of business do you think this is?' Harvey demanded. 'Some kind of fairground ride? Get up at ten, work an hour, then go home and party? This is hard labour. Celebrity never stops. Not for weekends. Not for sickness. Not for anything.'

'I understand that.'

Maggie shook her head.

'No you don't. No one can. Not until it happens.'

'You don't even escape it when you're dead,' Harvey said. 'Josh Jonah's people are looking at out-take footage of Allan Prime right now, seeing what they can CGI for the sequel. That's going to be an interesting one for the money men. Who gets the fee?'

'What?' Costa was unable to comprehend what he was saying.

'There's going to be a second *Inferno*,' Maggie told him. 'They can work up some of Allan's out-takes on computers.'

Harvey broke up with a moment of mirthless laughter.

'God knows what the storyline's going to be. How many circles can Hell have? Mind you, Roberto didn't bother so much with that for the original. Why worry now? After what's happened, all the publicity, the interest . . . this is no longer just a movie. It's becoming a sensation. And any sensation is a franchise. A brand. Like Sony or McDonald's or Leonardo da Vinci. They could maybe get eight years, a decade out of it. With or without Tonti. Or any of us. When something's this big no one's indispensable.'

The publicist took Maggie's hand again.

'And she – my friend and my client – will be a part of that brand. I'm going to make sure of that. A precious and important part. If we handle this story about the two of you well, it works in everyone's favour. Maggie's. Yours. The movie's . . .'

'I am not your client,' Costa said, suddenly angry. 'I am not in your business.'

'You are now,' Harvey retorted. 'Don't you get it? The moment those pictures of you two appeared in the papers you lost everything you ever had. Your privacy. Your identity. Your soul. It's all out there . . .' He pointed to the window. 'You've just become the livelihood of people you wouldn't wish on a dog. They feed their kids off you, they take their wives and their mistresses out to dinner on what you make for them. Break that deal . . .'

'There is no deal. This is not me.'

'As if you have a choice! It's too late for that. You're part of the story. Screw with my client's ability to fulfil her potential and . . .' Harvey bunched a fist and shook it in Costa's face. '. . . you will answer to me. *Capisce, sovrintendente?*'

'An intelligent man spends a year in Rome,' Costa observed without emotion. 'And still your accent sounds like that of a bad actor in a cheap gangster movie.'

'Don't push me . . .'

'Will you both shut up! *Will you . . . ?*'

She had her hands to her ears. Her face spoke of pain and fatigue. Costa felt something elemental tug at his heart, an emotion he hadn't known since Emily was alive. Guilt mingled with a deep, intense sense of misgiving about what might lie ahead.

'I was beginning to feel better until you two started screaming at each other,' she moaned, real tears in her eyes. 'What the hell gave you the right to walk in here and start bawling each other out like a couple of teenagers?'

'Nothing,' Costa said and placed the bouquet of roses on the bed. It seemed tiny and insignificant next to the vast displays of orchids and garish, gigantic blooms he couldn't begin to name ranged against the wall.

'Is this what you want?' he asked softly. 'Another year with Roberto Tonti? Another year being someone else?'

She turned to Harvey, kissed him quickly on the cheek and said, 'Leave this to me, Simon.'

The American left without a word, just a single, threatening glance in Costa's direction.

Maggie beckoned to him to take the empty seat. She held his hand, looked into his face. He wanted to ask himself who it was that he saw before him. Her? Or someone else, someone from a painting?

Costa felt oddly, reluctantly detached. As if someone were watching, directing this scene, one that was happening in some place that was apart from all that he regarded as reality.

'I'm sorry,' she whispered, looking so pale, so frail and fallible and human, eyes moist with fatigue and emotion.

'There's nothing for you to be sorry about, Maggie. Just rest. Take your time. Think things through.'

She laughed through her tears, and put her hand momentarily to her mouth.

'Time. I don't have any, Nic. I never have any. There are a million actresses out there screaming to take my place, most of them younger, smarter, better than me. Dino Bonetti wants to make this sequel. There's a lot of money at stake. I have to sign now, to commit. Otherwise . . .' She wiped her face with the sleeve of her dressing gown. 'Let's face it. Nobody knows who the hell Beatrice is anyway. All she does is stand there looking transcendental, promising Dante they'll be together one day, if only he lives a good life. It could be anyone in a blonde wig. I'm thirty-one years old. If it wasn't for all this publicity they wouldn't be offering me the part in the first place. I'll be thirty-four, thirty-five before it even appears. In this profession that's ancient. I can't say no.'

Her eyes stared into his.

'Also . . .' She hesitated. 'I'd be in Rome too. I thought . . . you might like that idea.'

'I'd like that very much,' he answered honestly.

She reached down and took the modest bouquet of roses,

smelled them and said, 'These are the nicest flowers anyone's ever given me.'

'The ones in Rome . . .' he said, and a picture entered his head that instant, of the two of them walking through the Campo dei Fiori, hand in hand, past the flower stalls, with not a single photographer in sight.

'Tell me about it. About you. About where you live. Your family.'

He sat on the end of her bed in a room that seemed like a suite in a hotel he could never hope to afford, staring down towards the city and the distant blue Pacific ocean. Nic Costa talked, as much to himself as to her. Of a quiet, difficult child taking lone bicycle rides on the Appian Way, of grapes and wine, of the countryside and the ruins, the tombs and the churches, the simple, modest rural life that his family had enjoyed as he grew up, watching their close-knit love for each other fall apart through sickness and age, however much he tried to hold back time, however hard he fought to paper over the cracks.

Some things were inevitable, even for the young.

He'd no idea how long he spoke, only that she never said a word. When he was finished his own eyes were stinging from tears. He felt as if some immense inner burden had lifted from him, one so heavy, familiar and persistent he had long ago ceased to notice its presence.

She was sound asleep against the pillows, her mouth open, snoring softly.

Costa picked up the roses and placed them next to the bed, in front of everything else. Then he let himself out of the room.

The staff were no strangers to celebrity. They guided him back to the side entrance where he strode out into the bright, cold July sun.

A sea of bodies surrounded him immediately. Reporters jabbed mikes in his face. Photographers aimed cameras, still and TV.

They followed him down the street. Across the road stood Simon Harvey. As Costa passed, Harvey tipped an imaginary hat and smiled sarcastically. This was his work. A publicist's way of saying, 'Do as I say or pay the price.'

Costa said nothing to anyone, simply smiled for the cameras and tried to look as pleasant and as baffled as he could.

When he reached the car he drove down the hill into Haight-Ashbury, found the nearest empty cafe and ordered a coffee. It was nearly four in the afternoon. He'd achieved nothing all day.

His phone rang.

'How is she?' Falcone asked.

'Recovering. Quickly.'

'Good. You should find that photographer you hit and apologize.'

'I am so very much in the mood for that right now.'

'Excellent. I'll give you the address.'

- 7 -

Teresa Lupo recognized the place the moment Hankenfrank's ancient Buick pulled up outside. Mission Dolores had changed very little in the fifty years since Hitchcock chose the church for a short but significant role in the movie. Not that the twins seemed much interested in that idea. All the way from Cow Hollow they talked of Dante and his numbers. Nothing else.

'So this guy of yours . . .' Frank went on. 'Quattrocchi . . . the snooty one we saw on the TV . . .'

'He's Carabinieri,' she declared from the rear seat. 'Not one of ours.'

Hank, who was at the wheel with his brother next to him, eased the old car into a parking spot then leaned back to look at her.

'Let's get this straight. You can't come over here with a million different police forces and expect us to understand what's going on. A cop's a cop.'

'What about the FBI?'

'They're not cops,' Hank pointed out.

'Neither are the Carabinieri!'

'Yeah well, they look that way to the SFPD and that's what matters.'

'Hank,' she said, taking his hand over the seat back and looking into his large, watery blue eyes. 'Try and understand. You're not reading a book now. This is not Sherlock Holmes versus Inspector Lestrade of Scotland Yard. Real life isn't fiction. It's all much more complicated and ragged at the edges. There are rarely neat symmetrical resolutions. People like me, the police, the Carabinieri . . . we just blunder around in the dark, hopefully with a little skill, creativity and luck, praying there's light somewhere around the corner. But don't quote me on that. Ever. It's supposed to be a secret.'

Frank let out a warm, throaty chuckle.

'Worst one you people have. We read newspapers as well, you know. If it wasn't for the scientists . . .'

'Science isn't everything. Trust me. I know. Did you ever read of someone getting murdered over poetry?'

'This is America. You need a reason to get killed?'

'But *poetry*?'

Hank perked up and punched his brother playfully on the arm.

'On the other hand, this isn't our case, is it? The whole thing began in Rome. In Europe. Maybe that's where it all comes from. And in Europe . . .'

'In Europe we don't murder people over poetry either.'

With his fondness for Victorian fiction, Hank relished the Dante story for the same reason Quattrocchi and the media did. It was colourful. It engaged the imagination. It told people that this in-volved more than low cunning, a vicious, heartless homicide. There was, Quattrocchi was trying to say, reassurance in the idea that some intellectual puzzle lay behind everything, a riddle waiting to be solved. This put an attractive skin on something ugly and old and familiar, simple, brutal violence. Which was all very well for a book, or someone who couldn't face up to reality . . .

Frank was looking at her, full of sincere curiosity.

'What do you murder people over back home?'

'The usual. Jealousy. Rage. We're not a different race; we just talk a different language. People everywhere kill each other for the same reasons they always have. We don't learn. We just make the same mistakes, over and over again. It's always something personal. A slight, an offence, even another crime, against ourselves or someone we love or feel responsible for. As a species we're selfish, vengeful creatures at heart. When something hurts us we like to hurt back.'

'Lots of people love Dante,' Hank pointed out. 'Some of them feel hurt by that movie.'

Frank looked dubious.

'But not many murderers, surely. And didn't I read somewhere that usually it's people you know. Family. Friends. Some guy round the corner. Those are the ones you need to worry about.'

'Usually,' she murmured. 'Whatever that means.'

'I disagree fundamentally, though in ways I am not yet able to articulate,' Hank announced. Then, after a long pause, he corrected himself. 'No actually. I don't. It's a ridiculous theory, if a little fetching. This stuck-up Quattrocchi guy's a professional. How can people like that ever begin to believe such stuff?'

'For the same reason you believed it,' Frank said. 'It sounds fun, and he's got that tame little Canadian monkey at his elbow reminding him of that fact whenever his resolve starts to fail. It doesn't mean he's a bad cop.'

Teresa bristled and pointed the wagging finger at them.

'He's not a cop. And if he was he wouldn't be a good one. Real cops are honest. I don't mean that in the obvious way. I mean they're honest with themselves, sometimes to the point of self-loathing.' She thought of Peroni, Nic and Falcone, and the way they couldn't ever really let go of anything until they'd shaken the thing into its component parts, however messy and painful that might be. 'It's not a talent to be envied or coveted. Some people have no choice, I suspect. Honesty's painful. But without it . . . what have you got?'

A curious sideways glance passed between the two of them, Hank in the driving seat, Frank next to him. One that was probably rare. It was a look of self-knowledge, of something fresh and different and challenging occurring between two people who knew each other better, surely, than most men knew their wives.

She stared into their near-identical faces and asked, 'Is there anything you two have been wanting to say to each other?'

'Yes,' Hank and Frank said simultaneously, then fell silent.

'OK,' she said after a while, pointing at Frank. 'You first.'

'That stupid fire engine is as clean as it ever was,' he blurted out. 'And we both damned well know it.'

Hank coughed and stared out of the window, a confused expression on his face.

'Not *quite* as clean . . .' he muttered, still gazing at the empty street.

'Clean enough. Why don't we get off those guys' backs? It's their job now. Not ours.'

Hank cleared his throat again, then turned to look at him.

'I've been trying to say that to you for months. I thought . . . maybe you'd have been offended. You started the whole thing. I wondered what we'd have without it.'

'I know I started it. And maybe I would have been upset. Stupid of me.'

Teresa Lupo was briefly speechless. For the first time, she finally saw them as two individuals, no longer the single identity Hankenfrank she had first met the day before. Their vivid mirror personalities, their almost exact physical resemblance, the near-identical clothes they wore . . . these visual cues had thrown her. It was almost a movie director's trick, one worthy of Hitchcock. The eye saw what it wanted to see. Just as Gianluca Quattrocchi and Professor Bryan Whitcombe looked at the events surrounding *Inferno* and beheld nothing but Dante, she had been fooled into thinking that Hank and Frank both thought and behaved as one. And in some ways, so had they. This automatic mental laziness intrigued her. She liked these two immensely and had to hide her amusement at the way they were now rubbing their eyes, one clockwise, one counter-clockwise, silent, embarrassed, but clearly relieved.

'You know, I would love to show you two around Rome some time. Will you come?'

'That's a date,' Frank replied, his voice a little cut up. To distract her – and Hank from noticing – he turned and glanced at the church along the road. It appeared to be divided into two parts, one relatively modern and grand, the second white, adobe style, and visibly older than anything she had ever seen in America. 'So why are we here?'

'To blunder creatively. And to see where Carlotta Valdes was really buried, before your friend in Chestnut Street stole her headstone. I want to see what's become of the grave of a ghost.'

- 8 -

Martin Vogel wasn't at home. So Costa drove the city, idly, meandering through the long, grey urban streets, up and down hills that seemed too steep for the automobile, dodging buses and cable cars, getting lost from time to time, then always finding something – the stretched silhouette of the Bay Bridge, the upright outline of Coit Tower, the Transamerica pyramid, the line of the ocean – that could give him some bearings. The previous night he'd got up and sat alone until three watching the movie he'd found lying on the coffee table next to the TV. Teresa had mentioned it briefly and received a fierce look from Falcone when she tried to expand on her theory that it might somehow have something to tell them.

As he cruised the city a day later, thinking of Maggie and a case that was not just baffling but also off-limits, he found it impossible to shake the memories of the movie from his head. It wasn't just that so many of the locations – the Legion of Honor, the Palace of Fine Arts, the same mundane landscape of small stores and offices – were places he'd visited with her. There was an atmosphere to the film, a sense of motion without obvious progress, yet with a hidden direction just out of reach, that was beginning to haunt him. Just as the thought of Maggie Flavier did.

Teresa had every right to be intrigued. There were obvious links. The car some stranger had loaned Maggie was the same model and colour as that driven by the principal female character in the movie. Costa had tried to find the vehicle but the studio security people said it had been taken away the morning after she'd been poisoned. Not by the police either. The Jaguar had disappeared, and when he

196

phoned her agent, who seemed both fascinated and appalled by the fact her client had been pictured in the papers gazing adoringly at a mere Roman cop, he discovered there was no paperwork, no trace of where it had come from or gone. Only a phone number, which turned out to be fake.

Something else bothered him. He was never good at flowers. But he was sure the oddly old-fashioned bouquet on the rear seat had been an obvious copy of the similar one in the movie, held by the dead Carlotta Valdes in a painting, and Madeleine Elster in real life. Not that it was the real Madeleine Elster. Or real life for that matter.

Everything about this case seemed steeped in the cinema. Roberto Tonti, Teresa said, had first learned his craft in the employ of Hitchcock as the director was making *Vertigo* in San Francisco. Everyone from Dino Bonetti to Simon Harvey, and even the young men in control of Lukatmi, had some kind of obsession with the moving image. A dependence – financial, perhaps, or something more personal – gripped them all.

He recalled Rome and a strange young actor dressed as a Carabinieri horseman, running through a performance that would lead to his death. And the end of Allan Prime, in the beautiful little Villa Farnesina. The links to Dante were everywhere, in the deadly cycle of numbers, the written warnings. The *evidence*.

Supposition and guesswork were dangerous friends. The tragic detective Scottie had toyed with them and lost everything in the end.

Costa's rented Ford kept nosing aimlessly over the city, from the tourist dives of Fisherman's Wharf to back streets and rich residential areas, and semi-abandoned industrial districts that looked as if they hadn't changed in years. He knew what he half hoped to see. An old green Jaguar with a blonde woman at the wheel, pulling into a dark corner, a dusty dead end where he might meet her and find some answers.

Somewhere along the way, he wasn't sure exactly, he stopped in a gleaming 1950s diner. A young south-east Asian girl in a white hat and anachronistic smock served him a weak milky coffee. She wore a badge that said 'The Philippines' and a broad toothy smile. San

Francisco seemed possessed of multiple personalities, all of them jumbled up together, one running into the many.

He looked at his watch. It was close to seven. A decent enough time to call. He phoned the Park Hill Sanatorium and waited as a woman who sounded like the smartest of hotel receptionists put him on hold.

'Miss Flavier discharged herself an hour ago,' she said after a long wait.

'You mean she's OK.'

'We can't discuss a patient's condition, sir. You appreciate that.'

'Where did she go? Who with?'

'I really can't add to what I've said. Good night.'

The line went dead. Costa realized he didn't even know where she lived. An apartment somewhere on Nob Hill. That was all she'd told him.

He called the agent. There was nothing there but an answering machine. He tried Falcone and finally got through to someone he could talk to. The man was clearly not in the mood for discussion. The inspector listened then said, 'If Maggie Flavier wants to go home it's none of your business.'

'She nearly died . . .'

'It was an allergic reaction. One she's had before. If she was really ill they would never have let her leave hospital. She'll have security. Relax.'

'I don't even know where she lives. Can you find that out?'

There was silence on the line.

'Yes. I can.'

Then nothing.

'Leo . . .'

'Leave it. You're fortunate the police haven't charged you with assault over that photographer. Don't tempt fate.'

He could feel his temper rising.

'You asked me to go and apologize to the man.'

'So why didn't you?'

He wasn't in, Costa told him. No one was around. The place looked deserted. But that was three hours before.

'Then try again. That's what we do, isn't it? No more calls, Nic. I'm off duty.'

'Yes . . . sir.'

He cut the call and uttered a short, meaningful Roman curse.

The Filipino waitress was beaming at him. She had a plate in her hands.

'Here you go. Veggie burger and fries,' she said, and the sight of it dispelled his appetite for good.

He gazed at the shining chrome and, plastered on the walls throughout the diner, posters for movies and stars he'd long forgotten. Marlon Brando in *The Wild One*. Robert Mitchum in *Cape Fear*. Cinema attempted to define modern life through allegory and mystery, in much the same way Dante sought to define his own medieval world. Fundamentally they were looking for the same, unreachable goals: happiness, peace, and a few good answers.

Then a familiar voice came over from the TV in the corner, very quietly.

He placed five dollars on the counter and asked, 'Can you turn up the volume on that thing?'

She glanced around her and said, 'A little. Why don't you move closer.'

He picked up his glass of plain water and sat in the steel seat directly beneath the screen. Roberto Tonti was on some news interview programme. It seemed to be live. A long clip from the movie – Allan Prime as Dante spellbound as Maggie, ethereal, otherworldly, strode through a nightmare universe of monsters and flame.

The waitress stopped work and watched it with him. The place was quiet anyway.

'Who's the boring guy?' she asked. 'What's he got to do with big stars like that?'

He told her the director's name. She looked puzzled.

'Never heard of him. He looks sick. Oughta be in hospital.'

'He directed the movie. It's his show.'

'No it's not. I don't go to the movies to see guys like that. I wanna see stars. Don't you?'

'They're just people. Like you and me.'

She stared at him and burst out laughing.

'Not like me, mister. Not in a million years.' Her eyes shone with amusement. 'No offence but . . . not like you either.'

- 9 -

They had spent more than an hour wandering around Mission Dolores. She couldn't have hoped for better guides. Hank and Frank were in love with their city and seemed to know every last corner. For Teresa Lupo, who temperamentally had no fondness for religion, the mission was a revelation. In Rome the Church was omnipresent, and seemed to have been that way for ever. Seated in the small adobe chapel of Mission Dolores she was, for the first time in her life, conscious of a world that existed before God, at least the one she'd grown up with. This had been a different, virgin environment, one conquered by a foreign host bringing what it saw as enlightenment and civilization, just two hundred and fifty years before, at a time when Rome regarded itself as the modern capital of a civilized, fixed universe in which everything was labelled, recognized and known. In Italy history seemed either distant or a part of the living present. Here the past existed just out of reach, tantalizingly near yet untouchable, alive yet gone too.

The place fascinated her so much that she forgot, for a while, why they came. Then Frank looked at her, with an amusing and deliberate mix of condescension and sympathy, and asked, 'So you really want to see Carlotta's grave?'

'Oh. Of course.'

They walked outside. It was getting cold and late. She wondered how much longer they could stay here. How much she could put off going back to Greenwich Street and admitting she had nothing to report, or suggest. A green car, some locations, a few possible coincidences . . . it added up to nothing and she knew it.

The cemetery was beautiful, still and peaceful, filled with roses, bold spikes of yellow cannas and flowers she couldn't identify.

The statues of dead monks ranged across the graveyard, pensive heads bowed over their own tombs, the long foreign grass rising up to their frozen grey waists. Misshapen conifers rose among the forest of headstones against the white adobe walls where two unequal towers, like decorations on a wedding cake, pointed to a fading blue sky above floods of purple and red bougainvillea tumbling down from the roofline.

The names on the graves seemed to come from everywhere: Spain and Ireland, England and the east coast of America. Some tombs were grand, most modest. Death and the relentless maritime climate were slowly reducing them all to leached and crumbling stone.

She wandered through a grove of roses and came upon a small dome-shaped reed hut, recently erected. A sign said it was designed to show the original kind of dwelling place used by the Ohlone, the indigenous people of the area before colonization. She closed her eyes, thought of the scene in the movie, Scottie, in a brown suit and a 1950s gentleman's hat, skulking by the overhang of the mission walls, watching from the shadow of a sprawling tomb, furtively spying on Madeleine as she gazed on a grave, a curious bouquet of roses in her hand.

'She knew you were there all along, Scottie,' Teresa said to herself.

'That she did,' Frank agreed.

'You like the movie too?' she asked.

His eyes clouded over with doubt.

'I suppose that's the word. It's not easy to forget and I don't know why. Or what it means, if it means anything, or needs to. The odd thing is I'm not sure about all these things in a different way every time I watch it. There's something . . .' He chose his words carefully. She noticed how Hank watched him, a quiet look of admiration in his near-identical face. '. . . there's something not quite right about it. Something obsessive. The way everyone seems to be watching that woman. Not just Scottie. The camera too. Us. The audience. It's unnatural and it's supposed to be that way. The thing draws you in and if you think about it, that makes you uncomfortable.'

'It's voyeuristic,' she suggested.

He broke into a broad grin.

'The very word! You know, for someone who comes from a place where they speak differently, you're very good with English.'

She shrugged.

'I've got the time. I'm off the case. Just another tourist. Words are all I have.'

Teresa put out her hand and touched the dry reeds of the Ohlone structure.

'It was here, wasn't it? Carlotta's gravestone? Before they moved it to that little cinema in the Marina?'

'*If* they moved it to that little cinema in the Marina,' Frank cautioned. 'You heard the guy. His uncle or whoever was a rogue. Movie hands always were. Maybe still are. Do you know no one has any idea where the painting went? The one of Carlotta? It'd be worth a fortune now. They think it just got scrapped. Thrown out with the junk. One more prop. That was Hitch. Finish one movie, get on with the next. Never look back. Only the present matters. Do you think people like Roberto Tonti treat the job that way?'

'Not for a moment. They've got egos the size of a whale. They're interested in their legacy.'

'Which is nothing more and nothing less than the movies they leave behind,' Frank insisted. 'I think Hitch got it right.'

His brother intervened.

'It was actually a little to the left.' Hank pointed to a rough patch where a few low annual flowers were trying to flourish in the dry earth. 'They couldn't use somewhere there was a real grave, for sure.'

'You saw it?' she asked them. 'When it was here?'

'We were still kids,' Hank replied. 'It was fun to go somewhere movie stars had been. To stand on the same spot. Like touching the hem of God. Not that we would have put it that way back then.' He nodded at the mission. 'Much more fun than that place anyway.'

'The funny thing is,' Frank went on, 'they left that fake gravestone there for a while. A few years if I recall right. It was a tourist attraction. The mission needed the money. You can't blame them. Then . . .' He glanced back at the little chapel again. '. . . someone said it was *disrespectful.* An insult to the real dead people here.'

'As if they're going to complain,' Hank added. 'Or their relatives. No one's been buried here in years.'

'Does that matter?' she wondered.

Frank shuffled, uncomfortable.

'I guess being Italian . . . and all. Teresa, we're not that way. Not anything. When you're dead you're dead. Only fools and children believe in ghosts.'

She felt the same way, usually.

'That's what Scottie thought. Was he right?'

Frank nodded earnestly.

'Yes. He was bang on the money, even if it did cost him. Is there anything else you need to see? Churches give me the creeps to be honest with you. Also if we're in time we can hit the happy hour at a little bar we know. There are alcoholic beverages which have been asking to be introduced to you. It would be impertinent to keep them waiting.'

'No. I don't think so . . .' she began, and then her eye caught the tree.

What was it Catherine Bianchi had said? In California almonds flowered at the end of February. That must have meant they would bear fruit during the summer.

Next to the place where the grave of the fictional Carlotta Valdes had stood was an old, crooked almond, little more than the height of a man, its leaves fluttering weakly in the early evening breeze, its feeble arthritic branches black with age and dead fungi. On each, still a little green from their newness, stood lines of nuts in their velvet, furry shells.

She took two steps towards the tree, reached up and tugged one from the nearest branch.

'You're going to get us in trouble,' Hank warned. 'Now aren't you?'

'Perish the thought . . .'

Teresa crouched down and found a stone. Then she placed the nut on its surface and cracked the shell open with a rock. There was a loud bang that ricocheted around the walls of the tiny graveyard. She looked at the shards of the inner fruit, white and mashed against the stone.

It was obvious what she had to do. There was no lab in San Francisco she could use. So she picked up the largest piece and put it in her mouth.

By the time she stood up she was coughing. It was painful. Someone – she couldn't see who – was patting her on the back. There was a new voice, a woman's voice.

With no grace whatsoever, she spat out every last piece of the almond she could. Even so the taste lingered.

It was the most bitter thing she'd ever known, until the face of a severe, dark-skinned woman of Mexican looks hove into view and began castigating her.

'What are you doing? *What are you doing?*'

'It was . . .' She began coughing and found it hard to stop.

Another woman, a sister, with a blue headdress, arrived, carrying a plastic cup with water in it. Teresa drank greedily and found herself spitting out more pieces of almond.

Things began to improve then.

'I'm sorry,' she said and found herself coughing again.

'Why did you do that?' the nun asked. 'This is a cemetery. Not an orchard.'

'I was curious. The fruit was very . . . harsh.'

The women were silent.

'It's a bitter almond,' Teresa asked. 'Isn't it?'

The nun crossed her arms in anger.

'They say the first fathers planted it. Two hundred and fifty years ago. Are we supposed to put up a sign saying, "Don't steal the almonds"?'

The woman touched the branches.

'It's dying. We feed it. We try to care. Nothing works.' She shook her head. Her eyes were grey and sad. 'Perhaps it's for the best. If people keep coming here and taking away what's not theirs . . .'

Teresa felt her heart skip a beat and prayed it wasn't a side effect of the bitter nut she'd just eaten.

'Someone else did this?'

'A man,' the Mexican woman said, as if it could have been no other. 'And he had a bag! He took many, and wouldn't give them back when we caught him.'

Hank and Frank were looking at her and licking their lips in anticipation. One right to left, the other left to right.

'This man?' she asked. 'Do you know who he is?'

'Who are we?' the woman asked. 'All-seeing, all-knowing angels?'

'I really need to know.'

The nun took the plastic cup and gave her a withering look.

'We don't have his name. We told the police, of course. This is a nice neighbourhood. We don't want people coming in and taking things. The police said we were wasting their time. There are larger crimes in the city than stealing almonds from a graveyard.'

'There are,' Teresa found herself saying.

The Mexican woman waved her fist in the air.

'But we had a photograph! *A photograph!*'

She wanted to laugh. But she still felt a touch giddy. The nasty taste wouldn't go away.

'Can I see it?'

The two of them stared at each other and said nothing.

'Please. It may be important.'

'The *parroco* has it,' the Mexican woman said. 'The pastor. He is out for a little while.'

'Then I'll wait.'

'Not here,' the nun ordered. 'In the basilica, please.' She patted the trunk of the withering almond tree. 'Out of the way of temptation, I think.'

- 10 -

Martin Vogel's apartment was in a recent block on what, for tourists, was the wrong side of Market Street, away from Union Square, the department stores and gift shops, the cable cars and the constant presence of street people pestering for money. It lay in a nondescript commercial building down a dark, dank lane. SoMa was, he understood from the guidebooks, a trendy part of the city, up and coming, aspiring to be cultural, in much the same way as Testaccio in Rome. In parts it had the same tough, rough urban aspect too. It was hard even to see where Vogel's apartment might be, until he found a discreet, half-hidden set of nameplates by a set of side doors. One, number 213, which he took to mean the second floor, had the scrawled name 'Vogel' by it.

His finger lurked over the bell push for a moment. Then Costa chose another name, a few doors along, pressed the button there and waited.

A woman's voice, taut, angry and hurried, barked out of the speaker.

'Pizz . . .' he began to say.

'Jesus Christ,' the woman screeched.

The buzzer on the lock sang. He wondered why he hadn't even got the chance to pretend to be the pizza man. Then he pushed the door open and found himself inside a spare, cool atrium that smelled of recent disinfectant and the cloying scent of a rose bush struggling in the thin light of the doorway.

Without thinking he patted his jacket. There was no gun there. He was just another civilian.

He walked upstairs, trying to think of something to say. He hadn't just broken the photographer's arm. He'd stood on it, determined to find out the exact location so that an ambulance might find them. This didn't worry him any more now than when it had happened. Vogel had been stalking them for reward and was determined to get out of there without helping once he had his pictures. Costa felt he'd had little alternative.

There was a sound from the floor above. A dog barking. A woman's cry. Music. From somewhere the shriek of a baby. There was the smell of stale food and rotten trash. Down the stairwell fell the noise of people arguing several floors up.

When he got to the top of the staircase he found himself in near-darkness. Two of the strip lights in the corridor ceiling had failed. A third flickered sickly, on and off.

The baby wailed again, its cries echoing off the walls so much he'd no idea from which direction the sound came.

Each door had a little light behind the bell push. The nearest read 256. He walked along. The next read 257.

The wrong side, and the wrong direction. It was turning out to be one of those days.

He wondered whether this was a good idea at all. Then he thought about what Falcone would say if he came back and admitted he'd pulled out at the last moment. The good mood that the presence of Catherine Bianchi instilled in the inspector was, like most things surrounding him, transient, and perhaps headed for failure. His private life consisted of a series of short, albeit intense, relationships followed by periods of mute, surly celibacy. The pattern was well established now. Costa didn't want to bounce it out of phase prematurely.

He recrossed the stairwell and strode down the opposite corridor. Only one light was out here. As he walked, the sounds of the apartment block receded. There were no crying babies in this part of the building, no angry voices. Nothing at all.

Costa reached the door of apartment 213. It was ajar, just a finger's width, enough to let a shaft of orange, artificial light stumble through and fall on the tiled floor in an eccentric shape.

Decisions, he thought.

He edged his foot forward until it reached the cheap painted wood that was supposed to keep Martin Vogel safe from the world beyond. The door moved steadily inwards at his touch, on hinges that needed a spot of oil.

- 11 -

The later the hour, the more uncomfortable Hank and Frank became. Churches really didn't suit them and the bar was calling. Finally, just before eight, she lost patience with their huffing and puffing and sent them on their way, out into the fast-falling evening. She could take a cab home. She could ride a bus. One went from the street outside all the way down to the waterfront at the Marina. She liked buses. They put you in touch with people.

Predictably, the priest appeared not long after her ride home had gone. She took one look at the man in the familiar black frock and felt her heart sink. He had a long pale face, Irish perhaps, pockmarked cheeks sagging with age. His eyes were sad and rheumy, as if they'd seen rather too much. A drink with the twins might be welcome relief after a little time in the gloom of Mission Dolores. She was glad she'd made a note of their favourite bar.

Then she told him who she was and where she came from. The priest opened his mouth and her opinion changed instantly. His voice did not match his appearance in the slightest, being bright and young and engaged, like that of some lively inner spirit trapped inside an older, more fragile frame. The *parroco* introduced himself as Dermot Gammon, originally from Boston, but a resident of Rome for several years before returning to the US and ending up in San Francisco.

'Where do you live?' he asked.

'Off Tritone.'

'Where exactly?'

'The Via Crispi.'

He rubbed his hands together and a beatific expression put fresh light in his eyes. A comprehensive list of local stores and restaurants and wine bars streamed from his lips.

'You know Rome well,' she said sincerely.

They spent a few happy minutes discussing her home city. Eventually the priest asked her why she had come. She told him a little about the case and the movie, then said, 'They told me you had a photograph. Of the man they found stealing something in the cemetery.'

His long, sad face fell into a frown.

'A bag full of almonds. The ladies . . .' He sighed. 'They have a sense of care for this place that occasionally goes to extremes. We exist to cater for souls, not bricks and mortar. They saw the man, they took some photos. I showed them to the police. Our local captain was not, I have to say, terribly interested or impressed.' He edged forward, as if making some statement in confession. 'Which pleased me greatly. I don't wish to see the mission in the newspapers. Not outside births and marriages and deaths, and a few charitable occasions. Certainly, not as part of something as serious as this awful case you mentioned. Am I making myself clear?'

'I'll be discreet. I promise. Besides, it's probably nothing. I'm shooting arrows in the dark, hoping one will land somewhere sunny.'

'That's work for a priest. Not a scientist.'

'I wouldn't presume to teach you your job, father. Science and religion aren't enemies.'

'Really?' He didn't look convinced. 'I must disagree. Nothing wonderful that I recall of Rome has to do with science.'

'Not the Sistine Chapel? Michelangelo thought himself more an architect than a painter. And Bernini. Those statues. How could he create them without knowing anatomy? Without *seeing*?'

'I was always a Caravaggio man myself. I like real human beings, frail men and women, not make-believe perfect ones. Without the fallible . . .' He opened his hands and looked around the dark interior of the mission. '. . . I'm out of a job.'

'Without mysteries we both are. Please, father. The photograph. Just to satisfy my curiosity.'

He excused himself for a few minutes. When he came back he sat down by her side and retrieved a snapshot from the inside of his gown. It was too dark to see much of it so she went and stood beneath the electric candles close to the altar.

The priest followed, looked over her shoulder and said, 'The gardener told me to chop the tree down two years ago. He said it's dying. Too old.'

She peered at the figure in the picture. The man was holding a supermarket bag that, from its bulging shape, appeared to contain a good collection of nuts from the tree. He was arguing with the Mexican woman she'd seen earlier, and looked as if he was coming off worse.

'I told them all, "It's a tree",' the priest went on. 'Not a human being. The thing is insensate. It feels no pain, has no consciousness of its impending end, or its present feeble state. We can wait a little while, I say. Not thinking . . .'

His glassy eyes stared into hers.

'I've been here thirteen years. We've never had a single person take something from the cemetery. Not something supposedly edible anyway. Now two in a matter of weeks.'

'It's not edible. It's a bitter almond. The original tree. Poisonous in quantity.'

He looked shocked.

'That's why the man took it?'

'Someone with a little knowledge might know, I imagine. The general shape of the branches is a little different. Not much else. Most people would simply see an almond tree. Though why you would want to steal from it . . .'

Its gnarled, failing form stood next to the patch of ground where the imaginary Carlotta Valdes's grave had been created for the film, and stayed, for a few uncertain years, in real life too, until someone deemed it unsuitable for a real cemetery. It was a link, one that, like the rest, seemed to lead into some opaque and unrelenting San Franciscan fog.

'Do you know the man?' the priest asked.

She gave him back the photograph.

'He's wearing sunglasses, father. And he's half turned away from the camera. If it were my own brother . . . perhaps. But . . .'

He took the snapshot from her and placed a guilty hand to his mouth.

'I'm sorry. I gave you the wrong one. Here. There's a better picture.'

Father Gammon scrabbled in his clothes. A crumpled packet of cigarettes fell to the floor. He apologized and looked a little guilty, then picked them up. In his other hand was a new photo which he passed over.

This was clear and distinct, even in the fusty yellow light of the electric altar candles.

'Do you know him now?'

'I believe so,' she answered. 'Will you excuse me, please?'

It was getting dark outside. Falcone was furious at being interrupted halfway through what sounded like a nervous dinner with Catherine Bianchi. But not for long.

- 12 -

Costa pushed the door as far as it would go. He needed what light there was from the corridor. It was pitch-black in the apartment.

There was a smell, though. Something familiar: the harsh odour of a spent weapon and behind it the faint tang of blood. From a tinny radio in a room beyond the entrance came the sound of music. *Tannhäuser.* He thought of the burly photographer squealing as he stood on his shattered arm. The man didn't look like an opera fan.

He stopped and listened. Not a sound except the music, but that was so full and insistent . . . Costa found the wall inside the entrance, making sure he stayed inside the shadow as much as possible. It wasn't a good idea to be a silhouette in a doorway. He couldn't see a thing. Then, in the middle of a line, the music stopped, as if someone had become aware of his presence.

'Police,' he said quietly into the dark, taking care to move position as he spoke.

Not a sound except for his own voice in the dark of an apartment where the smell of spent ammunition was so strong it seemed like the mark of some murderous feral cat.

When it came the racket made him jump. The electronic wail of the mobile phone cut through the black interior of Vogel's apartment.

It was the tone he'd set for Falcone. Costa swore, ducking further back into the pool of gloom by the door, desperate to avoid becoming an easy target.

He got the phone out of his pocket, and killed the call immediately.

There'd been a new noise. Someone moving in the blackness ahead of him. A new smell too, one he couldn't place at that moment.

Costa stared at the bright blue screen in his hand, got Falcone's number and texted four words, 'URGT VOGEL APT NOW'.

Then he threw the phone across to the other side of the room and backed hard against the wall. The same ring tone went off a moment after. The space in front of him was briefly filled by sound, the bellowing roar of gunfire fighting to escape the confined space that enclosed it.

He froze where he was, cold and sweating. Someone was scrabbling around on the floor, maybe three or four strides to the right, struggling to say something. The unseen figure's breathing was laboured, words unintelligible. He sounded sick or wounded, in some kind of trouble. He was still a man with a gun. Costa was pretty sure he wasn't the only one either, although it was hard to place anything in the darkness. The strong, noxious smell was beginning to overwhelm everything.

Finally he worked out what it was. Petrol.

Down the corridor someone screamed. The baby was crying again. Lights were coming on, voices were rising.

He wanted to kick himself. They'd called the police before. The woman let him in immediately, hearing just the first letter he'd spoken, because she thought he was the police. The gunfire had started before he'd blundered onto the scene. That was why everything was so quiet, so deserted. Sane people stayed out of the way.

As he moved a fraction further into the room Costa stumbled, found his fingers encountering the familiar hard metal frame of a photographer's tripod. He picked it up and threw the thing further into the darkness, towards where the window ought to be.

There was no shooting this time. He fell to the floor, managed to roll all the way, turning, turning, out into the corridor, scrabbling on hands and knees to get out of the deadly visible frame of the doorway.

Breathless and sweating on the hard floor, but outside the

apartment, finally, he heard nothing more. Then he started to scramble upright and found himself staring into the gun of a uniformed SFPD cop. The man was black, short and stocky, probably no more than twenty-five. He looked terrified. The weapon shook in his hands.

'I'm a police officer,' Costa said, slowly, carefully raising his hands. 'The ID's in my jacket pocket.'

'I don't recall ever seeing you around. What are you? Mexican?'

'A visitor.'

'Well Mr Visitor . . .' The gun got sweaty in his grip. He passed it from one hand to the other, then back, the barrel staying straight in Costa's face all the time. After that he nodded at the open doorway. 'You gonna tell me what I might find in there? And why you was looking?'

'There's a wounded man with a gun. I just came here to apologize. There was an incident. With the actress. Maggie Flavier. Maybe you read about it . . .'

The gun lowered a little. A flicker of recognition crossed the young cop's face.

'That was you? You looked bigger in the papers.'

'Thanks . . .'

There were more people behind him. The cop swung round nervously, waving the gun everywhere. Costa wanted to shout at him but it didn't seem a good idea.

He didn't need to anyway. It was Catherine Bianchi marching down the corridor, police ID held high, Falcone behind her with a face like thunder. She was bellowing at him to get his weapon down, in a voice that wasn't easy to ignore.

'Captain Bianchi . . . ?' the cop asked.

She was wearing a short cocktail dress with a scarlet silk scarf over her shoulders. The badge in her hand looked a little incongruous next to it.

'Yes. I have a life outside uniform. Who'd have believed it?'

She stared at Costa, then at Falcone, and asked, angrily, 'What the hell is going on?'

'There's a wounded man with a gun in there,' Costa said quickly, scrabbling to his feet, brushing off the dust from the floor. 'I urge . . .'

Caution, he was about to say, but the words stayed in his mouth. Someone was screaming, a high-pitched shriek of terror and pain. Inside Martin Vogel's apartment a light had appeared, a grim and familiar orange.

Costa strode down the corridor back towards the fire extinguisher and the box on the wall he'd felt as he made his way into the floor.

Catherine Bianchi let out a piercing yell when the man stumbled out of the door, body a bright, burning torch of flame from head to foot, leaping around like a victim of St Vitus's dance consumed by fire.

There was a blanket in the case by the extinguisher. Costa snatched the thing free and shook it in his arms as he ran towards the blazing figure.

'He's got a gun,' Catherine shouted at him, standing in the way, blocking any chance he had to move forward.

Sure enough there was a weapon in his right hand, which now appeared blackened and useless, gripping the familiar black shape out of nothing more than fear.

'I see it,' Costa said, and pushed her to one side, throwing the blanket over the shrieking shape in front of him.

A crowd was gathering. He got the flame-killing fabric round the man, tight, hugged him, trying to ignore the smell of burnt flesh and hair and clothing. The stricken figure in his arms fell to the floor, stiffening. Costa managed to look into the face. His skin was black with soot, red with livid burns.

He was recognizable, just.

'Medics,' Costa said, wondering if there was much life left in the man he held in his arms. Blood was beginning to seep through the blackened clothing. He was wounded, perhaps more than once. 'They're coming. Lie down. Wait . . .'

A noise escaped his blackened lips, a long, painful groan that blew the stink of burnt petrol straight into Costa's face. It was the last breath. He knew it. So did Josh Jonah, dying in his arms.

They were round him now, looking, unable to speak.

He let go of the rigid figure and didn't wait. Two steps took him to the door to Vogel's apartment, he found the light switch, tried to take in what he saw.

The place was wrecked. There'd been a fight, a bloody one. A scattering of money – fifty- and one-hundred-dollar notes – was spread across the table in the living room. It was a lot. Thousands possibly.

Falcone and Catherine Bianchi weren't far behind him.

'Let's put out a bulletin for Vogel,' she said, pulling out her radio. 'Then we work out how the hell I am going to explain all this to Gerald Kelly and keep my job.'

Costa tried to take in what he was seeing.

'I wouldn't make any hasty decisions. There were three people here. I heard them.'

He walked on through the scattered mess on the floor, into the bedroom.

The smell he'd first noticed, that of blood, hung heavy in the air, mingling with the harsh chemical stench of petrol. There was some-thing else too, its identity just out of reach.

A single naked bulb swung lazily over the bed as if someone had recently brushed against it. Martin Vogel didn't live in style. Or die that way either. The corpse was on the mattress. He wore nothing but a pair of boxer shorts and the plaster cast on his arm. A gaping wound stood over his heart like a bloody rose poking its way out from the inside.

'You can hold the bulletin,' Costa said, mostly to himself.

The window was open, just a fraction. He walked to it. There was a fire escape outside. Someone could have escaped undetected.

Maybe they did kill each other. Maybe it was meant to look that way.

Catherine Bianchi came in, looking lost. Homicide wasn't her field, and Costa could see that from her face. She returned to the living room, walked over to the table, picked up some of the notes and let them drop through her fingers. He watched Falcone biting his tongue, wanting to tell her not to touch a thing.

'What was it the Carabinieri's pet academic said?' she asked. 'Next we'd get the Avaricious and the Prodigal?'

She shook her head and cast a brief glance at the bedroom, and then the corridor, where Josh Jonah's corpse lay like a burnt and bloodied human ember escaped from some recently extinguished bonfire.

'How do you tell which one was which?'

The stink of petrol drifting into the room from around Vogel's bed was becoming overpowering. It must have been in the carpet, the curtains, everywhere.

So Josh Jonah wanted to set fire to the place and was caught by his own misdeed, shot by the wounded Vogel. Costa's mind struggled with that idea. The man was ablaze when he died. If he'd been close to the petrol trail he'd been laying that would have ignited too. There was a gap in the story somewhere.

'I think we should get out of here until the fire people take a look,' he began to say. 'This isn't a safe . . .'

Something hissed and fizzed in the corner and finally he managed to place the last unknown smell. It was one from childhood. Fireworks on the lawn of the house, bright, fiery lights in the sky. A fuse burning before the explosion.

In the corner of the room, safe on a chair above the fuel-stained carpet, sat an accordion-style jumping firecracker. A long length of cord had been attached so that it wound across the seat of the chair, lengthening the burn time. Most of it was now charred ash. Scarcely half a finger of untouched material remained, and that was getting rapidly eaten by the eager, hungry flame working its way to the small charge of powder that would take the incendiary and fling it into the room.

It was a perfect, home-made time bomb and it was about to explode.

He pushed Catherine Bianchi back towards the door, bellowing at Falcone and the young baffled cop to join them. When they were through, he heaved her sideways, away from the mouth of the empty space leading back to the apartment.

He just had time to see the other two scramble out into the corridor. Then the soft roaring gasp of the explosion hit. Costa felt the heat in his back, and threw himself hard down the hall.

An angry tongue of yellow, smoke-stained flame belched from the space they'd occupied only moments before, briefly licked the wall opposite, then retreated to rejoin the livid inferno that was growing inside Martin Vogel's apartment.

He struggled to his feet and went over to check the others. They were getting to their feet, speechless, eyes still glazed from shock.

The building fire alarms began to sound. They could hear people panicking down the distant corridors in the dark. Automatic sprinklers in the ceiling kicked in, dispatching a shower of water down onto their heads.

There was no way back. The flames had receded but the smoke was beginning to grow into a swirling plume working its way out into the hall. He was talking about what needed to be done, to himself as much as anyone else. They had to evacuate the building. They had to think about how to get four or five floors of people in a residential apartment block out into the street in safety. They had to . . .

He found himself interrupted by Catherine Bianchi, tugging on his arm, staring insistently into his face.

'Hear that siren?' she asked.

Somewhere outside there was a familiar wail, one that seemed to be multiplying into a chorus.

'It's called the fire department. Let's leave this to them, huh?'

- 13 -

An hour and a half later Costa found himself standing outside next to the engines and the emergency vehicles as they wound down their pumps and reported the entire building evacuated, without a single casualty.

Gerald Kelly had arrived, disturbed at dinner in formal dress, just like Falcone and his companion. The SFPD captain listened in quiet fury to a report from Catherine Bianchi and the fire officers. After that he took the two Italians to one side to demand an explanation, any explanation, for Costa's presence in Martin Vogel's apartment.

'I came to apologize,' Costa said simply. 'That was all.'

Falcone stood his ground.

'I asked him to do this, Kelly. I thought it might help.'

'Oh right. That's what you were doing. Helping.' He looked at them, desperation in his eyes. 'Well? Did it?'

'This isn't our case,' Costa said, before his superior had the chance to intervene.

Kelly eyeballed him and stifled a single, dry laugh.

'You guys really are something. I know it's not your case. If it was . . . what would you think? What you would do?'

Costa glanced at the narrow, badly lit street that fed back into the bright, busy district around Market Street.

'I'd be looking for a third man,' he said.

PART FIVE

- 1 -

Three days later Costa and Teresa Lupo sat at the door of the principal exhibition tent in the temporary canvas village by the side of the Palace of Fine Arts, watching Roberto Tonti and Dino Bonetti strut around the area as if they owned it.

The question had been bothering him for days. He knew he had to ask.

'What's the difference between a producer and a director?'

She stared at him and asked, 'Are you serious?'

'Deadly. I was never addicted to movies like you. I just see the finished thing. Actors. Pictures. I've no idea what goes into it.'

'What was the difference between Caravaggio and Cardinal Del Monte?'

Costa frowned and replied, 'One was an artist and the other was the man who made his art viable. By paying for it, or finding others to come up with the commissions.'

'One provides the art. The other provides the wherewithal. There. You answered your own question.'

He thought about that, and a nagging doubt that had been with him since the conversation with the Asian waitress in the diner.

'If you'd been Del Monte would you have loved Caravaggio or resented him? So much talent in one human being, something you couldn't hope to achieve yourself?'

Bonetti was striding past the huge marquee that was destined to house the audience for the premiere the following evening. Tonti was at his side, listening. Thirty years separated these men. One was in his prime: strong, both physically and personally. Tonti was dying;

his face seemed bloodless. His walk had the slow, pained determination of an old man resenting his increasing infirmity.

'I think I'd feel lucky to have known a genius,' Teresa replied. 'And a little jealous too from time to time.' She nodded at the two Italians. 'You think Bonetti might resent Tonti in some way?'

'Directors win Oscars. Producers don't win anything.'

'The kind of money they make they don't need to. Someone like Bonetti dips his beak in everything. He's Del Monte with a twist. He gets to sell the paintings he commissions and keep a share of them in perpetuity. What's some stupid little statue next to that?'

Something, he thought. But perhaps not much. Dino Bonetti was a powerful, confident man. It seemed far-fetched to think he would be offended by any fleeting fame attached to cast or crew.

'The question you should really be asking,' she added, 'is how much someone like Tonti resents his stars. I've been through the cuttings, read his biography. It's full of bust-ups with his cast. For some people that's a trademark. Tonti . . .' She frowned. 'He treats his cast as if they're just puppets. It's a shame he's so old. All this digital stuff they have nowadays . . . It can't be long before real actors become almost irrelevant for some directors. Just one more piece of software they can call up and manipulate on screen – so much more manageable than flesh and blood.'

Lukatmi was never far away from the story, he thought. The Italian director had been involved with the digital video company based near his home since the outset. The papers said that he provided some seed capital for its founding. Not that it was going to be worth much now. Lukatmi's shares had entered meltdown after the death of Josh Jonah. In seventy-two hours the company had gone from star of the NASDAQ to one more discredited and busted dotcom. The very day that the news channels and papers devoted huge amounts of coverage to the deadly inferno in the SoMa apartment of Martin Vogel, a series of lawsuits had been filed in the courts in California and New York. Given the speed with which they appeared, it was clear lawyers had been hovering at the edge of the company for some time, just as Catherine Bianchi had predicted. New actions seemed to be appearing almost by the hour, accusing the dead Jonah and his partner Tom Black of everything from stock option irregularities to misuse of shareholder funds. The newspapers claimed the District Attorney was mulling over a formal probe into the company over fraud, money-laundering and racketeering. The share price that had seemed so buoyant only four days before had fallen through the floor until, that morning, it had been suspended amid expectations of an impending bankruptcy announcement. Predators – old-school companies, the ones Lukatmi treated with such contempt – were now hovering ready to snap up what few worthwhile pieces might be salvaged from the corporate corpse on the waterfront at Fort Mason.

It was a great story for the media, one bettered only by a more astonishing revelation: as well as being a corporate crook, Josh Jonah had turned out to be a real-life criminal too, a man who'd been willing to murder a Hollywood movie star in order to save his company from collapse. All the evidence was there, or so Gianluca Quattrocchi had declared to the cameras, with Bryan Whitcombe in tow as ever. Gerald Kelly seemed somewhat muted in front of the press. But the arguments presented by Quattrocchi appeared solid: in spite of Costa's protests the evidence appeared to point to there being only two individuals in Martin Vogel's apartment in SoMa. Forensic believed that Jonah had fatally wounded Vogel, who had returned one shot before he died. That had crippled the billionaire as he started to spread petrol around the apartment to destroy any evidence.

'I still think I heard a third person there,' Costa said quietly.

She watched him; he was aware that he had, perhaps, protested this point too much.

'Back there again, are we? It was dark. You knew something was wrong. When people are under stress . . .'

'I know what I heard . . .'

'Enough! If you were sitting in Bryant Street now which way would you be leaning? Be honest with yourself.'

Costa didn't have a good answer for that. All the available facts suggested a failed murder attempt on Jonah's part. Cellphone company records showed that, shortly before Costa's arrival, the stricken man had tried to call his partner Tom Black from Vogel's apartment, presumably seeking help. That was speculation, though. Black had disappeared completely the evening his partner died. Kelly had let it be known to Catherine Bianchi that he thought the man was probably out of the US already. There were huge black holes in the Lukatmi accounts. The money was there to fund some covert flight from the country, enough to last a lifetime if Black was smart enough to keep his head down and choose the right distant location.

Quattrocchi's theory was, predictably, one the media was growing to love. Jonah and Black had hatched the plot to hype *Inferno*, employing Vogel as their legman. A phoney passport recovered from the wreckage in the photographer's apartment had a stamp proving he'd flown to Rome one week before Allan Prime died, and left the day after. The picture snapped by the furious women in the cemetery clearly revealed Vogel to be the man who had removed the almonds that nearly killed Maggie Flavier. Josh Jonah and Tom Black had enough access to security arrangements to provide Vogel with the means by which Maggie might be poisoned. His job as a paparazzo had proved the perfect cover to follow her afterwards. Records in Rome showed that he had also managed to obtain media accreditation there using his forged passport, giving him the opportunity to enter the restricted area by the Casa del Cinema and replace the genuine death mask of Dante with the fake one taken from Allan Prime that morning. Quattrocchi's team had, in what Falcone declared a rare moment of investigative competence, discovered that Vogel's alias was in an address book belonging to Peter Jamieson, the actor who had died in the uniform of a Carabinieri officer at the Villa Borghese. It seemed a logical step to assume that Jonah had recruited the man to scare Maggie Flavier, perhaps as a way of distracting the police from Allan Prime, perhaps calculating, too, that his act might provoke a violent response the unfortunate Jamieson had never expected.

The case remained open. Tom Black was still at large. There was still no sign of the woman calling herself Carlotta Valdes. Moreover, from the point of view of the state police, the genuine death mask of Dante was still missing, and causing considerable internal ructions with the museum authorities in Italy. But a kind of conclusion had been reached in terms of Allan Prime's murder. As far as Quattrocchi was concerned, nothing else really mattered. Jonah had used the cycle of Dante's numbers as a code for his attacks on those associated with the production, knowing that this fed the idea the movie was either somehow cursed or stalked by vengeful Dante fanatics seeking to punish those associated with the perfidious Roberto Tonti. It was all a desperate publicity stunt, though one engineered by those in Lukatmi, not within the movie itself. It had worked too. *Inferno* was on every front page, every news bulletin.

The pace of the investigation – one which had hung on the assumption that yet one more attack lurked around the corner – had slackened as the principal focus moved to the financial mess inside Lukatmi. They were now one day away from *Inferno*'s world premiere at an open-air screening for a select audience by the Palace of Fine Arts. Once that had occurred without incident, the cast and crew would begin to wind down by the weekend, handing over security arrangements entirely to the private companies. For Costa and his colleagues Italy would beckon.

Maggie Flavier had left innumerable messages imploring him to visit. He'd made a series of excuses, some genuine, some less so. In the hectic aftermath of the deaths of Jonah and the paparazzo Vogel, Costa had come to realize that he was beginning to miss Italy, miss Rome more than anything, with its familiar sights, the sounds of the street, the easy banter in cafes, the warm, comforting embrace of home. San Francisco was a beautiful, interesting and cultured city, but it could never be his. Rome was part of his identity, and without it he felt a little lost, like Maggie Flavier trying to find herself in the long-dead faces of the women in the paintings in the Legion of Honor. A movie was a temporary caravan, always waiting to disperse. If she came to Rome for some sequel she would be there six, nine months, perhaps no more. And then . . .

Life was temporary, and its briefness only given meaning by some short, often clumsy attempt to find permanence within the shifting sands of one's emotions. He knew that search would never leave him. He knew, too, that Maggie Flavier would struggle to feel the same way, seeking as she did character after character, personality after personality, through the constant round of work.

'I can't believe you're not even up to an argument over this,' Teresa complained, jolting him back to the present.

'We could be home in a few days. I'd like that. Wouldn't you?'

She screwed up her face in an awkward, gauche expression.

'Not yet. Not till it's over.'

'You just told me I was wrong to think there was more to this case than Gianluca Quattrocchi would have the media believe.'

'No. I merely said your supposition for the existence of a third party in Martin Vogel's apartment was difficult to prove. I do wish cops would listen more carefully sometimes.'

A familiar sly smile appeared.

'May I remind you of some things we do know? One chief suspect is missing. Thanks to the gigantic amount of publicity this has generated, a stack of money has been thrown up in the air and no one knows where it's going to fall. And you don't have your precious mask.'

Two points he appreciated. The third puzzled him.

'What do you mean about the money?'

'You should talk to Catherine Bianchi more. She has a firm grasp of finance. How you go about backing companies like Lukatmi. She even seems to understand how to raise money for movies, as much as anyone outside the business can.'

He watched the private security guards working on the installation of CCTV cameras on the nearest tent. The place was covered with the things. There were enough cameras to catch a squirrel sneezing out of turn. But the tempo of the investigation had changed. It felt . . . if not over, then more manageable, at least to some.

There was a minor commotion. Roberto Tonti strode through the door of the tent followed by Dino Bonetti speaking in low, confidential tones by his side. Bonetti didn't look his usual bouncy, arrogant self. This was surely going to be the most extraordinary and potentially lucrative opening he had ever produced. The newspapers were talking about a posthumous Oscar nomination for Allan Prime. The industry rags were predicting that *Inferno* could be the first movie to break the two-hundred-million-dollar weekend gross at the box office when it went nationwide.

Perhaps it was the strain, but neither man looked like someone on the verge of breaking every entertainment industry record in the book.

- 2 -

The two brothers stood at the entrance to the main hall of the Lukatmi building at Fort Mason. Removals trucks and bulky individuals in blue overalls appeared to be gutting the place. Furniture and phones and computer equipment were disappearing out of the door at an astonishing rate.

There was a supervisor by the entrance, his rank emphasized by the fact that he was so weedy he couldn't lift a thing except the clipboard in his hands. Hank Boynton went over and tapped the man on the arm.

'Didn't these guys own *anything* themselves?'

'Maybe a paper clip here and there. But we're taking those anyway. This place stinks of rotten debt. I'll have anything that's not nailed down.'

'The cops won't like that,' Frank suggested.

'The cops are in building two where all the accounting and e-mail stuff got kept. We're just taking the dweeb items they used to mess around with while they were pretending they were Fox or something.'

'Computers . . .' Hank said.

'*Work stations*,' the man emphasized.

'I was gonna ask if you had one going cheap,' Frank intervened. 'Not so interested now.'

'Can I help you, sirs?' he asked, and not nicely.

Hank pulled out his old ID from the station.

'We're safety officers here on an official visit. We'd like to check for fire hazards from any stray discarded pony-tails left behind after the train wreck. You know the kind of thing. Just routine.'

The man eyed the card and said, 'That thing's nearly a year out of date. There's got to be some law about impersonating a city official. Isn't there a bingo parlour or somewhere you two could go and while away the hours?'

Frank put his broad muscular arm around the little man's shoulders and squeezed a touch.

'You know,' he confided, 'I could say you'll live long enough to feel old and useless one day. But maybe I'd be lying. We're looking for a friend who quit the Fire Department for the joyous pastures of private enterprise. Jimmy Gaines. He did security here. We'd like to commiserate with him on the sad and premature loss of his stock options. Find him and we go away. Try to pretend we don't even exist . . .'

He caught Hank's eye, removed his arm from the supervisor, and said, 'Slip me some skin, bro.'

Then the two of them grazed knuckles and made rapper-like noises.

Mr Clipboard watched, looking worried.

'Folks keep going on about the young people these days,' Frank told him. 'Why? It's the old guys they got to worry about.'

The removals man walked into the front vestibule and yelled, 'Is there someone here called Gaines?'

To everyone's relief a sprightly upright figure in a dark uniform which contrasted vividly with his bright, bouncy grey hair emerged. He looked in their direction then started to dance up and down with glee.

'The old days,' Jimmy Gaines squealed as he came to greet them. 'It's like the old days.' He hesitated. 'Are they cleaning that engine good and proper yet? Like we used to?'

'Stop living in the past, you stupid old man,' Frank ordered. 'Our fire department days are over.' He watched the clipboard guy barking at his brutes to hurry up stripping the building. 'What the hell are you supposed to be guarding anyway, Jimmy? This place is going to be bare in an hour or so.'

'Nothing,' Gaines replied, setting up a brisk pace away from the military hall that had once been home to Lukatmi. 'Come round

233

the corner. There's a cafe. A real one. No pony-tails any more. No geeks or people drinking crushed wheat grass. If it was later and I didn't have a uniform I'd buy you a beer.'

'Coffee will do,' Hank said quietly.

'You look serious,' Gaines declared, as he cut behind the building, heading for a small door with the sign of a coffee cup above the threshold.

'We need to give a nice Italian lady a present,' Frank said as the brothers struggled to keep up.

'Chocolates,' Gaines suggested. 'I'm told they come with a guarantee.'

Hank caught up with him and placed his hand on Gaines's arm. The man stopped and looked at them. They were alone now. No one could hear.

'We want to find her a better present than that, Jimmy. We want to hand her Tom Black.'

Jimmy Gaines gave them a hard stare.

'And I thought this was a social visit? There's half the SFPD looking for Mr Black. I tried talking to them but they looked so bored having an old fart like me wheezing away I gave up in the end. What makes you think you can find someone they can't?'

'Because six, maybe nine months ago,' Frank said, 'we saw you and Mr Black out together. Him looking at you as if he had stars in his eyes and all manner of that fancy exploration gear you love in the back of your station wagon. You looked like good friends going somewhere remote. Two and two going together the way they do . . .'

'Hiking,' Jimmy Gaines snapped. 'We both belong to the Sierra Club and a couple other things. You suggesting something else?'

'Not for a moment,' Hank insisted. 'You always did love the wild side of life. The great outdoors.' The Boynton brothers liked Jimmy Gaines, mostly, though not so much they wanted to see him more than a couple of times a year. 'I remember you reading Henry David Thoreau on those long, empty night shifts. Things like that stick in the memory.'

'If more people read Thoreau we wouldn't be in the shit we're in now. The simple life and a little civil disobedience from time to time. You boys ever take a look at *Walden* like I told you to?'

'I'm allergic to poison ivy and air that doesn't have a little scent of gasoline in it,' Hank confessed. 'Wild things don't agree with me. Was Tom a Thoreau fan too?'

'Damned right. *Walden* was his favourite book after I showed it him. He isn't a murderer either. Don't care what those stupid police say. That Jonah bastard . . . nothing would surprise me about him.'

'That's what we heard,' Hank said, urging him on.

'Tom's a decent human being. Just a little lost kid who had too much in the way of brains and money and too little in the way of a life. Didn't have an old man. His mom was half crazy. Did you know that? Did you read that in the papers?'

'I guess we didn't,' Frank replied.

'No. Kind of spoils the story, doesn't it? So what do you really want? I'm going off the coffee idea rapidly.'

'We want to find him,' Frank said. 'We want to know the truth. If it's what you think it is – and our Italian friend believes that too – we'd maybe hope we can help get him off the hook.'

He sucked in the chill marine air, then said it.

'So where is he, Jimmy?'

Gaines shook with fury. He was fit and strong for his age. Sometimes, when much younger, he had been a touch free with his fists in a bar after work. Most people wouldn't see that now. They'd just see an energetic old man with grey, grandfather hair. Age hid things sometimes.

'I don't know! Why would he tell me where he was going? I'm just an old security guard he used to talk to about the mountains and the woods. When he wanted some new place to go usually. He liked being on his own. Poor kid thought he was soft on that actress woman for a while, not that *that* was ever going to go anywhere. She was a piece. Lead him on. Drop him gently at the door. Tom never should have got mixed up with that Hollywood crowd in the first place.'

Hank and Frank looked at one another.

'We need you to talk to us about those places you showed him,' Hank said.

Gaines nodded in the direction of the great red bridge along the bay and the wooded Marin headlands beyond.

'Why? You think he's up there somewhere? Scared and hungry and him a billionaire only four days ago?'

Frank folded his arms.

'I don't think he's in Acapulco. Do you?'

Jimmy Gaines swore, then screwed his eyes shut with fury.

It took a while before he looked at them again.

'It was Josh Jonah, all on his own, I swear it. Tom was just a starstruck idiot. He didn't understand the first thing about money. He actually believed all that new world crap Lukatmi used to spout. The kid's got one side of the brain as big as a house and the practical part missing in action.'

'We're sorry, Jimmy,' Hank apologized. 'Truth is you can insure against anything these days except stupidity, can't you?'

Gaines stared at them and asked, 'Insurance? What the hell are you talking about?'

'You know exactly what we're talking about,' Frank interrupted. 'Sorting this thing out once and for all. Please. Just tell us where to look.'

There was a short, unpleasant moment of laughter. Then . . .

'Yeah? *Yeah?* I remember you two struggling to find a simple house in the street back when we were working together and it was going up in flames.' He stripped off his jacket. He was still a big man, all muscle under the cheap white security guard shirt. 'This was my last day anyway. I guess I get to leave early. You two got good boots?'

Hank and Frank looked at each other.

'Just the old ones from the station,' Hank confessed.

'Best go get them. And something for poison ivy. Where we're headed things bite.'

– 3 –

Costa and Teresa Lupo got two cups of foul coffee from the food truck then went and sat on a bench by the lake in front of the Palace, listening to the ducks arguing, glad to be away from the ill-tempered crowd.

'Here's something to think about,' Teresa declared as she sat down. 'Josh Jonah told anyone willing to listen, including the papers, that fifty million dollars of Lukatmi money went into *Inferno*.'

'I know that.'

'Good. Well it's not there.'

He wondered why she was surprised.

'They've spent it, surely.'

'No. The SFPD can't find any proof much Lukatmi money went into the movie in the first place. All they can track is a measly five million in the production accounts at Cinecittà. The rest of it doesn't exist. Not in Rome anyway. They've located some other odd currency movements out of Lukatmi, substantial ones into offshore accounts, in the Caribbean, South America, the Far East. But not to Rome. Not to anything that seems to go near any kind of movie production. They think that was just Josh Jonah thieving the bank to put something aside for a rainy day.'

Costa found himself wishing he understood the movie industry better.

'If they didn't have the money how did the thing get finished? What did they pay people with?'

She shrugged.

'I don't know. Bonetti's the lead producer and he refuses to discuss the matter with the Americans. He says it's none of their business. Strictly speaking it isn't. *Inferno* got made by committee. A string of tiny production companies, all set up specifically for the purpose of funding the movie, all based in places where the accounting rules tend to be opaque. Cayman. Russia. Liechtenstein. Gibraltar. Even Uzbekistan.'

He couldn't believe what he was hearing.

'The company was Italian,' he insisted. 'I saw the notepaper. I saw the name on the posters. Roberto Tonti Productions.'

'Tonti put up half a million dollars to assemble a script, a cast and a budget. That's all. The real money came from ordinary investors, the mob, supposedly Lukatmi, God knows where else. We'll never find out. Not unless the offshore banking business suddenly decides to open itself up to public scrutiny.'

Costa tried to make sense of this.

'Someone must have paid the bills at Cinecittà. They couldn't have worked for six, nine months or so without settling at least some of what was owed.'

She grinned.

'Catherine says Bryant Street have checked through the Carabinieri in Rome. The urgent bills were settled by all those little co-production companies. One from Liechtenstein would handle catering, say. One from Cayman would pick up special effects. I'd place a bet on that being how the mob money got there. They like these places. None of it came from Lukatmi direct, and the Lukatmi accounts show just that five million I told you about going into the production to pay two months' studio fees at Cinecittà. Nothing more.' She paused. 'And for that they got exclusive world electronic distribution rights and stacks of publicity. Something that ought to have been worth, well, not fifty million dollars, but maybe twenty-five.'

Teresa had a habit of springing information on people this way.

'Why's Catherine confiding all this to you? Not Leo?'

'Because Leo, being Leo, is utterly fixated on this idea that the real story lies in that rotten money from the men in black suits. He's not the world's greatest listener, in case you never noticed. I am. Also I think Catherine likes stringing him along, on a couple of fronts. He's getting nowhere with her and it's driving him crazy.'

'Ah.'

Costa had gathered this from watching the two of them together. He'd never seen Falcone fail to get something he wanted in the end. It was an interesting sight, and an experience the man himself clearly found deeply frustrating.

'Enough of Leo,' Teresa went on. 'Here's something else . . . Josh Jonah *hated* old movies.'

'How can you possibly know that?'

'He told everyone! In a million media interviews. Anything that wasn't invented in this bright new century of ours simply didn't matter to him. There are three long articles a couple of friends tracked down for me. In them he gets asked to name his favourite movies of all time. They're all the same stupid, violent, computer-generated crap that passes for entertainment these days. Not a human emotion in any of them. No *Citizen Kane*. No Eisenstein. Nothing Italian. I doubt he'd even heard of Hitchcock.'

The director's name conjured up the cartoon image of the man, side on, lips protruding, and that funny old theme tune he'd heard so often on the late-night reruns put out by the more arcane Italian channels.

'If he'd never heard of Hitchcock, who invented Carlotta Valdes?' Costa asked.

'Who sent Maggie Flavier a green 1957 Jaguar?' Teresa replied. 'And told Martin Vogel to pick some bitter almonds from a tree next to that fictional grave at Mission Dolores?'

She turned round and pointed to the huge white mansion across the road that was the home of Roberto Tonti.

'He knows all about Hitchcock. So does Bonetti. His first movie in Italy was a cheap Hitchcock knock-off. Simon Harvey knows too. Maybe there's a movie fan among those mobsters Bonetti tapped for cash.'

'The Carabinieri say it's over.'

'We can argue about whether this was all about Dante. Or a bunch of Sicilian money from some people who were starting to feel they've been taken for a ride. Or a movie an old English director made here – *here* – half a century ago. But there's one thing even Leo can't argue about . . .'

Teresa watched him, waiting.

'Josh Jonah didn't know about any of these things,' Costa said.

'He could – and probably did – fix that awful snuff movie that made Lukatmi so much money when Allan Prime died. But that's about it,' she agreed. 'Whoever started this circus is still out there. Maybe they're going to go quiet now the SFPD want to lay the blame at the door of a dead computer billionaire. Maybe they feel the publicity they've got is enough. Maybe not.'

She looked at him.

'So what are you going to do now? Every case is unpacked. Every item accounted for.' She nodded towards the tents. 'You're surely not needed in there and you know it.'

He'd been warned to steer clear of Maggie Flavier, by both Gerald Kelly and Falcone, who was concerned that whatever little cooperation they could still count on from the SFPD was about to disappear.

'I'm supposed to behave myself.'

'Call her, Nic. Go and see her. No one's going to miss you. Even Leo and Peroni don't feel the need to hang around this place. Why should you?'

He hadn't been able to get Maggie out of his head for days. That was why he had hesitated.

Teresa reached into his jacket pocket, pulled out his phone and dangled her fingers over the buttons.

'Don't make me do this for you,' she warned.

– 4 –

It was almost three in the afternoon by the time Jimmy Gaines parked his station wagon in the Muir Woods visitor centre and pointed them up the hiking route signposted as Ocean View Trail.

'It all keeps coming round,' Hank said as he tied on his old fireman's boots. 'You ever watch *Vertigo*, Jimmy?'

'Couple of times.'

'Some of it was shot here. They give her a famous line. "I don't like it . . . knowing I have to die." '

'One more folk myth,' Frank cut in. 'Hitch shot that somewhere else.'

The two men turned and looked at him.

'You sure of that?' Jimmy Gaines asked. 'All them big sequoias. I'd assumed . . .'

'It's the movies,' Frank insisted. 'I've been reading up on things. The buffs call that part "the Muir Woods sequence" now. So I guess that's what it is. But it wasn't filmed here, I can promise you. It was shot at Big Basin, eighty-odd miles south. Hitch liked the light better apparently.' He watched Gaines pulling on a backpack with three water bottles strapped to the outside. 'Did Tom Black like *Vertigo* too?'

Gaines heaved some gear out of the car.

'Not that I know. He never talked about movies much. Just books. Thoreau a lot. *Walden* more than anything. All that stuff Tom used to spout to the media about how we could build a different world, one in tune with nature, with no real government and some kind of weird pacifism when it came to dealing with authority . . . it

241

came from Thoreau. That old crazy wasn't just a tree-hugger you know. He was an anarchist too.'

He stared into the forest of gigantic redwoods ahead of them.

'I never much liked to talk to Tom about that side of things. He was so young and naive there wasn't much point. Josh Jonah was the opposite, except when he wanted to appear that way to keep Tom happy. Just some money-happy creep. Josh liked movies where people died. We had a brief conversation about *The Matrix* once. When I told him I couldn't figure which way was up he looked at me like I was brain-dead and we didn't talk movies or much else ever again.' He stopped and scratched his grey mop of hair. 'Why are we talking about Hitchcock?'

'I don't know,' Hank confessed. 'It's just some crazy theory our Italian friend has. You know what Europeans are like.'

'Not really.'

They steered clear of poison ivy and listened in silence as Jimmy Gaines talked as they walked, mostly to himself, about the forest around, the redwoods and tan oak, the madrone and Douglas fir.

Frank Boynton caught his brother's eye after half an hour and knew they were both thinking the same thing. Or rather two things. This didn't seem the kind of place a fugitive would hide. The Muir Woods were popular. At weekends and on holidays, the paper said, it could be difficult to find a space in any of the parking lots dotted around the park.

And Jimmy Gaines looked like a man who knew where he was going.

After a while he diverted them into a side path deep in the thickest part of the wood. Frank glanced at the sign at the fork: they were on the Lost Trail.

It seemed well named. They began to descend through solitary tracts of fir that merged into thicker forest. The sun was so scarce the temperature felt as if the season had changed. For some reason, that line of Kim Novak's refused to leave Frank Boynton's head.

After what seemed like an hour of punishment Jimmy Gaines took them off the barely visible established path and led them directly into the deep forest where there was no discernible track at all. They stumbled down a steep mossy bank, further and further into the dense thickets where the redwoods stood over them like ancient giants. Gaines's eyes flickered constantly between the dim path ahead and a small GPS unit in his hand.

'They got animals here?' Frank asked.

'Chipmunk and deer mainly,' he said without turning round. 'Snakes. Lots of snakes. Don't believe the stories you hear about mountain lion. They're close but not that close. Too smart to come near humans mostly. We got ticks that carry Lyme disease. Rat shit with Hantavirus. Some of them mosquitoes might have West Nile Virus too.'

He stopped and watched them standing there, uncertain where to put their feet.

'Where's your insurance now, boys?' Gaines asked oddly, then checked something on the GPS unit. 'That's why no one's supposed to stay here after dark. It's dangerous in the wild woods. I thought you might have appreciated that.'

Gaines removed his backpack, pulled out the water bottles and handed two over. The Boynton brothers gulped greedily, watching him all the time.

'Doesn't feel like we're wandering around aimlessly,' Frank said. 'If I'm being honest.'

Gaines shook his head.

'You boys always were too clever for your own good, weren't you? Too greedy too. You just had to know what was going on.' He swigged at his own water bottle and eyed the dark, sheer trunks of the redwoods around them. 'I remember one time when there was a fire in some little baker's on Union. You two weren't even on duty. Didn't stop you coming round and watching, telling us what we were doing wrong while you stood there looking all censorious and stuff from the pavement.'

He opened up the backpack and took out a large handgun, old, with a revolving chamber. A Colt, maybe, Frank thought. He was never great at weapons.

The Boynton brothers' former colleague from the San Francisco Fire Department pointed the barrel in their direction and said, 'Tom and I are a little more than friends, truth be told. He's a good man. I never had a son. Never had a wife either. Just like you two.' He leaned forward and grinned, a little bashfully. 'Didn't you ever wonder?'

'Yeah,' Frank said straight away. 'But we didn't think it was any of our business. Still isn't. What's with the gun, Jimmy? We've known each other thirty years or more. You don't need that.'

There was a noise from behind them. Frank Boynton didn't turn to look. He wasn't going to take his eyes off Jimmy Gaines and the weapon in his hands, not for anything.

A dishevelled figure stumbled down through the high ferns of the bank by their side. Tom Black looked a mess. Like some street bum who'd been homeless for a good while, not a fugitive ex-billionaire who'd kept the company of movie stars only a few days before.

'Mr Black,' Frank said extending his hand. 'My brother and I are here to help.'

The young man turned and looked at Jimmy Gaines, fear and desperation in his eyes. And deference, too. Maybe Jimmy bossed him around in the open air the way Josh Jonah had inside Lukatmi's grim brick fortress by the water at Fort Mason.

'You got food?' was all Tom Black asked.

Gaines threw him the backpack.

'I showed you how to find things to eat in the woods,' he said, sounding cross. 'I can't be here for you all the time, Tom. That would just make them all suspicious.'

'Can't stay here all the time, either,' Hank cut in. 'Sooner or later you've got to come out.'

The young man ripped into a pack of trail mix, poured some into his throat and looked at them unpleasantly, as if they weren't quite real.

'What if we could make it sooner?' Frank added. 'What if we could make it safe?'

Black glanced at Jimmy Gaines, seeking some lead.

'Take their phones and throw them in the forest,' Gaines ordered. With his left hand he retrieved some rope out of the rucksack. 'Then tie them up good and tight.'

– 5 –

The apartment block was old and elegant and hauntingly familiar. Costa parked outside the grand entrance and talked his way past the uniformed concierge at the door. There was money on Nob Hill. History too. The connection came to him as he stood in the lift, waiting to get to the third floor where Maggie's apartment was situated.

Madeleine Elster had lived in this same block in the movie. He could recall the detective Scottie watching her leave the forecourt in a green Jaguar, identical to the one some unknown stranger had briefly loaned Maggie Flavier. Not that the Madeleine Scottie had known was quite who she seemed.

He went through a cursory ID check when he reached the floor – the movie company's security men were all flash suits and earpieces and very little in the way of brains – and she let him in.

Maggie looked as if she'd come straight from the shower. She was wearing a bright emerald silk robe and nothing else. Her blonde hair was newly dried and seemed to have recovered its gleaming sheen. It was still short, without the extensions that had caused his heart to skip a beat at the Palace of Fine Arts. She looked incredibly well, as if she'd never had a day's illness in her life.

'I wish you'd come when I asked,' she said. 'No need to explain. Help yourself to a drink, will you?' She pointed at the kitchen. 'I've got a vodka. I need to dress.'

He watched her walk into the bedroom and close the door. Then he found some Pellegrino in the refrigerator, returned with it and stood in front of a marble fireplace and the largest TV screen he'd ever seen, one that seemed to occupy much of the opposite wall. The place wasn't as big as he'd expected. A part of him said movie stars needed to live somewhere special, somewhere different. From what he could see there was just the one living room, a kitchen, the bedroom on the inner side of the building, away from the noise of the street, and a shining stone and steel bathroom next to it.

When she returned she was wearing a short, loose-pleated skirt, the kind he associated with teenage cheer-leaders at sports matches, and a polo shirt with the number seven on the front. No make-up, no pretence, no borrowed character from an old canvas in a museum. She looked little more than twenty.

'How long have you lived here?' he asked.

'For ever. My mother found it not long after we came from Paris. We rented back then. Not that she could afford it. There were . . . standards to be maintained. If you read the bios they'll tell you she spent our last thousand dollars trying to find me a break. That's not quite true. Not quite.'

'So that's . . . what? Ten, fifteen years ago?'

'Seventeen years in October. I remember how warm and sunny it was when we arrived. I thought San Francisco would always be like that. You should come in the autumn. It's beautiful. Different. What you'd expect of the summer.'

'You don't know how she found it?'

She shook her head and ran her fingers through the ragged blonde locks.

'No. Why should I? It was a good choice. When she was gone and I had the money I bought the apartment. It's just a one-bedroom bachelor-girl pad. I'm not here more than two or three months of the year anyway.'

'And when you're travelling?'

'Then the agency rents it. I hate the idea of an empty home. A place should be lived in. Why are you asking all this?'

'I've seen it before. This apartment block. It was in a movie.'

'It was?' she asked, wide-eyed, curious.

'*Vertigo*. Hitchcock.'

Maggie closed her eyes and fought to concentrate. Then she opened them, picked up her cocktail glass from the table and gulped at it.

'No. I don't think I've seen it. I know the name, of course. Hitchcock isn't really that fashionable to be honest with you, and a person in my position needs to know what's in and what's out. No one's going to give you any credit for name-dropping that one.'

'The woman in it lived here. She died. In the end.'

Maggie held out her drink in a kind of toast.

'Women in movies often do. You should congratulate me by the way. Dino Bonetti came round earlier to offer me the part of Beatrice in the sequel.'

'Did you sign?'

'What, on a social visit? I don't think so. All that stuff goes through Simon and then my agent.'

'Do they take a cut?'

She laughed, exasperated.

'This is show business. Everybody takes a cut of everything. I feed thousands . . .'

'How much?'

She hesitated.

'You're very curious. I don't know. I don't really want to. They put together some deal, I sign it when I'm told. Money goes in the bank.' Her eyes darkened. 'At least it's supposed to. Apparently I'm missing something from *Inferno*. My accountant was whining about something or other. It's no big deal. I'm . . .' She threw a hand around the room. '. . . rich, aren't I? After the first couple of million you stop counting. If there's a sudden hiccup I guess I can still do a hair ad. I'm not proud.' She hesitated. 'Why are you looking at me like that?'

'There's money missing in the production company accounts. A lot. And you haven't been paid?'

'Not everything. It's not the first time. Sometimes it takes months. They wait for the exchange rates to get better or something. That's why I didn't want to waste any time talking to Dino when he started pressing me to sign a new contract. Why should I? They can't screw me out of what they owe me for *Inferno*. It looks like it's going to be the biggest-grossing movie I've ever made. I'll get what I'm owed.' She glanced at the window. 'I want to live to enjoy it too. Are we all still supposed to be on someone's hit list? I can't believe I still have those goons outside the front door.'

He tried to sound convincing. And convinced.

'I don't think so. It still makes sense to be careful.'

'No rides through the Presidio? No visits to strange art galleries?'

'Not for the moment.'

She stood a little closer. Her perfume was subtle and mesmerizing. She didn't look so young close up, and he liked that.

'I have to do the premiere tomorrow. Then launch some old movie festival in the city at the weekend. After that . . .' The glass bobbed up and down, a touch nervously. 'I have a villa for three weeks in Barbados. No one but me. Private estate. Nearest house half a mile away, and that staffed with waiters running a lobster-on-demand service. Is that safe enough for you?'

'I'd think you'd be fine.'

'What I meant was . . .'

Another edgy shot of vodka disappeared. She was coughing hard, her hand to her mouth. Her eyes were wide open again with astonishment. His mind began to race, recalling her terrible collapse in the park.

Maggie fell back on the sofa behind them. He was next to her instantly.

'Damned drink,' she swore, still struggling to speak. 'Went down the wrong way. Must break that habit. Tomorrow. Definitely. Wait, I forgot something, Nic. Dino Bonetti! That movie! *Vertigo!*'

'What?'

'The first time he came here. He told me to watch it. He recognized the location too.'

She looked at him.

'Now you're saying the same thing. What's going on here?'

Costa told her a little of Teresa's ideas, and how the woman who

249

had first approached Allan Prime introduced herself after a character in the movie.

She sat on the sofa, bare legs tucked beneath her.

'Well I guess it's time I followed everyone's advice. Will you watch it with me? I know you saw it once. I'd still . . .' She closed her eyes and looked exhausted for a moment. 'I've been on my own so much since all this craziness began. It's getting tedious.'

'Where's the movie?' he asked.

She picked up the phone, called someone, and ordered a DVD. 'It'll be an hour or so. Are you hungry?'

'Starving.'

'I can order some food too.'

He looked at the kitchen, without thinking.

'You want me to *cook*?' she asked, astonished. 'I do bacon and eggs. And I'm really not that good at it. Nic . . . ?'

He got up. Costa knew he needed activity, something that would take his mind off Dante Alighieri and Alfred Hitchcock, Dino Bonetti and the shattered corpse of Josh Jonah, prone on the floor of a rundown SoMa apartment block.

Maggie followed him and watched as he rifled through the drawers and cabinets.

'You have food,' he said. 'That's a start.'

'*Old* food. One of the rental people must have left it.'

He found a small envelope of dried *porcini*, a packet of Arborio rice, a couple of shallots in the vegetable rack along with a chunk of parmesan wrapped in foil. Five minutes later he had the makings of a risotto. It felt good to cook again. It felt even better to have Maggie Flavier leaning on the threshold of the door looking at him as if she'd never seen anything like this in her life.

'Any wine recommendations?' she asked, nodding at the floor-length chilled cabinet filled with bottles that looked a lot more expensive than anything he usually drank.

'I'll leave that to you.'

She opened the glass door, peered inside and pulled out a bottle. 'I brought this from Rome. Is it any good?'

He looked at the 2004 Terredora Greco di Tufo and said, 'It'll do. Can I leave you to lay the table?'

'Men!' she exclaimed, and went to the kitchen drawers where she removed a well-ironed tablecloth and some place settings.

'After that . . .' he shouted through the open door, '. . . we need some cheese grated.'

It wasn't the best risotto Costa had ever made. But he didn't want someone else's food. Not with her.

They ate and talked freely and frankly of nothing at all. Towards the end she looked at him and asked, 'Did you use to cook? For Emily?'

He had to force himself to remember. There was now a distance between the present and the past. Perhaps it was San Francisco. Perhaps it was Maggie Flavier. Or both. But he could now see the winter's nightmare with some perspective, could stand back from it and feel apart from the pain and despair it had brought.

'Sometimes. Sometimes she did. Emily wasn't a vegetarian. If I was working nights I'd come home occasionally and I could smell steak in the kitchen.' He looked at her. 'Or bacon and eggs.'

'Were you cross?'

Costa found the idea odd, almost amusing.

'Of course not. It was her home too.' He could picture the two of them together, inside the house near the Appian Way. 'It used to smell good, if I'm honest. If I ate meat . . .' He shrugged. 'But I don't. I didn't like the smoking much. She went outside for that. I never asked. It just happened.'

Maggie held up her hands.

'I won't smoke inside either. Promise.'

'It's your home,' he said, and tidied the plates, ready to remove them.

'No it's not. It's just somewhere I live from time to time. Did you think about it? Being together? Did you ever . . . question whether it was right?'

'Not once. Not for a second,' he said immediately. 'We had arguments. We saw things different ways. None of that mattered. I can't explain. It happened.' A flash of recollection, of a cold, hard winter's day by the mausoleum of Augustus, ran through his head. 'Then it was over.'

She reached out and touched the back of his hand.

'I could feel something. Your sadness. Outside that little children's cinema. Before we went inside. Before I even knew who you were. It was like something tangible.'

'Not good for a police officer.'

'I wouldn't worry about it. I'm freaky Maggie Flavier. I see things other people don't. Lucky them.'

He got up and started to take the plates.

'No,' she insisted. 'You cooked. I do the hard labour of loading the dishwasher. Sit. Make yourself comfortable. I can manage that.'

She went back into the kitchen. He walked to the bathroom and looked at himself in the mirror, wondering what he saw, what he felt.

When he returned she was tipping the video delivery man at the door. After that she put the disc in some machine by the fireplace and turned the TV on. They sat next to each other, opposite the gigantic screen. She picked up a couple of remotes. The curtains on the apartment closed themselves slowly, the light fell.

Costa was on her right, stiff, a little awkward. The black and white titles ran: the logo of the Paramount peak, the awkward, jarring music he had come to associate with the movie. Then a brutal close-up of a woman, zooming into her eye with a cruel, unforgiving honesty, monochrome turning to blood-red, a swirling vortex spinning out from the black, unseeing pupil.

He felt cold. He felt lost and he'd no idea why.

- 6 -

It got cold quickly in the woods. At least, Frank Boynton assumed the way he felt was due to the temperature of the out-of-the-way patch of the sequoia forest, not some innate primeval sense of dread on his part. He'd read more *noir* books than he could count, watched the entire school of movies in the field. He'd thought he understood a little about fear from all that dedicated study, but now he realized he was wrong. There was a world of difference between theory and practice. Reality was a lot less complicated. It also seemed to happen a lot more quickly. He could almost feel the minutes slipping away from them.

So he sat there in silence, thinking, seated on the damp, cold ground, his hands tied behind his back, like Hank's, the two of them bound together so securely there really wasn't much point in contemplating escape. He couldn't run as well as either of their captors even if it was a straight contest, without ropes, without a slippery dark forest where the light was fading and he hadn't a clue which way to turn.

The Muir Woods weren't the overrun tourist destination he'd believed, not in this part anyway. They felt vast and timeless and desolate, an army of identical redwood monoliths stretching towards a darkening sky in every unfathomable direction. A place where a man could lie dead for months on end and maybe never be found.

Jimmy Gaines and Tom Black had gone off to a small clearing. They'd been there a long time talking out of earshot. Making the odd call too. Frank could hear the distant electronic beep of a phone and envied the way it communicated so easily, so swiftly with the outside world.

If he could just find his own . . .

They'd be dead by the time anyone came. The idea of rescue was one confined to the pages of fiction. In the real world there was no escape, except perhaps through meek, obedient submission. The brothers had told Jimmy Gaines and Tom Black what they knew: a good Italian woman thought Tom was innocent and might be able to help if only he'd get in touch. Then she'd pass him on to a friendly cop who, for once, didn't come with a bunch of preconceptions about presumed guilt. Frank had taken the lead, as he usually did in such situations, offering to make the call for the two men, promising he'd do nothing to compromise their location, or Jimmy Gaines's identity.

They'd listened then gone away. Something in the way they walked hadn't filled him with optimism.

Frank wriggled to try to get a little more comfortable. He wished he could look at his brother eye to eye. He wished he could under-stand what might be going on in Hank's head. Closeness could make you deaf and blind to things that sensitive, observant people spotted instantly. Over the decades their relationship had settled into an easy, unspoken rhythm. Frank was the practical one, the right-brainer, as Teresa Lupo had so cannily noticed. He dealt with money and work issues and the day-to-day problems of keeping the house in the Marina going: bills and taxes, repairs and improvements. Hank was the dreamer, the would-be poet, more interested in the San Fran-cisco of yesterday than now, more obsessed with the cerebral puzzles of Conan Doyle than the gutter reality of Dashiell Hammett which Frank preferred. Neither had much real preparation for their present quandary. Sherlock Holmes and Sam Spade were myths, ghostly actors in tales that chose entertainment over mundane, prosaic reality.

There weren't any memorable ends when it came to men with guns. Not in the Muir Woods. Not anywhere. Jimmy Gaines, when he wanted, would simply walk over and pop them, one after the other, straight in the head as they sat, tied together in a place that stank of moss and rotting vegetation. From waking to dead all in one go. A jerk of the trigger was all it took. He'd been thinking of Jimmy a lot in the hour or so since Tom Black had appeared from behind the sequoias, like a lost forest creature in search of salvation. Jimmy Gaines taking them to bars where they didn't really feel comfortable and never thought to mention it. Jimmy Gaines swinging hard and viciously at a stranger who'd said the wrong thing, thought the wrong thought, looked the wrong way. All it had ever taken when they were younger was a misplaced glint in the eye.

Like the idiots they were, he and Hank had walked straight up to him at Lukatmi based on that single sighting of Gaines with Tom Black weeks before when they had, now Frank thought of it, seemed the very best of friends. That was the trouble with the Marina. It was a community, a little village full of smart, engaged, occasionally difficult people, all living on top of one another. It was hard to keep secrets. Jimmy Gaines, a solitary bachelor who quietly declined to go to some of the bars the other guys did after duty, had never really kept his. People were simply too polite – too uninterested, frankly – to mention it. So when a secret became big, became important, a man just passed it by like all the others. Familiarity didn't breed contempt. It bred a quiet, polite ignorance, a glance away at an awk-ward, embarrassing moment, a cough in the fist, then, after a suitable pause, a quick smile while glancing at the ground and formulating a rapid change of subject.

All of which led them to the Muir Woods with a line from an old movie that kept running and running and running round his head like some loose carnivore circling the big, dark forest of his imagin-ation.

I don't like it . . . knowing I have to die.

It was a general statement, not a specific one.

Hank's elbow nudged him in the ribs. He felt his brother's bristly cheek rub up against his.

'How are you doing?'

'Never felt better.'

'This is my fault. Sorry.'

Frank racked his brain to work out where that had come from. They'd both decided to help Teresa once she told them about how useful Tom Black might be if he could only be found. They both liked the idea of delivering the young man as some kind of gift to her. She was fun. And Italian. She deserved a present.

'No need to apologize. We are jointly responsible for our own stupidity.'

Hank cleared his throat.

'May I remind you I am the junior, here?'

Frank so wished he could look his brother full in the face at that moment.

'By seven minutes, if you recall,' he pointed out, thinking it was a long time since they'd had this conversation. Maybe five decades or so.

'Seven minutes, seven years. It doesn't matter. It still makes me younger. Still makes you the old one. The serious one. The one who does things the way you do 'cos you think that's what's expected.'

They never argued. If there was cause for complaint they simply fell into silence and waited till the cloud lifted. It had worked this way for almost sixty years, since they learned to speak.

'So what?' Frank asked.

'So we're clever and stupid in different ways. Ordinarily I'd say you were the cleverer and me the stupider. But this isn't ordinary. Now is it?'

Tom Black and Jimmy Gaines were on the phone again. He was glad of that. They weren't taking any notice of the two old men they'd tied up next to a redwood tree.

'I am inclined to concur,' Frank said. 'Your point being?'

Hank shuffled round a touch more in his direction. Frank returned the favour. They could just about catch the corner of each other's eye, one left, one right.

'The point being,' Hank went on, 'whether this is a left-brain or right-brain situation. Whether it's one best handled by me.' The nudge in the ribs again. 'Or by you. And you think it's you. Because you're like that. No offence, brother. You are. That's fine.'

'Hank,' Frank said very calmly. 'This could be difficult. We might have a lot of talking to do. Talking's something best left to me. We've always worked that way.'

His brother shuffled against him, and there was anger and determination in that lone, bright eye.

'There you are wrong, brother. This is not about talking at all. Did they look remotely interested when you offered to call Teresa? Well, did they?'

He thought about this. He'd been a little scared when Jimmy Gaines had demanded her number. He just wanted to give the man anything he could if it kept that big old gun out of their faces.

Jimmy Gaines and Tom Black never asked them to do a damned thing once they had Frank's address book.

'No. They didn't.'

'Here's another thing,' Hank added. 'I can hear better than you these days, plus my good ear's beamed in on them. They weren't talking about Teresa. They kept using that cop's name, the one whose number she gave us. The good guy. Seemed like Black knew who he was already.'

'That's good.'

'No it isn't. That Italian guy doesn't know us from Adam.'

He felt scared again. Very.

'Listen to me, Frank. I'm telling you what's going on now. I don't know who they've called already but pretty soon they're going to call the Costa guy. Then Tom's going to go to see him and cut some kind of a deal. You know the thing. You read it a million times in all that stupid pulp fiction of yours. *I didn't know what was going on, officer. I just got scared and ran away. I got your number some time. You seemed a nice, gullible guy.*' He took a deep, wheezy breath. 'Whatever. And then . . .'

Hank's single eye peered at him. He marvelled at the fact he'd learned more new stuff about his twin brother this last week than at any time in the last twenty years.

'Then it's just Jimmy Gaines and us,' Frank replied. 'And us

257

knowing that was all a pile of crap, and that he was in there with them too, which Costa won't get told because Jimmy Gaines doesn't want to go to jail, not for anybody.'

'You old guys,' Hank muttered with some sly amusement. 'You get there in the end. Just listen to your little brother and do what he says.'

'OK,' Frank said, and was amazed how odd the word sounded.

'Good. They're working out their story. Their plan. Pretty soon Tom Black's going to make that final call then get out of here. After that Jimmy Gaines is going to walk over, say a brief apology, and blow our brains out.' He sighed. 'Or so he'd like to think.'

Frank Boynton watched his brother's lone eye wink the way it did when they were children.

'Good job the stupid, head-in-the-sky kid brother had the gumption to bring a knife, huh?' Hank asked lightly.

After that Frank didn't say a word. He stayed still and silent, hustling up a little closer to his brother so that the two men locked in conversation by the trees didn't get suspicious about what Hank was doing with his hands.

A little while later they heard Tom Black make one more call, and the name Costa came into that. It didn't last long. Then he left without once looking back.

Jimmy Gaines stayed by the big redwood and lit a cigarette. He smoked it slowly.

At least he seemed a little reluctant. Frank Boynton gave him that.

- 7 -

Vertigo lasted just over two hours. They watched in silence, Costa upright, Maggie reclining, her head on his shoulder, hair brushing against his mouth, sweet and soft and full of memories of another. They had nothing to say, nothing to share except the same sense of fearful wonder watching what was taking place on the screen, a fairy tale for adults imagined long before they were born.

The day started to die beyond the curtains. The lights in the streets and adjoining buildings began to wake for the evening. He scarcely noticed much except the movie and the presence of the woman by his side, so close she was almost part of him, and equally rapt in the strange, disjointed narrative playing out in front of them, one which meshed with their identities and the city beyond in ways that seemed beyond any rational analysis.

Maggie let out a sharp, momentary gasp at the scene outside the Brocklebank, with the green Jaguar pulling away, Kim Novak at the wheel, made blonde by Hitchcock. Some parts made her shiver against him; Madeleine falling into the bay at Fort Point, not far from the Marina, and Scottie rescuing her, an act which was to establish the bond between them; again when she was wandering among the giant redwoods, lost, uncertain of her own identity; Madeleine in the Legion of Honor, facing the painting of Carlotta Valdes, seeming to believe this long-dead woman somehow possessed her own identity, in her hands a bouquet identical both to the one in the painting and to that left in Maggie's borrowed car.

Most all she was affected by what happened at the old white adobe bell-tower of San Juan Bautista, erect in a blue sky like some biblical monument to a warped sense of justice, the place where the real Madeleine fell to her death, and the woman who usurped her identity – and Scottie's love – followed in the cryptic, cruel finale.

Her eyes were wide with shock at that final act, unable to quit the screen. Together they watched Jimmy Stewart, tense and tragic, frozen in the open arch high above the mission courtyard, his own vertigo cured, but at a shocking price: the life of the female icon – not a real woman, in some sense – whom he'd come to love, obsessively, with the same voyeuristic single-mindedness with which Hitchcock himself pursued her through the all-seeing eye of the camera.

When the credits rolled she got up anxiously from the table and took her glass into the kitchen. She hadn't touched it all through the movie. Maggie came back, a fresh cocktail full of ice and lime and booze in her left hand, another glass of wine for him in her right.

'I need a drink after that,' she announced, and sat down, putting just a little distance between them. 'Don't you?'

He left the Greco di Tufo on the table and looked at her.

'I don't know what I need.'

Maggie gulped at the vodka, let her head drift back onto the sofa, rubbed her neck against the fabric, breathing deeply, rhythmically, as if to calm herself.

'What does it mean?' she asked, her green eyes suddenly alive with interest.

That question had never left him from the moment the spectral figure of Madeleine Elster walked across the screen, through a world that seemed so like the one they now inhabited.

'Perhaps what Teresa said all along. Someone, somewhere is using the movie as an analogy, a kind of template for what they're doing. A riddle, a reminder, a taunt . . . The way the Carabinieri think that Dante is being used. Maybe they're both right.'

There was a half-smile on her face, and an expectant look. Costa knew he hadn't said enough.

'There's nothing here that could possibly interest the SFPD. I'm a cop like them. We don't think along these lines. We don't watch movies for inspiration. Or read books of poetry. We do something real, something concrete and direct. It's all we know. If a case gets inside your head that's usually when it all starts to go wrong.'

There was another problem, though he didn't want to say it. There had to be more. Some link, some individual inside *Inferno* who was the catalyst. Whether what had happened was a simulacrum of *The Divine Comedy* or *Vertigo* – or both – some event, some conversation, perhaps recent, perhaps long forgotten, must have given life to the dark, convoluted story that began in the park of the Villa Borghese.

She moved closer again.

'Like it went wrong for Scottie? They said he was a good cop. He might have made commissioner of police. Then along comes a woman who isn't what she seems . . .'

'You could put it that way.'

'Nic.' Her green eyes shone with bright intelligence. 'I was really asking about the movie. What does *that* mean?'

'Next to a murder investigation? Nothing.'

She sighed, disappointed.

'What I wanted was for you to tell me about Scottie. About Madeleine. The woman he thought he loved, who didn't really exist. Then that sad little thing who did and was happy to pretend she was her simply because that was what Scottie wanted. That could make him happy, so that he would love her in return.'

'I don't know what it's about,' he confessed. 'It's supposed to be enigmatic. Art's not there to give you answers, not always. Sometimes it's enough simply to ask a question.'

'What question?'

He thought about Scottie and the way he looked at the woman he believed to be Madeleine Elster. How he'd undressed her while she was unconscious after rescuing her at Fort Point, and waited expectantly by his own bed as she woke, naked, beneath his sheets.

'I don't know,' he said, guessing, racking his head for answers. 'Questions about how Scottie can't extricate himself from his desire for Madeleine, even though a part of him knows it's not real. The way he's always following her, watching, thinking. Hoping. It's the pursuit of some hopeless fantasy. Like . . .'

He felt cold. He felt stupid. He felt more awake, more alive than at any time since Emily had died.

'It's like Dante's *Inferno*,' he said, and could feel the revelation rising inside him. 'Scottie and Madeleine Elster. Dante and Beatrice. It's the same story, the same pilgrimage, looking for something important, the most important thing there can be. The big answer. A reason for living.'

Costa shook his head and laughed.

'Why couldn't I see this before? *Vertigo* is *Inferno*. Just a different way of looking at the same question. Scottie . . . Dante . . . they're both just everyman looking for something that makes them whole. Some reason to live, beyond the mundane.'

'I don't like it . . . knowing I have to die,' Maggie Flavier said, quoting from the movie in the same quiet, lost voice, one so accurate she might have been the woman they'd just watched on the screen.

'Do you know what Simon told me once?' she asked in a whisper. 'When I asked him what *Inferno* was really about? Not the movie. The real thing.'

'What?'

'He said it was about knowing you never got to see the truth, to get a glimpse of God, until you're dead. That everything up to that point is just some kind of preparation, a bunch of beginnings. You live in order to die. One gives meaning to the other. Black and white. Yin and yang. Being and not being.'

She snatched at the glass.

'But none of it's up to us, is it?' she asked, and there was a quiet note of bitterness in her voice. 'That's for God and if we play *that* role we lose everything. Scottie tried it on for size, tried to make the woman he wanted out of nobody. In the end that killed her. A man's just a man. A woman can only be what she is.'

'What did you say? When he told you that?'

'I damn near slapped his face and told him not to be so stupid. I don't believe in anything except here and now. Don't ask me to trade that for some kind of hidden grace I only get when I'm dead. Don't ever do that.'

The blonde hair extensions he'd seen at the Palace of Fine Arts were there on a low coffee table. She picked them up and held them to her head. There was a movement in her eye, an expression she had somehow picked up from that photo in his wallet, something else he couldn't define because, unlike her, he'd never consciously noticed . . .

Instantly the associations rose for him, ones that were both warm and worrying.

She wasn't Emily. She could pretend to be, though. If he wanted.

'I'm just like the woman in the movie, aren't I? I can be anything you like. That's what I do.'

He felt uneasy, he wondered whether it was time to leave, whether that was even possible.

'Is that what you'd like, Nic? Would it make things easier?'

'I want you to be you.'

She threw the false hair onto the table brusquely as if she hated the things.

'That's very noble. What if I don't know who I am?'

'Then it's time to find out.'

'Doing what? Commercials? Too cheap. Theatre? I'm not good enough. Get them to revive *L'Amour LA* so I can stare into the camera one more time and say, "But 'oo can blame Françoise?"'

Her eyes were glassy. This was a conversation she both needed and feared.

'Or become one more suburban housewife who used to be something. Getting pointed at in supermarkets while I buy the diapers. Getting pitied. I don't think so.'

'Doing whatever you want.'

She took a deep breath, looked him in the eye and said, 'The only thing I want right now is you. I've wanted that ever since the moment I saw you in the park, looking lost and sad, not knowing who the hell I was and still wanting to help me, protect me, in spite of all that pain you had inside. That's never happened before.

263

Something so selfless. Not anything like it. And I've seen them all, Nic. The filthy rich, the astonishingly beautiful.' She pushed away the glass on the table. 'I've been drunk on this shallow little exist-ence since I was thirteen years old and it was only when I got to know you I realized I might as well have been dead. Or a creature from someone's imagination, like the woman who pretended to be Madeleine Elster.'

It had to be said. He couldn't avoid it.

'I'm just a Roman police officer going nowhere. I do what I do in the place that I know. That won't change. Not ever. That's me.'

'I know,' she replied, still staring at him. 'But that's not what scares you. *I* scare you. What you think I am. Some being from a different planet. Out of your reach.'

He felt the need for a drink and reached for the glass of Greco di Tufo. It tasted warm and a little too complex. There were cheaper wines he preferred. Cheaper places than this luxurious apartment in a city where he didn't belong. He'd lost track of time. He'd no idea where any of his team were, or whether they'd simply given up on him.

'I was never much interested in anything that couldn't last,' he said, and found he couldn't look at her when he spoke those words.

'Because of what I am?' she asked. 'Some perfect untouchable movie star? Listen to the truth.' She lifted her hands to her face. 'This is an accident and maybe not a lucky one. I'm the most flawed, most damaged human being you're likely to find. I've been off the rails more times than you could imagine. I've woken up in the wrong place, the wrong bed, so often I don't even have to blot out the memories any more, there are so many they do that for themselves. I'm weak and pathetic and stupid. Someone can even poison me with an apple. Remember? Without you I might be dead.'

'I remember.'

She got on her knees on the sofa next to him and hitched up her skirt.

'Does this look like perfection to you?'

The mark of the hypodermic pen was still livid on her thigh, darkening purple at its centre, yellow at the rim.

'If I was naked on a set with a million men pointing lights and cameras at my body they could cover that with make-up. It doesn't mean it isn't there.'

She took his head in her hands. Her eyes were wide open and guileless, her fingers felt as if they were on fire.

'I bruise, I bleed. I weep. I ache . . . I need. Just like you.'

His fingers reached and touched the mark on her leg. Her skin felt soft and warm, like Emily's, like anyone's.

She leaned forward, took his head more firmly, pulled it towards her.

Her breath was hot and damp in his ear.

'You can kiss it better if you want.'

His hand spread over her leg without a single, deliberate thought.

'Please,' she whispered.

Costa bent down and brushed his lips gently again the mark, then let his tongue fall to the warm flesh. She tasted of something sweet: soap and perfume. His fingers ran around her torso and felt the taut, nervous strength there.

Then he got off the sofa, picked her up in his arms and carried her into the bedroom. Her frantic kisses covered his neck, his face, her hands worked at his shoulders. Gently, he placed her slender frame on the soft white cotton coverlet. She looked at him, pleading in silence, unmoving, arms raised.

He removed her shirt with a slow, deliberate patience. She was naked beneath. Her hands tore anxiously at his clothes. Under the low orange lights of the bedroom they found each other, not seeing anything else, not caring.

There hadn't been many women in his life, and all of them had mattered. But not like this. Maggie Flavier sought something in him he'd never been asked for before, in ways that were new to him.

He lost count of the times they struggled with each other in the half-darkness on a bed so gigantic he couldn't hear it creak, however physical their efforts. There would never be a time, he thought, when he could forget these moments, the sight of her sighing beneath him. The gentle curves of her legs with their moist dark triangle at the apex, the dark corona of the areola of her breast as she arched above him, straining with a gentle insistence, seeking to prolong the sweetness between them.

Eventually Costa rolled to one side, closed his eyes, threw back his head against the deep pillow and laughed.

She was on her elbow at his side when he looked again, poking at him with a long fingernail.

'So it's funny, is it?'

'No. It's ridiculous.'

'I like the ridiculous. I feel at home there. So will you one day.'

She rolled over and looked at the bedside clock.

'It's nearly ten. What do we do now?' She ran a finger down his navel to his thigh. 'Chess?'

'I haven't played chess in years . . .' he began to say.

The phone rang from somewhere and he had to think about it.

His jacket was strewn on the floor with all his other clothes. He struggled to find it.

'Oh God,' she moaned. 'You really are a cop, aren't you? I suppose I should be glad this didn't happen ten minutes ago.'

'Or ten minutes before. Or ten minutes before *that*.'

Costa picked up the phone, sat down on the bed and said, without thinking, 'Pronto.'

'What?' asked a young, uncertain voice on the other end. 'Who is this?'

'I'm sorry. My name is Nic Costa. I'm Italian. I wasn't . . .' He glanced at Maggie who was upright with her arms folded, watching him with an expression of mock anger on her face. At least he thought it was mock. 'I wasn't thinking straight.'

'Please start, Mr Costa. I need your help.'

'Who are you?'

'My name is Tom Black and someone wants to kill me. Be at the viewing platform above Fort Point. Eleven on the dot. Be alone and for God's sake tell no one or I'm as good as dead.'

The call ended abruptly. Costa hit redial. The number was withheld.

'Who was it?' Maggie asked.

'He said he was Tom Black. Wants to meet me. The viewing platform above Fort Point.'

He'd seen the old brick fortress when they'd been sightseeing. The building was half hidden beneath the city footings of the Golden Gate Bridge, like some ancient toy castle discarded by a lost race of giants. It was there that Scottie had fished the supposedly suicidal Madeleine Elster out of the San Francisco bay. The spot seemed so remote and shut off by the great red iron structure above he'd no idea how it could be reached.

'How do I get there?'

'You don't,' she said very severely. 'You tell the police and let them do it. This isn't Rome.'

'I know that. Tom Black's no idiot. He won't come straight out and give himself up if he sees the police there. He's scared and he wants to talk. With me for some reason.'

'Nic . . .'

'If he disappears this time we may never see him again.'

She swore and gave him an evil look. Then she said, 'Get on 101 as if you want to go over the bridge. Just before you do there's a turnoff to the right with a parking lot.'

'How public is it?'

'You're right next to the Golden Gate Bridge. There'll be traffic.' She sat up in bed and hunched her arms around herself. Naked, she seemed smaller somehow, and vulnerable. 'But not much if you turn off the road, I guess.'

She took his hand.

'Don't go. Stay here with me. We can drink wine and play chess. Anything. I don't mind. Leave this to someone else.'

'Who?'

'Anyone. I don't care.'

He couldn't read the expression on her face.

The hot, human scent of sex hung around them, and that sense of both embarrassment and elation he'd come to recognize when life took a turn like this. It was about so much more than their exertions on these crumpled sheets. Something had changed in a subtle and mysterious way. The barriers were tumbling down, like leaves caught in an autumn storm. A part of him, he knew, wanted to run.

Costa gripped her fingers then kissed her damp forehead.

'Stay here. I'll call,' he promised.

- 8 -

Jimmy Gaines smoked three cigarettes by the redwood tree, none of them quickly. As darkness fell a waxy yellow half-moon began to emerge above the forest, and the dense wilderness became drowned in a cacophony of new sounds: birds and animals, insects and distant wild calls Frank Boynton couldn't begin to name. He and his brother watched everything like hawks. More than anything they sought to measure every breath of the man by the tree or perhaps, he reflected, they were simply counting away their own.

Without Gaines noticing, the two had talked together in low tones, about the lie of the land and the possibilities ahead of them. Somewhere at their backs they could hear motor vehicles passing through Muir Woods. Not many. This was a deserted part of the forest, and their number had diminished as day turned to night. But there was a road somewhere back there up the slope. Both men were sure of that.

In the opposite direction, downhill, beyond the sequoia trees looming opposite their captor, was, Hank said, a steep, sheer drop, one he'd seen as they arrived. Frank had never noticed. He'd been too worried by that stage to take much notice of anything except Jimmy Gaines. Now, though, thanks to his brother's unforeseen acuity, he could tell it was there by the way the just-visible foliage faded to nothing in the mid-distance, and from the faint sound of running water somewhere distant and below. There was a creek maybe. It was difficult to tell. Even more difficult as dusk disappeared altogether and gave way to the weak sheen of the moon, which fell lazily on the forest, placing dim shafts of light between the thick trunks of the sequoias, making the area beneath the high, dense tree cover seem even blacker than before.

Neither man felt at home in the forest. All they had between them were two small torches and some vague idea of where the road might be. That would have to be enough. If they could escape Jimmy Gaines and his old, black gun, they would head uphill, back towards the Lost Trail, then try to find headlights that might lead them back to the city and civilization.

If . . .

Frank was wasting time tossing this thought around when it began, so quickly he had no time to react or even much of an idea what to do.

Jimmy Gaines threw his last cigarette into the black space ahead of him where it disappeared like a firefly on speed, then came tearing towards them, swearing and stomping his big boots on the damp, mossy ground.

They could see in the flashes of moonlight that the big gun was low in his right hand. Soon Gaines was pacing up and down on the gentle slope of slippery moss and dirt in front of them, calling out every curse word under the sun.

'Why can't you keep your noses out of things that don't bother you?' the old fireman demanded after a while, when the language had calmed down a little.

The gun was in his right hand, dangling at forty-five degrees, halfway between the two of them. Hank had cut both their sets of ropes and left them there so Gaines wouldn't see what had happened. Frank wondered whether that mattered so much. A gun was a gun.

'We're sorry, Jimmy,' Frank said. 'We didn't know.'

'You still had to come looking!'

'Blame me,' Frank continued, nodding at his brother. 'Not him. He was never the brightest one. You know that. It was always me who got to you. You don't need to bring Hank into this.'

'Hank, Frank, Tweedledee, Tweedledum . . .' The gun was getting higher and starting to look more purposeful. 'You're both the same. What's it got to do with you anyway? What Tom Black and me get up to? He's a good guy. It was Josh who got him into all this shit. Josh and *them*.'

'What shit?' Hank asked straight out.

The gun rose and pointed at his head.

'There you go again,' Gaines moaned. 'Mouth on overdrive. I suppose you think I might as well tell you now it doesn't matter. All this movie shit. Those bastards from Hollywood who ate the two of them up and spat them straight out. They were doing OK when they just stuck to being computer geeks. Somebody would've come along and bought the company when the money ran out. They didn't need to move in those damned circles . . .'

The weapon wavered.

'It's got nothing to do with us,' Frank agreed, trying to sound calm. 'Our Italian lady said she could help Tom. That's all. So we thought maybe . . .'

Jimmy Gaines let out a despairing wheeze. The cigarettes weren't a good idea, not for a man of his age, however fit he thought he was.

'If they put Tom and me together we're done . . .' Gaines muttered, mainly to himself. 'I don't want to die in jail. I don't deserve that. I was just looking for a little security when I retired. That and a little companionship.'

'We won't tell them,' Frank insisted.

'We don't even know what's going on, do we?' Hank said meekly. 'We just thought we were doing your friend a favour, Jimmy. Isn't he going to see our nice Italian lady?'

'Never mind where he's going. None of your business.'

Frank thought about this.

'I couldn't agree more there, Jimmy. But she's going to think it's a little funny if we don't turn up for our regular coffee tomorrow morning. She's like us. Inquisitive.'

Gaines moved on the wet moss and a shaft of moonlight caught his face. It was taut, anxious, locked in something close to a snarl.

'As if I don't know you two. Always the smartasses. You wouldn't tell someone what you were doing before you went out and did it. Not if you thought you'd get some brownie points at the end when you turned round and said, "Look at us. Look at the Boynton brothers. Clever little bastards all over again." '

Jimmy Gaines bent down and leered in Frank's face.

'You didn't tell her where you were going, did you? Or any of this stuff. Admit it. You were always lousy liars. Don't try that on me. I've known you too long.'

'We didn't tell her,' Frank agreed. 'All the same . . . two and two.'

'Screw two and two. If Tom can get a few days free once he's spoken to the police that's all we need. We'll be gone. They say Laos is nice.' He grimaced. 'If that jerk Jonah hadn't locked up the money so tight we'd be gone by now anyway.' He laughed, not pleasantly. 'I owe you that, boys. You provided us with a way out. Just a pity . . .'

The gun arced through the air, from Frank to Hank and back again. To give the man his due, he didn't look keen on any of this.

'Tell you what. Let me do you one last favour. You choose who gets to go first. If you'd like . . .'

'Him,' Hank said straight away, nodding at his brother. 'He got to come into this world seven minutes before me. Only right I get to even things up a little.' Hank stuck his head up at the figure above them. 'Don't suppose I could claim those seven minutes back too, could I, Jimmy? I mean . . .' One more nod to his side. '*After* . . . We could talk.'

'What?' Frank bellowed with heartfelt outrage. '*What?* You're asking him to keep your miserable skin alive for seven minutes so you can *talk?*'

Hank screwed round trying to look at him.

'Would be downright stupid not to say something, brother. Given the circumstances and everything.'

Frank shuffled up against him, remembering not to disturb the loose ropes.

'He'd have just killed me!'

'So who else am I supposed to exchange my final words with?' Hank objected. 'The frigging chipmunks?'

'Generally speaking, chipmunks are only active by day,' Gaines pointed out. 'Too many predators at night. Also . . .'

'Shut up, Jimmy!' the Boynton brothers yelled in concert.

Gaines shuffled in his big forest boots.

'Maybe it wasn't fair of me to offer you a choice,' he said a little mournfully. 'I mean, it's not like I'm proud of this, you know. It's just . . . needed.' The gun swung towards Frank and Jimmy Gaines said, 'Oh hell . . .'

It was the loudest noise Frank had ever heard. Like a sonic boom that rang throughout the forest. Unseen creatures skittered across on the ground around them, crashing through the leaves.

Hank had caught Jimmy Gaines's shin hard with his foot as the weapon was coming round. More through luck than anything else, the gun was rising upwards, above them both, when the explosion came.

Frank guessed Jimmy Gaines wasn't really a gun type. The recoil on the old handgun seemed tremendous, and the upward forty-five-degree angle pushed it all back into Gaines's shoulder. The force bucked him away from them onto the slight slope towards the red-wood that had, until recently, been wreathed in his cigarette smoke. One stumbling step behind took over from another. Soon Gaines was running backwards downhill, arms flailing and cartwheeling through the air, old gun flying high into the moonlight, trying to stay upright, screaming and swearing until he finally toppled over.

The two brothers got up and watched, helpless. Momentum could be a terrible thing. He'd fallen past the lip of some projecting plateau in the forest floor and flipped over the edge like a tree trunk rolling downhill. In the gashes of wan light visible through the sequoia branches they could see Jimmy Gaines's body tumbling round and round on the moss and grass and rocks as the incline grew steeper and steeper, and the trees got more slender and scarce.

They stood together in silence. Then there was a long, solitary cry and Jimmy Gaines's fast-turning shape disappeared from sight altogether.

'Damn,' Hank muttered, and pulled out his little torch. The

battery was low. The light was the colour of the idle moon. Frank got his instead and ordered him to turn it off. They might need it later.

They held hands like children to make sure they didn't lose their footings, stepping gingerly down the slope towards the place where Jimmy Gaines had vanished.

After a little while Frank put out an arm to keep his brother back. The incline was turning too sheer. There was no point and they both knew it. Jimmy Gaines lay somewhere below, a long way, close to the tinkling waters of the creek that they could now hear very clearly. Frank doubted even a skilled mountain rescue party could reach him quickly in conditions like this.

He pointed his little torch back up the hill. They waited for a minute or two. Then there was the faint sound of some kind of vehicle and the flash of far-off headlights rounding an unseen corner.

'You walk carefully, little brother,' Frank Boynton said, still holding on to his arm. 'This has been a very eventful day.'

A loud and repetitive electronic beep burst out of the lush undergrowth beneath the beam of his torch, one so unexpected it made him jump with a short spike of fear.

'My phone,' Hank said. 'See. I told you there was a point to having different rings.'

The sound was so insistent they managed to find the thing almost immediately.

Frank picked it up, looked at the caller ID and said, 'Pronto.'

– 9 –

There were no other vehicles in the parking lot by the bridge. Costa got out and walked to the edge of the bluff overlooking the Pacific. Fifty years before, somewhere below, a fictional Scottie had seen Madeleine Elster fall into the ocean, diving in to save her, sealing his and her fate. The movie he'd watched with Maggie wouldn't leave his head. Or what had happened after.

In the distance to the right there were lights in the Marina and Fort Mason, where the Lukatmi corporation was now a corpse being dismembered day by day. Further along a vivid electric slur of illumination marked the tourist bars and restaurants of Fisherman's Wharf. A few boats, some large, bobbed on the water. It was the noise that took him aback, rising into the starry sky, the gruff, smoke-stained roar of a constant throng of vehicles on the highway behind. Their fumes choked the sea breeze rising over the headland, their presence almost blotted out the beauty of the ocean.

The Mediterranean couldn't compete with this scale. Maggie had been right that night she bit into the poisoned apple. In San Francisco the world felt bigger, so large one might travel it for ever without setting foot on the same piece of earth twice. This idea appealed to her. He found it strange and foreign. There was, and always would be, a conflict between two people like them, between his insistence on staring at a small, familiar place, seeking to know it – and by implication himself – better. And Maggie always fleeing, always looking to lose herself entirely in something vast and shapeless, to pull on any passing identity she could find before the next film, the next ghost, entered her life.

He climbed the steps of the viewing platform and stopped. Alcatraz stood like a beached fortress across the dappled water of the bay. It was now two minutes past eleven. Tom Black was late. Perhaps he'd never show. Maggie was right. He should have called the police.

All the same he wished this was his case, not theirs, and, most of all, not the Carabinieri's. So many opportunities had been lost through Gianluca Quattrocchi's insistent belief that the core of the investigation lay within the cryptic poetry of Dante. The *maresciallo* had taken a wrong turning from the start. How did *The Divine Comedy* begin?

'For the straightforward pathway had been lost,' Costa said quietly to himself, remembering his school days, long hours in the classroom.

Criminal cases, like lives, could so easily follow a false route, a deceptive fork in the road that seemed so attractive when it first emerged. Quattrocchi loved the publicity. The media adored a story that came with both a real-life cast of stars and a deadly narrative seemingly stolen from the spectacular piece of cinema that had brought them together. Everything was an illusion.

His phone rang.

'Costa.'

'You're alone.'

The voice was young, concerned and American, mangled by the bellowing rumble of traffic behind it. He couldn't be far away.

'Is that a question?'

'Not really.' The man sounded uncertain of himself, aware of that fact, desperate to hide it. 'Listen. There's an unlocked bike at the back of the parking lot. Take it, then go to the pedestrian gate on the bridge. Buzz the security people. They'll let anyone through with a bike. Ride across until I meet you. Don't try to walk. They don't allow pedestrians at night. You won't even get past the gate.'

'We could just meet here.'

'I want to see you first. I want to make sure you're alone.'

The line went dead.

Costa walked around the parking lot until he found the bike. He had the same unsettling feeling he'd had in Martin Vogel's apartment: that he wasn't alone. Maybe it was Tom Black watching him. But then . . .

He tried to shoo these thoughts from his head. It was an old road-racer model, with lots of gears and lots of rust. He wheeled it around the footpath and reached the gate. There was a button there, and a security camera. He hit the buzzer, a voice said something impenetrable from a hidden speaker, and then the barrier opened on electric hinges.

Wondering how long it had been since he climbed on a bike, Costa got on the saddle and rode slowly onto the bridge, alongside the northbound traffic in the adjoining lane a few yards to his left. The noise grew so loud he could scarcely think straight. In the middle of the great span he paused. It was an extraordinary view. The entire southern side of the city was visible, and the communities on the far side of the bay. The bridge was well lit. He could see all the way along the pedestrian footway to another closed gate at the Marin end.

He waited a good minute for the phone to ring.

'I'm in an old station wagon doing twenty in the southbound lane going back to the city. If I like what I see I'll slow up to a stop when I'm in the middle. Jump the barrier, cross the road and get in the back. You with me?'

In the distance on the far side he could just make out a vehicle being driven with the kind of caution one expected of the elderly. It was hugging the inside lane and getting passed by everything on the bridge.

'Where are we going?'

'For a drive and a talk. Yes or no?'

When the car got closer Costa stepped over the low iron barrier, waited for a gap in the traffic, and crossed to the other side.

It was an old, battered station wagon and it slowed even further as the driver saw him. The thing was scarcely at walking pace by the time it got close. Costa began to run to match its speed. He found the handle, threw open the back door and leapt in.

– 10 –

The vehicle stank of tobacco and age. It wasn't the kind of transport he would previously have associated with Tom Black.

Physically, he was a big, powerful man. Costa looked at his shaken, lost face in the mirror as they pulled away. He seemed different now Josh Jonah was gone. Uncertain of himself. Desperate. Black had to struggle with his shaking hands to take out the card to get them through the toll gates on the southern end of the bridge.

'What do you want?' Costa asked, then sat back, listened and found himself in fantasy land.

Tom Black had a list, one so ludicrous it was impossible to know how to begin the task of bringing him down to reality. The man wanted immunity from prosecution. He wanted access to his frozen funds. An immediate appointment with a lawyer before being asked any questions by the police. A phone call to his mother in Colorado. Finally . . .

The figure in the front seat turned round and looked at him hopefully, with an ingenuous schoolkid's hope in his eyes.

'I have a ticket for the premiere tomorrow. Lukatmi money paid for that. I don't want it revoked. I want to be there.'

Costa shook his head and laughed, aware of the scared young eyes watching him in the mirror.

'You're in a car with a stranger going nowhere,' Black grunted. 'You find this funny?'

'How else am I supposed to feel? You're wanted for murder and more financial crimes than I can put a name to. Now you want me to fix tickets for the cinema?'

'Lukatmi . . .'

'Lukatmi didn't pay, Tom! That's the point. Why don't you just drop me off and I'll find a cab home. This is a waste of time.'

They followed 101 off the bridge, cutting into the city past the Palace of Fine Arts where the lights were still on in the exhibition tents, and on to Lombard where the highway turned into a broad city street. Then Black turned down towards the waterfront, past the bars of Fisherman's Wharf. It was just lazy driving, the kind you did when you wanted to talk or think or convince yourself you could stay out of harm's way for ever.

Costa thought of the sensation he'd felt while hunting for the bike, of being watched. If it was true, it couldn't have been Tom Black. There was no way he could have got to the north side of the bridge and driven back in time.

'That ticket's mine, man. I want to be there. It was part of the deal. I'm owed.'

They passed a parked police car on North Point Street. Costa watched the way its lights came on afterwards. Discreetly he turned his head to glance out of the rear window and saw it move into the road.

'Who does this vehicle belong to, Tom?'

'I'm not bringing anyone else into this. Don't even think of going there.'

'Is it stolen?'

Black turned round and looked at him like he was crazy. Then, to Costa's dismay, he lifted his right hand and showed him something. It was a handgun. A black semi-automatic by the looks of things.

'*This* is stolen. That's all you need to know.'

'You don't look like a gun person to me. You don't look like someone who could fix all this on your own either. Who gave it to you? Is he following us?'

'Shut . . . up!'

He sat back and watched the piers of the northern waterfront go past the passenger window. They were on the Embarcadero now. He liked this road. It led to the Ferry Building, a piece of architecture that had caught his eye the moment he first saw it. The tall clock tower reminded him of Europe. Somewhere in Spain.

'So what do you say?' Black persisted. 'I'm being reasonable here.'

'Pull over, give me the gun, promise to tell the nice people in the San Francisco Police Department everything you know, and it's possible I can keep you alive. Maybe even out of jail. I'm only guessing. You haven't told me who wants to kill you. That complicates matters somewhat.'

The semi-automatic came up again, as if it had something to say.

Costa put up his hands and said, 'Fine. We're done here.'

They passed Lombard Street and another patrol car pulled out into the road. Costa looked back. They were holding off. Waiting for orders.

'Pull the car over, Tom. I'm getting out.'

'I want . . .' He looked ready to crack.

The Ferry Building was approaching. There was no traffic coming in the opposite direction. Costa knew what that had to mean. Soon they could see it. A line of police vehicles straddled the road, blue lights flashing.

'You told them, you bastard,' Black yelled, and the weapon was up again, jerking wildly in his free hand.

'I didn't tell them anything. Do you think they would have waited till now?'

'Then . . . ?'

'What about the guy who gave you the gun? The one who set this up? Put that bike out for me? Did he follow us too?'

'Got to know who to trust . . .' Black whimpered. 'Got to know.'

Up the street there were uniformed men by the patrol cars. Costa snatched a look at the beautiful, illuminated clock tower and realized where he'd seen something like it before, where the architect must have got the idea. It was the Giralda in Seville, the Moorish tower attached to a Catholic cathedral that had consumed the mosque that went before. All generations pillaged what they inherited. Roberto

Tonti had stolen from Dante. A murderer had somehow found inspiration in a film that was half a century old.

'Give me the gun and I will deal with this,' Costa ordered.

Black was starting to slow down. They were edging closer to the roadblock. He could hear Gerald Kelly's voice booming through a bullhorn, all the commands Costa would expect of a situation like this.

Stop the car. Get out. Lie down.

'I'm dead,' Tom Black mumbled at the wheel.

'If you step out of that door with a gun in your hand you will be.'

The vehicle rolled to a halt twenty yards from the police line. Costa couldn't begin to guess the number of weapons that were trained on them by the dark figures crouched next to the line of vehicles blocking the street beneath the tower of the Ferry Building.

'If you're in jail for a couple of years, what's it matter? You'll still be alive. Still got a future in front of you. Maybe there's a lawyer who can get you off scot-free too. The world's like that. Money talks. You'll find some.'

Black turned round and stared at him.

'That's what Josh thought. He just wanted to pay off that blackmailing bastard Vogel once and for all.'

'See. That's a start. Keep talking and you'd be amazed how popular you can get.'

'You don't understand the first thing about what's going on here, do you?'

'True. So tell me.'

He looked out of the window, lost, forlorn.

'Once you sign up with these people you never get free. It's a contract, right? *A contract.* Break it and you die.'

'Is that what happened with Allan Prime?'

'I don't know what happened with Allan Prime and neither did Josh. It was never supposed to end that way. It was just a deal. Don't you see?'

The weapon was near, but not enough to snatch.

'Give me the gun, Tom. I'll throw it out of the window. Then we crawl out of here and go straight down on the ground, faces in the dirt, hands out, not moving a muscle until they tell us. That way we both stay alive.'

'Just like the movies,' Black mumbled sarcastically.

He was so close. One more minute with this man and he'd be there.

'What's wrong with the movies?' Costa asked.

The man at the wheel turned and stared him with eyes that were dark, bleak and full of self-loathing.

'They screw you up. They . . .' He was mumbling. Costa could scarcely make out the words. 'They screw everyone. Scottie. Me. I never thought this'd happen. Not when we went to Jones . . .'

He threw back his head, closed his eyes, groaned, in despair.

'Jones? Who the . . . ?' Costa was starting to ask.

The bullhorn burst into life again, and this time it was loud and close enough to shake the vehicle.

'Get out of the car,' Gerald Kelly's metallic voice bellowed.

Black leaned out of the open window, abruptly furious, waving the weapon around, screaming, 'Shut up, *shut up, shut up!* Lemme think.'

Costa sat back and watched him subside. They had time. Getting the weapon off this scared young man might take an hour. More maybe. But it was achievable.

'We know about Jimmy Gaines,' Kelly shouted. 'We need you to come in. You and your accomplice. Leave the vehicle. Get on the ground.'

Something changed in Tom Black's demeanour. His face hardened. Costa's spirits sank.

Black thrust his head out into the night.

'What the hell have you done to Jimmy? This was nothing to do with him. Blame Josh and me. Not Jimmy.'

'Who's Jimmy Gaines?' Costa asked.

He didn't get a reply. Black was screaming into the street again.

'What you done with Jimmy? You bring him here. I wanna talk to him. This isn't his doing. I want him free.'

Kelly didn't come back on the bullhorn straight away. That was odd.

'Let's just get out of the car like they say,' Costa began. 'This will be so much easier in someone's office, where it's warm and they have coffee and lawyers and people who can help you.'

'I can't bring you Jimmy Gaines,' Kelly said, and there was an edge to his voice even through the electronic medium of the bull-horn. 'There was an accident. Let's not have any more.'

Costa stiffened back into the old, uncomfortable seats of the station wagon and watched Black fumble at his phone, calling someone who didn't answer, and that made him more furious than ever.

'An accident . . . an accident . . . what the hell does that mean?'

'If we talk to them . . .'

It was no use.

'Bring me Jimmy Gaines,' Black screeched out of the window again.

There was a pause, then Gerald Kelly's piercing, metallic voice said simply, 'We can't. He's dead.'

Costa closed his eyes and wondered why words always had to give way to deeds. Why he couldn't talk people out of things, and couldn't accept his failure in that regard. It had cost Emily her life. It had almost robbed him of his sanity. He'd done everything he could to reason with Tom Black, and might have managed if Gerald Kelly – a good, intelligent police officer, Costa didn't doubt that – hadn't intervened with the wrong words at the wrong time. Yet it would all have been so much simpler if he'd never tried in the first place. If he'd simply overpowered this odd, confused young man, got the gun off him, taken him down to Bryant Street and let Kelly's men throw him in an interrogation room.

He rolled over on the back seat and thrust himself deep down into the floor space. He could smell what was coming in the stink of sweat and fear and panic that was rolling off the man in the front.

The driver's door opened and Black was out, screaming obscenities. Costa steeled himself for the sound. It didn't come. Not immediately. Kelly was shouting. So was Tom Black. Then . . .

A single shot. One loose round begets a host.

When it began, he found himself racked with pain and anguish, trying to force his fists into his ears to keep out the volley of gunfire enveloping this quiet, beautiful patch of the city outside the Embarcadero Ferry Building.

The place never mattered. It was the same, always. In the grubby gardens surrounding the mausoleum of the emperor Augustus where his wife died. In the grounds of the Villa Borghese as an actor posing as a carabiniere was brought down because he didn't understand how jumpy police officers get when they see what appears to be an armed individual intent on violence.

There was a short, high scream, then the shooting came to a halt. It was immediately replaced by that angry, taut chorus of shouts that followed almost every act of violence he had witnessed. A part of him felt he could hear the life of Tom Black depart the world, a single human soul lost for eternity, for no good reason Costa could imagine. This hurt him. He had no such recollection of the moment of Emily's death. That instant was black and bleak and empty and would always remain so.

Crushed face-down in the rear seat of the vehicle, hands now tight on his head, waiting, he was aware of them tearing at the doors, screaming at him, wondering themselves whether he was armed too and might take a life of their own.

Strange voices assaulted him, strong hands gripped his arms. Before he could begin to get up Costa felt himself dragged from the back seat and thrown face-down onto the hard ground. He thrust out his arms as they ordered. The gravel scraped his cheeks, the familiar pain from childhood, of stone entering the skin, flesh on dirt. He kept his hands out wide. A couple of them aimed kicks, one quite powerful, deep into his stomach. He grunted and didn't move, not an inch. After a while the noise and the violence subsided. He heard Kelly's voice say to another man, 'Let's see what we've got.'

They used their feet to turn him.

Bloodied hands still up over his head, Costa opened his eyes to see the SFPD captain's shape obscuring the grey stone tower of the Ferry Building.

'What in God's name are you doing here?' Kelly asked, shaking his head in amazement.

'I was trying to bring you a witness. I did my best. Sorry.'

To his surprise Kelly held out his hand and helped him upright. He had a strong grip. It hurt when it pushed the gravel further back into Costa's torn palm. A bunch of men was standing over the body of Tom Black looking at it, shaking their heads. Sirens were wailing somewhere along Market Street. Costa brushed himself down. He felt detached from this situation. The pain from his hands and the kick in his gut helped.

Kelly offered him a clean handkerchief.

'There's some blood on your face. You might want to get it off.'

Costa wiped his cheek with the back of his hand. He'd had worse.

'Did he tell you anything?' Kelly asked.

He tried to remember.

'I'd have to think about that.'

Kelly put an arm around his shoulder and walked him towards the doors of the terminal. A small crowd had gathered behind the tape barrier erected by Kelly's uniformed men. The traffic was beginning to back up along the Embarcadero.

'Please,' Kelly said. 'Think hard.'

'How did you know he was in the car?'

'Your pathologist called us. A couple of guys she knows were playing PI and got themselves kidnapped by this Gaines character. Seems he and Black were very good friends indeed. So good Gaines thought he'd get Black out there to cut some deal with you, and then pop off these friends of hers in the meantime.'

Kelly shrugged.

'Didn't work out that way. So they called her. And she, being a sensible, helpful lady, called me.'

The SFPD captain scratched his grizzled head.

'It never really occurred to me you might have got there first.'

'We keep trying to do you favours. It doesn't buy us any credit, does it?'

'Not much.'

Nic Costa closed his eyes and tried to imagine himself back in Rome. It was impossible.

'Did you happen to witness Tom Black taking a shot at us?' Kelly asked out of nowhere.

'I was in the back of the car with my head in my hands. I didn't see a thing.'

'Sensible man.'

'So?'

'I didn't see Tom Black use his weapon. In fact I'd say the first shot I heard took him down, and that didn't come from us. After that something popped a window on one of our squad cars and . . .'

He shrugged.

'When guns get used like kids' toys anything can happen. I'd like you to make a statement to one of my officers now. The basic details of what happened here. Tomorrow . . . maybe we should speak again.'

PART SIX

- 1 -

He was woken by the phone. It was Maggie wanting to know what had happened. The incident outside the Ferry Building was on the morning news. *Inferno* had hit the headlines again.

Still trying to throw off his drowsiness, Costa told her and fought for some questions he ought to ask. They weren't there. It was gone nine and he still felt exhausted. Outside the window of his bedroom the light in Greenwich Street looked different, less bright, more diffuse. There wasn't a sound in the house, only the noise of the boombox from the Mexican decorators who'd spent most of the previous week painting the front of the building next door.

'You could have been killed,' she said, and there was an accusatory note in her voice.

'Tom Black asked to see me. Alone. He didn't wish me any harm. If he'd listened he'd still be alive and we might have a clearer idea of what's been going on.'

'That makes it worthwhile, does it?'

'Sometimes. He sounded as if he needed help.'

'And now he's dead too.'

'I'm sorry.' The memories of those last moments on the Embarcadero were starting to come back. 'I don't understand what happened. You liked him.'

There was a moment's silence on the line.

'Not really. Tom was a sad man. He hung around me for a while like a lot of men do, not that he seemed terribly convinced. I think he felt he was meant to do that kind of thing. If Josh had told him to jump off the roof he would have. Tom didn't have the courage to ask for what he wanted, which makes him stand out from most so-called associate producers I've met.'

The job was news to him.

'Tom Black was a producer?'

'Associate producer. Lukatmi put in money, didn't they? Collect enough tokens, you get free candy.' She hesitated. 'Did they have to shoot him?'

He thought about Gerald Kelly's odd question.

'I didn't see what happened. Tom was a man with a gun who looked ready to use it. Just like that idiot in Rome. I tried to talk him out of it. I failed.'

'This is getting to me, Nic. I can't wait to get the hell out of here. There are a couple of events at the weekend and then I'm gone.'

He wasn't sure why he asked, but then he added, 'Do you know if you've been paid yet?'

'What the hell does that matter?' she asked, incredulous.

'Maybe it doesn't. Have you?'

She sighed.

'Only what I got at the start. Sylvie my agent's jumping up and down about it. This is partly my fault. I let Simon deal with the money stuff when it all got complicated.'

'Complicated?'

'Not enough money to pay the bills at Cinecittà. People asking for favours. Don't take your fee now. Take it later, in instalments. That kind of stuff. Normally you get it before the movie starts shooting. Not part-way through. I didn't want to know. Simon was in Rome. Sylvie was in Hollywood. Like she should care. She still gets her cut.'

She sounded perplexed.

'Why's my money important?'

'It probably isn't.'

'Did Tom say anything about what happened?'

Costa thought about that, and then said, 'Nothing useful.'

'You wouldn't tell me, would you? Even if he did.'

This conversation always came up, in every relationship he'd had. With Emily it had been easy. She'd worked in law enforcement too. She understood.

'No. I wouldn't.'

'OK. I'm starting to get the picture.'

'I wish I was. When will I see you?'

'Tonight, I hope. At the premiere. Will you be working?'

'If you can call it that. Looking after a set of glass cases. We're still irrelevant here. Come Saturday when the exhibition goes back to Rome, we don't even get the rent paid.'

She waited, then said, very slowly, 'I thought we had an understanding. Barbados. Wall-to-wall lobster. Remember?'

There was always that gap between what was said in the spur of passion and what was felt in the cold light of day. Costa didn't doubt his emotions there for a moment. He wanted to be with Maggie Flavier. Anywhere would do.

'Wall-to-wall lobster,' he said. 'Let me talk to Leo.'

'Do that. And another thing. An actress can't walk down the red carpet at a movie premiere on her own.' A pause. 'Do I really have to ask?'

'I'm working.'

'Two minutes of your time. That's all it takes. Then you can go back to standing around your glass cases. Two minutes.'

He didn't know what to say. He was trying to picture it in his head, all those images of glittering affairs on the TV, shots of the Oscars, celebrities laughing and joking . . . The sea of paparazzi who had been trying to capture them all along, given what they wanted, on a plate.

'If you'd prefer not to . . .' she began.

'There's nothing I'd rather do in the world.'

'Really?'

'Really. I will smile for the cameras and wear a flower in my lapel. I will hold your hand, if that's not too forward. Be my director. Tell me what to do.'

There was a low, throaty giggle on the line.

'I'd rather leave that till later if you don't mind. The photographers will go to town. You realize that, don't you? They'll say we're a couple, official. Privacy will be confined to the bathroom from now on, and I can't always guarantee that.'

'I can live with it if you can.'

'You say that now . . .'

'Yes. I do.'

'If that's true you'll be the best damn man I've ever known,' she said rapidly. 'Got to go . . .'

He tried to imagine her in the Brocklebank building, wondering what she would wear for the premiere. Who she might be. Herself or someone stolen from a wall in the Legion of Honor.

Costa walked downstairs. The small, timber-boarded house was empty. On the table was a handwritten note, scribbled in the familiar, precise hand of Leo Falcone.

I say this as much as a friend as your commanding officer. To absent yourself on a whim last night, without informing any of us of your intentions, was stupid, selfish and unacceptable. I do not wish to see you today. Try to amuse yourself in a way which causes no one any concern or harm.
Falcone

He read the message twice, then screwed it up into a tight ball and threw the thing into the kitchen bin. Once again there was no coffee. Costa sat down at Teresa's computer with a glass of orange juice and got the number for Sylvie Brewster, Maggie's agent, from a Hollywood directory. He had to talk his way through three assistants to reach her, and then she asked, 'You're asking me to discuss the financial affairs of a client? And you not even an American cop with a warrant or something?'

'I'm a friend. I'm concerned.'

'Oh right. I'm being slow here. You're that one. Nic.'

'This is important. It may explain why she was attacked. I don't know.'

The woman waited for a moment and said, 'Whoever did that thing to Maggie deserves to be eaten alive by rats. What can I tell you?'

'I don't know anything about the movie business. I don't understand how a film can go into production, go as far as having a premiere, and still the cast haven't all been paid. Is that normal?'

'No,' Sylvie Brewster replied, and nothing more.

'Then how did it happen?'

He heard a long groan and then the sound of someone drawing on a cigarette.

'OK. You will never pass this on to another soul, right?'

'Agreed.'

'I haven't a clue. The first thing I heard was when the deal was already done. I started screaming all round but it was like I was an idiot. They'd had some financial crisis. Tonti and that evil bastard Bonetti had fixed it. Then it was done and if I tried anything I might be running the risk of bringing down the whole damn thing. For good. Not just no money but no movie.'

'Could they make a threat like that?'

'They thought so. Dino Bonetti broke every rule in the book. Those bastards took Maggie to one side in Rome. Leaned on her. Begged her. Next thing I know she's signed some papers and it's all settled.'

'Have you seen the papers?'

'Nope. And if I didn't love Maggie she'd be an ex-client now. To hell with my cut. This is not the way the business is supposed to work.'

'Simon Harvey organized the deal, didn't he?'

'So I hear. Can't get into directing. Maybe he fancies himself as a producer now. Best he doesn't come near my clients – I'll carve his eyes out with spoons. Unless he's got funding, in which case we'll do lunch.' She laughed.

'Thanks for the insight.'

'I'll tell you something else too. I was talking to Allan Prime's agent the other day. This is a small world. I wanted to commiserate.'

'He cut the same kind of deal,' Costa guessed. 'Outside the usual rules. No money on the table. No money anywhere.'

Sylvie Brewster sounded impressed.

'Maggie said you were a smart one. Be kind to her while it lasts, won't you?'

Then she was gone. Costa went to the waste bin and retrieved Falcone's note. He was still reading it, half furious, half ashamed, when Teresa came back with two bags full of shopping.

She saw what he was doing and said, 'Well, look on the bright side. At least you escaped getting it face to face. He was pretty mad with you. Even for him.'

'Sorry. I'll have to find him and apologize.'

'No rush. Leo Falcone's life consists of a series of small explosions. It always will. Particularly when he keeps getting knocked back. A woman who doesn't fall for his well-oiled charms. We had to come all the way to California to find one.'

She didn't say it with much relish.

'Is he upset?' Costa asked.

'About Catherine? He's beside himself. It's not the usual arrogance either. I think the poor thing's actually smitten. I'd like to say it serves him right for treating Raffaella Arcangelo so badly.' She screwed up her face. 'But I don't feel that way. Must be getting old. It's difficult to work up the energy to be vindictive these days. He'll get over it when he's back home in Rome.'

She took the note from his hands and put it back in the bin.

'Look. Leo wrote that thing out of hurt more than anything else. It's forgotten now. You should do the same. Don't expect me to make you coffee either. I'm not stopping. I have identical twins to scold. And for that I do have the strength. Jesus . . .'

Costa didn't say a word.

She sat down opposite him and grumbled, 'Oh for God's sake, what do you want?'

'I want to talk this through.'

Teresa put a finger to her cheek, gave him a questioning look and said, 'Let me make a suggestion. You have been granted the day off.

There is, it seems to me, someone in your life again. You're in a beautiful city most people would pay good money to visit. Why not go out and enjoy yourself? See the sights. Take Maggie for lunch. Do something normal for a change.'

'I do normal things all the time,' he objected.

'That is the stupidest thing I've ever heard.'

She left without another word. Costa thought about what she'd said. He'd never invited Maggie for a coffee, let alone a meal. In Rome it would have been different. No, he corrected himself, in Rome it *will* be different.

He was about to call her when the phone rang.

'We need to meet,' Gerald Kelly said. 'Right away.'

- 2 -

Teresa Lupo had summoned them to their usual table at the cafe in Chestnut. She couldn't work out whether to feel mad or relieved. Hank and Frank sat there sipping coffee and picking at a couple of doughnuts, staring at the ceiling as if pretending that nothing had happened. Their hands were covered in scratches. Hank's right cheek was red and inflamed from what he said was a reaction to poison ivy. Frank's eyes were watery and bloodshot as if he hadn't slept all night. They looked a mess, and as guilty as a couple of schoolboys found pilfering from the neighbourhood store.

'What were you thinking?' she asked in the end.

'That maybe we could help,' Frank responded.

'It was his idea,' Hank jumped in.

'Don't try that with me,' she warned. 'You two work as a pair. I'm not stupid.'

'We did help, didn't we?' Hank seemed quite offended. 'In a messy kind of way.'

The death of two men had clearly upset them, in spite of Jimmy Gaines's murderous intentions. It was impossible to escape the consequences. The shooting of Tom Black had led the bulletin on the morning TV news, but the recovery of Gaines's body from a ravine in the Muir Woods hadn't been far behind. Hank and Frank had spent half the night being interviewed in Bryant Street and then, on the advice of the SFPD, found themselves somewhere private to stay in order to avoid the attentions of the news crews. 'Somewhere private' had turned out to be a cheap motel in Cow Hollow, just round the corner from where they lived. Frank called it 'hiding in plain sight'. Hank described the decision as pure laziness.

'If they hadn't shot that poor boy . . .' Hank grumbled. 'He could have told them something.'

She was not going to take this nonsense.

'Someone who comes racing towards armed police holding a gun is asking for trouble. Don't blame anyone else for that. Least of all yourselves.'

'So is that it?' Frank asked. 'Is it over? It was Josh Jonah, Tom Black and Jimmy Gaines doing all this stuff? Along with that photographer guy who got killed?'

Teresa shrugged her shoulders.

'Criminal investigations are based on assumptions,' she said, toying with some strange Middle Eastern pastry the cafe owner had thrust upon her. 'They have to be. It's how we make progress. We assume that when a series of killings occur inside the same circle like this, it's all down to the same individual or group of people.'

'That makes sense,' Hank agreed.

'But what if the assumptions are wrong?' Teresa asked. 'What if one person killed Allan Prime and another one tried to poison Maggie Flavier? I've said it before. I'll say it again. They don't look like the same person's handiwork to me. Not for a moment.'

Frank looked uneasy.

'I don't like complicated ideas. There's a gratifying shortage of people willing to go round knocking off their fellow human beings. What are the odds of them all turning up in one place like this, all at the same time?'

Hank nodded.

'I'm inclined to agree. If this were fiction . . .'

'It isn't fiction!' she hissed. 'If you'd got killed last night you'd have known that.'

The brothers stared at her, eyebrows raised in the same surprised, amused expression.

'You know what I mean. Don't ask me what people think right now. I have no idea.'

'What did Tom Black tell your young friend?' Frank asked.

'Not a lot. Yes, there was a conspiracy to hype the movie. No, they didn't think anyone would get hurt. That's about it.'

Hank finished his doughnut, wiped his fingers daintily on a napkin and said, 'I still don't know why Jimmy Gaines wanted to put us out of the way. Why he couldn't just let us go once Tom got into police custody and started to tell his tale. He must have known it would have come back to him in the end.'

'He'd have been gone the moment he was out of Muir Woods,' Frank muttered. 'Murderous bastard . . .'

'Yeah but why?' Hank shook his head. 'He didn't like the idea of shooting us. If he'd been a touch more single-minded in that regard we might not be here. He didn't need to kill us, did he?'

Frank scratched his nose, a sign, she'd learned, of discomfort.

'No,' he agreed. 'He didn't.'

Teresa watched them struggle with this idea, then suggested, 'There has to be some reason. Something you knew . . .'

'Like what?' Frank demanded. 'We were wise to the fact Jimmy knocked around with Tom Black. If I'm being honest with you we knew Jimmy was gay, or at least hanging round in those circles. That's no big deal. If he wanted to keep it to himself that was his privilege. Nothing worth killing for.'

'Frank's right,' Hank added. 'No answers there.'

'Then it must have been something you said.'

The two men grumbled to each other, then folded their arms in unison and gazed at her.

'Think about it,' she continued. 'When you went to see Jimmy Gaines at Lukatmi. He surely wasn't thinking of popping you two in the Muir Woods the moment you turned up.'

'He looked pleased to see us,' Hank agreed. 'Turned a touch cooler when we told him why we came. Not that *that* helps us any. He was keeping a big secret. Only understandable.'

'Find the moment,' she told them. 'Think back. Was there some point in the conversation when the mood turned?'

The brothers looked blank.

'What about later?' Teresa persisted. 'On the way to the woods? When you got there? What did you talk about?'

'*Vertigo* and how it wasn't really shot where everyone thought it was,' Frank answered. 'Oh, and Thoreau. Tom Black loved *Walden*. I don't think those secrets merit killing two old colleagues, not really.'

'He'd already made up his mind by the time we got there,' Hank said. 'Think back. It was in his eyes.'

Frank nodded.

'You're right. He was odd with us even before we crossed the bridge. I can't believe we were so stupid to just walk into that forest with him.'

She didn't like seeing them like this.

'Never look back, boys. Stupidity is God's gift to the world, ours to do with as we please. You're dead tired. Are you going to go back to that motel of yours? Come round to our place if you like . . .'

They didn't budge. Something she said had set Hank thinking.

'This is insane,' he said finally.

'What is?' she asked.

'The moment. When Jimmy Gaines got a look in his eye. I think I got it.'

'You have?' Frank asked.

'Maybe. Remember at Lukatmi? When he wanted to take us off for a coffee?'

'So?' Frank said, shaking his head.

'You made some crack about there being no insurance against stupidity. Jimmy looked at you funny the moment you used that word. He asked what you meant.' Hank leaned forward. 'Remember what you said?'

Frank grimaced.

'I told him he knew exactly what I meant. It was just a saying.'

'He didn't get the joke, brother. Not at all.'

The three of them looked at each other.

'Insurance?' Teresa asked, bewildered. 'Is that the best you've got? I've spent the last few weeks screaming at people about how the human race doesn't go around murdering itself in defence of poetry. They, in return, have been yelling at me for having the temerity to suggest it might have something to do with a 1950s movie. Now you're throwing insurance my way?'

Hank called out for more coffee and added, 'Barkev? Is it OK if we use your machine out back?'

The cafe owner walked to the rear of the room and opened a door to a tiny and very tidy office where a smart new computer sat on a clear and well-polished desk.

'I don't imagine either of you has ever read much Robert Louis Stevenson except for *Treasure Island* and *Kidnapped*,' Hank stated.

She exchanged glances with Frank.

'I think I can speak for both of us when I say no,' Teresa responded.

Hank got up and stretched his scratched and swollen fingers, as if readying them for action.

'There was a book called *The Wrong Box*. He wrote it with a friend. Read it years ago. Funny story, comedic funny that is. Cruel and heartless too.'

He peered through at the office.

'Guilty people get touchy, I guess,' Hank Boynton said. 'They see spooks round every corner. Get twitchy at the slightest, most innocent of things. Maybe . . .'

He looked at them, still working this out for himself.

'Just maybe, it's all in a name.'

- 3 -

Gerald Kelly owned an ordinary black sedan and drove it sedately through the city by a route so circuitous Costa couldn't begin to identify any of the neighbourhoods they passed. This was a conversation the SFPD captain had wanted with someone for a long time. Listening to him spend the best part of an hour outlining what he knew, it was obvious why. Without Gianluca Quattrocchi's conspiracy theory, homicide had precious little left to work on. There was a genuine crime inside Lukatmi – missing money, and offshore agreements that were impenetrable to the US authorities, and probably would remain so now the two founders of the company were dead. But those entailed financial offences and fell to a different team of investigators, probably the federal authorities in the end. Kelly was a homicide man through and through, and in that field he was struggling for daylight.

They travelled slowly down a long straight street. At the end the Pacific ocean sat in a pale blue line on the horizon.

'What do you think Tom Black was trying to tell you last night?' Kelly asked.

'That there was a conspiracy within *Inferno* designed to generate as much publicity as possible. As far as he was concerned that's all it was. Allan Prime wasn't supposed to die.'

Kelly reached the intersection, pulled in to the side and stopped.

'Don't you love the sea?' he asked. 'It's so beautiful. I could sit here for hours. Used to when I was a street cop and there was nothing to do. You'd be amazed what you get to learn that way.' He looked at Costa in the passenger seat. 'Or maybe you wouldn't.

Here's something that came in from the overnight people. James Conway Gaines. Our onetime fireman who wound up working security at Lukatmi and seems to have become some kind of lover-cum-father figure for Tom Black. He had three convictions for violence, bar brawls, the usual. Some rough gay places mainly. Also . . .'

Kelly's mobile phone rang. He took it out of his jacket, answered the call, told someone he was busy and would be back within the hour.

'We never would have found this out without you putting him our way. Jimmy Gaines was in Italy for two weeks right when all this fun began. In Rome. We found an entry in his passport and stubs for some fancy hotel that ought to be beyond the reach of someone on a security guard's wages. Flew back the day after Allan Prime died.'

He wound down the window and breathed in the fresh sea air.

'James Conway Gaines was crew too, but for the publicity stunt, not the movie set. Alongside our dead photographer friend Martin Vogel. Gaines fell over a cliff. Pretty clear it was an accident and those two friends of your pathologist got lucky. But why did Vogel get killed?'

Costa thought of the conversation in the back of Gaines's station wagon. There were so many questions he wished he'd asked.

'Vogel was blackmailing Josh Jonah. However much he got paid to start with it wasn't enough. Jonah went round to see him. Maybe to kill him. Maybe to reason with him and it turned into a fight. Maybe . . .'

He couldn't shake the memories of that night.

'I still think there was someone else there.'

Kelly watched a gull float past on the other side of the road, stationary in the light marine breeze.

'I know you do and I wish there was one scrap of evidence in that burnt-out mess to back you up. So let's assume it was the fight idea. I don't see those two geeks getting into the hit business. Dino Bonetti, on the other hand . . .'

'Everything we have on Bonetti we gave to you. Falcone made

sure of that days ago. Our people in Rome had plenty of information. The mob connections. The history of fraud.'

'Yeah. We had stuff of our own too. Does it help? I don't know. The guy's a movie producer. Most of that business is clean. Some parts are as dirty as hell. Bonetti's been dining with crooks here and back in Italy for two decades or more. There was a time when the Feds were thinking of refusing him entrance into the US on grounds of his connections. Not that it happened. Maybe a movie wouldn't have got made or something.'

'What about Tonti?' Costa asked.

'We all know he's got mob links. His wife's left him so maybe brother-in-law scarface isn't too happy. But I don't buy it. This is California not Calabria. It's not worth going to jail for wasting an in-law who's a jerk. Tonti's Italian by birth, living here and he's got friends with history. Doesn't add up to much.'

He waved his arm along the seafront.

'There's a dozen restaurant guys not a mile from here I could say the same thing about. We have no proof, only guesses. I'm sick of those.'

He started the car and took a right along the seafront road. Ahead was an expanse of green hillside. It looked familiar.

'Also,' Kelly added as they settled into a cruise at around twenty-five mph, 'there's the health thing. Roberto Tonti has advanced lung cancer. He wasn't hopping in and out of Martin Vogel's apartment when the shooting started. The guy's got maybe three or four months max. Little movie industry secret, one they'd like to keep quiet while they're raising dough to make a sequel. Yeah, I know. Sometimes a dying man feels he's been given the right to kill. We'd need a little more evidence than that though. And a reason.' He shook his head. 'We need that more than anything. Killing Allan Prime got these guys what they wanted. Why did they need more than that? How rich do you have to be? If it had stayed at Prime maybe Lukatmi wouldn't have collapsed, not with all that nice publicity to keep it afloat.'

He stomped on the horn as a skateboarder crossed the empty road directly in front of them.

'Kids.' He peered at the ocean as if wishing he were on it. 'Am I missing something?'

'Carlotta Valdes,' Costa stated.

They began to climb uphill. Costa had a good idea where they were headed. Kelly didn't say a word for a minute or so. Then they drove past golfers playing through wisps of fog drifting in from the sea and drew up in front of the elegant white building at the summit. The Legion of Honor looked just as he remembered it. Images of the paintings it held, Maggie's ghosts, flitted through his head.

Kelly turned and pointed a finger in his direction.

'I was not forgetting Carlotta Valdes. By the way, kindly tell Falcone I am mad as hell at him for mentioning that damned movie in the first place. Just when I was trying to think straight after listening to Bryan Whitcombe talk poetry crap non-stop. It was a distraction. So Tonti worked with Hitchcock fifty years ago. What are we supposed to make of that? What's the connection?'

Costa took a deep breath.

'Think about it. They're the same story. *Inferno* and *Vertigo*. A lost man looking for something he wants. An ethereal woman he thinks can provide some answers.' He thought of what Simon Harvey had told Maggie. 'For both of them it ends in death. Beatrice waits for Dante in Paradise. Scottie sees the woman he's created in the image of Madeleine Elster die in front of his eyes, and stands alone in the bell-tower, staring down at her body. He's lost everything. Including the vertigo that's been cursing him, that got him into the case in the first place.'

Kelly seemed unmoved.

'You're starting to sound like Bryan Whitcombe now.'

'Not really. If someone's obsessed with one it's understandable he might be obsessed with the other. There's a connection. It's obvious when you think about it. What it means . . .' His voice trailed off. He'd spent hours trying to make sense of the link. Something was missing. 'I can't begin to guess.'

Another memory returned.

'Tom Black said something. About how the movies screw you up. Someone called Scottie. Someone called Jones . . .' He shook his head, trying to recall the jumble of words he'd just managed to catch during those final moments.

'One more alias from *Vertigo*,' Kelly suggested. 'Is there a guy called Jones in the movie too?'

'There was an actor. He played the creepy coroner. He's long dead.'

Kelly gave him the kind of look Costa had come to expect from Falcone.

'Are we shooting in the dark or what? I'll check if the name Jones means anything inside the movie crew. You sure you heard it right?'

'Not really.'

'Let's deal with something practical, shall we? Where's Carlotta? Back in Rome and paid off? Dead?'

'You tell me.'

'*Cherchez la femme*. We don't have one. Not anywhere.' He caught Costa's eye. 'Except for Maggie Flavier. We're supposed to think someone's tried to kill her twice, except neither time was quite what it appeared on the surface. Personal feelings apart, do you think it might possibly be her? It could have been, you know. I checked Quattrocchi's files. Carlotta Valdes turned up at Allan Prime's home first thing in the morning. Maggie Flavier was at home in her apartment until two in the afternoon. On her own. No witnesses. That name could have been a joke.'

'Whoever it was made a real death mask,' Costa pointed out. 'Does that sound a likely skill for an actress?'

'Maybe. Have you asked?'

'No. No more than I asked whether she poisoned herself either.'

The captain didn't flinch.

'If you wanted to put on some kind of show isn't that the way you'd do it? Carrying a hypodermic along with you and a tame cop to help out?' He leaned over the seat and said, in a low, half-amused voice, 'You don't mind me saying this, do you?'

'No,' Costa answered, refusing to rise to the bait.

'You don't think it hasn't run through the minds of your colleagues, do you? They're not dumb.'

'They're not dumb. The Carabinieri were wrong when they told you Maggie Flavier had no alibi for that morning. She had flowers delivered around ten. Ordered them herself. Signed for them herself. We have a copy of the receipt back in the Questura and a statement from the delivery man. Little details like that probably never occurred to Quattrocchi. He already knew the story, didn't he?'

Kelly stared at him in bewilderment.

'When the hell did you know that?'

'I took the delivery man's statement myself before we even left Rome. Maggie Flavier could not have been the woman who signed herself in as Carlotta Valdes in that apartment in the Via Guilia. It's simply impossible.'

The man in the driving seat creased with laughter.

'Jesus . . . *Jesus* . . . And I picked Gianluca Quattrocchi . . .'

He started the engine. They drew away, in the opposite direction down the hill. The Golden Gate Bridge emerged in the distance. The car was headed for the Marina. He'd seen this road before, in *Vertigo*.

'I've got to go back to the office soon. I'm enjoying myself too much here,' Kelly said, bringing the speed up to something like normal. 'You want to know the truth? There's only one thing we're sure of right now. There was a conspiracy to hype *Inferno*. Somehow, somewhere along the way it turned murderous. So where do we begin?'

Costa shrugged and said, 'Any way you look at it one of three people has got to be at the heart of this case. Roberto Tonti, Dino Bonetti or Simon Harvey. If they'd been cab-drivers or office clerks they'd have spent a couple of days in Bryant Street being sweated until they couldn't sleep. Instead . . .'

'Nothing doing. Tonti and Bonetti are Italian citizens. They insist Gianluca Quattrocchi is present if we so much as ask them the way to the bathroom, which is about as far as the conversation ever gets.'

'And Harvey?'

'Like juggling with eels. You know the kind of people they are. The kind with the right numbers in their phone books. I leaned a little hard on Harvey right at the beginning. One hour later I'm getting calls from God down asking me why I'm wasting my time. There's not a scrap of hard evidence linking them into the case and you know it.'

Despite his words, Kelly still looked interested. 'You think you can do better?'

'I can try.'

'How?'

'By getting in their faces. The way I'd do if they were plain ordinary human beings like everyone else. When they don't want it. Before they can call up a lawyer.'

They had reached a bluff overlooking the bridge. Kelly pulled in.

'Now there's something you don't see often,' he muttered, pointing at the ocean.

A long white, smoky finger of mist was working across the bay ahead.

'If you're the sailing type I'll take you out there some day. We call that place "the slot". It runs from the bridge to Alcatraz. Windy as hell sometimes, and you don't have a clue what's going on until you're in the middle of it.' He shook his head. 'Fog? Now? I'd expect it from the west. And later. But hell. Welcome to summer in San Francisco.'

He took off his jacket, removed the tan holster and held it out, gun first, to Costa.

'Expecting things to turn out like they should is something stupid people do. If you plan to go visiting, and I hope you do, I would like you to have this.'

Costa didn't reach for the weapon.

'Men who work with me do so armed,' Kelly insisted. 'I've lost three officers in my career and that's three too many.'

'It's illegal for me to carry a weapon.'

'I'll look the other way. I know this city and I have my rules when dealing with it. We both understand there are still people out there with blood on their hands. I'd hazard a guess they'll shed a little more to keep us from knowing what exactly has gone on here. This is not a subject for discussion, Nic. You take the gun or I drive you home and you stay there.' The handgun didn't move. 'Well?'

Costa grasped the cold butt of the weapon, felt the familiar weight.

Kelly turned on the radio and kept the volume low. Strains of Santana drifted into the car.

'Oh,' he added, as if it were an afterthought. 'One more thing. That crossbow that killed Allan Prime. Unusual object. You won't have seen the forensic, I guess. Quattrocchi is a little reticent with these things.'

'The crossbow?'

'It was a Barnett Revolution.' He looked at Costa. 'It's a hunting crossbow, made for killing deer. Very powerful. Not generally available in Italy. It was bought used through eBay. Guy paid cash and met the seller in a car park in south San Francisco one month before Prime died. He wore a hat and sunglasses. That's as good a description as we could get. My guess is it got shipped to Rome along with some of the equipment they took out for that event there, not that I can prove it.'

'A month?'

'None of this happened on the spur of the moment, did it? Now here's one more interesting thing. We recovered three shells from Tom Black's body. Two of them were ours. One wasn't.'

Kelly squinted at the bright horizon.

'The shooter was in a parking lot across the street. I guess he must have been following you from when you came off the bridge. When he saw the roadblock he pulled off, set up position, then popped one into Black as he walked towards us, and another through the windshield of a squad car just to make sure we returned fire. Clever guy. I'd put money he was the ghost in Vogel's apartment, that he somehow fixed that meeting, shot the two of them, left them the guns, and got panicked when you arrived.'

He looked at Costa.

'That makes for two occasions when he could have had you in his sights. Consider yourself damned lucky and keep hold of that gun.'

'Anything else I should know?' Costa asked.

'Here's the last remaining fact I have. We have the bullets and we have spent shells from the Embarcadero – .243 Winchester. He had a long-range hunting rifle.'

Gerald Kelly winced, thinking about something.

'The kind you use for shooting deer. Which is not my idea of sport, though marginally kinder than a crossbow, I guess.'

– 4 –

Hank had a pair of half-moon glasses for sitting at the computer. Frank, similarly afflicted, preferred a pair of modern square plastic frames. Both men squinted at Barkev's Mac and made baffling complimentary remarks on its newness and speed. These things seemed important in San Francisco. The average pair of sixty-year-old Roman twins newly out of the fire service would probably have struggled to do much more than send an e-mail. The Boynton brothers sailed through a sea of information sources in front of them with a speed and ease that reminded her of Silvio Di Capua back in Rome, a thought that gave her a pang of homesickness. She'd experienced too little yelling and too much being yelled at of late.

Finally Hank found the page he wanted and once they'd read it, Teresa said, 'One more coincidence. It has to be. We're talking nearly four hundred years ago.'

'Let's see.' His fat fingers clattered across Barkev's pristine keyboard. 'Yep. It's a coincidence. Lorenzo di Tonti. Born in Naples. Got into trouble there. Moved to Paris. Died penniless.'

'Offspring?' Frank asked.

'Two of note,' his brother replied, placing a large finger directly on the screen.

Teresa scanned the article next to a black and white portrait of a man with long, flowing black hair and elegant nobleman's clothes.

'So Roberto Tonti can't be related,' she declared when she skimmed to the end.

His fingers ran over the keyboard again.

'Seems not. Even the name changes. Lorenzo became *de* Tonti when he moved to Paris. Two sons wound up over here. One expired penniless of yellow fever in Mobile, Alabama. The second helped to found Detroit and died in disgrace. Was calling himself de Tonty by then. They didn't have a lot of luck these guys, did they? Mind you, all that from an argument in Naples. Interesting lives. Makes me feel quite small.'

'So,' she repeated, 'Roberto Tonti the movie director can in no way be a descendant of Lorenzo di Tonti the dubious seventeenth-century banker.'

'Agreed,' Hank said straight away. 'But does that matter? Use your imagination. Roberto certainly does. It's his job. Lorenzo invented the tontine that's named after him. Who doesn't Google themselves these days? How many other people have surnames describing an idea that's killed a good number of idiots over the years?'

Tontine.

She vaguely knew what the word meant. It reminded her of old stories of tortuous conspiracies and unbelievably clever detectives. All the kinds of things real-life law enforcement agencies never met in the mundane world of hard, cruel fact.

Hank looked uncomfortable.

'I've got to be honest. I looked up Tonti a few days ago. I went hunting after you put all this in our heads. Type in Tonti and pretty soon you get to tontine. I apologize for not mentioning any of this earlier. It seemed irrelevant. I thought the same about tontines too. Maybe I was wrong. Here.'

She went through another page he'd found, feeling a welcome mild rush of excitement and possibility.

Teresa dimly recalled a tontine as an agreement between a group of individuals to share some kind of bounty, usually a crooked one, leaving the illicit prize to the last surviving member of the circle. This proved fundamentally wrong in many respects. Lorenzo di Tonti, the man who shared Roberto's name – though not, it would seem, his blood – hadn't set out to make his fortune creating a secret profit-sharing scheme for criminals. He was an ambitious banker trying to establish a new form of investment vehicle of general benefit to those who had the wherewithal to take part in it.

Teresa read the details and tried to recall what little she knew about investing for the future. Money was never one of her strong points, which was probably why the true tontine appeared eminently sensible. Each member made a contribution to the fund. The total was then invested in legitimate enterprises. Any dividends from those holdings were shared equally among the surviving members of the scheme, until the penultimate one died, at which point the entire sum, dividends and capital, fell to the ownership of the last in the group.

The only flaw she could see was the obvious one; there was a substantial incentive on the part of tontine members to murder one another in order to ensure they claimed the richest prize. According to the documents Hank found, this had happened, and not just in fiction either. The schemes were made illegal in most countries by the nineteenth century, and passed on as fodder for novelists.

'Fine . . .' she said quietly. 'The connection being?'

Hank found another article, one from the *Financial Times* the previous year.

'I remembered this one because it made me think. Take a look.'

It was a long and very serious piece about the nature of life insurance.

'You see the author's point?' Hank asked after they scanned it. 'If you leave out the temptation-to-murder part, what old Lorenzo actually invented was the very first pension scheme. The only differ-ence is he didn't let newcomers in, so that big final payout remained. In practical terms it's not much different to what happens today.' He nodded at his brother. 'We're in the fire department pension scheme. The pot for that depends on the stock market or something magical, I guess. When one of our colleagues bites the dust, that's one less mouth to feed. We all profit from each other's deaths. We always have. Lorenzo just said all that out loud, and put it in a way that prompted a few people to bring on some of those deaths a little earlier than might otherwise have happened.'

She knew what he was getting at even if she wasn't quite sure how it could be made to work.

'So there was a tontine,' Teresa suggested. 'The people who were trying to hype *Inferno* were all in it.'

'That's a possibility. Plus Josh Jonah and Tom Black, and Jimmy Gaines. Jimmy wasn't the brightest of creatures. I doubt anyone could have sold him on a tontine. But if they said it was some kind of fancy insurance, one that might give him and Tom Black a tidy return each . . . ?'

'What did Jimmy Gaines have to put into a movie?' Frank asked.

Hank shrugged.

'A little muscle, maybe, like that photographer guy. What you have is what you contribute. And what you take out is . . .'

There he was struggling. Frank looked sceptical.

'Let me try and ask some practical questions,' he said. 'Imagine this is true. Why would they do it? They're making a movie. What these people need is money. Money pays people. You don't pay people, you don't get the job done.'

'They didn't pay people,' Teresa interjected. 'That's the point. The money wasn't there. Nic told me Maggie Flavier was still owed most of her fee. Lots of other people too.'

'I still don't see it . . .' Frank sighed.

But she did. Or at least she thought she might.

'Imagine you're Allan Prime. They come to you. The movie's halfway through. You've been working for six months but the big reward is still down the line, when it comes out. They say there's no money left to pay you what's owed. But if you're willing to exchange your fee for something else . . .'

'Insurance?' Hank suggested.

Frank shook his big, tired head.

'Prime would tell them to take a hike! These guys aren't stupid. It's the movie business. Getting paid's the first thing any of them would want.'

'But if you won't get paid anyway?' she asked. 'If they say you take this deal or the whole thing collapses? Everything with it? The merchandise cut, the residuals from the TV and DVD rights, the cosy promotional tour around the world? If there's no movie Allan Prime loses a lot more than his fee. He loses everything that might come after.'

Frank still wasn't happy.

'I still don't see how someone like Jimmy Gaines would get mixed up in something like that. What the hell would he know about the movie business?'

Barkev came in with some more coffee. Teresa gulped it down quickly.

'They weren't dealing with the movie business,' she said quietly after Barkev left the room.

The two brothers watched her and didn't utter a word.

'The movie people were dealing with Lukatmi. Don't you see? We've been asking the wrong question all along. When Roberto Tonti needed real money, he went to the mob. They stumped up enough to keep the production alive, barely, but it still couldn't be finished. We're pretty sure of that. Dino Bonetti has been taking finance from criminals for years. You don't need to be a genius to understand they'll certainly be expecting their return. Lukatmi was different. They came in later, when Tonti was looking at the whole project collapsing. Everyone's turned him down. He's desperate. And Lukatmi turn up offering . . .'

What? It was clear there was precious little money behind the doors of their hangars at Fort Mason by that stage. Josh Jonah and Tom Black hadn't bailed out *Inferno*. They didn't have the cash.

Frank – practical, logical, rational Frank – got there first, naturally.

'I know what I'd do. I'd go quietly to all the people I owe money, not just the big guys like Allan Prime. I'd say, skip the fee and we'll give you something else. Something that might be worth a whole lot more than some risky horror flick if you play along.'

She wanted to pinch herself. It was so obvious.

'This wasn't about investing in a movie,' Teresa said. 'It was about cutting your losses, keeping *Inferno* alive and getting a chunk of the next big dotcom float coming round the corner. One that could make you richer than you could ever dream of even through Hollywood. Josh Jonah and Tom Black were paper billionaires. Allan Prime couldn't even contemplate money like that and he was a huge movie star. So you put together a secret little scheme to hype *Inferno* to the heavens and make Lukatmi even more lucrative at the same time.'

Frank was scribbling down some notes.

'I get it. Whatever paperwork's involved resides in one of these funny-money places in the Caribbean. A limited number of members with the payout based on status. Obviously it won't be equal. Allan Prime's going to expect a whole lot more than poor little Jimmy Gaines, that's for sure. Martin Vogel thought his efforts merited a bigger cut and started blackmailing Josh Jonah. But it's still a fund. A secret one. It has to be. You can't invite in more members otherwise you go to jail. You get it?'

Not quite yet, she thought.

'It's a tontine by default as much as by design,' Frank said. 'When the numbers start to fall because people are dying, where else can the money go except to the original members? Tonti could have sold the whole thing to these people without saying the word "tontine" once. It was what he said it was. What Jimmy got told. Insurance.'

Hank put down his coffee cup. He had a sour expression on his face.

'This world sickens me. All these people screwing one another. Josh Jonah and Tom Black thinking they were robbing the movie crowd so's they could keep their tinpot company afloat. The movie people kidding themselves they'd all get rich on some dumb kids' dotcom dream. Yuk . . .'

He looked at the door and yelled, 'Barkev. I need a beer.'

The dark face appeared.

'Hank,' the man said. 'This is a cafe. If you want a beer go find a bar.'

'That I shall. Someone going to join me?'

Teresa stared at him in astonishment.

'We are about to get some insight into this case, finally, and you want to go to a bar?'

He looked puzzled.

'You can think of a better time? What's there left to talk about? Half these people are dead. Josh and Tom and Jimmy. That photographer guy. Allan Prime. Anyone else who's involved . . . why would they do anything now? What for? The money's gone. Lukatmi's dead, worthless. Their grubby little deal won't get them a penny. That's as much justice as any of us can expect.'

She caught his arm.

'You're missing the point. This is offshore. It can't be part of Lukatmi any more otherwise they'd be able to find it. From what Catherine Bianchi told me even the Federal people think they'll never trace where the company's assets really ended up.' She needed to get this clear in her own head too. 'That part of things is not dead. It's very much alive, out there somewhere. Just reversed. Lukatmi's the turkey and *Inferno*'s the golden goose. One that's in the names of a diminishing group of people who, between them, now own a chunk of the biggest movie in decades.'

'Do the math,' Frank suggested. 'Say there's four of them still alive. One dies. Your share just went from . . .' He paused to do the sums in his head. 'Twenty-five per cent to thirty-three.'

'Two left and you just doubled your money,' Teresa added, pulling out her phone. 'Winner takes all. It's worth killing for now more than it ever was.'

- 5 -

The call came through as Kelly was driving him through the foot of the Presidio. Costa got dropped off in Chestnut and met Teresa and the Boynton brothers in a tiny cafe he'd never even noticed before. Outside the grubby windows the light was changing. Fog was reaching the city, bringing with it a filmy haze that was dimming the bright blue sky.

Teresa and the two somewhat eccentric twins spoke of what they'd discovered. He listened.

When they were finished, she said, 'We thought you ought to know.'

He took a deep breath, smiled and said, 'It's a good theory.'

They waited and waited for something else.

'That's it?' Teresa asked, incensed. 'That's all you have to say?'

'You can't base a case on some information you've picked up on Google.'

'Nothing else fits,' said one of the brothers. 'Does it?'

'That doesn't make it true. Without some evidence from a place that's beyond our reach, or a confession, which seems just as unlikely, we've nothing.'

'A confession of murder,' the other brother said. 'Sure. No one's going to own up to that easily. But . . . am I really the only one who sees this?'

'Yes, Hank,' Teresa said. 'I believe you are.'

'You don't need to get someone to own up to killing one of these people. All you need is to get them to own up to the deal. The insurance scheme. The tontine. If he – or she – does that and gives you the names of the members you've got a shortlist. Someone on it has to be your man.'

Teresa looked at him and asked, 'Why on earth would anyone confess to that?'

'Because they can't all be murdering bastards. This was an accidental tontine, right?' He looked at Costa. 'Tom Black told you that himself, didn't he? They surely didn't start out to kill people. Why would they? Just to get a movie made? Someone somewhere's got to have a conscience. Even in the movie business.' He clutched his empty coffee cup. 'Either that or they've got to be scared. Looking round at the others wondering, "Was it him? Am I next?" No sane human being's happy in that kind of situation.'

Their attention was all on Costa.

'Know anyone who fits the bill?' Teresa asked.

'I'm not sure,' he replied. 'Thanks for your time.'

Then he threw some money on the table and left.

- 6 -

Costa walked out into Chestnut and looked west, past the stores of the street's commercial area, towards the flat green that fronted Fort Mason. The temperature seemed to have fallen a few degrees in the brief time he'd been inside the cafe. Gerald Kelly was right about the weather.

In the early days after they'd arrived in San Francisco he'd checked the whereabouts of everyone involved in *Inferno*. Everyone except Maggie, since that would have felt prurient. Roberto Tonti lived just a few hundred yards away in his bleached white mansion opposite the Palace of Fine Arts. Dino Bonetti usually took a suite in the Four Seasons on Market.

And Simon Harvey had a long-time rent of an apartment on Marina Boulevard, not far from the Lukatmi building.

Someone somewhere's got to have a conscience.

Even if it had to be pricked.

He phoned Maggie. She was trying on some clothes for the premiere in a downtown store, surrounded, she complained, by plain-clothes police. The two of them made small talk then she asked, 'Why did you really call? It wasn't to check what I was going to wear now, was it?'

'I need to know something. A straight answer. It's important and it's not what it sounds.'

He heard her move somewhere more private.

'That has an ominous ring to it.'

'Was your relationship with Simon Harvey ever more than pro-fessional? Is it over, and if it is, how does he feel about that now?'

319

He could hear the quick, disappointed intake of breath down the phone. He could imagine the pain this question caused.

'Oh, Nic. You're not going to do this to me all the time, are you? Asking about the past? If you do that you've got to know. There are a lot of questions and not many answers you're going to like.'

'It's never going to happen again. I wish I didn't have to ask now. But I do. It's important.'

'To you?'

'In the sense that it concerns your safety . . . yes. Someone tried to harm you.'

'Not Simon, never Simon. That's ludicrous . . .'

He hesitated. He really didn't want to know.

'You know that?'

'Yes. I do. We had an affair five years ago on that pirate nonsense he told you about. It lasted a few months and then he joined the long line of ex-lovers who couldn't take my behaviour any longer. I hurt him. A lot. I know because he's told me more than once. He thought . . .' Costa wished he didn't have to hear this. 'Simon thought he could save me from myself. Some men do. It still pains him. From time to time he tries to pick up the pieces. Why do you think he was there in the sanatorium that day? Why do you think he gets so awkward when you're around?'

'I'm sorry I had to ask.'

'I'm sorry too. Don't ever do it again.'

The phone went dead.

- 7 -

Simon Harvey's apartment was on the ground floor of a Spanish-style block close to the yacht moorings that adjoined the eastern face of Fort Mason. The fog was rolling in from the bay with a steady momentum, the first grey fingers seeping onto land. There were three uniformed SFPD cops outside the door. They didn't give him any trouble once they saw his ID. Kelly must have put round the word.

Harvey didn't answer the bell straight away. When he arrived he didn't look like a man preparing for the movie event of his career.

'What the hell did I do to deserve this?'

He kept the door half open, blocking Costa's way.

'I thought perhaps I'd need a publicist, now you're setting the paparazzi on me.'

Harvey's hair was shorter, freshly cut. The vaguely hip, student-like appearance was gone. He was trying on a tuxedo over a pair of jeans and a white dress shirt.

'Does this look like a good time to you? I'm getting dressed. For a big occasion.'

'It's a good time for me . . .' Costa began.

Harvey swore and began to close the door. Costa got his foot in the gap and his arm up against the wood.

'What the hell is this?' Harvey yelled. 'Some Roman punk can't come here and start harassing me.' He stared at the three uniforms by the front gate, beyond the small, immaculate lawn of the garden. 'Hey. *Hey.* Do I get some protection here? *Well? Do I?*'

One of the men turned briefly and shrugged.

Costa leaned forward and said, 'Just a minute of your time, sir . . .'

'You don't deserve a second of it.'

'Simon,' Costa interrupted. 'I *know*.'

The pressure on the door relaxed a little. Harvey's bright, intelligent eyes narrowed a little.

'What's that supposed to mean? You know what?'

'I know about the deal. The tontine that Roberto Tonti had you and Dino Bonetti run up. The one that got *Inferno* made even though you didn't have the money. Just a treasure chest offshore, one part Lukatmi, one part *Inferno*. All under-the-counter, half of it worthless, half . . .'

Costa watched the man's reactions. He recognized the taut, nervous strain of denial.

'. . . worth what? Killing for?'

Harvey scowled at him.

'You really are something else. You mess with one of my stars. You almost get her killed. And now you stand on my doorstep accusing me of murder. Get out of here . . .'

Costa launched himself forward, pushed Simon Harvey hard back through the entrance, kicked the door shut behind and held him tight against the wall, elbow to his throat. It was dark in the entrance to the apartment. This close he could smell some rank, harsh spirit on Harvey's breath. It seemed rather early in the day for vodka.

'I don't care about you,' Costa murmured. 'Not for one moment. I don't care who it was turned murderous. Or that he may still have your name left on the list of people standing between him and the pot of gold waiting in Grand Cayman or wherever.'

'Get out of my home,' Harvey began. Then he shut up.

Costa had never done this before but there were lots of things he'd never done until San Francisco. He had the service revolver hard against Simon Harvey's right temple. He was looking into his terrified face, searching for something.

'Do you know what it feels like? To get shot? I do. It hurts. Not the way you think. It's a big hurt. It aches and aches. Long after the blood's gone. Long after the scars. It's not like the movies. Life isn't. It's real and cold and hard. If you lose someone you love the taste of it stays with you for ever.'

'Don't threaten me. I could pick up that phone . . .'

He stood back and let go, then he shouldered the weapon.

'Pick it up. Didn't you hear me? I *know*. I know you didn't just cut yourself in on this deal. Somehow you got between Maggie and her agent and put some part of her fee into that grubby little scheme of yours. That's why she's wondering where the money is now. What's she going to think when she finds she got robbed by some . . .' He waited to let the words have some power. '. . . old boyfriend? One who still won't let go?'

'You're remarkably out of your depth.'

'Maybe,' Costa admitted. 'Doesn't it bother you, though? The idea that this isn't over?'

'Of course it's over. The Carabinieri said so. Those creeps from Lukatmi. Josh Jonah. Tom Black.'

'They're wrong. What if someone gets to Maggie first? Would you even care?'

'What the hell are you talking about? Where'd you get this crap?'

'Maggie told me. About you two. And the money.'

Harvey stared at him, remembering something, some pain, some anguish.

'Big deal. She tell you anything else? About what it was like? What she did?'

'No . . .'

'You've got all that to come, friend. Nothing I can do will warn you off it either. Listen. I'm not a thief.'

'What else do you call it?'

'I call it looking after people who can't look after themselves.' He glared at Costa. 'I call it keeping her alive, making sure the last movie she was ever going to get didn't fold beneath her. That's the truth of it. Maggie's career has been on the skids for years. *Inferno* was her only chance to keep her name up there. If it never even made it to the screen . . .'

There was a distant look of resignation and regret in his face.

'You weren't there. You can't begin to understand. Some of us put in years for that movie and there it was, ready to fall apart. No way past go. No fairy godmothers on the horizon. Everything was in hock. Our homes, our reputations. Everything.'

Costa waited.

'And if you tell anyone I said that I'll call you a liar to your face,' Harvey added. 'In a police station. On the witness stand. Anywhere. This is America. We've got lawyers who could free the Devil if he got found eating babies on Main Street. I'm sorry. You can't win. Not with me. Not with Maggie either. We're all out of your class. Best you see that and cut your losses.' He nodded at the door. 'Best you get out of here.'

'Best I know my place,' Costa said, not moving.

'If that's the way you want to see it.'

He took out the weapon again and closed on the man. The barrel stayed close to Harvey's throat.

'You're not listening to me. Maggie knew nothing of all this. You made her a part of it. You put her in danger. She nearly died.'

The shadow of the weapon fell towards the window.

'Whoever killed Allan Prime is still out there. He killed Martin Vogel and Josh Jonah. He shot Tom Black dead before the police got a chance.'

The blood drained from Harvey's face.

'What the hell are you talking about? The cops shot Tom.'

'No they didn't. He was killed by a single bullet from some distant gunman. They've recovered the shell. They know what kind of rifle he used. A hunting weapon. Like the crossbow that killed Allan Prime.'

Harvey was shaking his head like a man on the brink.

'This is not possible, not possible. The Maggie thing . . . it had to be an accident. I couldn't . . .'

'There are no accidents. None. Every time someone in this deal of yours dies the rest of you get richer. I don't care what he does to you. But . . . if it's Maggie he finally finds this time . . .'

'Not going to happen, not going to happen,' Harvey whispered, eyes closed, screwed tight shut. 'It's inconceivable . . .'

'If it does – it doesn't matter where or when – I will find you. I will walk up to your dinner table in whatever fancy restaurant in New York or Cannes or LA, anywhere . . .'

He nudged the barrel of the gun back towards Harvey's temple.

'. . . and then in front of your friends I will shoot you through the head.'

Costa felt he was listening to the voice of another. He lowered the weapon and put it back in Gerald Kelly's leather holster. Then he turned towards the door.

A hand touched his arm.

'Don't go.'

Simon Harvey was slumped against the wall. He looked drained, lost, defeated.

Then he walked into the living room, picked up a bottle of Grey Goose from the cocktail cabinet by the window, poured himself a large glass, and said, 'Sit down.'

- 8 -

'It was never meant to turn out this way,' Harvey murmured, clutching at the glass. 'The whole thing was just something to get us through. Out of the mess.'

He sat on the sofa opposite Costa staring at the mirror on the side wall, as if trying to convince himself. 'Maggie wasn't the only one with everything to lose. Roberto's terminal. There was never going to be another movie. I wasn't sure he'd live long enough to complete this one.'

'I didn't realize the movie business was so sentimental.'

'Don't patronize me!' Harvey screeched. 'I've worked alongside these people for years. They're more to me than a pay cheque. Even Roberto. Sure, he can be an asshole. They all can. But he's an artist too, one of the last. The people he worked with . . . Hitchcock, Rossellini, De Sica. We don't see them any more. Those days, when it was all about film, nothing but film, they're over. Roberto's all I ever really saw of them, and when I looked at him . . .'

His bleak eyes never left Costa's face.

'You won't understand. I grew up with all those movies from the Fifties. Roberto lived them. You could talk to him, about how Hitchcock would chase the light he wanted, how Rossellini could coax a performance from some two-bit actress who hadn't the talent to speak her own name. *Inferno* was always going to be his last movie, and when he dies a piece of history goes with him.'

He threw back more vodka.

'After that all we have left are kids who think you can direct a movie with a computer and a mouse. Who see some bum performance then bring in CGI to save it. Maybe *Inferno*'s a piece of shit. But there's still some art in there, somewhere. I see it, even if no one else does.'

Outside the fog had swept in across the bay. Costa couldn't even see the cops by the gate any more.

'It wasn't supposed to happen.'

'But it did. Maybe it will again.'

'No.' Harvey shook his head wildly, as if the long curly student hair was still there. 'It won't. I guarantee that. I'll make sure of it. This has gone far enough.'

'You need to make a statement.'

'Yeah, yeah, yeah,' he grumbled, waving Costa down. 'And in return . . . ?'

Costa felt the ground turn shaky beneath him.

'I can't negotiate on behalf of the SFPD. You need to talk to them direct.'

'Fine. But when the premiere's over. Not before. Roberto's owed his moment. We all are. Maggie too.'

'Whose idea was it?' he asked.

'I said after . . .'

'I know. But I want to hear it. Just for me.'

'Just for you.' He shook his head, bitterly amused by some internal thought. 'Do you have any idea how long I've wanted to tell someone this?'

'I'm starting to,' Costa said honestly.

'I really don't recall. I was drunk at the time. I thought *Inferno* was dead. We'd been everywhere. Dino had begged every last penny he could out of his mob friends and they were starting to get heavy thinking the whole thing was about to turn into some train wreck. Maybe it was him, maybe Roberto. One or both. I just woke up one morning and it was there. We got the movie, and maybe down the line we got paid too.'

Harvey scowled at the glass and put it on the table in front of him, half finished.

'How'd you say no to something like that? We all knew Roberto was sick. He told us he was rolling in his fee as collateral, knowing full well he'd never get to pick it up. Lukatmi was going to go sky-high. So there was an instant profit for all of us the moment he croaked, even if the movie bombed.'

'Whose names were on the contract?'

Harvey stared at him as if it were an idiotic question.

'What contract? What do you think this was? A corporation? Some listing on the New York Stock Exchange? It was just some grubby little deal to breathe life back into a dying movie. These things happen all the time. Maybe not quite like this.'

'Who . . . ?'

'I didn't know all the names. I didn't want to. Allan put in the balance of his fee. That took a little persuading but Dino offered to sort out a few personal issues he had somewhere. What's a producer for? I waived what I was owed. Same with Dino. Josh and Tom put in some special form of Lukatmi stock and a little cash to keep the wheels turning. Those of us on the movie side thought that would turn out to be the real cream. How dumb can you get, huh? We thought we were robbing the geeks when the truth is it was the other way round. Robbing murderous geeks too . . .'

He cleared his throat then, looked at Costa and asked, 'And now you're telling me that's not the case?'

'I don't think so. Do you know anyone who hunts?'

'In the movie business? Are you kidding?'

'Then the people you used.'

'I made damned sure I stayed clear of that side of things. Fraud's as far as I was prepared to go. Dino handled the rough stuff. He seemed comfortable with it. He had the contacts. Tom and Josh knew some guy from Lukatmi who came in as crew. All I did was get Martin Vogel on board. That creep would screw his mother for five dollars. The only other thing I handled was Maggie. I gave her a few drinks and talked her into signing her fee away into some fictitious offshore production company. She didn't have a clue what she was doing. Money's never been her thing. I had her name on the paper before her agent got to know. Nothing anyone could do after that.'

His phone rang. Harvey took it out of his pocket, looked at the number, then turned the thing off.

'She wasn't going to get robbed either. Not as far as I was concerned. All of us expected what we were owed at the very least. Maybe more if Lukatmi's stock went through the roof. Dino handled the money and contract side of things. He could do that better than anyone. I didn't understand a word of what he was doing. All any of us cared about was the fact this gave us a chance to make *Inferno* happen.'

He looked at his watch and shrugged.

'I've got to get dressed soon. Really.'

'Who put it all together?' Costa asked.

'We just did what we'd been doing all along. I'd been hyping *Inferno* from the start. Would the academic community be pissed off by it? Was the thing cursed? The media loved all that crap. The story had legs. So we decided to build on it. This idea that someone was stalking the movie and leaving clues straight out of Dante. We forged a few e-mails.' He stiffened. 'Someone hired that guy to wear a Carabinieri uniform and create some kind of incident the day of the premiere in Rome. No one was supposed to get shot.'

'Allan Prime . . .'

'I damned near told you all this then. But that would have killed the movie stone-dead. All I understood was that Tom and Josh had cooked up something to get us some publicity. They never told me what. I don't know about the others. Afterwards . . .'

He fell silent.

'What?' Costa asked.

'I thought the rest of them didn't understand it either. Allan was supposed to disappear for a while, get that mask nonsense made, then put on that little show in front of the camera as a stunt and get rescued by the cops. They were going to portray it as some kind of warped attack. Allan was in on the plan. They told him on the day.

329

That's what they said. They'd no idea why he got killed. They thought maybe something went wrong . . .'

'He was murdered, deliberately, in cold blood, in front of millions of people. It almost kept Lukatmi alive.'

'Josh said it was never meant to happen. That's all I can tell you.'

Harvey tapped his watch.

'When the premiere's over, come and see me and I will make a statement. I'll want a lawyer there. Don't freak out over that. This has gone far enough already. I don't want anything else on my conscience. Besides . . .'

He caught his own reflection in the mirror and the traces of a smile creased his face.

'. . . it's a hell of a story, isn't it? Biggest I've ever run. Could make a movie some day.'

Something was still missing.

'There was a woman involved. She went to Allan Prime's apartment the morning he died. She made the mask. She left with him.'

Harvey waved away the idea with his hand, 'I don't know of any woman. Except for Maggie, and she didn't know the first thing about what was going on. Can't help you there.'

Costa kept his eyes on him and said, 'She called herself Carlotta Valdes.'

Simon Harvey blinked and said, 'What?'

'Carlotta Valdes? Do you know the name?'

'Of course I do. *Vertigo*. It was shot right here. Roberto worked on it. He's talked about it, often.'

Harvey sat hunched on the sofa, silently removing his tuxedo.

'What do you think it means?' Costa asked.

'That some punk in this whole mess still has good taste in movies, I guess.'

- 9 -

The security cordon ran from 101 all the way down to the waterfront stretch of Marina Boulevard. Bright red barriers and yellow tape blocked off all the normal entry routes. Photographers and TV camera crews who hadn't managed to beg media accreditation wandered the perimeter like mangy starving lions. Uniformed SFPD officers stood at the two entry checkpoints, patiently checking the credentials of the lines of men in evening suits and women wearing elegant, expensive dresses gathered for the premiere, shivering in the chilly mist. Once they were approved the guests were then forced to walk through a portable airport-style metal detector to check for weapons, an unusual addition to such an event, Costa thought, and one that clearly engaged the attention of the photographers.

The crocodile of expensively clad bodies was steadily working through the system. Costa walked round the entire enclosed area once, then stopped by the lake that fronted the main structure of the Palace. Even this close up he could only just make out the domed roof of the structure across the water. Soon that would be gone. *Inferno* would be launched, appropriately enough, in a cloud of San Francisco fog. He wondered if the grey cloud might seep into the gigantic tent erected for the private screening by the side of the lake, and if it did whether those at the rear of the seats would have much of a view at all. Perhaps that wasn't the point. More than anything this was an occasion to be seen at. The lines of long dark limousines drawing up by the checkpoints contained more than a few faces he had come to recognize from the TV since he'd arrived in San

Francisco, politicians and media figures, actors and other celebrities, and a constant stream of beautiful women on the arms of men in evening dress.

He looked ruefully at his own crumpled dark blue suit, bought from the usual discount store in Vittorio Emanuele, near the bridge to the Castel Sant'Angelo. Costa tightened his tie into a half-passable knot, which was as good as it got. When no one was looking he stepped into a nearby flower bed, stole a red rose from one of the bushes there, and placed it in his lapel. Then he took out his Roman police ID card and, after the uniform on the gate checked with Gerald Kelly, made his way into the world premiere for *Roberto Tonti's Inferno*.

After a brief search he found Falcone, Peroni and Teresa in the tent that housed the main historical exhibits from Florence. The three of them looked bored and out of sorts, yawning next to a set of glass cabinets full of illuminated medieval manuscripts. Only a handful of visitors had wandered into the place. The rest were outside, with the stars and the free drinks. Compared to those, some old documents seemed insufficient to warrant anyone's attention.

Falcone cleared his throat and said, though with precious little in the way of displeasure, 'I was under the impression, *sovrintendente*, that you were off duty today.'

'I am.' He flashed the envelope Maggie had sent to the house in Greenwich Street. 'Someone sent me a ticket for the main event.'

'Lucky you,' Peroni observed.

'Thanks.'

'I meant,' the big man went on, 'lucky you getting away with all that nonsense last night. It would be nice if we knew where you were sometimes, Nic.'

He shrugged and apologized.

'I hadn't really expected things to turn out the way they did. Also . . .' He wondered how much to tell them. '. . . I was hoping for a little gratitude from Gerald Kelly when I brought him Tom Black. It wasn't the fault of the SFPD that things went wrong.'

Not at all, he thought, remembering the hunting weapon, and its link to the crossbow that had killed Allan Prime.

Teresa reached up and did some more work on his tie.

'If you're on a date, and I suspect you are, you really ought to take a little more time with your appearance.'

'Been busy,' he said, fighting shy of her hands.

They caught the unintentional note of satisfaction in his voice.

'Good busy or idle busy?' Peroni asked suspiciously.

'Good.'

He left it at that.

Falcone looked at him and said, 'How good?'

There was no way to say it except simply.

'Possibly as good as we're likely to get. When the show's over Simon Harvey wants to make a statement. He'll confess to being a part of a financial conspiracy to hype *Inferno* by making bogus threats to those involved, with their knowledge usually. They needed the money. They needed the movie to be a success. Also . . .'

'No details, not now,' Falcone said, suppressing a wry grin.

Teresa smiled.

'Will he name anyone else, perchance?'

'Allan Prime. Josh Jonah. Tom Black. Dino Bonetti.' He paused. 'And Roberto Tonti.'

'A tontine?' she asked.

'Effectively. Harvey says that Tonti made his illness one of the lures. It was obvious he wouldn't survive to pick up his share, so that would give the others an instant profit. In return he was allowed to make his final movie.'

Falcone pointed a finger at him.

'What did I say about details?' He glanced around. They were on their own. 'Harvey's told you all this already? And you say he's willing to repeat it all?'

'After the premiere. He feels they're all owed their moment of glory. After that he's had enough. He's a decent man.'

Peroni huffed and puffed and grumbled.

'*Now* he's decent! And if he changes his mind?'

Costa pulled out the tiny MP3 player he'd bought from Walgreens in Chestnut on his way to Harvey's apartment. It had been tucked into his jacket pocket, set to record, throughout their conversation. The histrionics with the gun had been intended, in part, to make Harvey so nervous he might not notice its presence. For twenty dollars the thing did a good job; he'd checked through the little earphones on the walk back to the Palace of Fine Arts. He still didn't quite recognize his own voice at times, particularly in those moments when he had the gun in his hands.

'If he changes his mind then I just give this to Gerald Kelly and let nature take its course. The entire conversation is recorded, from beginning to end. I'm not sure how much of it will pass the evidence rules in America . . .'

They were grinning like Cheshire cats, all three of them.

'I mean that about the evidence, Leo. It would be best all round if the man confesses . . .'

'Let me worry about that.' The inspector hesitated then asked, 'No more names to give me?'

'Maggie Flavier was defrauded of her fee. She never knew a thing about what was going on. Harvey's admitted that in detail. It may be Kelly's opening shot. At the very least he can charge them over that.'

'At the very least,' Falcone agreed, then took the audio player from Costa's fingers. 'Thank you very much.'

Costa stood his ground.

'And you intend to do what with it, sir?'

Leo Falcone stiffened, straightened his own tie, and looked outside the door at the thickening mist.

'I intend to find Gerald Kelly and tell him what you've just told me. You can't spring this on the San Francisco Police Department the way you sprang it on us, however pleasant that would be. I want to leave this place feeling we did our job as well as could be expected in the circumstances. Not in the middle of some argument over who deserves the credit.'

'And me?' Costa asked.

Falcone frowned as if the question was ridiculous.

'You're off duty and you've got a date. Make the most of it. As for you two . . .'

He glanced at Peroni and Teresa, then waved at the glass cabinets and their ancient manuscripts.

'. . . watch this stuff, will you?'

– 10 –

Falcone found Gerald Kelly alone a little way from the mob of photographers and reporters jostling one another by the red carpet runway to the premiere. The tent was now a ghostly grey shape in the fog. Through the doors he could just make out the brightly lit stage with mikes in front of the screen, like the podium for some cut-down copy of the Oscar ceremonies. A half-familiar face from the TV was due to start a warm-up for the evening. Then there would be the movie, and, some three hours later, a closing speech from Roberto Tonti.

The Roman inspector wished to see none of it. He knew his own force could take no part in what followed, even if the crucial information was to come from them in the first instance. This was Gerald Kelly's case, one that would, if it came to court, be prosecuted through the American authorities, not those in Italy. If Falcone could return home with the missing mask of Dante Alighieri then he would be content, though he did not expect this happy conclusion to be reached.

'Are you planning to watch the movie?' Falcone asked as he arrived.

'Not if I can help it.'

'I understand.' The American had a very piercing gaze. 'Are you pleased with arrangements, captain?'

Kelly frowned.

'As much as anyone could be. The glitterati don't like going through metal detectors much but they can learn to live with it. We're doing what we can.'

Falcone thought of how Maggie Flavier was poisoned by someone working in a catering truck, an individual with a fake name and no ID. There were limits to how much security one could put in place for events of this nature. Without months of preparation and the vetting of everyone concerned – neither of which had been practicable – some loopholes had to remain.

He didn't mention this because he knew Gerald Kelly understood the problem just as well as he did. So, with no further ado, he told Kelly in summary what he had learned from Costa and passed on the audio player, then asked to attend any interview with Simon Harvey to put the necessary questions about the missing death mask of Dante Alighieri. After that – barring any new discoveries – the work of the Roman state police in San Francisco would be done. They could return home at the weekend with some sense of achievement, even if the public prize would doubtless fall to others.

This news did not appear to surprise the American police captain, which Falcone found odd. But Kelly thanked him politely for it, agreed to Harvey's conditions, and asked for Falcone to meet him with the publicist at the temporary police control truck after Roberto Tonti's closing speech. Then he said no more.

Taking the hint, Falcone left to amble idly round the crowd, determined not to return to a tent full of glass cases and mouldering pieces of paper.

Finally, not consciously realizing that this was what he intended all along, he found her. Catherine Bianchi was standing beneath the dome of the Palace, a radio in her hand. She wore a dark suit that was tight on her slender figure, and might have been mistaken for a guest herself had she not spent so much of her time alone, watching the crowd with the careful attention he recognized in all good police officers.

'Leo?' she said as he approached.

'It's a foul evening for a movie premiere. They should have chosen a cinema.'

'It's only a movie. A few hours of fantasy and then it's over.' She smiled at him. She looked different somehow. More at ease. More

. . . alluring perhaps. Falcone found this odd and a little disconcerting. He had scarcely given Catherine Bianchi a second thought all day, possibly for the first time since he had arrived in San Francisco.

'I'm through at nine,' she said. 'I know a warm place for dinner. We should go to North Beach. You've been avoiding Italian food ever since you came here. It's time to try something new.'

He laughed.

'I don't think I've done anything else since I came, have I? And now . . . ?'

'Now you're going. I can see it in your face.'

'Is it that obvious?'

'You're very transparent. You all are. Peroni. Nic. Teresa. I'll miss that. It's unusual. You're unusual.'

'Perhaps. Perhaps we're just out of place.'

'When do you go?' she asked.

'At the weekend, I think. I haven't given it much thought to be honest. Nic said something about wishing to tack some holiday on the end. It's fine by me. I have some reports to deal with in Rome. Internal reorganization. You know the kind of thing.'

'When they close down Greenwich Street,' she said, 'they want me downtown. Bryant Street. With all the others.' She glanced around at the columns of the Palace. The distant quacking of the waterfowl on the lake echoed through the mist. 'I'll miss the Marina. It's my little village.'

There was a burst of laughter and applause from the stage, which was now almost invisible in the fog.

'You'll never leave Rome, will you?' she asked.

'No more than you'd leave San Francisco.'

'Kind of makes things hard, doesn't it? When two people are fixed in their ways like that?'

'Why? We have what time we have. We do with it the best we can.'

'Not everyone. You're Roman. My family are old Catholics from Campania. Cautious. Traditional. Set in their ways.'

'I never saw you like that,' he said, surprised.

'No. You didn't. I could tell.'

He opened his arms in a gesture of despair. A part of him had sought this woman's affection with an ardent desire he'd not known for a long time. Now that Italy beckoned, that passion had dissipated almost as quickly as it had arisen in the first place. Yet there was a look in her eyes . . .

'I'm sorry if I offended you, Catherine. That was never my intention.'

'I wasn't offended. I was flattered. But you try too hard, Leo. And also . . .'

She looked a little guilty.

'I have a rule. I don't date cops.'

He blinked.

'Ever?'

'Ever.'

She was smiling at him.

'At least I haven't since I made the mistake of marrying one briefly a decade or so back.'

'Ah . . .'

'But we could have dinner in North Beach tonight. Since you go home so soon . . . And this isn't Campania, is it? We're in California. We're free as birds. After the premiere . . . ?'

Falcone felt briefly lost for words. Then he tapped his watch and said, rather more bluntly than he wished, 'I'm afraid I can't fit you in. Business, unfortunately. It may go on for a while. We should meet for a coffee some time. That would be good.'

The radio burst into life. She held it to her mouth and began speaking. He could see she hadn't even touched the press to talk button. The conversation had come to a close.

Feeling somewhat bemused by this unexpected and tardy approach, Falcone walked to the edge of the cordoned area, found a quiet place with a seat. He was acutely aware of something that surprised him. He would miss this city. He would regret, too, the overzealous and childish way he had chased Catherine Bianchi without ever once asking himself what she might seek in return.

Cries of surprise and a ripple of applause drifted through the mist from the nearby runway into the premiere.

Falcone walked to the edge of the crowd, close to the road, and, with the deft elbows of a Roman, worked his way politely but forcefully to the front.

The cameras and the reporters had only one thing on their minds, and that was the couple walking slowly along the red carpet.

He stood behind the yellow tape, and found himself beaming with a mixture of pride and emotion at what he saw. Nic Costa looked as if he belonged with the beautiful young woman on his arm, even though his cheap Roman suit seemed somewhat shabby next to her long, flowing silk gown, a flimsy creation for such a chilly, fog-strewn night, not that Maggie Flavier, being the consummate actress she was, showed one iota of discomfort.

As the reporters shouted her name, she simply smiled and waved and held herself like a star for the cameras, always clutching Costa's arm. He held himself with quiet, calm dignity, and didn't respond to their calls either.

As they slowly passed, Falcone, to his own amazement, found himself crying out, '*Sovrintendente! Sovrintendente!*'

The couple stopped. Nic Costa turned and stared at him with a quizzical look.

'*In bocca al lupo,*' Falcone shouted, with a sudden and entirely involuntary enthusiasm that took him aback.

'*Crepi il lupo!*' Maggie Flavier cried back at him.

And then they moved on.

In the mouth of the wolf. Foreigners always found it a curious way to wish someone good luck. He was impressed that Maggie Flavier knew the correct response too. *To hell with the wolf.*

The wolf had hung around Nic Costa long enough, Falcone thought as he watched them disappear into the mist.

– 11 –

Gianluca Quattrocchi wore his finest Carabinieri dress uniform with a white carnation in the collar, determined to look his best at this glittering event before his return home. He had already rehearsed in his head the report he would give to his superiors. Of the uncooperative intransigence of the American authorities, unable to relinquish their grip of the case sufficiently to allow the Carabinieri to do their job. Of the meddling of the state police too, constantly obstructing and interfering with Quattrocchi's investigation. He would single out Falcone by name, in the knowledge that remark would get back to the higher echelons of the state police and perhaps earn the man a deserved reprimand.

There was, for Gianluca Quattrocchi, a point at which a failed case turned from a mystery demanding solution into a disaster requiring containment. The death of Allan Prime and the sequence of events that had followed now fell entirely into the second category. It would be for the American authorities to pursue whatever slim, time-consuming half-leads and connections they could find in the financial affairs of the two dead men involved in the dotcom bubble of Lukatmi. The Carabinieri had neither the time nor the resources to become involved in such work, not least because any resulting case would surely be heard in America and benefit the Italian authorities not one whit.

This was not the outcome Quattrocchi had sought. He had, for a while, genuinely believed that the Canadian professor Bryan Whitcombe, who had pressed himself upon the Italian authorities with such adamant enthusiasm, might hold some insight into the case.

That idea had waned of late, and he'd begun to find the man somewhat creepy. Whitcombe had turned up for the premiere in a garish white suit and taken to bearding starlets with his earnest and lascivious gaze. The man had even announced to the media that he intended to write a book on the affair of 'Dante's Numbers', as he had dubbed it. According to that morning's papers, an outline for the work was now being hyped around American publishers by one of the book world's more notorious agents. Law enforcement work often had unforeseen consequences. The elevation of Bryan Whitcombe to the status of unlikely media star was one he could never have predicted.

None of this did much for Gianluca Quattrocchi's mood as he sipped his free champagne. He began quietly to plan his exit from the proceedings so that he might miss the screening altogether, merely returning for the closing ceremony. Then he saw Gerald Kelly, a man for whom he felt no affection whatsoever, stomping towards him like a bulldog intent on its victim.

'We need to talk,' the American announced. 'Somewhere private.'

He followed to an empty area close by the lake and listened. As he did so he felt the bitter taste of envy rise in his throat.

The SFPD captain was right to tell him of this development. He was in charge of the Italian investigative team. Falcone should have come to him first with this news, and allowed Quattrocchi to pass it on to Kelly.

The American finished with the suggestion Quattrocchi join him and Falcone for the interview with Simon Harvey after the premiere.

'Of course I'll be there,' Quattrocchi insisted. 'We're joint investigating authorities in this case. It would be highly improper to commence without me.'

Kelly glared at him.

'You know I never got round to saying this to your face until now. But this is our country, not yours. We interview who we like, when we like, and I don't care whether that pisses you off or not.'

'And Tonti? What do you propose with him?'

'I'm feeling generous. And I don't want this freak show getting any worse. He's a sick old man going nowhere. He can turn up with his lawyers at Bryant Street in the morning. No reporters. No leaks. Not a word to anyone.'

The *maresciallo* nodded at the pack of photographers now corralled into a specific section of the secure area by the stage outside the screening tent.

'You think they'll be happy with that?'

'I don't care what they'll be happy with. That's the way it's going to be.'

After that he marched back into the crowd.

Americans amazed Quattrocchi. Their incapacity for a little common deviousness from time to time was quite bewildering.

He found Roberto Tonti in the middle of a group of besuited movie company executives. The man looked more gaunt and haggard than he had even two weeks before. His eyes were invisible behind sunglasses as usual. His grey hair appeared stiff and unreal. The director was finishing a cigarette as Quattrocchi arrived. Immediately he lit another and said nothing as the suits around him gossiped and argued.

Quattrocchi got next to him and said in Italian, 'Tonti, it is important we talk.'

'I doubt that very much.'

The Carabinieri officer nodded at the men with them.

'Do they speak Italian?'

There was a long, slow intake of breath, then Tonti said, 'They're producers. Most are still struggling with English and it's their native tongue.'

'Listen to me well. Once this premiere is over it is the intention of the San Francisco Police Department to arrest you on suspicion of fraud and conspiracy to murder.'

Tonti took a long drag on the cigarette, looked at him and said nothing.

'They have a witness,' Quattrocchi continued. 'A member of your . . . tontine. He has told them of your arrangement already. The man has agreed to make a statement, doubtless in return for some kind of immunity or preferential treatment.'

The man led him to an empty area by the side of the stage.

'Who?' he demanded.

'This is not an appropriate time.'

'I wish to avoid embarrassment this evening. You must understand that.'

'Of course. All the same . . .'

'Shut up. I am thinking.'

Gianluca Quattrocchi fell silent. There was something chilling in the authority of this man. Something decidedly odd.

'What do you have to offer me?' Tonti asked in the end.

'You're an Italian citizen. If you give yourself up to my authority I can arrange these matters through our courts, not theirs.'

'You don't understand Americans. They don't like to lose.'

'Kelly is feeling sentimental. He will invite you for interview tomorrow morning. Were you to leave the country immediately after the premiere and arrive in Italy in due course . . . It would not be difficult. A private jet would have you in Mexico in a couple of hours. After that, what could they do?'

Quattrocchi coughed into his fist, praying none of this conversation would ever go any further.

'Extradition proceedings take years. You will receive much fairer treatment in your native country, surely. If you plead guilty to some minor financial transgression we can spin things out for a long time . . .'

'I'll be dead before summer turns,' Tonti said with a matter-of-fact certainty.

'Then die in Rome, where you belong. In bed. In a house, not some prison cell in California.'

'Without a name I shall not agree to this.'

'I cannot . . .'

'Without a name I shall go to the Americans this instant. I shall tell them everything, and inform them of your approach and your offer. Perhaps they can better it.'

Quattrocchi felt his temper stretching to breaking point. The premiere would begin in a matter of minutes.

'I believe they have an appointment with Simon Harvey,' he muttered. 'I did not tell you this.'

'Of course, *maresciallo*. This is kind of you.'

'No. Merely practical.' He tried to gauge some expression in the man's haggard features. 'So we have an arrangement?'

'How could one deny the Carabinieri?' the director replied effusively. 'It would be impertinent, no?'

Gianluca Quattrocchi did not expect thanks from this individual. Nor did he anticipate or enjoy condescension.

'I shall endeavour to make your time in Rome as comfortable as possible,' he replied, aware that he was speaking to the long, thin back of Roberto Tonti as he returned to the suits and evening gowns, the mayhem of the premiere of *Inferno*.

– 12 –

They watched the movie from the darkness of the VIP seats at the front. Not long after the start he felt her head slip onto his shoulder, her hair fall against his neck. Costa turned his head a degree or two and stole a glimpse at Maggie Flavier. On the screen she stood five metres high, the ethereal beauty Beatrice, Dante's dead muse, offering hope as the poet faced the horrors and travails of the circles of Hell, just as the idea of the unworldly Madeleine Elster had appeared to bring solace to the lost and fearful Scottie. For most of the movie, the real woman behind Beatrice was fast asleep against him, mouth just ajar, at peace. He scarcely dared breathe for fear of waking her. However loud the commotion on the screen above and ahead of them she seemed oblivious to it all, slumbering by his side like a child lost in a world of her own.

He felt happy. Lucky too. And like her he took scarcely any notice of the overblown cinematic fiction that had brought them there. Costa's thoughts turned instead to the events of the past few weeks, and the returning conviction that the roots of this genuine drama lay, somehow, in the fairy tales these people created for themselves.

The making of the conspiracy lay in the ability of men like Roberto Tonti and Dino Bonetti to invent some fantastical story out of dust. He still failed to understand how that trick had come to shift from some desperate marketing ploy into a murderous actuality, but the seeds were there from the outset in the way those involved danced between one world, that of everyday life, and another in which fiction posed as fact.

Maggie was an unwitting part of that fabrication. In ways he didn't wish to understand, it had damaged her.

This dark, unsettling thought dogged him as the movie finally came to an end. Costa was about to nudge her gently awake as the lights came up. There was no need. Her head was off his shoulder even before the waves of applause began to ripple around the audience.

By the time Roberto Tonti was striding onto the stage with Simon Harvey by his side most of the audience was on its feet. In the way of things, Costa found himself following suit. Maggie rose next to him. He leaned down and asked her when the cast would join Tonti on the platform.

She had to cup her hand to his ear to make herself heard over the din. 'This is Roberto's moment. We were all told that. He's the director. We're just his puppets, remember?'

It still seemed unfair, Costa thought, half listening to Harvey run through a fulsome tribute to Allan Prime followed by a lengthy homily about Tonti's determination to see the project completed. The years of struggle, the script revisions, the financial difficulties, the threats, the tragic events of recent weeks. Above all, said Harvey, the fight for artistic and creative control, without which the movie in its present form could never have been conceived, least of all made.

It was florid hyperbole delivered with a straight face. Within the space of the next thirty minutes Harvey would either be making a statement to the SFPD incriminating Tonti in the conspiracy that had brought about at least four deaths, or else Falcone would be handing over the audio evidence to justify his arrest and interrogation on these same charges. One way or another the riddle would be brought to some kind of resolution.

Then Harvey stepped back. Slowly, with a pained, sick gait, which a cynical part of Costa's mind felt might be half-theatrical, Tonti walked to the microphone and stood there alone, listening, only half smiling, to the wall of clapping hands, catcalls and whistles of the crowd.

It was tedious and artificial. Costa was becoming impatient, wishing for an end to this show. As he fought to stifle a yawn something caught his attention and he found himself lost for any thought, any idea on how to interpret what he now saw.

A woman was walking towards Roberto Tonti from the far side of the stage. In her hands she held a gigantic bouquet of roses, carnations and bright, vivid orchids.

Costa blinked, trying to convince himself this was not some flashback out of a dream, or a night in front of the TV in the house in Greenwich Street.

She was of medium height and wore a severe grey jacket with matching slacks and white shirt high up to her neck. Her build was full, almost stocky, her hair was perfect, dyed platinum blonde, unyielding, as if held by the strongest lacquer imaginable. As she turned to present the flowers to Tonti, Costa could see that the wig – it could be nothing else – was tied back into a tight, shining apostrophe above the somewhat thick form of her neck.

In spite of the weather she wore a pair of black plastic Italian sunglasses, so large they effectively obscured her features. Yet Costa knew her. She was the character from *Vertigo*. Kim Novak as Madeleine Elster, or rather a fake Madeleine who posed as the doomed wife Jimmy Stewart's Scottie came to love and hoped to save.

It also occurred to him that she matched exactly the description of the woman calling herself Carlotta Valdes who had visited Allan Prime in the Via Giulia, ostensibly to create a death mask.

He found himself fighting to get through the cordon around the stage. Maggie clawed at his arms.

'What are you doing?' she asked.

'Stay where you are. Don't go near the stage.'

He pressed forward and the large hand of a security guard shoved him hard in the chest. Costa fell backwards with a lurch. Maggie only just caught him. He stumbled and found himself guided by her back into a seat.

'Nic,' she said, exasperated, 'you can't go up there. Roberto owns that stage. No one's going to take it from him. Those bouncers wouldn't let God himself through unless he had a pass.'

The crowd was still on its feet, whooping and cheering.

'There's something wrong,' he muttered and dragged out his Rome police ID.

She gazed at the plastic card in his fingers and said, 'Well, that's going to work, isn't it? For pity's sake, what's the matter?'

He struggled to his feet and wondered, for a moment, whether he was going mad. The woman was gone. Roberto Tonti was at the front of the stage alone, with Simon Harvey a couple of metres behind. The director held the gigantic bouquet and waved and nodded to the joyful, over-the-top roar of the crowd.

'My ego's done, thank you,' Maggie whispered into his ear. 'Five minutes of this and we're out of here.'

He prayed more than anything she would be proved right.

The tall, gaunt figure on the stage mouthed something into the microphone. Costa knew what it was. A single word in Italian, an exhortation, a command.

Silenzio.

– 13 –

'Once upon a time, in a land far away . . .' Roberto Tonti began.

He clutched the bouquet to his emaciated chest, then he removed his sunglasses and tried to squint at the audience beyond the bright floodlights.

'You come to me for stories.' The man's voice sounded distant and hollow and sick. 'Children begging for gifts. Did you get them?' The noise of the audience diminished a little. Tonti waited. He took hold of the microphone and in his hoarse, weak voice tried his best to bellow, 'Did you get them?'

The strained sound of his words, the accent half-American, half-Italian, carried into the night with a deafening clarity. The space inside the tent turned silent.

'Did you appreciate the cost?' he croaked. 'Allan Prime. A poor actor. A weak man. Nothing to be missed. He died. Why not? Where's the loss?'

His skinny, weak arm moved across them as he spat out his words.

'See what I must work with? See how I make something precious out of clay? What do you want of me? What else do you expect?'

Maggie murmured close up, 'I can't take this any more . . .'

She slipped away from him, and still he couldn't take his eyes off the stage.

Simon Harvey tried to move towards the director. Tonti turned and stopped him with a single magisterial glance.

A low, murmur of disquiet and astonishment began to rise up from the crowd.

Tonti reached into the bouquet of flowers and withdrew something that stilled every voice in the room. A small black handgun emerged from the orchids and the blood-red roses. He cast away the bouquet to give the weapon emphasis, held it high for the camera rigs floating over the stage, wandering around him like robotic eyes, fixated on a single subject.

'Watch me,' he said to the giant, peering lenses. 'Focus, always, always.'

Costa scanned around the crowd. Gerald Kelly was at the edge of the platform on ground level with a group of uniformed officers, holding them back for the moment.

Tonti's arms waved, as if beseeching them for something, some kind of understanding.

'Listen to me. Listen! This once I tell you the truth. Some impertinent hack once asked Fellini . . .' The tip of the black barrel caressed his cheek, like a thoughtful finger. '*Che cosa fai?* What do you do?'

'Enough, Roberto . . .' Harvey said, and took one step closer. The gun drifted his way. The publicist froze.

'Fellini answers . . . *sono un gran bugiardo*. I am a big liar. Pinocchio writ large. See my nose! See my nose!'

He was gripping his own face, laughing, and the movement brought about a spasmodic cough that briefly gripped his frail frame.

Tonti struggled back to the microphone.

'Fellini, Hitchcock, Rossellini . . . Tonti, too. This is what you demand of our calling. That we are liars, all, and the more distance we put between your dreams and the miserable mundanity of your sad little lives, the better we lie, the happier you are.'

The man tried to swallow. His voice was cracking with some kind of emotion and it was impossible to say whether it was anger or grief or some deep-rooted sense of fear.

'*Mea culpa. Mea culpa.*'

His hands held in front of him, he bowed low before the audience.

'I am the director. All you have seen of late, on screen and off, is my creation. From Allan Prime dead in the Farnesina to some pretty little clothes horse choking for life from a poisoned apple. This is my doing, my orchestration, and listen to me now . . .'

He coughed again, and it was raw and dry and rasping.

'No man gets a better final scene than this. Better than any I gave any of these two-bit hacks. See . . .'

He indicated the cameras, following his every movement.

'See! This is the last of Roberto Tonti. Greater than any of you. Any of them.'

Kelly had nodded to his men. They were starting to make their way on to the stage. Tonti knew what was coming, surely.

'Not Dante Alighieri, though,' he added. 'Listen to me, children. Listen to the final words of *Inferno*, that I never gave you on the screen, for they are beyond your comprehension.'

He drew himself up, closed his eyes and began to recite, slowly, in a sonorous, theatrical tone.

> *'The Guide and I into that hidden road*
> *Now entered, to return to the bright world;*
> *And without care of having any rest*
> *We mounted up, he first and I the second,*
> *Till I beheld through a round aperture*
> *Some of the beauteous things that Heaven doth bear;*
> *Thence we came forth to rebehold the stars.'*

Roberto Tonti paused, and gazed at the rapt, still, silent crowd in front of him.

He was shaking with laughter, and his eyes, now open and dark and alert, glistened with moisture as they fixed the camera lenses following his every move.

'Through a round aperture . . . to rebehold the stars,' Roberto Tonti repeated and swept his arm along the rows of glitterati and celebrities before him. 'Such as they are.'

Simon Harvey was getting closer, hands out, pleading for the gun.

'Yet,' Tonti added, 'each and every story deserves a twist, some small epiphany at the close.'

Without warning he swung round to face Harvey. The publicist stopped where he was, looked at the director and asked, 'Roberto?'

'Traitor.'

The word, the final key in the ninth circle, the last of Dante's Numbers, came out in a flat, unemotional tone.

He began to fire, repeatedly, deliberately, into the torso of the flailing, tumbling publicist.

A woman screamed behind Costa.

When the gun clicked on empty Roberto Tonti stopped and took one last, disgusted glance at the shattered body on the stage.

Then, seizing the microphone, he gazed up at the cameras.

In a calm, disinterested voice, he ordered, 'And . . . *cut*.'

PART SEVEN

- 1 -

It was Saturday morning. The weather was warmer. August beckoned. Costa woke in Maggie Flavier's apartment then drove to
Greenwich Street to help the rest of them pack. Their flight home
would be late that afternoon. He would travel to Barbados the
following Monday. There were still some private business events in
her diary. The job never seemed to disappear completely. Simon
Harvey's death continued to stand between them like some unspoken
obstacle. Perhaps time would deal with that, and a move to a different
place, one with no connections, no memories. He was unsure.

But at least the case appeared to be, if not closed, at least partly
resolved, probably as much as it ever would be. Roberto Tonti had
scarcely ceased speaking to Gerald Kelly and his team since he was
taken into custody. The SFPD had passed on the details to Falcone,
since Gianluca Quattrocchi had been recalled to Rome with his
officers to face an internal inquiry. Quattrocchi's private approach on
the night of the premiere was only one of the revelations the director
was now minded to disclose. He had also confessed to being the
originator of the tontine scheme to save the troubled movie in Rome,
and to diverting Harvey's secret publicity scam about fictitious threats
to the production into a real and murderous conspiracy. His motive,
he said with no apparent shame, was purely selfish. *Inferno* was by no
means a guaranteed success, even with Harvey's incessant hype.
Something else was needed and, since Tonti knew this was the last
movie he would ever make, he was prepared to go to any lengths in
order to find it.

He had named Josh Jonah, the dead photographer Martin Vogel

357

and the Lukatmi security guard Jimmy Gaines as the principals in the plot to murder Allan Prime. Vogel had arranged the poison for Maggie Flavier. Jonah had then approached the photographer after being blackmailed over his involvement in the plot. Tonti had promised them Prime would be the only victim. He had hoped that would be the case, and that the half-hearted attempt on Maggie Flavier's life, which he had not expected to be successful, would simply gain yet more publicity to keep the movie in the headlines. The deaths of Jonah and Vogel he regarded as accidental, if fortuitous. He claimed to have shot Tom Black – who had never understood the true nature of the scheme – himself, from a viewpoint near the Embarcadero, and then disposed of the weapon.

Dino Bonetti's role remained unclear. The producer had disappeared on the night of the premiere and was now the subject of arrest warrants for fraud and attempted murder. Tonti, however, steadfastly refused to discuss his involvement in the conspiracy, dismissing it as minor. The credit, as he saw it, was to be his.

In spite of the man's age and frailty he remained in custody, though Kelly was minded to waive any objections to bail at some stage provided Tonti surrendered his passport and reported to the police on a daily basis. The medical reports indicated that he had, at most, a few months to live, and would never face trial. There was no question, either, that the man would wish to flee to Italy, in spite of Gianluca Quattrocchi's promises. The truth, Kelly felt, was that Roberto Tonti had achieved what he wanted.

Even during his interrogation the SFPD phone lines had burned with calls from TV networks and newspapers pleading with Tonti to go on air or give lengthy press interviews. From the major serious newspapers to the primetime celebrity shows, he was suddenly in demand, and this, it seemed, was worth a succession of lives, none of which he deemed of any great value. Only his own reputation, his heritage, mattered, and by force of circumstance that would always be tied to a single movie, *Roberto Tonti's Inferno*.

Hank and Frank Boynton had been round for breakfast when Falcone returned from Bryant Street to brief them on what he'd heard from Gerald Kelly. All of them at the table – the Boyntons, Teresa, Peroni and Costa – listened carefully, and then the Italians stayed silent.

Hank, however, raised a long forefinger and said, by way of objection, 'But just a minute . . .'

'Not now, Hank,' Teresa stopped him, mid-sentence. 'We're finished here.'

'But . . .'

'Not now.'

'The movie business,' Frank grumbled. 'He couldn't take being behind that camera all his life, watching others get the fame. What was that line from Dante he spouted after he killed that poor bastard in front of everyone?'

' "Thence we came forth to re-behold the stars," ' Costa said.

'Envy. Greed. This insane craving for fame.' Frank Boynton shook his head then got up from the table. 'Come on, brother. These people have things to do.' He looked at Teresa. 'That invitation to Rome still stands?'

'Whenever you boys want it.'

'Good. Have a safe journey home. All of you.'

They watched the two men leave. Ten minutes later Catherine Bianchi arrived and offered them one last drive round the city before a farewell lunch in the Marina.

- 2 -

Costa almost fell asleep in the people mover as it wound through a city landscape he felt he now knew well. The views across to Marin County, the great bridge, the hulking island of Alcatraz . . . It would be hard to shake San Francisco from the memory for many reasons, good and bad. Then he remembered he had something to return. It was sitting in a supermarket plastic bag he'd brought along for the purpose. When they stopped at some lights he reached forward and placed it on the ledge between the front seats.

'That belongs to Gerald Kelly. Tell him thanks but I didn't need it.'

Catherine Bianchi took a look at the handgun in its leather holster.

'Lucky you.'

Her dark eyes wandered to the tall lean figure in the passenger seat. Something had changed between these two. Falcone sat next to her looking relaxed and perhaps a little bored. He was no longer the ardent pursuer and had already talked wistfully that morning of work back in Rome. Yet, as his eagerness waned, Catherine Bianchi's, it seemed to Costa, was beginning to surface, rather too late in the day.

'Is everything good?' she asked with a brittle, edgy ease.

The question was principally aimed at the man next to her. He scarcely seemed to notice.

They were travelling along Union towards Russian Hill, trying to make a left turn, when, after her third attempt to start a conversation, Catherine finally lost patience.

'Listen,' she snapped. 'I may never see any of you guys again.

Ever. And all you can do is sit there moping. What the hell is the matter now? What did I do wrong?'

'Nothing,' Falcone remarked, turning to look at her, somewhat puzzled.

'Then why are you . . . all of you . . . ?'

She muttered something beneath her breath, then added, 'You might at least look a little grateful this mess is over. That someone's in custody, admitting to the whole damned thing. Loose ends all tied up. Case closed.' She glanced at Falcone. 'Tickets home all booked.'

The Italians shuffled uncomfortably on their seats.

'The loose ends aren't all tied up, Catherine, and you know that as well as the rest of us,' Teresa said before anyone else could. 'All that's happened is that Tonti's stuck up his hand and said, "Send it all my way." Which is very convenient in the circumstances. But . . .'

'But what . . . ?'

She was too late. The dam had burst. Peroni got in next, aware, perhaps, that there was likely to be a queue.

'I was under the impression we weren't going to talk about this. But since we are let me say just one thing. Tom Black was shot from a considerable distance by someone using a hunting rifle. Either Roberto Tonti is quite a marksman or he got very lucky. Have you seen his eyes? How he shakes? I don't believe he could do that. Not for one moment.'

He was getting into his stride.

'Also . . . how did he know Tom Black was in that car with Nic in the first place?'

'He says Black called him beforehand asking for help,' she snapped.

'But why?' Peroni asked. 'If Tom Black knew Tonti was behind the whole thing . . . Oh . . . I give up.'

Falcone smiled pleasantly in the passenger seat and said nothing.

'Carlotta Valdes,' Costa added. 'Who was she? Where is she now?'

Catherine Bianchi turned round, looking cross.

'He won't tell us, Nic. The guy's just put up his hand to

everything and that's that. Are we supposed to lose sleep over it? Whoever that woman was she didn't do much. Maybe roped in Allan Prime and brought Tonti a gun on stage at the Palace of Fine Arts. One more fake ID among many. Trust me. Kelly's people have checked. They could spend a lifetime chasing someone who was nothing more than some bit-part courier. They will for a little while. But not for long. Do you blame them? Don't you have priorities in Rome too?'

'It's the name,' Costa emphasized, not quite knowing what he meant, trying to place a memory. 'Why that one?'

'Because of Hitchcock,' Teresa insisted. 'As I've been trying to tell you all along. Tonti worked with him. It was all here . . .'

The vehicle came to an abrupt halt by a busy junction. Catherine Bianchi slammed her hands angrily on the steering wheel.

'You people make me want to scream. Why, in God's name, do you have to make everything so hard?'

Falcone finally took his gaze off the ocean horizon.

'We didn't. We never had the chance. The fact that the film was made here . . .'

'This is San Francisco! Movie central!' she yelled. 'Haven't you noticed? Watch.'

She jerked out into the street, cut left onto another road, then bore right again.

'*Dirty Harry*,' she chanted. '*Bullitt. Mrs Doubtfire, The Joy Luck Club* . . .'

'Eastwood and McQueen I can take . . .' Teresa cut in.

'Shut up! *Harold and Maude, Freebie and the Bean, Pal Joey* . . . Am I making my point here? It's not all dark and bloody. Remember, Jesus, *The Love Bug?*'

The Italians stiffened and glanced at each other.

'*The Love Bug?*' Teresa asked eventually. 'You mean the kids' movie?' She winced. 'The Disney one?'

'The Disney one.'

'Like *Bambi*,' Costa murmured, trying to place the recollection that was haunting him, one that was buried somehow in that dark night that had ended in bloodshed outside the Ferry Building on the Embarcadero.

He was amazed to see that the road they had entered bore the name Lombard, just like the highway that became Route 101 as it swept towards the Golden Gate Bridge. Here it was narrow and residential. Then they crossed a broad street and Lombard became a winding, single-track lane that turned into a crazed series of steep switchbacks winding downhill past grand Victorian mansions and newer apartment blocks.

'Tourist time,' Catherine said as she wheeled the big Dodge around the tight hairpins, the vehicle grumbling over the brick road. 'America's crookedest street. Architecturally speaking, naturally. Most of the people around here are upstanding citizens, with plenty of cash too.'

The bends finished, the street straightened and became smooth asphalt once more. She pulled in by the junction at Leavenworth and looked back over her shoulder at the winding lane behind. It was so familiar, from so many movies. It made her point.

'Recognize anything?' she asked. 'That little Beetle Herby came down here. Lots of movies came down here. After LA, this city is the biggest movie stage in the world. So what's the big deal if someone steals the name of a movie character now and again? Why wouldn't they?'

He wasn't looking back. His eyes were fixed straight ahead, seeing something he recognized. There was a city map in the seat back in front of him. Costa took it out, scanned the index, found what he wanted, ran his finger across the ganglion of streets that criss-crossed the crowded, confined peninsula of San Francisco, a complex patchwork of neighbourhoods, each running into the next, overlapping, obscuring the obvious.

She calmed down a little and began to turn right, back towards the Marina. Costa reached over and tapped her shoulder.

'Drive on, please. Ahead. Indulge me.'

The view ahead changed shape, becoming more like the one he expected. Costa asked her to stop at the next junction. Opposite was a plain two-storey house with scaffolding along the side obscuring the long windows of what must have been some kind of living room. The curtains were closed. A builder was working on the exterior, setting up a cement-mixing machine.

Tom Black's words kept coming back to him.

They screw you up . . . they screw everyone. Scottie. Me . . . I never thought this'd happen. Not when we went to Jones . . .

There was a scene in the movie in which Jimmy Stewart's character stared out from his living-room window across towards the Bay Bridge, admiring this very view fifty years before from the building across the road. This was Scottie's old home in Lombard, the very building Hitchcock had used. The front, with its long living-room window, was on a street called Jones. Someone who didn't know might think that was its real address.

Tom Black hadn't been talking about a man, Costa realized, cursing his own stupidity. He'd been remembering a place. Somewhere he'd met a movie-obsessed individual who'd stolen his name from *Vertigo*.

He climbed out of the car and walked over the road. The builder was a big man, his hands covered in plaster, his face wary, full of suspicion.

'I was wondering if Scottie was in,' Costa asked as if it was the most natural question in the world. 'I heard the lucky bastard had got some nice old car from somewhere. He promised to show it me when I was in the neighbourhood.'

The man looked him up and down carefully.

'Only his friends call him that. Not seen you before.'

'Been a while.'

'Mr Ferguson went out this morning. I don't expect him back while I'm here, and I'm here all day.'

'The car?'

He didn't drop his guard.

'Remind me . . .'

'Green. Jaguar. Nineteen fifties. He said it was a beauty.'

That broke the ice.

'Oh it's a beauty. I guess that's why it hardly ever gets out of the garage. Today being an exception. Sorry to disappoint . . .'

'Where . . . ?'

'I don't know.' He took off his yellow hard hat and scratched his head. 'Maybe at that cinema of his. I don't know . . .'

The others had arrived and were listening. This didn't make the builder any more relaxed.

'The cinema?' Costa asked.

'That weird deadbeat little place in Chestnut, down the Marina. The one with the tower. How the hell Scottie manages to make a bean out of that dump . . .'

Costa picked up a steel-headed mallet from the side of the concrete mixer.

'Now,' the builder said, 'let's not do anything hasty . . .'

The door looked so old he felt sure Jimmy Stewart had touched it. People made things well back then. It needed three swings to smash through the hardwood slab.

- 3 -

The package arrived at ten, along with the man from the movie festival offering to give her a ride to the event. Maggie Flavier looked at the box in his hands and asked, 'Costume?'

He seemed early thirties, medium height, sturdy and very clean-shaven, with soft, pale skin that belied his heavy, calloused hands. The dress was standard suburban movie festival fare: worn jeans and a white T-shirt. The only thing that stood out a little was the pair of thick-set black plastic sunglasses that sat on his face. It was bright outside but something about the man told her they lived there permanently.

'The festival people said . . .' he began.

'They didn't mention anything about costume to me.'

She didn't know what they'd said. She couldn't remember. This engagement had gone into the diary through her agent weeks ago when she was in Rome.

He took off the glasses. Bright blue eyes. Too blue. She wondered if they were coloured contacts. Hangers-on at the fringes of the business sometimes had affectations too.

'I'm sorry.' He put down the box. 'If it's a problem . . . forget it. They went to a lot of trouble to get this dress. They said it was important. But if they screwed up . . .'

'What am I doing again?'

'My name's John,' he said, smiling pleasantly, and holding out his hand. 'John Ferguson.'

She shook it. He had the strong grip of a workman.

'What am I doing today, Mr Ferguson?'

'It's the Marina Festival of Fifties Noir. Sponsored by one friendly local organic supermarket, a bank branch and some nice kind arts people in the city. Opened by Miss Maggie Flavier. Fifteen minutes in public, a couple of smiles and you're done.' He peered at her. 'You do *know* the Marina Odeon, don't you?'

'Sorry. Movies are work, not leisure. Also, I never quite hit the Marina scene. It's a way from here.'

'Ah . . .'

'Noir?' she asked.

'We open with *Touch of Evil* and close with *The Asphalt Jungle*. Talk about doing things backwards, but I just fetch and carry. Programming's all down to someone else.'

He took out a piece of paper.

'According to my schedule you cut the ribbon for the opening at 1.30, then we show the Welles film at two. Stay if you like. The choice is yours. We got the message from your agent about not wanting too much in the way of media there.'

'Good . . .'

'That's all arranged, Miss Flavier. We have one reporter and one TV crew. No one else will be allowed inside.' He glanced at the clock on the wall. 'And if we get there quick no one's going to be outside either. The festival people would like to get a few words from you for some DVD they're putting together first. It just involves marks and a few prepared questions.'

He nodded at the box.

'It's all for charity, you know. One sweet dress. They said the pictures would make all the mags. I got the limo round the corner.'

'Why do I have to wear a dress?'

'Came from some society lady in Russian Hill. Of the period, or so they say.' He sighed. 'I'm just the messenger here. Nothing else. I'm sorry. After all this awful stuff in the papers, I understand if you don't feel up to it. If you want to cancel, just say so. I can tell them . . . It's no problem.'

'No, no . . .' She hated letting people down. It seemed so selfish given the money and acclaim she got in return for what, in truth, was a small amount of talent and a lot of luck.

She opened the box, took out the garment there and found herself wondering for a moment whether to believe what she had in her hands. The dress was a long, voluminous silk evening gown, low-cut, the kind of thing women wore in old movies. It was a dark, incandescent green. The same green as the one in *Vertigo*. Almost the same dress if she remembered correctly. It was so beautiful she could scarcely take her eyes off it.

'What is this?'

'They said it's a copy of one Janet Leigh wears in *Touch of Evil*.'

That was a film she did remember. The sight of Orson Welles's fat, sweating face looming out of the Mexican darkness was hard to lose.

'I thought that was made in black and white.'

'Well I guess the movie was. Not the people. What do I know? Don't shoot the messenger, remember?'

She hesitated. The death of Simon Harvey and the dark succession of events that preceded it continued to haunt her. She felt tired and uncertain about the trip to Barbados. Maggie Flavier knew what Nic thought; she needed time away from the movie business. She understood, too, that he was right, and also that he failed to comprehend why that was so difficult for her. There had been nothing else for as long as she could remember. The idea of a blank, unwritten future extending into the distance, disappearing into the mist . . .

She remembered Scottie's nightmare from the movie, of falling into a deep, shapeless abyss. Vertigo. It wasn't just fear of heights. It was fear of the unknown too.

'We need to go, Miss Flavier,' the man insisted. 'If you want to. The limo can't wait for ever.'

One last engagement, and then some space.

'Do you want me to put it on now?' she asked, looking at the green dress.

'No need. There's a dressing room at the theatre.'

He carried the box carefully in his arms, following her all the way down to the parking lot.

'We're around the corner,' he said, beckoning her to the back of her apartment block.

It was a long way. Past dumpsters and parts of the building she'd hardly ever visited. Then, with him very close behind, they turned a corner and she saw the car.

The green Jaguar gleamed in the half-shade of a neighbouring block, sleek and old and full of memories. She remembered the smell of the leather and the drive with Nic up into the heights beyond the Legion of Honor.

'What the hell is going on here?' she started to say, turning to look at him.

The sunglasses were back on. He'd dropped the big cardboard box. He was grinning at her. There was no one near, not a window overlooking this place.

He was getting something out of his pocket.

'It's the final act,' the man who called himself John Ferguson said. Suddenly he was on her, strong arms around her neck, a hand pushing some cloth that stank of damp, corrosive chemical into her face.

She tried to struggle. Then she tried to breathe. Her arms flailed wildly, to no purpose. She could hear him laughing over the sound of a very heavy car trunk getting popped.

From the corner of her eye she could just make out the sun, bright and wild in a pure blue Californian sky. The world started to turn dark. Her head fell into some buzzing, insensate place, one where her body got bundled into an awkward, half-crouching position and there was a stench of oil and the kind of fusty fabric you got in the backs of old cars.

For one short moment the sun glittered high above her. Then the cloth came down once more and with it went everything. She couldn't breathe. She couldn't feel. He held the thing over her mouth, choking her until she submitted and fell into the dark.

- 4 -

Once inside the house, Costa wasted fifteen seconds fumbling for a light switch, then went straight to the main windows. There he threw open the curtains on the long flat panes that covered the corner of the room abutting Lombard and Jones, revealing a view that, through ancient Venetian blinds, took him back to Maggie Flavier's apartment, watching *Vertigo* for the second time in a matter of days, both of them feeling the past tapping on their shoulders like some recent hungry ghost.

This wasn't just the same building. It was the very room they'd seen in the movie, with its beautiful hillside vista out to Coit Tower and the ocean. The furniture had been carefully selected from the same era: a pale fabric sofa, long, low chairs of a similar 1950s design. Even a small TV set with manual rotating dials and switches and a bulging, pop-eyed screen. An old movie channel was playing there: something black and white, the sound turned down as if the room needed to be inhabited by the cinema even when no one was present. It was a sanctuary, a kind of temple, and it was obvious what was being worshipped.

The walls were plastered with movie posters from floor to ceiling. All from the Fifties to Seventies. American, English, international, Italian . . .

Teresa went round them methodically, finger on the old paper, checking the names.

'Roberto Tonti worked on every one of these,' she murmured, half to herself. 'Whoever this man is he knows his stuff. Tonti doesn't even get a name check on the *Vertigo* poster and it's up there along with all the Italian horror flicks he actually directed. We have a fan here. *The* fan.'

There was an open kitchen leading onto the main living area and perhaps two or three other rooms down a short corridor. Catherine Bianchi began to make worried noises about Bryant Street. Falcone ignored her. He was busily rooting through documents on a compact antique desk against the wall next to the TV.

'Rome,' Falcone declared holding up some papers. 'He went there one week before Prime died and returned home the day after. Just like Martin Vogel and Jimmy Gaines. There are air tickets in the name of Michael Fitzwilliam, the bill for a hotel near Termini, cards for restaurants and bars. A receipt for a pair of sunglasses from Salvatore Ferragamo in the Via Condotti.' His grey eyebrows furrowed in bafflement. 'Ferragamo don't make men's sunglasses, surely . . .'

'So we've found one more member of the team?' Catherine Bianchi asked.

'It would appear so. Ferragamo . . .'

'You're right. They don't make men's sunglasses,' Peroni said, returning from inside a spacious walk-in closet with something held carefully across both outstretched arms. It was a set of woman's clothing fresh back from the cleaners, pressed and spotless inside plastic wrapping. A grey jacket with matching slacks. The same clothes they'd seen worn by the woman who handed a bouquet of flowers, with a gun inside, to Roberto Tonti on the stage by the Palace of Fine Arts. The same clothes apparently worn by the mysterious Carlotta Valdes when she appeared at the apartment of Allan Prime in the Via Giulia.

'He keeps his ladies' things in the same cupboard as his best men's stuff. There's make-up and a mirror. This is a bachelor apartment with a difference. Also, there's this . . .'

He held up a photo of a man in hunting gear with his foot on a dead deer.

'When he's not dressing up he likes to go shooting. Lots more like this out there, and what appears to be a locked firearms cabinet that could house a couple of rifles.'

'OK,' Catherine Bianchi said. 'Now I am calling Gerald Kelly.'

Falcone had been poking around in the desk. From the bottom right drawer he retrieved what appeared to be a plastic refuse bag bound with duct tape. He picked up a pair of scissors and cut the fastenings. From within he pulled out something wrapped in white tissue paper. It had a familiar, tantalizing shape.

As they watched he unwrapped the death mask of Dante Alighieri.

Each of them gathered round, leaving a gap to the window so that the bright Californian light fell on the object Falcone was holding gingerly through the tissue paper. The mask seemed very old and fragile, almost careworn by the long journey from Italy to California, a place Dante could never have guessed existed. Costa looked at the closed eyes, the face in peace after so much pain, the long, bent nose, the thin-lipped, intelligent mouth, and knew in an instant that it was genuine.

'This is our case as well,' Falcone said with obvious satisfaction. 'Call Kelly. Tell him we need an immediate check to find out this individual's real identity, and a discreet distribution of his description.'

He gave her the kind of look he gave policewomen in Rome, one she hadn't seen before.

'I do not want to see this in the media. Not even on a police station wall. If this man can change identities so easily and convincingly he'll be gone the moment he hears.'

'Sir . . .' she said caustically. 'Anything else?'

Falcone ignored her. Teresa Lupo had returned from the kitchen.

'We need forensic,' she said. ' "Scottie" may be finicky about his fancy clothes but his work gear is stuffed into one big pile in a basket just like any other bachelor slob. Maybe for a few weeks, some of it. That side of him doesn't seem too unusual.' She looked at them. 'There are items in there with what I'd swear are bloodstains on them. And a pair of jeans that still smell of petrol. Martin Vogel's apartment. There's a lot here, Catherine . . .'

'OK, OK, OK. I'll call . . .'

But she still didn't. She looked at them.

'Who the hell is this guy? Some kind of obsessed fan they took up as a foot soldier or something?'

Costa walked over to look at the shelves in the corridor. There seemed nothing unusual among the collection of personal belongings. Souvenirs, from Mexico and Italy, some small pieces of pottery, a few photographs in cheap plastic frames. Everything was so ordinary. If you took away the posters and the incriminating evidence this would simply be the apartment of a wealthy bachelor with a penchant for 1950s style.

He moved closer and picked up one of the photographs. It showed a tall, erect figure with a full head of dark, perhaps dyed hair, standing on the waterfront near Fort Point, beneath the grand span of the Golden Gate Bridge, squinting at the sun. He had his arm around a tall, spindly boy of perhaps ten or eleven. Neither was smiling. The man was a younger Roberto Tonti, in his late forties perhaps. The boy wore faded shorts, a cheap T-shirt, the clothes of someone who came from a different class. His hair needed cutting, his face was frozen in an expression of fear and anger.

There was a catch on the back of the frame. He unlocked it and took out the print. It was sufficiently recent to have a printed date still faintly visible on the rear: August 24th, 1987. Scribbled in thick, grey pencil, the kind artists used, an adult hand had written a line Costa recognized from *Inferno*:

> *Said the good Master: 'Son, thou now beholdest*
> *The souls of those whom anger overcame.'*

'Does Roberto Tonti have children?' he asked Teresa.

'Only married once. Without issue as they say.'

'The right side of the sheets anyway,' Peroni said, looking at the photo. 'That's a man and his son. Take it from me. They don't see each other much. They don't like each other much, I suspect. But the same blood's there and they know it. You can see it in their faces, can't you? One of those meetings distant fathers have with their sons. Out of duty. Out of habit, both sides hating it, but going along with the idea all the same.'

Costa thought he could make out some slight physical resemblance in their narrow, lost faces.

'Scottie . . . Ferguson,' Peroni went on. 'This man is Roberto Tonti junior living and working under another name just a mile or so from his father. For what? All his life? He must be thirty or more by now.'

Catherine Bianchi was finally starting to punch the buttons on her phone. She looked up at them, excited, maybe a little anxious too.

'So Roberto's still an Italian at heart. When in trouble, turn to your family. Even if it's one you've probably ignored for years. Best not touch anything else, folks. My severance payment could count on a few plus points once they realize I had this guy under my nose all along and never even noticed.'

Costa replaced the photograph.

'No one would have noticed. That was the point. He was just one more extra in his father's scheme.'

A player who, like the others, ceased to discern the line between what was real and what was invented. Everything in the apartment . . . the posters, the photos, the old movies on the TV, the frantic scribbling on the walls . . . spoke of obsession. A compulsion that had prompted him to take at least two false identities, one of them the name of Jimmy Stewart's character in an old movie in which his father had been a minor technician, to buy an old green Jaguar and lend it to an actress in the hope of . . . what?

He thought of the mythical Scottie dogging Madeleine Elster through the San Francisco of fifty years before, peering at her compulsively through the windscreen of his car as his curiosity turned to an irresistible desire, until the moment she fell in the ocean and then woke naked beneath the sheets in a scene meant to take place in the bedroom of this very apartment.

The SFPD had picked up the call. They were trying to find Gerald Kelly.

Some memory tweaked an anxious nerve. In *Vertigo*, Scottie had watched the sleeping, naked Madeleine avidly from the sofa in the living room, through an open door. The real one was closed, in a private way that seemed out of place in a bachelor apartment.

Costa opened it and walked in. The place was almost pitch-black with just the barest fringe of light coming in through what must have been a large window opposite, one blocked by heavy opaque blinds.

He found the switch and flipped it. In his astonishment he was only just conscious that they'd followed and stood behind him in much the same kind of silence.

This was the bedroom from the movie, copied with a precise and compulsive eye for detail. There was the same set of chestnut drawers by the door, four small framed paintings on the facing wall, a plaid chair in red and white and brown.

And the bed. A double bed with a high walnut veneer foot. The sheets and pillows were as crumpled as they had been when Madeleine Elster was woken from beneath them by a phone call, puzzled, but not entirely ashamed of her nakedness after being rescued by Scottie from the bay. In his own mind Costa half-believed he could smell the ocean at that moment, rising from the creased linen.

The others stood there still not saying a word, just looking. It was the walls. They were covered in photographs. Not of Kim Novak or anything else from *Vertigo*. It was Maggie Flavier, everywhere, so different in some that he barely recognized the pictures until he found the courage to stare into the frozen eyes of the distant figure they depicted and see that same mixture of courage and fear and resignation he had recognized in her from the start.

Some were so old they must have pre-dated her career. There was one in which she stood with a group of schoolgirls outside Grace Cathedral on Nob Hill, not far from her home. Maggie was immediately recognizable even though she couldn't have been more than thirteen. Just another child among many, prettier, more striking than the rest, with a woman behind her, pale, sick-looking, a hand on her shoulder.

He turned away and forced himself to look at the others. It was like walking through the halls of the Legion of Honor again. Maggie as a bright-faced girl on a farm, as a poverty-stricken teenager, as a rich young lady in an English mansion. And then the new images. The adult woman: her beauty strangely marred, as she fell through a series of roles that, seen in this cruel linear fashion, in this gloomy private shrine, seemed to denote her fall from the innocence of childhood into a fragile, haunted maturity. No longer smiling, staring at the camera, sometimes with a hatred that was pure and vitriolic, her face looked back at them from the walls. And her body too, in some of the more lurid shots, blown up to display every open pore, every inch of her skin, its minor imperfections, the faint, discernible penumbra of blonde hair rising above a posed, bare arm.

There was scarcely an inch of the room that wasn't covered with her presence in one way or another. They spanned, as far as he could make out, almost two decades, from child to woman. Costa couldn't take it any more. He pushed his way through them, trying to grasp the memory that lay just out of reach.

When he tried to call her there was no answer. He phoned Sylvie Brewster, the agent, and after a long wait got through.

'It's Nic,' he said quickly. 'Where's Maggie's appointment today? I need to know.'

'You mean you didn't think to ask over breakfast?'

He hadn't and now he hated himself for that. He didn't want to talk about her work. She was happy with that too, and he couldn't explain why.

'Please . . .' he begged.

She went away for a moment then came back and told him. Costa knew already somehow, and what he'd do. There could be no more police stand-offs. The actor Peter Jamieson had died after that outside the Cinema dei Piccoli. So, in a way he still didn't fully understand, had Tom Black.

The rest were still in the bedroom, probably staying away from him out of embarrassment. He could hear their quiet, low voices, Falcone's more prominent, more commanding.

The team from Bryant Street couldn't be more than a few minutes away.

Without saying a word Costa walked over to the desk, found Catherine Bianchi's bag and took the keys to her Dodge. Quickly, silently, he walked through the open door and down the stairs.

The sun was brighter than ever. The builder was back at work, puzzled but keeping his head down. Costa slid into the driving seat and worked the unfamiliar automatic vehicle out into the road with a rough, rude lack of skill. As the vehicle wound round the side streets back to Chestnut and the long straight drive to the Marina his hand reached over into the passenger side, found the glove compartment, flicked it open and fumbled inside.

Gerald Kelly's gun was still there.

– 5 –

She woke beneath the wrinkled sheets of an uncomfortable old double bed pushed hard against the corner of a cramped office that smelled of damp and sweat. As she tried to clear the fumes of the drug from her nose and throat, choking and nauseous, Maggie Flavier felt at her own body automatically, fingers trembling, mind reeling. She ached. She felt . . . strange.

Then she opened her eyes, knowing what she'd see. John Ferguson, whoever he was, sat opposite, on a chair turned round, his arms leaning easily on the back, watching her squirm and lurch as she tried to force herself upright on the stiff, creaking mattress. It took one look at herself to confirm what she suspected. She was now wearing the strange green dress and nothing else, nothing underneath, nothing on her feet. He must have stripped her while she was unconscious, then put on the old silk garment.

She tried to move but something stopped her and it hurt. Rough brown rope, the kind construction people used, gripped both her wrists. She turned. He'd tied her to the iron bedhead with a length for each arm, loose enough to let her move a little, but not much. Not enough to get off the bed entirely.

He had an expression on his face that suggested he knew this knowledge was running through her head at that moment, and a part of him liked that idea. But there was some uncertainty there too. He wasn't, it seemed to her, entirely at ease.

'I told you it was a nice dress,' he said, then reached for a packet of cigarettes tucked into the sleeve of his T-shirt, took one out, the last one, lit it, scrunched up the pack and threw it on the floor. After that he sat there, smoking easily, like a worker on a break. The grey cloud rose into the blades of a rotating ceiling fan performing lazy turns above them. The room felt as if it belonged to another time, not far enough away to be foreign, not quite.

'Who are you?' she asked. 'Where the hell am I?'

'You had an engagement. Don't you remember? Booze and boyfriends getting to the old grey cells now?'

'There'll be people here soon. You just let me go now and I'll forget this ever happened.'

He closed his eyes for a moment as if he despaired of her.

'That's what I love about the movie industry. You're all so damned wrapped up in yourselves you never check stuff out, do you? Someone calls and says . . .'

He put on a high-pitched girl's voice, like Shirley Temple on drugs.

'Miss Flavier. Oh *Miss Flavier.* We love you so much you just *got* to come open our little Noir festival in some flea-pit movie theatre you wouldn't normally . . .' The real voice came back . . . '*deign* to set foot inside. And you don't think to check the times you're given.'

He flicked a finger at the face of his watch. His expression was deadly serious.

'Why I say, I say . . .' She recognized the new voice. It was a cartoon character, fake Southern gentleman, Foghorn Leghorn. '. . . I *say*, boy . . . festival folk don't turn up in truth till four in the afternoon. Till then ain't nobody here but us chickens.'

After that he leaned forward and said, very earnestly, 'I hope you enjoy my voices, Maggie. I've been working on them for a while. All my life if I'm being candid.'

She hitched herself up on the bed, knees together beneath the sheets, taking the rope as far as it could before the harsh hessian began to bite into her skin, and said, 'Your voices are very good.'

'We have scarcely scratched the surface, dahling . . .' he groaned lasciviously.

She recognized this new look. Very well because it was one she'd known since she was a pretty little teenager. He was staring at her as if she were meat.

'Here's a question,' he added. 'You wake up naked aside from that dress and you realize some guy you don't seem to know put it on you. At least there *is* a dress. Not like Madeleine, huh? There she was all . . . *bare* . . . in Scottie's apartment . . . nice apartment by the way, play your cards right and one day maybe you get to see it. Well?'

'Well what?'

'Why didn't Madeleine scream? Some complete stranger takes her home, puts her in his bed, takes her clothes off . . . and . . . well . . .'

She didn't rise to the bait. This flustered him.

'I mean he sure looked, didn't he? Maybe a little more. Would you know? If you were out cold like that?'

He wriggled and looked awkward. A pink flush briefly stained his cheeks.

'Would you know . . . If . . . if . . . he'd d-d-done the *real thing*. All the way. Sure you would. You'd feel something. I guess.'

She still didn't say anything.

'But what about if he just kind of . . . fiddled around.' He sniggered. 'Got some touchy feely in there.' He shook his head, laughing out loud now. 'You think of that? Jimmy Stewart perving all over Kim Novak while she was out like a light and him all hot fingers, runny, runny . . .' He was licking his hands, slobbering all over them. '. . . Runny . . . runny. And she never gets to know.'

He stiffened up on the chair and stopped laughing.

'Or does she?'

John Ferguson, which was, she now recalled, the real name of the character Jimmy Stewart played, leaned forward and bellowed at her, '*Does she?*'

'They were actors. None of it was real.'

His plain face, which had seemed so ordinary, wrinkled with hate and disgust. Then something new, the demeanour of a doctor or someone officious.

'Now who's being naive, Miss Flavier? You of all people. Telling me a little of the story never makes its way into real life. Truly, I am shocked.'

Besides the bed there was some kind of storage cabinet. On it stood film cans lined up like books next to a small office desk with a phone on it, a cheap chair and not much else. A dusty window almost opaque with cobwebs. A single door opposite that led . . . she had no idea. They had to be in the movie theatre. But even so she could only picture one part of it in her head: the big white bell-tower looming over Chestnut.

If she could just get to the door, fight him off long enough . . .

She'd no idea whether that was remotely possible, so she stalled and asked again, 'What do you want?'

He shook his head as if that was a way of changing something, whichever character possessed him.

The voice altered again.

'You talkin' to me? You talkin' to me? Then who the hell else are you talking to?'

Taxi Driver.

'I don't know who I'm talking to but I don't think it's John Ferguson,' she said quietly. 'Or Travis Bickle.'

His head went from side to side in that crazy fashion again. He blubbed his fingers against his lips and made a stupid, childlike noise.

'Yeah. That's the problem. You don't know, Maggie. And you should. Because knowing means you get to answer the conundrum.'

'The conundrum?'

'You know. *The* conundrum.'

She stared at him in ignorance. He sighed as if she were a stupid child.

'The fuck-you-kill-you conundrum.'

Maggie Flavier's mind closed in on itself, refused to function.

'You do know what that is, don't you?'

'Tell me.'

'Fuck you *then* kill you? Fuck you *or* kill you.' He placed a finger on his lips, hamming a philosophical pose. 'Kill you *then* fuck you,

381

even?' He giggled. 'Though if I'm being honest the fuck-you part is a little moot. Whatever way things work out that's gonna happen, let's face it.'

He leaned forward, looked very sincere and added, 'I've been waiting a very long time for that. Keeping myself . . . pure, to be truthful. While you got banged by anything that took your passing fancy.'

There had to be a weapon somewhere. Or something she could use. A ball-point pen even. Anything she could stab him with when he came close.

'Who . . .' she asked very slowly, '. . . are . . . you?'

'Like you want to know.'

'I do.'

'Really?'

'Really.'

He shrugged, got up, walked over to the little desk, rudely swept away a pile of papers from the surface and then scrabbled around at the back until he found what he wanted. Then he came back, sat down again, eyed her once more. Maybe not quite so hungrily. Not quite.

'My name . . . my *real* name,' he said quietly, 'is . . .' the voice turned Irish now . . . 'Michael Fitzwilliam. Fitz, in the Gaelic sense, meaning bastard, *sans père* for you Froggies, illegitimate, mongrel, wrong side of the blanket, born out of wedlock, or even love child, if you happen to be of a humorous or gullible disposition.'

She found it hard to breathe. She was remembering something from a very long time ago.

'Sure the name has jogged a little memory now, I'm thinking.'

It was a terrible Irish accent and meant to be.

He had something in his hand. She didn't want to see it. But there was nowhere to run, and she felt hot and tired and weak beneath the old dress that was tight in the wrong places.

Michael Fitzwilliam – Mickey, they had called him that, surely – threw a piece of fabric on the bed and she couldn't not look at it, couldn't take her eyes away.

382

Notre Dame des Victoires was in Pine Street, four blocks from the Brocklebank Apartments, though that wasn't why her mother chose the school. It was the only one in the city that offered daily tuition in French conversation and writing. A small part of her felt guilty about dragging them from Paris. That part wanted the young Maggie to keep some distant contact with their mutual roots.

She stared at the school badge, faded with age. A white fleur-de-lys inside an oval shield with a red and blue crown at the centre. She thought of the name Mickey Fitzwilliam again. Now the distant memory had a face attached to it, that of a sad, lonely, unexceptional child, one who bragged constantly of his famous father yet always refused to name him.

'I'm sorry,' she murmured, and felt this was owed him, even after almost twenty years.

His head lolled around his shoulders, his eyes rolled in their sockets, a bad comic actor's 'come again?' routine.

'Is that it? "I'm *sorry*." Me, the poor little bastard you all laughed at, teased and fucked with. No dad. No money. Just a drunk for a mom and a . . .'

She could hear it before he even spoke, rattling around her head from across the years.

'. . . a st-st-st-st-st-stutter . . .'

Mickey Fitzwilliam, who so wanted to be the same as the rest of them and never could. She'd made sure of that.

'I'm sorry,' she said again.

'You will be. You've got to be. *Really* sorry, Maggie. Not acting sorry. I know the difference. I had a director for an old man and in between times, when he was pretending I didn't exist, I got to watch him and learn. Got to feed off his money and know how he worked. Got to learn your *tricks* over the years. No fooling Roberto Tonti's kid now, is there? Not for some two-bit actress who got where she is by handing out a quick fuck on the casting couch to any wrinkled old producer who demanded one.'

'That is not *true*!' she screamed.

He sat there, smiling, unmoved.

'No. It's not. So what really got you where you are, Maggie? Do you remember?'

She'd heard that question a million times, from a million different showbiz hacks.

'A little good fortune,' she said automatically. 'A little bit of talent.'

Mickey Fitzwilliam gazed at her and shook his head.

'You've got to remember better than that, Maggie.'

He reached down beneath the foot of the bed and came back up with a knife in his hands. The blade was long and clean and shiny.

'It's what the fuck-you-kill-you conundrum hangs on.'

- 6 -

It was Saturday morning, shoppers' hell. The traffic started bad and got worse all the way. He was still a good ten minutes from the cinema when it finally ground to a halt. Up ahead he heard the wail of a siren and his heart fell. Then a couple of very shiny red fire engines fought their way into the angry mass of stalled machines blocking the breadth of Chestnut some way short of the turnoff towards the ocean. Costa pulled the Dodge into the side of the road and got out.

People were coming out of stores and offices to stand in the street to look. There was a cop there, in uniform, looking bored.

Costa caught his attention.

'I'm in a hurry. Can you tell me what's going on?'

'Got some blaze down at Fort Mason. Stupid contractors lousing up or something. Or maybe the insurance. That place always was bad news.'

A fire. Not a call to the cinema further down the road in Chestnut. He had some time.

'Is the street going to be blocked for long?'

The cop pulled a sarcastic face and said, 'Sadly my psychic powers fail me there, sir. You can't dump your vehicle like that, by the way. You'll just have to wait for this train wreck to clear like everyone else.'

He'd put on Gerald Kelly's leather shoulder holster. The black handgun sat snug against his chest. If this man had been any use he should have seen it already.

'Thank you, officer,' Costa said and went back to sit behind the wheel.

When the blue uniform crossed the road, fighting his way through the choked cars and buses, he climbed out again, looked down the street, past the idle bystanders on the sidewalk. In the far distance crowds of shoppers were milling on the road close to the store, weaving through the stalled cars the way Romans did in the Corso on a Saturday afternoon, ordinary human beings on foot deciding there came a time when pedestrians deserved precedence over metal.

He took one look at them, saw the cop was returning, looking angrily at Catherine Bianchi's abandoned Dodge, and then began to move, falling into a steady pace as he wound through the growing throng of bodies, on into the Marina.

– 7 –

She did remember. It was all there. Just hidden, waiting to be let out into the light of day like an old poltergeist freed from the basement.

It must have been September. She could still feel the heat. Seventh-grade boys and girls, out on a trip to Crissy Field, doing the things schoolkids did. Working a little. Playing a little. Teasing . . .

Maggie Flavier could picture herself on that bright distant morning, thin as a rake but tall for her age and with a look about her that turned men's heads as they walked down the street. She tried not to notice. Her English still wasn't that good. She felt alone and a little unhappy in San Francisco. This was her mother's idea, not hers. To flee Paris and an estranged father, to try to find some new life halfway across the world in a city where they knew no one, and had, as far as the young Maggie could see, no clear idea of what the future might bring.

She'd danced at the stage school in France, and men looked then. Her mother had watched and taken note.

They were so kind in the church school on Pine Street. They smiled a lot and listened to her. They didn't mind that she hated trigonometry and algebra and preferred to dress up and play on the stage instead, always inventing something, stories, characters, voices, situations, imaginary people she created to fill the void inside.

These small and seemingly useless talents mattered, her mother said. Because of the auditions. She spoke the word as if it possessed some magical power. As if it could save them. The young Maggie had no idea how. All she understood was that she possessed a burning, unquenchable need to be popular, to be noticed, to be applauded. By her peers. By her mother, more than anything. Through singing and dancing. Through acting and taking part. By doing what others – her mother and the older girls – said was right and cool and proper.

The notes had been coming for weeks, always unsigned, always written in a crude childish hand on cheap school notebook paper. They were, she thought, beautiful in a simple, babyish way. Flowery language. Sometimes bad French. Sometimes, she thought, better Italian, which she recognized from lessons in Paris. They were never coarse or dirty, like some she'd received, and some the other girls sent from time to time. All they spoke of, carefully, indirectly, was love. As if there were an emotion somewhere waiting for her to discover it, like a hidden Easter egg, a secret buried in the ground. Something ethereal, something holy, distinct from the hard, cold physical reality of the life she knew. She didn't really understand the words or the poetry, some of it so old she found the verses unread-able. So she threw them away mostly, until the last.

Had this unseen admirer written, simply . . . *Margot Flavier, je t'aime, je t'aime, je t'aime* . . . then, perhaps, she would have tried to understand. But nothing was that clear and sometimes the language was so florid, so strange, she thought it was a joke. Sometimes it scared her a little. Always, she treated it with some intellectual distance, almost disdain, that seemed the easiest reaction. She was young, she was exiled in a foreign land, with a strange and unhappy mother who wished to push her into a career about which she felt unsure, not that her doubts mattered for one moment.

Naturally, she told the girls. Barbara Ronson. Louise Gostelow. Susan Shanks. The trio who ran the class.

Naturally, when the final note arrived, they had an idea.

That last message came the day after she'd gone to the first successful audition of her life, taking time off school for the short flight to LA with her mother, spending hours reading the scripts, trying to make her fast-improving English bad again for a group of men and women who seemed to demand that. Afterwards, when they waited at LAX for the flight home, her mother had made a call on a public phone. She'd pushed and pushed, and Maggie had the part. Françoise in *L'Amour LA*. A life mapped out in a single day, not that she knew that then, not that she felt anything much at all, except pleasure that this had produced some small joy in her mother.

Maggie had been surprised. She thought she'd fluffed her lines. She had felt slow and stupid in front of them. And still she got the part.

The next morning she came into school and found the note tucked into the seam of her locker. It read, *Tomorrow at Crissy Field I will reveal my love.*

Barbara and Louise and Susan had gawped at the scrawled, nervous handwriting, giggling, and then concocted the plan.

Out on the hot, dusty sand dunes of the Marina the following day they'd played it out. While the rest of them walked with Miss Piper, making notes about the grass and the lizards and the birds, Maggie had detached herself, looking distracted, knowing full well what would happen.

Finally the teacher headed for the public washrooms, ordering them to wait. Maggie walked to one of the small huts owned by the park service and stood in its shadow, out of the burning sun. It only took a minute. Then he was there, staring at her, his plain, simple face going redder and redder, voice tripping over itself, his eyes, which were not unattractive, locked on the pale, drifting sand.

'Maggie . . .'

At that moment she didn't even remember his name. He was the lost boy. The one with the stutter and the cheap clothes, and the father who was something big and famous, not that anyone was allowed to know his name.

'*Oui?*' she'd asked, hearing a giggle being stifled from the other side of the hut.

He bowed his head, held out his hands and tried to speak.

All that came out was, 'I lu . . . lu . . . lu . . . lu . . .'

It happened so quickly she didn't have a chance to intervene, even if she'd possessed the courage. The three of them burst out from their hiding place and formed a ring round him, hands locked, eyes wild with glee, chanting.

Strapped to an old, hard bed in some place she thought was a cinema in the Marina, the adult Maggie Flavier could hear that heartless song, see them dancing round him, a jeering circle of coarse, hard cruelty, eyes wild, cackling, taunting, chanting rhythmically in their sing-song voices . . .

I lu . . . lu . . . lu . . . lu . . .
I lu . . . lu . . . lu . . . lu . . .
I lu . . . lu . . . lu . . . lu . . .

She could see the way he'd stared at her, accusing eyes starting to fill with tears.

Then the boy ducked beneath their arms and she'd watched, heart beating wildly in her chest, as he ran away down the beach towards Fort Mason, shrieking with shame and fury until his cries mingled with those of the gulls that hung in the sea air as if pinned to the too-blue sky.

She didn't speak much to Barbara and Louise and Susan afterwards, though she blamed herself for showing them the letter in the first place. The boy, Mickey Fitzwilliam, never came to school again, which she regretted since she wished, more than anything, to apologize. It was impossible. He had no friends. The teachers, when she asked, refused to tell her where he lived. For a while he was a burden on her conscience. Then other cares intervened. Trips to LA to the TV studios. Work. Progress. A career. Her mother's growing frailty.

From that point to now . . .

She tried to imagine the distance, the journey, and couldn't. Not for herself. Certainly not for Mickey Fitzwilliam.

- 8 -

'I lu . . . lu . . . lu . . . loved you,' he stuttered, clutching the badge from all those years before.

'We were thirteen. We were children.'

'I loved you!' he roared.

She couldn't think of anything to say.

'Did you never ask yourself why it was *that* day? Why then?'

'I was a child. I didn't ask myself anything.'

'He was the p-p-producer. Roberto. My dad.' The head was shaking again but there was only one voice left now, a young, frail one that sounded hurt and damaged. 'He gave us money. He came by from time to time. Didn't want to see me. He just wanted my mom. That's all.'

'I don't understand . . .'

'He wanted to give me something. To ease his conscience. So I told him about you. About how you danced and acted and sang. How your mom wanted to get you into show business. Everyone knew that. I got him to give you the audition. I begged him to give you that part. That was me.'

'Thank you,' she said simply.

'You were good, even then. Everyone wanted to look at you. They couldn't stop.'

She whispered, 'But 'oo can blame Françoise?'

'Don't play those games with me,' he snarled. 'I saw you. On the TV. Going round town. You never even noticed me. I watched you grow up.' He stared hungrily at her. 'I watched you change. All those nice parts in the beginning. The good girl. Disney and stuff. Sweet dreams and apple pie. Then . . .'

'Then you keep on working,' she cut in, knowing where this was going. 'Any way you can.'

'That first time you . . . t-t-took off your clothes.'

'Mickey . . .'

'Do you know what that did to me? Do you even care?'

She shook her head and said, 'I did not know you then. I do not know you now. If I had . . .'

'While you were banging half of Hollywood I was there. Didn't touch another human being. Not once. Waiting.'

'Mickey, please . . .'

'I stood outside the Brocklebank all night long sometimes. I knew what was going on, behind those drapes. I could picture in my head, every one of them. In your bed. None of those bastards loved you. Not your actors and your rich guys and your pimps. Not some stupid Italian cop . . .'

'Stop this now!'

'I watched you every day of your life one way or another. On the screen. In the papers. On the net. Next to you in a store somewhere, an elevator, at the movies. Anywhere else I could find. You never noticed, did you? Never had a clue what you owed me. Why the hell do you think Roberto cast you for *Inferno* in the first place, huh? Some washed-up has-been dodging in and out of rehab so fast even the papers gave up on you in the end? Why'd he pick you of all people?'

'Because I can do my job,' she insisted, mainly to herself.

'So can a million other pretty women, all of them younger than you too. I asked him. I *begged*. One more favour for the bastard son. Keep him quiet. Ease an awkward little situation. Got to say that about my old man. He still has a Catholic sense of guilt somewhere, even when he's murdering people. Here's something else. You know when he came along and wanted someone else removed from that cute deal of his, to bring down the numbers a little more and keep up the coverage in the papers?'

She didn't want to listen to this. She didn't want to think about it.

'I screwed it up on purpose. I sent out Martin to get that almond stuff knowing you had that hypodermic handy.'

'I could have died that night.'

'If I'd wanted it, you would have. Don't you see?'

It was the last thing she needed but the tears were beginning to prick in her eyes.

'In God's name . . . what is it you expect me to do?'

'Fuck-you-kill-you . . .' he whispered. 'Lu-lu-love you. I waited so long for this. Nearly twenty years. I didn't want you to hate me. I made you, Maggie. I saved you. I still can. There's just the three of us left in the deal now. Me, you, and my old man – and he won't be around much longer. Millions and millions and millions of dollars. It could last a whole lifetime. For the two of us.'

'What deal?' she asked, exasperated. 'I don't understand . . .'

'*The* deal, dummy. The one that jerk Harvey wrote you into when you were too bombed to notice. Your name's there anyway. Once my old man's dead there's a place in the Caribbean we can fly, walk in a bank, pick up the whole lot, everything that was meant to go to him, to Harvey, those Lukatmi losers, Martin . . . It's ours. No more work. No more worry. You don't need to go down on some jerk in a director's chair. I don't have to slave away in construction until my old man calls and tells me to go do his dirty work. Everything winds up fine. Perfect. Don't you see?'

He didn't stutter when he felt confident. He didn't even look terribly threatening.

'Talk to me some more,' she said. 'Come closer.'

Mickey Fitzwilliam laughed nervously, then patted down the sheets at the foot, away from her, and sat down, very stiff, very nervous.

'See, Roberto said this whole deal was all for me in the end. The money. The tontine. All I needed was to round down the numbers a little.'

He snickered like a child and looked briefly proud of himself.

'Well, a lot actually. Josh and Martin . . . that was pure improv. They came round my place bleating about how it was all going wrong . . . how *scared* they were. Pissed me off. Next day I just sent Josh a stack of letters demanding money and made it look like they came from Martin. Easiest thing in the world. Morons. They thought I was there to, like, mediate. You believe that? Then that idiot Tom Black calls me when he's on the run.'

Another voice, high-pitched. Terrified.

'Scottie, Scottie, ya got to help me. Like you promised . . .'

A dark, malevolent gleam flashed in his eyes.

'I hate dumb people. Told my old man afterwards. Know what he said? I got lucky. I oughta shut up. He'd take care of it all in the end. See me right. Call that luck? Does anyone get that lucky?'

'I'd call it fate.'

He smiled.

'Me too. This was *meant to be.*'

He scanned the room as if he was looking at something he despised.

'Roberto gave me this dump as some kind of stupid present. A "legacy". Bullshit. He couldn't make any money out of the place. All these things . . . they were supposed to be his way of saying sorry. I'm not stupid. It was always about him. That deal was just like . . . his *pièce de résistance*. His big moment. Going out in some big blaze of glory. Look at me, Ma! Top of the world! All those years behind the camera. All those years watching actors get the applause. It got to him . . .'

'I saw that.'

'You did?'

'It was obvious. Tell me more.'

He inched a little closer and looked at her left leg, bare, half askew on the bed.

'I never touched a woman before. Not till today. When you were sleeping.'

Maggie Flavier gave him a stern look.

'That's not nice. Touching a woman when she doesn't know.'

'I'm sorry. I just . . .' He shook his head as if someone else was trying to climb in there. 'I couldn't stop looking at that movie after my dad gave it me back when I was a kid. *Vertigo*. It was the first piece of work he did in America, you know. I watched it straight away. Had to. He told me so. Said it was his movie too, in a way. Then I saw you and you lived in the same place. It was like . . .'

He ran his tongue over his lips as if they were dry.

'I'd watch it every day. Twice, three times sometimes. Got it in French and Italian too. I could sit here and tell you every second, read you every line.'

He gazed at her, frankly, greedily.

'After a little while it was you I saw, not some dumb old actress no one's ever heard of. You in that car. In that dress.' He blushed again, looked younger. 'In bed, in that apartment. *My* apartment. Bought it with my own money. Robbed a bank in Reno. Self-made man. Wasn't taking everything off Roberto. I got my dignity.' He squeezed his eyes shut for a moment. 'That movie . . . it kind of got inside me.'

'They do sometimes.'

He edged closer still and, as she watched, gingerly put his hand on her knee, looking all the time, anxious for her approval. His fingers closed on her skin, squeezing, as if she were some kind of lab specimen.

'Not hard,' she said. 'That's not nice.' She held up her arms, with the rope dangling from the wrists. 'This isn't nice.'

She leaned forward as if to kiss him. The rope was just short enough to stop her. She moved back to where she was with a sigh.

'A woman can't make love tied to a bed. Not a good woman. That's what hookers do. Dirty women. I don't want to be a dirty woman. I won't do that. Not for anyone.'

'I-I-I d-don't want that, Maggie. I *never* wanted that. All that fuck-you-kill-you stuff. Jesus . . .' The head shook again. 'All I wanted was to be with you. Like we should have been from the start. Now we've got the money, we can . . .'

His words drifted into the nothingness of acute embarrassment.

'We can what, Mickey? Tell me. Please.'

'We can be like normal people. A couple. We can live where we want. On a desert island maybe. Or Paris. Or a farm in the country with a-a-animals . . .' He closed his eyes tight shut and started to turn bright red. 'Kids maybe. All in good time. We don't have to do it right now. I don't expect that. I just . . . sometimes. Sheesh. Sometimes I'm not me.'

He took his hand off her knee, stared at the sheets, then mumbled, 'We don't have to do it till after we're married. I'd like that. It would be proper. In the circumstances.'

'In the circumstances . . .' she echoed, cursing herself for letting a little of her fury show, glad he didn't notice.

'I can't kiss you if my hands are tied, Michael. Can I call you Michael? Is that OK?'

'If you like.'

He looked at her, mouth open, a little idiotic. Then he went back to the chair, scrabbled on the floor, came back with the knife and sat next to her on the bed.

'The reason I never messed with girls is my old man told me. They screw with you. They fuck your head. They eat your whole life until one day there's nothing left.'

'Some girls. Not all.'

She held out her hands.

'It depends how you treat them.'

'Yeah.'

He reached over and sawed through the loop of rope on her left wrist, then her right.

'I didn't tie them tight, you know. I didn't want to hurt you. Not ever.'

'I realize that.'

She took his right hand, the one with the blade, slipped forward, angled her body against his, heard his breathing turn short and excited.

'Are you going to hold a knife when you kiss me?'

'Oh . . .'

He looked at the thing, shamefaced, then let go. She heard it clatter on the floor and that was enough. Before he could even look at her again Maggie Flavier was on her feet, trying to remember some of the things she'd learned in the few self-defence classes she'd taken a couple of years before.

Nothing returned so she did what came naturally. She jerked back her arm and elbowed him hard in the face with such force the blow sent something electric running up and down her funny bone, and she was the one to scream first.

Mickey Fitzwilliam fell to the floor clutching at his nose. Blood was leaking out between his fingers. He was moaning like a little kid.

She didn't wait. She ran to the door, jerked on the handle, found nothing moved. There was an old-fashioned key in the lock. In her mind's eye she was already rushing outside, into the bright, safe world, screaming at the top of her lungs for all her life was worth.

The trouble was the key wouldn't turn.

He was on the floor, glaring at her, a different Mickey again, the one who'd been there when she came to. The one who snatched her, stripped her, put her inside someone else's old dress, dreaming, dreaming, dreaming.

His hands were away from his face. He didn't care that snot and blood were pouring down over his lips, dripping off his chin onto his knees.

'Guess that solves the conundrum,' he said in a dreamy nasal slur.

- 9 -

What puzzled her when she looked back was the other door, one she'd never noticed, in the wall to the right of the bed. It looked bigger. More serious somehow.

He was getting up and walking towards a glass cabinet on the wall. It was marked 'In case of fire' and contained an axe, set diagonally against black fabric, like some kind of exhibit in a museum.

Mickey Fitzwilliam dashed his fist through the broken glass. Blood shot out from his fingers as he did so. He didn't seem to notice.

Praying to any god she could think of, she fought with the key. It turned. The door opened and she dashed through. It was pitch dark. Her hand flailed against the wall, her fingers found a switch. A bright light burst on her from a single bulb that dangled from a wire not more than a hand's width from her face.

Escape had taken her into a small, square room entirely without windows, nothing but plain whitewashed brick walls. A winding, rickety-looking wooden staircase rose against the white, dusty wall opposite. A dark corridor led off to the right, maybe to nowhere.

A picture came into her mind's eye, one kept there from the times she'd driven down Chestnut on the way to the shops or Roberto Tonti's grand mansion opposite the Palace of Fine Arts.

She knew where she was instantly. Inside the fake bell-tower of the Marina Odeon, the one pretending to be the *campanario* of San Juan Bautista.

Trying to think straight, she shot her hand back round the handle, ripped out the key, got back to the tower side and slammed the old wooden door shut. It closed with a hefty ring. Hand shaking, fingers fumbling, she got the key in the lock and managed to turn it. She put her head to the edge of the frame and whispered, 'Michael, Michael . . .'

There was no reply. Not a word.

'I'm sorry,' she said very purposefully. 'You're sick. Let me . . .'

Was she serious? Was she acting? She'd no idea.

'I can help. There are doctors . . .'

Silence. She tried to catch her breath. She looked up the narrow wooden staircase winding up the interior of the fake bell-tower.

Face against the wood, trying to sound calm and in control, she said, 'Talk to me, Michael. Please . . .'

The blade of the axe crashed through the flimsy old timber next to her face and rested there, shining brightly under the glare of the single light bulb. She shrieked. The sharp, gleaming metal withdrew, and he began battering again, repeatedly, maniacally, tearing a hole through the panel, sending splinters and dust everywhere.

She retreated to the other side of the tiny chamber, staring at the growing breach he was tearing in the last barrier of defence she possessed. The world was closing in on her and it was one that seemed to be composed entirely of clips from movies, remembered scenes, flashes of recognition that veered between fact and fiction, never quite knowing which was which.

The next thing she knew she was stumbling down the dark little corridor that led off to the right, praying there might be some way out at the end. The light disappeared altogether. Her fingers crawled along the damp plaster around the same height as the switch she'd found earlier. Finally they found something that felt the same. She flipped it and felt a raw, painful scream leap into her throat.

Ahead of her was a naked man, one a part of her panicking mind could recognize and name, though he looked so different, so changed. Dino Bonetti was trapped upright in some kind of tall glass cabinet, the kind they had in restaurants for desserts and ice cream. He was still alive, barely, moving a little, mumbling wordlessly. At his feet was a round papery object the size and shape of a football. It seemed to be spewing a constant stream of yellow and black shapes that flew in and out, only to find themselves cornered in the cabinet alongside Bonetti. A cloud of furious wasps buzzed around him, crawling across his florid, swollen face as if feeding, pulsing thick, like a living carpet, on his chest.

His fist banged weakly on the padlocked glass. He could see her, just. There was a putrid, vile smell leaking from somewhere. She edged back, towards the foot of the tower.

As she stumbled against the door joist there was a brutal, vicious crack. He was through, his face a rictus of amused savagery, cheek against the axe blade, so close she could feel the spittle from his mouth fall like hot rain on her skin as he leered crazily through the gap.

There was nowhere else to go. She stumbled towards the staircase, knowing what he would say next, placing the resonant link: Jack Nicholson in *The Shining*, a performance twice removed, an actor mimicking something else from the real–unreal world of show business.

'Here's J-J-Johnny,' Mickey Fitzwilliam screamed, then took three more swipes at the door, got the gap there big enough to squeeze his hand through and lunged down grasping, groping, hunting for the key.

- 10 -

At the end of his long run to the movie theatre Costa found the front door locked and not a light on anywhere front of house. To one side he saw a low, unlocked wooden gate. He went through and worked his way to the back of the building.

There was no obvious entry point at ground level, only rough plaster walls and the white tower rising three storeys or more into a cloudless sky. Close by – this he hardly dared look at – stood an old cemetery headstone over a grave marked out by pansies and daisies with a grey urn at the centre filled with red roses and a green sash wrapped around the stems.

Out of breath, lost for a way inside, he heard a scream, then another, and the sound of crashing timber.

Then he heard Maggie's voice. A man's name, over and over again.

Michael, Michael, Michael . . .

From the echoing, muffled tone he knew in an instant where she was: behind the fake adobe wall, just a few short steps away, trapped with the man who'd covered the walls of his bedroom with two decades of her portraits.

Next to the base of the tower was a small window so grubby and littered with cobwebs it was impossible to see through. He searched the trash-filled back yard until he came across an old discarded sink, hefted it in his arms, stumbled through the rusting junk back to the building, then, with a desperate lurch, managed to throw the thing through the glass. It landed on the far side with a muffled crash. Costa picked up some old, bent piping and roughed out a gap through the sharp fingers of remaining glass, wrapped his right fingers in a handkerchief, reached inside, found some purchase on the other side and pulled himself through. He found himself half spread-eagled across an old office desk, reached ahead, gripped the edge of the wood and dragged himself forward until he was mostly free of the spikes and scattered shards.

Trying to catch his breath he looked around. There was a bed in there, the smell of sweat, and a misshapen red puddle on the grimy floor.

Some second sense made him turn to see a man in a doorway at what appeared to be the foot of the stairs of the tower. He had a bloodied face and hands and wore an expression of surprise and contempt.

His right arm was racing into view, and it held a long, workman-like fireman's axe which, as he scrambled from the desk, began to fly, turning, turning, turning, towards him through the air.

Costa fought to drag himself off the desk and get upright, pulled too far and found himself dropping like a sack onto the hard concrete floor. Bells chimed, pain flooded into his temples. Maggie was there, beyond his assailant somewhere, shrieking again. After a brief, sickening moment of blackness Costa found himself on the ground amidst a sea of shattered glass trying weakly to recover the gun from Gerald Kelly's leather holster inside his jacket. He'd taken the fall on his right shoulder, which hurt like hell. Maybe something was broken. Still trying to get his fingers round the weapon, he rolled and came face to face with the axe. The blade had driven itself deep into the wood just an arm's length away from his head. The fall, painful as it was, had probably saved him.

When he got half upright, onto a single knee, gun in hand, with a clear view back towards the tower, he was alone.

Costa staggered towards the tower, his head throbbing, his body convulsed in a single painful ache.

'Police!' he bellowed, stumbling through with the kind of unguarded, careless bravado that would have got him screamed at in the state police academy in Flaminio. '*Police.*'

Laughter drifted unseen down the rickety wooden staircase.

Maggie cried in an echoing scream, 'What do you *want?*'

There was a noise to one side, down a gloomy corridor, a sound like someone rapping on glass. Costa glanced that way automatically, seeking its source. What he saw sent his mind reeling into a black, crazy space. At the end of the narrow passage, illuminated by a bulb swinging close by, stood a large, upright glass cabinet that looked as if it had been looted from a grocery store. Inside a naked individual, one that might have been Dino Bonetti, was banging weakly on the door. A heavy padlock stood on the handle. Around the trapped man's bloated, livid body swarmed a thick, angry cloud of buzzing insects.

'No time,' he murmured and pointed the gun very visibly at the cabinet. He heard a thin frightened screech from the figure locked inside, then saw him fall, crouching, arms around his head, to the ground.

Costa loosed off two shots, as high into the structure as he could make them. The cabinet shattered with a sharp, loud explosion. Glass, wasps, and finally the bloodied, torn husk of a human being fell outwards, into the hot, fetid air of the corridor.

He couldn't wait to see any more. Trying to take the stairs two steps at a time he stumbled, fell down the dry timber planks, splinters tearing at his fingers, the pain in his shoulder getting worse, so bad that in the end the gun slipped rattling from his grasp. Back at the bottom again he recovered the weapon and set about the climb once more, slowly, this time, at a speed his aching frame could manage.

'What do I want?'

A man's voice. Not one racked with anger. More outrage.

Costa staggered ever upward, round and round the twisting corners of the staircase, until, panting, exhausted, he reached some bright, sunny platform, holding on to the banister for support, aware that, finally, he wasn't alone.

Maggie was crouched in the far corner wearing a strange old-fashioned dress the colour of an emerald. Above her stood the bloodied man, a knife in his hand, his face full of pain and fury.

'Put down the weapon,' Costa yelled. 'Stand by the wall. Do as I say and no one will get hurt.'

The man across the room didn't even hear.

'What do I *want?*' he asked again. 'To be happy, Maggie. Is that so freaking much, huh?'

The blade was high over her, stationary, gleaming. A spiralling swarm of wasps rising from below was beginning to work its way into the room.

'You're sick, Michael. I'm sorry. Please, listen to me . . .' She was weeping, choking, and there was more than fear in her voice, there was regret there, some kind of recrimination and self-hate. 'Let me help. Let me do something . . .'

Costa snatched a frenzied glance around him. Ahead rose a single arch the height of the room, open to the blue sky, with a ledge outside so small it scarcely counted.

'Do what?' the man with the knife demanded.

Maggie crouched in the grime on the floor, knees bunched up before her, arms around them, a tight and terrified ball of misery.

'Whatever's needed,' she said in a low, weak voice. 'Whatever . . .'

Costa took out the gun and aimed straight through the shaft of bright sun that separated them. A cloud of yellow and black insects danced in the dusty golden air.

'Move away from her,' he ordered. 'Do as I say.'

Not a word. Not a sign he even heard.

'He's sick . . .' Maggie whispered, still cowering. 'Please, he's . . .'

A voice came into Costa's head, and it was Emily's, repeating the words she'd uttered moments before his hesitation ended her life by the side of a crumbling monument that stank of cats and the homeless, a rank, compound smell that would never leave him.

'Don't beg,' he said, so quietly he knew this was for himself, not her. 'You never beg. It's the worst thing you can do. The worst . . .'

The knife didn't move. The weapon in Costa's grip didn't waver, not even when something small and dry crawled across his extended hand, paused, and thrust its sting into the soft, taut flesh between his index finger and thumb as he gripped the gun.

A hot, sharp spike of pain that he barely noticed.

The man ahead shifted position, just a fraction, turning to look at Costa, his face frozen, something new, a look of doubt maybe, in his eyes. Another vicious yellow and black creature crawled across Costa's forehead, stabbed its poison into him, got crushed in an instant as he swept its carapace into his skin with the back of his hand.

'You know . . .' The voice didn't match the tortured face of the figure with the knife. It was anonymous, anybody's, nobody's. It drifted dreamily around the bell-tower. 'I was thinking . . .'

Costa's first bullet took him somewhere in the left arm, near the elbow. The shattered limb jerked like that of a rag doll. The jumping man screamed. So did Maggie Flavier.

The force of the second threw his shaking body hard against the white rotting wall and Costa didn't know where he'd hit him, not for a moment. So he kept on firing, jerking on the sweaty trigger constantly, trying to empty the weapon into this husk of a man as the pained shape jerked and shrieked across the room until he came to block the searing California sun at the long bright archway, still upright, just, still holding the weapon.

'He's sick . . .' Maggie screeched through her hands, crouched in a bundle of agony, beseeching someone, him, the man.

Costa wasn't sure. He wasn't really hearing anything at that moment, except for his dead wife's voice and the buzzing of a million tiny wings.

'Drop the knife.'

It was spoken quietly, calmly, and he didn't wait for a reaction.

He pointed the gun across the room, dead straight, hand steady, and pulled the trigger. The shot caught the man who called himself John Ferguson in one life, and Carlotta Valdes in another, full in the chest and the impact blew him clean out of the tower, backwards into the unforgiving brightness of the day.

The room went quiet. He could hear her weeping and knew, in a sudden revelatory instant, there would never be anything he could say to heal the hurt.

Costa crossed the room. He walked out onto the narrow ledge three storeys above the tiny garden that sat among the junk and debris in the shadow of the bell-tower of the Marina Odeon.

Heights didn't scare him. Nothing scared him much any more. Only the big unknowable things, life and closeness and the fragile bond of family. He stood stock-still in the high open arch of the counterfeit *campanario* of an imaginary San Juan Bautista and peered directly down over the dizzying, exposed edge.

Below, on the ground, broken, torn, and bloodied, next to a shattered grey urn strewn with scarlet roses, a man's body lay exposed before the headstone of Carlotta Valdes, like a corpse that had worked its way out of the grave below.